Praise for
Igniting the Reaches
and
Through the Breach

"Drake uses military language fluently to create vivid combat scenes." —*Publishers Weekly*

"A violent, hard-nosed swashbuckler, set forth with discernment and skill. —*Kirkus Reviews*

"His forte lies with the tales of the military in the far future, but he also creates believable characters with real conflicts and inner depth surprising for the genre."
—*Fort Lauderdale Sun-Sentinel*

"Hard-hitting adventure—a tale that will appeal to fans of military SF." —*Library Journal*

D0191397

FIRESHIPS

DAVID DRAKE

ACE BOOKS, NEW YORK

This Ace Book contains the complete text of the original hardcover edition. It has been completely reset in a typeface designed for easy reading, and was printed from new film.

FIRESHIPS

An Ace Book / published by arrangement with the author

PRINTING HISTORY
Ace hardcover edition / June 1996
Ace mass-market edition / February 1997

The Putnam Berkley World Wide Web site address is
http://www.berkley.com/berkley
Make sure to check out PB Plug, the science fiction/fantasy newsletter, at
http://www.pb.plug.com

ISBN: 0-441-00417-2

ACE®
Ace Books are published by The Berkley Publishing Group,
200 Madison Avenue, New York, New York 10016.
ACE and the "A" design are trademarks
belonging to Charter Communications, Inc.

PRINTED IN THE UNITED STATES OF AMERICA

10 9 8 7 6 5 4 3 2 1

To Carolyn Ross

Who's a long way away, but only physically

FIRESHIPS

ABOVE LILYMEAD.

"We can get one more aboard, Sal," called Tom Harrigan from the hatch of the lighter across the temporary orbital dock from the *Gallant Sallie.*

Captain Sarah—Sal—Blythe checked her vessel's hold and said, "No, let 'em go, Tom. We've got two turbines and the crate of spare rotors left, so there'll be a part-load anyway. Tell them to start bringing the return cargo on the next lift, though. We can have the last of this waiting in the dock and our hold clear by the time they get back up."

The access tube connecting the lighter to the dock was three meters long. The valve at the inner end of the tube opened automatically when the air pressure on both sides was equal. The system formed a simple airlock while the outer end was attached to a ship's pressurized hold or cabin.

Technically the business of shifting cargo after a vessel docked was the responsibility of the planetary staff, but Lilymead wasn't really set up to handle cargoes in orbit. The ships that traded to Near Space colonies like Lilymead put down on the unimproved field and waited for tractors to haul lowboys full of stevedores to them over dirt blasted by the exhaust of other vessels.

The huge freighters in which the North American Federation voyaged to the Reaches touched in Near Space only when leakage and slow progress forced them to resupply their reaction mass and atmosphere. Those monsters rarely dared to land on ports without hardened pads and full facilities. Lilymead had a remotely controlled water buffalo to ferry water and air up to them.

1

Harrigan—Sal's mate—and the starboard watch of eight crewmen slid from the lighter's hold with the delicacy of men experienced with weightless conditions. The Federation lighter's own crew of two wasn't enough to handle cargo as massive as these turbines, even if Sal had been willing to wait while the locals did the job. The dock was processed cellulose, constructed as cheaply as possible to be abandoned after a single use. Inertia would tear a turbine that got away from its handlers right on through the fuzzily transparent walls.

"Say, what's that?" Harrigan said in astonishment as he saw the featherboat that had grappled to another of the dock's four access tubes while he and his men were striking cargo down in the lighter.

The 30-tonne vessel was too small to have an airlock of its own. As Sal and the mate watched, the dorsal hatch opened. A group of civilians caromed out with the spastic overcorrections of folk who thought of gravity, not inertia, when they moved.

"Some local merchants, they said," Sal explained. "Asked to come aboard. We've got a return cargo, but I didn't see any harm in talking to them." She grimaced. "We could use a little extra profit to cover repairs to the attitude jets."

"Oh, Sallie," Harrigan said uncomfortably. The mate never jibbed at her orders, but he couldn't help treating Sarah Blythe as the captain's daughter rather than as the captain in her own right. Harrigan had always assumed that when Marcus Blythe's arthritis grounded him for good, Thomas Harrigan would marry Sal and captain the *Gallant Sallie* himself—while his wife stayed on Venus and raised children as a woman should. "I don't think that'll be much, just a bad connection somewhere, only . . ."

The *Gallant Sallie*'s three bands of attitude jets kept the vessel aligned with the direction her main thrusters were to drive her. On the voyage out to Lilymead, the jets occasionally failed to fire as programmed. The problem forced Sal to go through the trouble and added expense of lightering down her cargo, rather than landing in the port where two other Venerian vessels took advantage of the relaxing of the Federation's embargo on trade with its Near Space colonies. If the jets—most likely their controls—glitched during transit, the error required recomputation and lengthened the *Gallant Sallie*'s voyage. If the problem occurred during landing, well . . .

Captain Sarah Blythe was rightly proud of her reflexes and piloting ability. Since she had the choice, though, the only landing the *Gallant Sallie* would make this voyage would be back on Venus, where dockyard mechanics could go over the vessel and cure what the crew's repeated attempts had not.

The featherboat's passengers, five men and two women, spun in the slight turbulence as they entered the dock's main chamber. None of the seven was a spacer, though Sal was by no means sure they were all the civilians their clothing proclaimed.

Her eyes narrowed. The dark speckling on one woman's cheek was a powder burn. While the stiff leg of the group's leader could have come from any number of causes, the puckered skin of his right forearm was surely a bullet scar.

"Captain Blythe?" the leader said to Harrigan. "I'm Walter Beck. These are my associates in the trading community here on Lilymead."

The *Gallant Sallie*'s working party watched the Fed delegation with the amusement of spacers for landsmen out of their element. Brantling, a senior man who'd have been bosun except for his jealousy of Harrigan, snickered loudly.

"There's our captain!" Tom Harrigan said, anger at Brantling's laughter turning the words into a snarl. "Deal with her if you've business here."

Beck was holding out a bottle of local liquor. He swung it from Harrigan to Sal at arm's length. The gesture set his whole body pivoting away in reaction. Sal caught Beck's cuff and said, "You're welcome aboard the *Gallant Sallie*, miladies and sirs. Left up the passage from the hold, please. We'll speak in the cabin so that my crew can continue their duties."

Sal's gentle tug sent Beck through the hatch ahead of her. Without needing direction, Harrigan and the rest of the work party caught the other Feds and pushed them after their leader like so many billiard balls into a pocket. A few of the thrusts were more enthusiastic than kindly; Sal, still gripping the coaming, braked those Feds with her free hand. The powder-burned female pinwheeled wildly because she'd swiped at the head of the sailor who pushed her off. Brantling again . . .

"Brantling," Sal ordered. "Put a helmet on and check the nozzles of all twelve attitude jets again. Now!"

"Aye aye, Captain," Brantling said, cheerful despite the unpleasant, dangerous, and (at this point) useless task he'd just been set. Brantling never failed to use Sal's title with due deference, because he believed it irritated the mate to hear her called "Captain."

He was wrong. Tom Harrigan couldn't understand Sal's refusing his hand nor her insistence on sailing as captain in lieu of her father; but he had neither jealousy nor anger toward her. He'd been ship's boy when Marcus Blythe brought his two-year-old infant aboard the *Gallant Sallie* for the first time.

Sal seated herself at the navigation console and hooked a tie-down across her lap to keep her there. "What can I do for you, Master Beck?" she asked.

The *Gallant Sallie* was a freighter of standard Venerian design with a nominal burden of 150 tonnes. She had a main hold aft; it could be pressurized, but the large outer hatch was single-panel, not an airlock. The cabin forward served as crew quarters and control room. There were stanchions to help people direct themselves in weightlessness, but the light screen around the toilet in deference to the captain's sex was the only bulkhead within the compartment. There was an airlock near the navigation console in the nose. Hatches at either end of the two-meter-long passageway between the hold and cabin (through the air and water tanks amidships) turned it into an airlock as well.

The visiting landsmen hovered awkwardly in the cabin, stared at by the off-duty crew members. In weightless conditions, all the compartment's volume was usable; but by the same token, gravity didn't organize the space in an expected fashion. One of the Feds started noticeably when he realized his ear was less than a finger's breadth from the feet of a spacer floating in his sleeping net.

Beck looked around before replying. His eyes lingered on the four 10-cm plasma cannon, dominating the cabin by their mass despite being draped with netted gear at present. Beck still held the liquor bottle. It couldn't be used in orbit without a pressure vessel, which Sal pointedly didn't offer. She'd decided that whatever these folk were about, she wanted no part of it.

"I'm sorry for your engine trouble, Captain," Beck said. There was little distinction between the sexes in Fed service, but a female captain on a Venerian ship was unusual enough to arouse interest. "Are you sure you wouldn't like to land and see if our crews couldn't put it to right? You know how clever some Molts can be, almost as if they were human."

"We'll manage," Sal said curtly. "We've got plenty of reaction mass for the return trip. In Ishtar City the people who installed the system can troubleshoot it."

She didn't like Molts; the chitinous aliens made her skin crawl. There weren't many on Venus, but the North American Federation used Molts as slaves to do much of the labor on their starships and the colonies those ships served. Because Molts had genetic memory, they could operate the machinery remaining across the Reaches where mankind had abandoned it after the Rebellion and the Collapse of civilization a thousand years before.

No denying the Molts' value, but—they stank; the food they ate stank; and so far as Sal was concerned, the Federation that depended on Molt abilities stank also.

"As you please," Beck said with a shrug. He grabbed a bundle of dehydrated food to keep from drifting away. "You know," he added as if it were a new thought, "I see that you've got plasma guns. Our port defenses could do with some improvement. Would you—"

"Not interested," Sal said loudly, awakening two of the crewmen who were still asleep. Brantling, who'd pulled an elastic pressure suit over his coveralls, paused beside the airlock without donning his air helmet.

"We could offer a good price," said the powder-burned Fed. She sounded calm, but the cabin wasn't warm enough to have beaded her forehead with sweat.

"Not interested," Sal repeated sharply. She rose from

her seat in obvious dismissal. "You know the old saying: 'There's no law beyond Pluto.' Without the great guns, we'd be prey for any skulking pirate we chanced across."

And for any Federation customs vessel; which she didn't say and didn't need to say. The *Gallant Sallie* was a merchant ship, not a raider; but only a fool would put herself and her crew at the mercy of Federation officials who had been bloodied so often and so badly by the raiding captains of Venus.

"Well, we're only here to offer you the hospitality of Lilymead," Beck said. "Now that the embargo for Near Space is lifted, we hope to trade with you and your compatriots often."

He offered the bottle of liquor again. Sal took it. It was some sort of local brew, perhaps of native vegetation. The contents were bright yellow and moved as sluggishly as heavy oil.

"Thank you, Master Beck," Sal replied. "I certainly hope we will." The profits were too good to pass up, but she didn't know if she'd touch down the next time either. Too much about the conditions on Lilymead made her uneasy.

Harrigan came up the passage from the hold. "Tom," Sal said, "help our visitors back to their vessel. I'll bring up the rear."

With the loading done, the starboard watch was returning to the cabin behind Harrigan. The mate didn't bother to send his men back into the hold ahead of the visitors, as Sal had meant he should. The passage was a tight fit for people passing in opposite directions, even when they all were experienced spacers. Sal heard curses. One of her Venerians responded to a bump by kicking a Fed hard down the passage into the woman ahead.

The lighter had already cast off. As Sal entered the dock, she saw the little vessel's thruster fire. The bulkhead's translucence blurred the rainbow haze of plasma exhaust. Lilymead hung overhead, its visible continent a squamous green as distinctly different from that of Terran vegetation as it was from the ruddy yellow cloudscape of Venus.

Tom Harrigan was a tall, rawboned man, bald at age 35 save for a fringe of red hair. He glared as the visitors closed the hatch of their featherboat behind them. "If I never see another Federation toady," he said, "it'll be too soon."

Sal glanced at her mate without expression. She was a short, stocky blonde, 24 years old. Earth years, because the folk living beneath the crust and equally opaque atmosphere of Venus had never measured time by Venus years or the yearlong days of the second planet. "I expect to turn around for Lilymead again as soon as I can get another cargo from home," she said mildly. "There's a good profit on glazing earths."

"Glazing earths!" Harrigan said. "The real profit's in microchips from the Reaches, and President Pleyal claims all those for himself. Why, the only reason the Feds even opened their Near Space colonies to us is that Captain Ricimer's raids made Pleyal be a little more reasonable about trade!"

The featherboat cast off from the dock. It continued to hang alongside while the Molt pilot waited for a reentry window. A few stars were bright enough for Sal to see them through the dock's walls.

"All I know," Sal said, a trifle more crisply than before, "is that there's money to be made hauling manufactures out to Lilymead and glazing earths back. That's the trade the *Gallant Sallie*'s going to carry so long as the embargo's lifted and nothing better offers."

The featherboat's thruster flared. Its iridescent brilliance was brighter than the sun until the vessel dropped well within the ball of the planet.

"I'll tell you though, Tom," Sarah Blythe said in an appraising tone. "If that lot comes back again, see to it that I'm awake and the whole crew is on alert. I'm not sure what they've got in mind is trade."

ABOVE LILYMEAD.

Sal watched through a magnifier as her fingers fed new coils through the narrow slots of an electric drill's stator. She'd cut and teased out the shorted coils on the previous watch while waiting for the lighter to return; now she was rewiring the unit. When she was done, the drill would work again—and as an activity, it beat recomputing the course back to Venus for the umpteenth time.

Rickalds, on watch at the navigation console, straightened up sharply and said, "Captain, the lighter's on course. They're not two minutes out, I swear."

"Haven't they heard of radio?" Sal snapped as she struck the repair tools and pieces of drill down in a canvas bag. Otherwise the bits would drift into all corners of the ship while she was away from the task. "See if you can raise port control and see why they didn't warn us!"

"Port watch to the dock to load cargo!" Harrigan called, his voice echoing in the hold and up the passageway to the cabin. Tom must have noticed the lighter's braking flare through the cellulose walls. The lighter wasn't scheduled to return for another twenty minutes; based on past experience with the Lilymead personnel, Sal hadn't *expected* them for an hour at best.

"Captain, it's two ships, I think," Rickalds said. He squinted at the holographic display instead of trying to sharpen the view electronically. Rickalds was alert and a willing worker, but he was ill at ease with any tool more complex than a pry bar.

"I've got the controls, Rickalds," Sal said, pushing the

8

spacer from the console. "Airley," she said to the senior man of the starboard watch, "stand by to take over here."

The *Gallant Sallie*'s optronics were original to the vessel and thus older than Sal herself. As built they hadn't been as clear as one might wish, and it took a practiced hand to bring the best out of their aged chips now.

Sal focused, raised the magnification, and rolled a ball switch with her hand to correct for drift as the console's electronics were unable to do. "Damn their fool souls to *Hell*," she snarled.

"Sir?" said Airley.

"Take over!" she said as she left the console and propelled herself down the passageway in a pair of reflexively precise motions. Two vessels were approaching. The lighter was five hundred meters out, still braking with its thruster to match velocities. The featherboat that had brought Beck in the morning had arrived again also, and it was already coupled to the temporary dock.

Harrigan was organizing his eight cargo handlers in the hold, nearly empty now that the rest of the outbound freight had been shifted to the temporary dock. Sal brought herself up on a stanchion and said, "Tom, keep the men aboard and ready the ship to lift. I'm going to see why Beck's here again. If I don't like his reasons, we're out of here!"

She pushed off, using the hatch coaming to correct and brake her motion. "Sal?" Harrigan called to her back. "If we leave, we miss the return cargo."

"Bugger the return cargo!" Sal said.

If the *Gallant Sallie* cut and ran, Sarah Blythe would spend the voyage home worrying about what she'd say to the note-holder, Ishtar Chandlery. She might even have to decide whether it'd be worse to lose the ship than to call on a noble named Samuel Trafficant and . . . beg his kindness. For the moment, though, her concerns were much more immediate.

The *Gallant Sallie*'s arms locker was strapped to the rear cabin bulkhead. Sal wondered if she should have paused long enough to open the locker and take one of the six rifles or the shotgun inside. At least she should have grabbed one of the powered cutting bars that spacers used for tools or weap-

ons as circumstances dictated. She hadn't thought of that till
she noticed how lonely the empty dock seemed.

Sal used the crate of turbine spares to halt her. Its mass
didn't visibly move when it stopped her 55 kilograms.

The featherboat's hatch, a two-meter-by-one-meter section
of the upper hull, lifted as soon as the dock's attachment lips
were clamped around the coaming. Atmosphere from the
featherboat filled the access tube. The valve started to open
inward, toward Sal.

A dozen figures from the featherboat entered the tube.
They were armed. Three of them—Beck and two other of
the morning's visitors—wore the white uniforms of Federation officials. Six of the others were Molts, their purplish
exoskeletons unclothed save for one draped in a pink sash-
of-office.

The other three invaders were human also, but they were
garbed in clothing cast off by Federation colonists. These
last were obviously Rabbits, the human remnants of Lilymead's pre-Collapse population; sunken to savagery, and
now slaves of the Federation like the Molts beside them.

"Harrigan, close the hatch!" Sal shouted in a cold, clear
voice. She propelled herself toward the access tube. The
valve had sprung open when the featherboat equalized pressure, but perhaps she could jam it—

A Molt caught her wrist with three chitinous fingers. Sal
twisted. The Molt wasn't as strong as she was, but he raised
the cutting bar in his free hand. The surfaces of his triangular
face were expressionless.

"I've got this one, bug!" shouted a pudgy human with
CUSTOMS SERVICE in tarnished braid on the collar of his uniform. He socketed the muzzle of a revolver in Sal's left ear.

"Don't you move, bitch, or I'll paint your brains all over
the walls!" the Fed added, his face centimeters from hers.
His breath stank of fear and unfamiliar spices.

Sal heard shots and a cry of pain from the *Gallant Sallie*'s
hatch. Beck, wearing a tunic with gold epaulets and holding
a rifle awkwardly, crossed the dock with the aid of two
Molts.

The lighter was disgorging more armed Feds up a second
access tube to join the force from the featherboat. The two

Fed vessels were much of a size, but the lighter had greater internal capacity because it didn't need the equipment and hull strength for interstellar travel. There seemed to have been forty or fifty personnel, mostly Molts and Rabbits, packed into the lighter's hold.

"We are here under a valid contract, approved by the Bureau of Out-System Trade in Montreal!" Sal said. "You'll answer to President Pleyal for this piracy!"

"Shut up!" cried the Fed officer. "We've got orders, and by Mary and the Saints, we've got the power!"

He forced his revolver harder against Sal's ear. The two of them rotated slowly. Sal could now see the backs of the attackers entering the *Gallant Sallie*. A gunshot lighted the hold red. Cutting bars whined. There were several more shots in quick succession, but this time the muzzle flashes were obscured.

A Molt drifted from the hatchway. The creature's head had been dished in. The edges of the wound dripped brown ichor.

The Fed holding Sal gaped. There was a hollow *thoonk*. His face bulged and something sprayed Sal, half blinding her. A bullet had taken the officer in the back of the skull and exited beneath his left eye. The projectile went on out through the wall of the temporary dock, leaving a black void in the center of a 20-centimeter bulge stressed to white opacity.

Sal wiped her eyes. The corpse was floating away from her. She twisted the revolver out of fingers that had clamped when the Fed's brain was destroyed.

The *Gallant Sallie* had a sprinkler system, nozzles in the hold fed directly from the tank of reaction mass behind the midships bulkhead. Somebody opened the valve briefly. An opaque cloud of water vapor filled the hold and gushed from the hatch. It was doubly blinding in the low-pressure atmosphere.

Federation personnel retreated gasping through the gray mass. They collided with the reinforcements continuing to arrive from the lighter. Beck reappeared, shouting an unintelligible order. A woman in Federation uniform bumped him into a somersault as she pushed past.

Another bullet came through the wall of the dock from outside, from vacuum. This round smashed the thigh of a Molt with an impact that spun the creature's legs above its head.

Orbit around Lilymead brought the *Gallant Sallie*'s port side to the sun again. So illuminated, the vessel's ceramic hull was clearly visible through the dulling medium of the cellulose walls. Everybody in the dock could see a gunport open and the muzzle of one of the 10-cm guns appear.

Sal knew that the cannon couldn't be safely fired before the ship cleared for action; the gun probably wasn't even loaded. The Federation groundlings didn't know that, and the blobs of blood and ichor floating about them had drained their morale anyway. As a mob, they broke and forced their way up the tubes to the vessels that had brought them.

Tom Harrigan appeared in the hatchway, veiled in dissipating water vapor. His forehead was gashed and the pry bar in his right fist was bloody. Nedderington paused beside the mate, fired a shotgun at the backs of the fleeing Feds, and recoiled into the hold.

Sal crouched against the side of the dock, holding herself steady by expert, tiny motions. Brantling, still wearing his pressure suit and helmet, stood in the cabin airlock with a rifle. He fired again, this time killing a Rabbit about to reenter the featherboat. Panicked Feds pressed the corpse aboard with them.

Beck, unable to control his body's spinning, drifted close to Sal. She aimed the revolver at him and tried to fire it. The trigger wouldn't move: the ill-maintained weapon was rusted solid. The Fed leader screamed in terror. Sal grabbed Beck by the collar and used the revolver to clout him twice above the ear. Beck's eyeballs rolled up in their sockets.

The lighter pulled away with a blast of its thruster. The dock jerked before main force broke the seal. The lighter's hatch was open, and there were still people trying to board through it.

The dock's inner door closed. The last of the air in the tube puffed the bodies into hard vacuum, their limbs flailing momentarily.

The featherboat separated also. The Fed pilots were terrified by the plasma cannon, whose blast at this range could turn either vessel into a fireball more gaseous than solid. No one was in the featherboat's access tube, but a uniformed human and two Molts were trapped in the dock as the valve closed.

"Sal, are you all right?" Tom Harrigan said. He launched himself to his captain's side across the blood-spattered dock.

Sal straightened, using Beck's mass to control her motion. The Fed leader was coming around. The other Fed survivors stared at Sal and the weapons in the hands of the Venerians joining her in the dock.

"Cooney, give me a hand with the captain!" Harrigan ordered, taking Sal's silence for proof she'd been incapacitated. "Leave these other bastards here to see how well they breathe vacuum!"

"No!" Sal said. "Bring them aboard. And fast—I want to be out of this system in five minutes!"

Harrigan took her arm anyway. He pushed off the wall of the dock, guiding her as if she was a landsman who couldn't navigate in weightlessness. "I say leave them, Sal," he repeated. "They killed Josselyn, and there's a couple more might not make it home."

"No, don't leave me!" Beck pleaded, trailing behind Sal like a heavy dufflebag. "I'm the Fiscal of Lilymead, the President's representative. I'm an important man!"

They entered the hold. Obedient to Sal's orders, her crewmen had policed up all the Fed survivors and were following with them. She thrust the revolver down the throat of her tunic and caught a stanchion.

"You lying bastard!" Harrigan snarled in Beck's face. "If you're Pleyal's representative, why didn't you honor the safe conduct Pleyal gave us?"

Sal kicked forward, up the passageway and into the cabin. Josselyn floated in midair with his throat cut. Bealzy was trying to stuff a loop of intestine back through the bullet wound in Kokalas' abdomen.

"We had orders from Montreal," Beck whimpered behind her. He patted the pocket of his uniform blouse. Paper crackled. "I'm carrying them right here with me. We're to confiscate all Venerian vessels which arrive, regardless of their

safe conducts. President Pleyal needs them to help equip the
fleet he's gathering to end the Venus rebellion for once and
for all!''

"Rebellion?" Harrigan said, too amazed at the term for
the impact of the whole statement to register. "Why, we're
not rebels, we're citizens of the Free State of Venus!''

Sal thrust the Fiscal of Lilymead into a net that still held
a day's supply of rations for the crew.

"Stay here, don't move, and you'll live even though you
don't deserve to," she ordered savagely. To Harrigan she
added, "And I mean it, Tom, I want him to stay alive all
the way back. There's a lot of people on Venus who need
to hear his story!''

Sal strapped herself to the navigation console. While the
hard-used electronics moaned to life, she dabbed absently at
the grit on her face.

The main hatch clanged shut. Crewmen called to one another as they seated the manual dogs and completed the other
familiar business of liftoff.

The holographic display settled to a creamy saffron,
picked out by a few strobing points where a circuit misfired.
Very shortly the ready prompt would come up and Sal could
initiate the first transit sequence.

She glanced at her hands. What she'd wiped from her face
was bits of the skull of the Fed who'd been holding her in
the dock. The chips were tacky with a slime of fresh pink
brains.

Sal managed to turn her head so that her sudden rush of
vomit didn't cover the navigation keyboard.

ISHTAR CITY, VENUS.

The woman who entered the pantry didn't notice Stephen until she'd closed the door behind her and cut off the burr of voices from the party in the function rooms down the hallway. When she saw the big man in the corner holding a bottle of slash, liquor distilled from algae, her eyes widened in startlement. "You're Stephen Gregg," she said.

Stephen looked at her without expression. "I'm not too drunk to remember my name," he said. His eyes flicked from the woman to the bottle in his hand. The slash was vaguely gray in hue. "In fact I'm not drunk at all, though that's not for lack of trying."

"Do you mind if I . . ." she said. She nodded toward the closed door. "I needed to get away from that. They're all over me like lice, each one trying to get his drop of blood."

Stephen smiled faintly. He recognized the woman as Sarah Blythe, the captain who'd brought to Venus notice of the treachery, the latest treachery, of the North American Federation. Identifying her was no great trick. Though the gathering had a social gloss in a mild attempt to mislead President Pleyal's spies, the attendees were principals and agents only; they'd left their consorts at home. Only a handful of the several score persons present were women.

"I'm not the most social of people myself," Stephen said in smiling understatement. He found a glass on the shelf beside him, started to pour, and paused. "Will you have a drink?" he asked. "I only brought slash with me when I ran the servants out, I'm afraid."

"Slash is fine with me," she said. She wore a pale blue

15

jacket and jumper over a ruffed blouse. The outfit was in unobtrusive good taste. Though it was inexpensive by the standards of the guests in the function rooms, Blythe didn't stand out the way a space captain in the midst of a gathering of magnates could be expected to do. "Ah, I'm Sal Blythe. I apologize for the way I—greeted you."

She wasn't a beautiful woman, but she was interesting in appearance as well as personality. Gregg had the impression that Blythe had started to reach for the bottle to drink from it straight, the way he'd been doing. She took a healthy swig from the tumbler he handed her, grimaced, and said, "Paint thinner. But you know, it was what I grew up with, and nothing else seems like a drink."

She looked at him appraisingly. Not the way a man would have done, because when strange men looked at Stephen Gregg, there was always a touch of fear or challenge in their eyes. Very few people could say honestly that they knew Stephen, but almost every adult on Venus knew *of* him. . . .

"I never thought I'd meet you," Blythe said, drinking more of her slash. "And Captain Ricimer's out there as well." She grinned wryly and added, "I'd say that it was worth being attacked by the Feds, but then there's the rest of the pack. They all want the Commission of Redress they expect I'll be issued for the damage the Feds did me on Lilymead."

Blythe's face lost its chubby softness and became momentarily as hard as her eyes. "They don't seem to hear the word 'no' when a woman's saying it," she said.

"Oh, it's not a word they hear very easily from anyone, some of them," Stephen said with a shrug. He took down another glass for himself. "From those who don't have as much money as they do, at least, but that's most people."

As Stephen poured, the door behind Sarah Blythe opened in a blast of sound. "Go away!" he snarled without looking up.

"Oh!" a male voice said. "Terribly sorry, Mister Gregg!" The last syllable was trimmed by the door's firm closure.

"Who was that?" Blythe asked in surprise. All she would have seen of the intruder was the sleeve of a gorgeous coat.

Stephen grimaced and tossed off his slash. "I'm afraid

from the voice it was Blenrott of Laodicea,'' he said. ''Our host. I can't seem to get drunk, and that makes me . . . even less tactful than usual. But there's no excuse for me behaving like a—''

He shook his head and smiled without humor. ''Rabid dog, I suppose. Well, I'll make it up to him.''

Stephen wondered just what it was that Blythe saw when she looked at him. He was 32 years old, taller than most men, and stronger than almost anyone he was likely to meet. His features were regular, and his short hair was a blond so pale that the long scar on his scalp showed through clearly.

At one time Stephen Gregg had been considered a handsome man, but he couldn't imagine anyone found him so today. He'd lost track of the number of people he'd killed over the past ten years. Hundreds, certainly. He knew there was nothing inside him but a lump of cold gray ice, and he was sure that others had to see through the shell of him to that emptiness as clearly as he did himself.

''I'm going out with the commission myself,'' Blythe said harshly, hunching over the liquor glass. ''It was me the Feds attacked, me and the *Gallant Sallie*. It's us who'll take redress from them, by *God* we will!''

She was embarrassed by the outburst. To cover it with a mask of small talk, Stephen said, ''I feel the same way about slash. No other run has quite the taste of Eryx slash, though.''

He smiled minusculely and added, ''If I didn't think it was too affected for words, I'd have my brother ship me a case every week or so.''

''That's your hold, Eryx?'' Blythe said. She was watching him over the top of her glass, but he wasn't sure she'd taken another sip.

''The family hold,'' Stephen said deprecatingly. ''My brother Augustus is the factor, and it's a very small place, Eryx is.'' But with a flush of the pride that never ceased to amaze him, he added, ''There've been Greggs of Eryx since the Collapse, though.''

''You don't live at the hold, then?'' Blythe said. Because she knew she was edging beyond the bounds of proper discussion with a stranger—a famous man, a powerful man—

she looked at Stephen's elbow rather than his face as she spoke. Her eyes were pleasantly blue with brown rings about the irises.

"It didn't really work out," Stephen said, pouring more slash. "They were more than kind, but I made the family nervous and that made me, you know, more uncomfortable. I've got two rooms in Betaport. On holidays I make day-trips to Eryx so the kids can climb on their Uncle Stephen. But I don't sleep over."

"Two *rooms*?" Blythe repeated. This run of slash proved on the order of seventy five percent ethanol. Whether she was used to the liquor or not, it had stripped some of the subtlety that might otherwise have overlain her question.

Blythe's eyes probed Stephen's clothing again as she considered whether her initial appraisal had been wrong. He was in court dress, suitable for wear at functions in the Governor's Palace. The colors were muted, beige and russet, and the cut of the garments was looser than the mode; but the fabric was Terran silk, and the ensemble had probably cost more than a set of eight thruster nozzles for the *Gallant Sallie*.

Stephen laughed, a harsh sound that he hated to hear. "You think that with my share of the loot we took from Pleyal and his thugs in the Reaches, Piet and I and the rest, I ought to be able to afford a place like this myself?"

He gestured, indicating not the pantry in which the two of them were hiding but the suite of which it was a part. The measure of wealth on Venus was the volume of one's dwelling. There'd been an enormous recent growth of trade, fueled directly and indirectly by the microchips that raiders like Piet Ricimer brought home from the pre-Collapse automated production facilities in the Reaches. Men like Blenrott, who'd invested heavily and been lucky, had huge sums to sink into town houses like this one on the fringes of the capital.

"And so I could," Stephen continued. "But if I wanted to have a lot of people around me, Captain Blythe, I'd be out there in the function rooms, wouldn't I?"

"I, ah," Blythe said. Her glass was empty. Stephen leaned toward her to refill it, but she waved him away. She'd already had more than was probably good for her discretion. "I assumed you had a wife or, ah . . ."

"Are you offering?" Stephen said in a cold, professional tone.

Sarah Blythe set her glass on the terrazzo floor beside her. She could have thrown it without much risk of breakage. Metal-poor Venus had developed ceramics technology to levels undreamed of before the Collapse cut the planet off from Earth and the Asteroid Belt. She straightened, took a step forward, and slapped Stephen as hard as she could.

Stephen let the blow land, though it jolted his head to the side. He'd been hit by men who put less steam into their punches. "I'm sorry," he said. "That was stupid and uncalled for. I'll try to make amends."

Blythe swung again. He stopped the blow with the fingers of his left hand. Her eyes widened when she realized how quick the motion had been. "Captain Blythe," he said with the least tremble of emotion, "I apologize."

She'd had a right to hit him, but the impact had taken Stephen Gregg's mind into another place: the place he tried to forget about by drinking. He could control his actions, but couldn't help the suffusing golden joy at the thought of killing again *soon*.

Blythe stepped back and drew a shuddering breath. "I apologize too, Mister Gregg," she said. She didn't meet his eyes. She massaged her right palm with her left hand. If she'd closed her hand into a fist, she'd have broken at least a knuckle. "My question was improperly pers—"

He held out the bottle.

"No, no," she said. "Not for me. I've obviously had too much already."

"Yes, well, maybe I have too," Stephen said, stoppering the bottle. There wasn't much left in it anyway. "You're owner as well as captain of the ship involved in the incident on Lilymead?"

"The *Gallant Sallie*, yes," Blythe said. "My father's still alive, but he assigned the title to me when he had to retire. So that I could pledge a security interest in the ship during out-system trading."

Stephen nodded his understanding. He'd gone into space

as a merchant, a supercargo looking out for the interests of his uncle, Gregg of Weyston, an investor in the voyage. Piet Ricimer was a junior officer on the same ship. Amazing the changes that ten years could bring; good and otherwise.

"Marcus Blythe is my father," Blythe said. Then—perhaps because she'd slapped him and wanted to punish herself for reacting the way she had—she went on crisply, "And he *is* my father, in every way that matters. I was born while Dad was on a two-year voyage to Southern Cross colonies in the Reaches. I'm told my mother saw a lot of Samuel Trafficant during the time Dad was gone, I don't know. But Marcus has always been a father to me!"

Stephen nodded again. "Samuel . . ." he said. "That would be the brother of Trafficant of Trafficant?" He'd met Factor Trafficant once, years ago; a heavyset man with hair the same shade of blond as Sarah Blythe's.

"Uncle of the current factor," Blythe said with a deliberate lack of emotion. "I'm told Samuel controls some of the family investments, but I don't really know."

She looked directly at him. "*I* live in Ishtar City near the Old Port with Dad. My mother died before I was two."

Stephen shrugged away the challenge in the stocky woman's gaze. "What's the burden of your *Gallant Sallie*, then?" he asked. "If you're—"

There was a knock on the pantry door. "Stephen?" called a familiar voice through the panel. "Can you join us for the ceremonies?"

"Of course, Piet," Stephen said. "That's why we're here, after all."

He reached past Sarah Blythe for the latch. It wasn't until the door opened, though, that she realized the plumpish, youngish man whom she faced close enough to kiss was Captain Piet Ricimer, the most famous spacer on Venus— and the man whose name President Pleyal was said to scream in his nightmares. "Oh!" Blythe said.

"Captain Blythe," Stephen said with a bland smile for the humor in the situation, "permit me to introduce you to my friend Factor Ricimer. Piet, this is Sarah Blythe, the captain of the ship which escaped during the incident on Lilymead."

Piet shook Blythe's hand with every sign of approval. Piet

Ricimer believed that only idolators like those of the Federation permitted women to do the work of men, but he was rarely impolite—or impolitic—when he could avoid it. Piet's purpose in life, the return of mankind to the stars in furtherance of God's plan, eclipsed every other belief and feeling within him.

"A very good job, Captain," Piet said. "I've noticed that your report gives the credit to your crew, but they wouldn't have reacted as you describe without proper training and a captain they were willing to fight for."

Behind Piet stood Guillermo, Piet's Molt servant. Referring to Guillermo as a slave was one of the few things that brought Piet to instant, open anger. So far as Piet was concerned, Molts were human and the slavery the Feds practiced in the Reaches was a sin against God.

Crewmen who'd served with Piet on his long voyages treated Guillermo as a fellow and a dab hand with a starship's controls, almost the equal of Captain Ricimer himself. The Molt wasn't much good in a fight, but that didn't matter. Not in a ship with Mister Gregg aboard, it didn't.

Behind Piet and Guillermo stood a servant in Blenrott's livery, pale and purple. The houseman watched Stephen in obvious nervousness. Stephen caught Piet's eye and nodded to indicate the servant.

"Factor Blenrott put him at the door of the pantry with orders not to permit anyone to disturb you, Stephen," Piet explained dryly. "That's why I had to come fetch you myself. And speaking of that, the others are probably waiting for us."

Stephen grimaced with disgust at his own conduct. It doesn't matter how you feel or why you feel that way, you don't take it out on innocents. In this respect at least, Kaspar Blenrott was surely an innocent. "I'll make it up to him," he muttered again.

He fell into step a half pace behind Piet and as much to the side. In this gathering, there was no need for the shoulders and grim visage of Stephen Gregg to clear the way.

Guillermo was on Piet's other flank. Stephen, for reasons he didn't care to examine, gestured Captain Sarah Blythe up between them so that they walked in clear association into the hushed assembly room.

ISHTAR CITY, VENUS.

Sal Blythe was personally acquainted with only a handful of the folk gathered in the assembly room. Captain Willem Casson was a contemporary of her father's; not a friend, exactly, but a man who'd sat with the Blythes in a dockside tavern, speaking of voyages to the Reaches in which he searched for worlds whose pre-Collapse wealth was not yet claimed by the Federation or the Southern Cross.

The other attendees Sal knew to speak with were bankers, every one of them. People from whom she'd raised—more often tried to raise—money for this or that requirement of the *Gallant Sallie* over the years. She wondered if now would be a good time to broach the subject of the additional loan she'd need to fit the vessel out to raid Federation shipping under the Commission of Redress she hoped to be granted.

Piet Ricimer mounted the dais in a light flurry of applause. Sal knew of the two men already on the dais, though they were too powerful for her to have had any dealings with. Councilor Duneen headed the Bureau of External Relations; he was said to be Governor Halys' chief advisor on matters of foreign policy. Duneen was much of a size with Piet Ricimer and less than a dozen years older. The councilor moved with grace and an easy assurance of his own great power, but there was a fire in the soul of the space captain that the courtier lacked.

Alexi Mostert stood beside Duneen. His brother, Siddons Mostert, was in the front rank below, along with Stephen Gregg and many of the most powerful shipping and financial magnates on Venus. Alexi rated the dais because for the past three years he'd been Chief Constructor of the Fleet, the man primarily responsible for the design and building of state warships.

The Mosterts were able and intelligent men who'd expanded a modest shipping firm into the spearhead of trade from Venus. Alexi's purpose-built warships were handy and powerful, each of them supposedly more than a match for one of the much larger vessels of the North American Federation.

Supposedly: the truth wouldn't be known until the outbreak of open war between Venus and the Federation. That test couldn't be long coming, however, if the result of this gathering was what Sal expected it to be.

Ricimer bowed to Councilor Duneen, then called to the assembly in a ringing voice, "Fellow citizens, fellow patriots—I could tell you how serious a threat the Free State of Venus faces today, but I prefer to yield to a man who can speak far more eloquently. I give you Fiscal Walter Beck, until recently the Federation's chief representative on Lilymead and the man responsible for executing President Pleyal's orders there!"

The curtain behind the dais rustled to pass Beck, flanked by a pair of tough-looking sailors. The guards were a dramatic effect: Beck wasn't a threat to anyone. The fiscal had aged a decade in the days since Sal last saw him. The governor's interrogators didn't appear to have physically harmed him, but his skin was gray and his eyes faced a future in which there was no hope.

"I received orders from Montreal, signed by the president and authenticated with his code," Beck said. His tone was singsong because he'd repeated the story so frequently. "The papers being passed around the room are true copies of those orders. They required me to seize all Venerian vessels which called at Lilymead, despite the announced lifting of the embargo on foreign ships trading with us. The orders stated that the North American Federation had need of Venerian ships and particularly their guns for a Fleet of Retribution that would finally end the rebellion of Venus against the proper rule of President Pleyal."

The words, though familiar by now and spoken without

affect, stabbed like cold steel through Sal's chest. The North American Federation, which five years before had incorporated the Southern Cross in a lightning sweep, had twenty times the population of Venus and drew on the resources of a hundred colonial worlds. If that power were focused, how could the Free State of Venus survive?

Beck shuffled away at the end of his practiced spiel and disappeared behind the curtains with his guards. A servant offered Sal a copy of the orders captured with the fiscal on Lilymead. Sal took the sheet absently, though God knew she'd studied the original long enough as the *Gallant Sallie* ran for home.

Councilor Duneen stepped forward with a fierce, solemn expression and said, "Individual citizens of Venus have been harmed by this action of President Pleyal. Two ships were captured on Lilymead, four others have failed to return from similar voyages to Federation colonies in Near Space, and"—he nodded in Sal's direction—"the vessel which escaped to give the alarm was damaged in the Feds' treacherous attack and lost the value of its cargo. In all cases, the interested parties will receive Commissions of Redress by the grace of Governor Halys, authorizing them to recoup their losses from the citizens and facilities of the North American Federation. There is another dimension to this event, however."

The room was tensely still as Duneen gazed around his audience. Many of the folk assembled had spent most of their lives grasping for profit. There was a leavening of sharks like Ricimer, like Casson; men who'd fought the Federation already and whose hope had been open war in which all Venus fought together to smash the tyranny of President Pleyal.

Both groups waited in a hush for the words they'd been assembled to hear. No one who opposed the government's plan had been invited; but, as with guests at a wedding, everyone present knew that the future might bring disaster.

"Governor Halys," Duneen continued, "has determined to send a squadron to retrieve the vessels unlawfully held in Federation ports. She will provide two ships from the State service, but there will be many opportunities for patriotic citizens to join in the expedition for the usual share of any profits accruing from the voyage. I won't discuss the details of the makeup and outfitting. That will be in the hands of the man Governor Halys has appointed as General Commander of the squadron: Captain Piet Ricimer!''

The cheer that greeted the announcement was spontaneous and general. Rather, almost general. Stephen Gregg stood at the base of the dais in part-profile to Sal behind him. Gregg's face was expressionless. Only the one gray eye Sal could see had life, a terrible glee that shocked her more than the muzzle of the Fed's revolver touching her head had done.

"Gentlemen and ladies,'' Piet Ricimer called, his voice riding with the enthusiasm instead of trying to overshout it, "through the generosity of Factor Blenrott, there are tables against the back wall here and separate rooms for those who would prefer to deal amongst themselves in greater privacy. I suggest we break up now and see how we can best put profit and patriotism at the service of the Lord God Almighty!''

Bowing again to the company, Ricimer strode at a swinging pace toward the table where Guillermo already waited. Stephen and the Mosterts fell in behind him. The gathering broke into a score of discussions milling like eddies of bubbles beneath a flume.

A young man in severely muted tunic and trousers—probably an agent rather than a principal—matched his step to Gregg's and began to talk earnestly. As the fellow spoke, he gestured with a notebook open to a page of numbers in column.

"Yes, but is that FOB Ishtar City, or for orbital loading?'' Stephen replied in a coolly precise voice. "If it's orbit then yes, we might well be interested.''

He didn't sound like the swashbuckling killer that common report held Stephen Gregg to be. He didn't sound like the tortured man Sal had met in the pantry, either.

If Sal tried to see Councilor Duneen in his palace office, she would have to bribe her way through phalanxes of attendants. Here there were only a few magnates with the councilor. On the strength of Duneen's nod to her in his presentation, Sal decided to ask how and when her Commission of Redress would be issued.

She was a hair too slow to approach the dais. Hollin, Grouse, and Richards, the three most importunate of the folk who'd pestered Sal till she took cover in the pantry, closed about her in a ring as close as minimal politeness permitted.

"I've told all you gentlemen my position," Sal said sharply. "I'm not interested in dealing with you."

"Yes, but there've been developments since then," Hollin said. The trio were money men, not shippers; bankers in a large way and reputed to be well known in the Governor's Palace. "In particular we've made an arrangement among ourselves so that the three of us aren't in competition, so to speak."

"We've also looked into your circumstances in detail, Mistress Blythe," Grouse added. "You can't afford to pay the gift Councilor Duneen will expect to release your commission, much less outfit your ship for a raiding voyage. The commission won't exist unless you see reason and transfer your rights to us—for a very respectable sum. We've agreed to pay you three thousand consols—cash, not discounted bills."

Sal turned angrily. Richards stood in that direction, a disdainful sneer on his lips. She wondered what the banker would do if she slapped him the way she'd slapped Stephen Gregg.

The advantage of a Commission of Redress was that the holder was exempted from the Governor's Fifth, the levy on cargoes brought to Venus from beyond the Solar System. If Sal sold her commission to the consortium surrounding her, they stood to greatly increase the value of prizes awarded to ships they owned in the course of the coming raid. Given the fabulous success of Piet Ricimer's previous expeditions, an extra twenty percent could be worth a fortune. Three thousand Venerian consols was a derisory offer, even if Sal had been willing to deal.

"We've called in some favors, Blythe," Richards said harshly. "You'll get no credit in Ishtar City or any of the other ports. And if you're thinking of raising the money you need from some pawnbroker out in the sticks—forget it!

They'd need to pass the loan back to a respondent in Ishtar City, and they'd learn that nobody was willing to negotiate your paper."

Grouse frowned a little at Richards' open threat. He gestured calmingly and said, "There's another matter you should consider, Mistress Blythe. Your vessel operating alone is unlikely to make any significant prizes from the Federation. Probably not even enough to pay the expenses of your voyage. The chance of real profit is with the squadron forming now. I shouldn't have to tell you that General Commander Ricimer is far too good a Christian to permit a ship captained by a woman to serve with him."

Sal jerked upright. She felt suddenly sick with frustration. "Listen, you!" she said. "I'm as good a Christian as any man in this room! Show me where the Bible says a woman can't captain a starship. Show me where it says a woman can't do *any* damned thing!"

"I'm sure President Pleyal and his toadies would agree with you, *Mistress*," Hollin said. "I'm equally sure that Captain Ricimer would not. Now, if you'd like us to take up the outstanding loans on the *Gallant Sallie* and leave you without a ship at all, then—"

"Good afternoon, gentlemen," said Stephen Gregg, looming like a fang of rock behind Richards. "I heard you discussing business with my partner, Captain Blythe, here, so I thought I ought to come join you."

He smiled. If Death had a human face, thought Sarah Blythe, it would wear a very similar expression.

ISHTAR CITY, VENUS.

AUGUST 10, YEAR 26.
1707 HOURS, VENUS TIME.

"Your *partner*, Mister Gregg?" Hollin said. Richards, who'd jerked around as though he'd been stabbed, said nothing. Grouse twitched backward. His reflex, barely controlled, was to try to vanish into the crowd.

"Why, yes, Factor Hollin," Stephen said. He continued to walk forward in a curving path. His advance forced the bankers to move away from Blythe and, not coincidentally, put Stephen's own back to the wall. There was no physical need for that precaution here, but at the psychic level Stephen felt better for it. *We live in our minds, after all.*

He knew the three bankers better than he liked them. They were the new breed of financier, young men who'd made their mark in the current expansion of commerce. Grouse was of an age with Stephen and Piet, and the other two were only in their forties.

Stephen had heard the trio described as ruthless, but the word means different things to different people. *Ruthless means firing into a compartment full of people because somewhere among the screaming civilians is a Fed soldier with a gun. Ruthless is—*

Stephen focused back on the present, on the three well-dressed men staring at him in horror and the woman with a look of concern. Blythe's left hand was raised to touch him, to call him back from where he'd gone for an instant.

"I was sure there'd been a failure of communication," Stephen said. By the end of the sentence, his voice was back to its normal pleasant tenor, free of the rusty harshness that made the first words sound as though they'd been vocalized

28

by an ill-programmed machine. "None of you gentlemen would have insulted my honor by knowingly trying to undercut my arrangements."

"Good *God*, no, sir!" Richards blurted as he backed away. The banker didn't have a high reputation for honesty, but there was no doubting the simple truth of his words this time.

Stephen smiled at the statement, but the bankers missed the humor of it. They bowed their respects and scuttled into the crowd, avoiding one another as well as their former quarry.

Sarah Blythe still stood beside him. Stephen scanned the assembly, looking over her head instead of at her. Not necessary, but—

"Those three had a good notion of what it costs to outfit a commercial vessel for raiding," Stephen said. "They should, after all, since they've had shares in at least a dozen raiders in the past five years. They work with the Mosterts, often as not. Were they right about your own financial condition?"

Blythe nodded, her expression deliberately blank. "Credit's tight, yes," she said. "Credit *was* tight before I came back from Lilymead with an empty hold, though I thought— I think that I'll be able to raise the necessary on the basis of the Commission of Redress."

She cleared her throat. "I . . ." she said. "Ah, thank you for what you did."

She was looking at him, but he continued to view the room. "My pleasure," he said. He laughed, a sound like that of bricks clinking together. "It's a pity, I suppose, but that's really true."

Blythe cleared her throat. "Well, thank you again. I need to see Councilor Duneen, so—"

"We have business to transact," Stephen said crisply. "If you're amenable, I'll take a silent partnership in your venture. You'll retain full control of the *Gallant Sallie*—captain her, engage the crew, all as you've been doing previously. I'll undertake to outfit the vessel for the voyage at my own sole charge, and to provide expertise."

He gave her a businesslike smile. "You'll need an expert,

me or someone like me. I assure you, a raiding voyage is very different from the commercial endeavors in which you've been engaged to present."

She nodded back. "I can see that," she said. She didn't really understand, though. She thought he meant differences in staff and equipment. . . .

"The relative value of the ship's share and the backer's share will be determined by survey of the vessel," Stephen continued, speaking with the seamless precision of a man at one with his subject. "We'll each appoint a surveyor, the pair to choose the third man themselves. Captain's and crew's shares aren't affected, of course."

"I'd want to discuss this with . . ." Blythe said, but she let her voice trail off as she reconsidered. Her father, Stephen assumed, though there might well be a man in her life. There deserved to be.

"Alternatively," he concluded, "I'll put a consol down and you'll double it to me on your return. For honor's sake."

He grinned. Her face lost the thoughtful animation of a moment before and became guarded again.

"I told those three that I was your partner, you see," he explained. "So I need to put something into the expedition."

At the back of the room, Piet shook hands with Kuelow of Thorn, leaning across the table to clap the magnate on the back. Piet's eyes met Stephen's in a quick flicker. Stephen flared the fingers of his left hand in an all's-well signal; Piet nodded and switched the full force of his personality to the next man waiting to talk with him, the agent of a syndicate of Betaport shippers.

They'd been looking out for each other for a decade now, he and Piet. One way and another.

"Why are you making this offer, Mister Gregg?" Sarah Blythe said. She wasn't quite able to hide the unintended challenge.

"My uncle is Benjamin Gregg," Stephen said in a mildly bantering tone. "Gregg of Weyston, Weyston Trading. Uncle Ben would disown me if I turned down a business opportunity like this when it dropped in my lap. And there's also . . ."

Stephen looked at Captain Sarah Blythe, feeling the sadness at what so easily might have been: Stephen Gregg, merchant. Stephen Gregg, managing partner in Weyston Trading by now, though Uncle Ben wasn't the sort to give up titular control while life was in him.

"There's also the fact that I said I'd make amends for my boorishness," he went on, rubbing his cheek where she'd hit him.

Blythe snorted. "I'd say running those three off put the debt on my side of the ledger," she said, nodding dismissively toward Factor Richards, glimpsed across the room.

"I said that was a pleasure," Stephen repeated. "God help me, but it was."

"Very well," Blythe said. "My hand on the bargain then, Mister Gregg."

Her grip was firm, but her palms were sweating. If she had not been nervous, that would have meant she didn't understand what had been going on.

"I'll talk to Calaccio about the survey," she went on. "He's the primary noteholder. Ishtar Chandlery, you know."

Stephen nodded. "I'll get one of Uncle Ben's people and tell him to contact Calaccio," he said. "Oh, and if you'll ask Calaccio to turn over the vessel's full supply and maintenance logs to my representative, I'll get to work at once on my end. And let me take care of Duneen."

"I should hit men more often," Blythe said with a straight face.

"If they behave the way I did, you should indeed," Stephen replied.

Blenrott, beaming with the success of the affair he was hosting, turned from a group of courtiers and caught Stephen's eye. Stephen gave him a full bow.

"On Thursday," Stephen said in a voice that Blythe leaned closer to hear, "I'll attend Factor Blenrott's levee. My presence will make his peers think he stands a meter taller; which is stupid, but it's the truth nonetheless."

"I think my friend Mister Gregg can best supply those estimates," Piet said in tones pitched to carry across the five meters of conversation separating the two of them.

"Duty calls," Stephen said, gesturing with his left hand but looking directly at Blythe for the first time since he'd

driven away the bankers. "Blenrott's affair will be excruci-
atingly dull," he went on in the same soft voice as he'd used
when he discussed their host before. "That's good. I believe
a person should be punished for acting badly. It makes it
unlikely that he'll do that particular thing again."

Stephen bowed to the woman and returned to where Piet
needed him for a discussion of share percentages.

ISHTAR CITY, VENUS.

AUGUST 13, YEAR 26.
0317 HOURS, VENUS TIME.

Marcus Blythe opened the street door cautiously, but he dropped his walking stick with a loud clatter before he managed to close the door behind him. He froze.

"It's all right, Dad," Sal said. "I'm up working, so you haven't bothered me."

"Ah," said Marcus. He turned around and saw his daughter seated at the table in the common room of the suite. He'd thought the light was on merely to guide him back to his bed as usual. "Ah."

"Do you need . . ." Sal asked.

"No, I'm quite all right," Marcus said in a tone of injured innocence. He bent carefully to retrieve his stick, fumbling it several times in the process. That was as much his arthritis-twisted hands as the drink, though. In truth, he wasn't drunk by his standards or those of the Old Port District more generally. "I was out toasting the success of our new venture with a few friends, you see."

He began to tremble. Sal rose quickly from her seat, bumping the table and disarranging the array of small parts on it. "Dad?" she said.

"No, I'm all right!" Marcus said with a touch of the fire appropriate to a space captain and shipowner; rarely heard since he became a cripple who spent his time drinking with other has-beens.

Sal put her arms around her father anyway, holding him close. There were tears at the corners of his eyes. Marcus wasn't an old man, but to himself—not to her, never to her—he was a useless one.

"Is it really going to happen, Sallie?" he said.

Sal used the bandanna with which she secured her hair in private to dab at the tears. "I don't think Mister Gregg lies about things, Dad," she said. "I don't think he could imagine a reason he'd want to. Now, if you're really all right, why don't you wash up before you go to bed? I've changed your sheets—and not before time."

"Yes, I'll do that," Marcus agreed humbly. He didn't move for a moment. "It . . . Sallie, it's so hard to believe that my own daughter is in partnership with Stephen Gregg. Mister Stephen *Gregg*!"

"Yeah," Sal said. "It is very hard to believe."

She hadn't let herself feel anything. She didn't know what she even ought to feel. Elation? Fear? There was reason enough for those and any number of other emotions; she just didn't know what was right.

"It means we'll be rich, you know, Sal," he said. "When I was young I thought—well, you're young, you know. But—"

"I don't know that we're going to be rich," Sal said, almost completely concealing her nervous irritation at hearing her father tempt fate. "All we have is a chance, a *chance* to recoup our losses on the last voyage."

"Oh, it's better than that, girl!" Marcus said, irritated in turn at having his hopes discounted. "Why, Gregg is Captain Ricimer's right-hand man! Gregg's cut his way to a dozen fortunes in the Reaches. You think he's not going to make sure this latest investment doesn't turn a profit too? A profit in a rich *gentleman's* terms!"

Sal swallowed. "I know that Mister Gregg is a skillful businessman, Dad," she said. "I just don't want you to get your hopes up. Would you like a hand to the corner?"

The bathhouse was at the junction with the main corridor three doors down.

"And I want you to know," Marcus bumbled on, "that nobody thinks the less of you for . . . what you've done. Your mother was a good woman at heart, a truly loving wife while we were together, and—"

"Dad, shut *up*," Sal said in a voice like a dragon's. "You're drunk and you don't know what you're saying."

She turned her father around in a curt movement better suited for shifting furniture and opened the door for him. Men were shouting at one another in slurred anger somewhere in the night, but they could have been blocks away. When there weren't crowds of pedestrians to absorb sound, it echoed long distances in the underground corridors of the older Venerian settlements.

"I'm not drunk!" Marcus protested feebly. "Sallie, what did I—"

"Sweat *all* the booze out of you before you come back here!" Sal said. "In the future, don't tell foolish *lies* to your drunken friends, and especially don't tell them to me!"

Puzzled, shocked completely sober, Marcus Blythe stumbled into the street. "Sallie, I'm sorry for—" he called.

She slammed the door on the last of his words and stood trembling against the inside of the panel for a moment. Were they all saying that she was Gregg's mistress? If her father said it to her face, then they probably were.

Sal sighed. It didn't matter. Most folk assumed the only use for a woman on a starship was to service the sexual needs of the crew. She'd lived with that all her life, so she could live with this too.

She sat down at the table and began to sort the parts into groups by subassemblies. She'd tacked a high-intensity lamp to the wall to work by. Its glare made her eyes sting; she switched it off and rubbed her forehead, swearing softly at nothing she could put a clear name to.

After a moment Sal turned the light back on. She dipped the copper bristles in solvent and resumed brushing the rust off the sear.

Spread before her on the table was the completely disassembled revolver that she'd pulled from the Federation officer's death grip. After she had it completely cleaned, she would treat the external surfaces with a corrosion-resistant phosphate finish.

When Sarah Blythe went beyond Pluto the next time, she would go armed.

BETAPORT, VENUS.

Piet Ricimer rose from the table in the back room of the Blue Rose Tavern and stretched with a groan. "I'm going to complain to the landlord about how hard the chairs in this room are," he said.

"They were comfortable enough six hours ago," Stephen said. "Maybe we've just worn them out."

The Blue Rose was on Ship Street, facing the port's transfer docks. The tavern had been Piet's headquarters from the beginning, long before he'd bought the freehold with a small fraction of the profits on his most recent raiding voyage.

Business was good tonight. A gust of laughter from the public bar rumbled its way through the wall. Guillermo was outside, acting as doorkeeper in case an important message arrived in person rather than by telephone.

"Six hours?" Piet echoed. "So it is. Shall we take a break?"

"Ten minutes more," Stephen said. He typed a string of commands on the keyboard, then rotated the holographic screen so that the display faced his companion. "I want to run through the last of the ships offered to the squadron."

Piet sat down again, his expression neutral. "All right," he said.

In the public bar, three sailors sang in excellent harmony, "*There were ninety and nine who safely lay—*"

"The *Gallant Sallie*," Stephen said. He leaned back in his chair so that his shoulders touched the glazed tiles of the wall behind him. "A well-found vessel of a hundred and fifty tonnes. A crew of sixteen plus the captain and mate.

36

She mounts four ten-centimeter guns, sufficient for the purpose we'd want her for—which I take to be transport rather than combat. She could easily be up-gunned, of course.''

"No, we don't need another fighting ship," Piet said. He looked at Stephen rather than the display. "If I recall correctly," he continued evenly, "this vessel's owner and captain is a woman."

Stephen got up, turned to face the corner behind him, and forced his palms hard against both walls of the angle. "Governor Halys is a woman, Piet," he said in a tense, clipped voice. "We serve a woman."

"We serve mankind, Stephen," Piet replied. His arms were spread, his right hand on the console and his left draped with deliberate nonchalance across the back of his chair. "I hope that we serve God as well, by executing His plan to return mankind to the stars. But I take your point."

Piet was speaking softly. His face, no longer neutral, bore a look of concern similar to that of an adult with an injured child.

Stephen sighed, turned, and wrapped his arms around himself. He was trying to find a position that relaxed him. "It's not just Lilymead, Piet," he said without meeting his friend's eyes. "I've looked at the *Gallant Sallie*'s maintenance records. I may not know the first thing about piloting, but I can see from repair invoices whether the captain's been beating a ship around. She's good."

"By now, perhaps the *first* thing," Piet said with a smile.

Stephen laughed, glad of the release. "All right, I'm a gentleman and can't be expected to touch my delicate fingers to a navigation computer," he said.

Piet stood. He put his right hand on the back of Stephen's hand and his left on Stephen's right shoulder. "Are you asking me to do this, Stephen?" he said.

Stephen met his eyes at last. "Yes, I am," he said.

In the public bar, dozens joined the trio to roar, "*Rejoice, for the Shepherd has found His sheep!*"

The *a cappella* rendition ended in a general cheer.

"All right, Stephen," Piet said, sitting down again. "Let's run through the rest of these and get something to eat, shall we?" He grinned. "Perhaps to drink as well."

"That's the last," Stephen said. He breathed out a sigh of relief more intense than anything he'd felt outside of combat. The feeling took him completely by surprise.

He looked at his friend. "Thanks, Piet," he said.

"It's little enough to do for you, Stephen," Piet said. He was dressed in flashy style even now, closeted with a friend doing bookwork. His tunic was black plush crossed by triple gold chevrons, in contrast to Stephen's worn blue garment with one of the buttons missing. "You came out beyond Pluto with me the second time because I needed you. Even though you knew what it would cost."

"No, by then it wouldn't have done me any good to stay home," Stephen said. "That's not, that's nothing for you to worry about. I—"

He glanced toward the door. The voices of sailors beginning "*Three Old Whores from Betaport*" didn't penetrate his consciousness, though his ears filed the information.

He looked down at Piet again and said with lilting simplicity, "Since the first voyage, the only time I'm really alive is when I'm killing something. That's not your doing, Piet. Best I ought to be out in the Reaches where enemies come with proper labels, isn't it? Otherwise—"

Stephen shrugged. His mouth smiled, but he couldn't control what his eyes showed to those who watched him at times like these.

Piet stood up. "We'll get something to eat," he said, gripping his friend's hand. Then he said, "Stephen? Do you know why you want the *Gallant Sallie* in the squadron?"

"Not really," Stephen said. He chuckled. "In my case, introspection isn't a terribly good idea, you know."

He opened the door to the public bar. "Dinner, Guillermo," he said, putting his free hand on the Molt's chitinous shoulder. "Blackie's as usual?"

Sailors cheered and doffed their caps to Captain Ricimer and Mister Gregg. In Betaport, Piet Ricimer stood just below the throne of God—and Mister Stephen Gregg was the angel with the sword.

"I've been checking prices on provisioning the squadron from common stores and deducting the cost from the captains' shares,'' Stephen said to his companions as they squeezed toward the street door. "I think it's workable. If we leave it to individual captains the usual way, some of them are going to skimp—which hurts us all. . . .''

BETAPORT, VENUS.

OCTOBER 4, YEAR 26.
1404 HOURS, VENUS TIME.

"My friends, my fellows; some of you my comrades of many years," said Piet Ricimer. He spoke in distinct periods so that his amplified voice, echoing across the huge storage dock, was nonetheless clearly audible. "Our purpose today is the same as that of former years, to free the stars from the tyranny of President Pleyal and the North American Federation."

Sal and the crew of the *Gallant Sallie* stood in a tight group in the midst of nearly two thousand sailors. The storage dock held eighteen starships with room for forty or more. On Venus, all starship operations except takeoff and landing took place in vast caverns like this one. Internal cargo was transferred, repairs were carried out, consumables including air and water for reaction mass were loaded—and finally the crew reported on board. Only then was the vessel winched complete along one of the tunnels to a transfer dock whose dome could be opened to the Venerian atmosphere for launch.

The assembly was being held here because a storage dock was the only volume in Betaport sufficient to hold the numbers involved, the crews of all the Betaport vessels that were part of the squadron. Ishtar City was the capital and financial center of the Free State of Venus, but Betaport and the settlements of Beta Regio were the heart of trade to the Reaches—and resistance to the Feds' claim to own everything beyond Pluto. Though ships would lift from Ishtar City to join the squadron in orbit, most of Ricimer's vessels were in this dock.

40

"With the help of God, we will take prizes on this voyage," General Commander Ricimer said. So that he could be seen by all, he stood in the open hold of the *Wrath*, a purpose-built warship that Governor Halys had provided to the expedition. "This time, however, we voyage not as raiders but as the champions of Venus and mankind. Our purpose is to harm our enemies rather than to enrich ourselves as individuals."

Ricimer wore half armor, the helmet and chestplates of a hard suit. He was under no threat here, but the gleaming metallized surfaces made his floodlit figure splendid.

"What's he mean, then?" Cooney asked in a whisper loud enough to be sure that Sal heard it. "Does he mean we're supposed to get our knackers shot away for bare wages?"

Tom Harrigan clubbed Cooney silent with the side of his knobby fist. If some of the Betaport sailors standing nearby had heard the question/complaint, they might have used a length of pipe instead. In Betaport, you didn't argue with a statement of Piet Ricimer's.

The *Gallant Sallie* was docked in Betaport now because Stephen Gregg chose to have the refit work done by workmen and suppliers who knew him well. The ship had been gutted to the bare hull and built back again with the newest and best equipment. It wasn't just a ploy of the co-owner to run up the assessed value of his share, either. Sal had gone over the figures. She knew that she couldn't have gotten the work done herself for anything close to the amount Stephen claimed to be paying.

"I hope to make you all rich," Ricimer continued, as though he'd been listening to Cooney himself. The general commander had been a sailor all his life, and he knew how his fellows thought. "But nothing can take precedence over the needs of Venus and God on this expedition."

The *Wrath* and most of the squadron's bigger vessels were carrying soldiers, landsmen whose specialty was war instead of being sailors with guns. Stephen Gregg, the expedition's vice commander, was no sailor, but neither was he merely a soldier. Like Piet Ricimer himself, Mister Gregg wasn't merely anything.

Stephen waited in the back of the hold behind his friend

and commander now. His head was barely visible from where Sal stood.

"My comrades, my *friends*," Piet Ricimer boomed. "We go out as a flame—a beacon to all friends of freedom, and a torch to the enemies of God! Let us pray for His help in our endeavors!"

As she bowed her head, listening to the deeply felt sincerity of the general commander's words, Sal wondered what it was that Stephen Gregg might pray for.

LILYMEAD.

The fields to the north and west of the community grew Terran crops irrigated from deep wells, but the street was shaded by local succulents that spread their thick leafless stems in intricate traceries against the sky. To Stephen, it was like walking under cool green nets.

Besides Piet, Stephen, and Guillermo, the Venerian "embassy" consisted of Sarah Blythe—for her local knowledge—and the mates of the other two freighters, comparable to the *Gallant Sallie*, that had set down with the flagship.

Locally, it was mid-morning. Members of the colony's government were drawn up in front of the Commandatura, a modest building distinguished from its neighbors only by having a coat of stucco over the adobe brick.

Close to three hundred people, a good percentage of the town's population, sat or stood in the street beyond. The humans, generally in front, wore their best clothes, an odd assortment of Terran and locally made finery. The Molts were naked except for an occasional sash-of-office. The tone of the aliens' chitin ranged from yellow-brown to near purple.

A few Rabbits, human by genetic inheritance, sauntered from alley to doorway or back. Their patent unconcern was in contrast to the sharp tension of the rest of the crowd.

Four of the six Fed officials wore white tunics; only the sixty-ish woman and the much younger man at her side had uniform trousers to match. The five Molts standing behind the humans were probably principal clerks in their departments, since they wore varicolored sashes.

43

There were no weapons visible.

Stephen grinned with inward humor at the thought: there were no Fed weapons visible. The Venerian contingent was escorted by fifty soldiers and an equal number of armed sailors, the *Wrath*'s B Watch close-combat team. The warship's broadside of 20-cm plasma cannon dominated the community from the nearby spaceport.

"I don't guess they're going to try anything, Mister Gregg," said Dole, who commanded the sailors. He was the *Wrath*'s bosun and a companion of Piet's from the days Piet was the mate of a tiny intrasystem trader.

"Did you think they would?" Stephen said. He scanned the shuttered windows up and down the town's single street. His palms tingled on the grip and fore-end of his flashgun, a heavy monopulse laser.

There'd always been a chance that some fanatic would decide that shooting the devil Piet Ricimer was worth the total destruction of the colony that would surely follow. At the least hint of a threat, Stephen would act, as he'd acted before.

Piet, wearing a complete hard suit except for the gauntlets and lower-leg pieces, faced the uniformed woman and said, "Are you the Fiscal of Lilymead?"

"Ah!" the woman said, blinking in confusion. She was terrified, they were all of them terrified. "I'm, I'm—"

"Factor Ricimer, I'm Fiscal Dimetrio," the young man at her side blurted with an anguished expression, "but Prefect Larsen is in charge. Mister Beck was merely filling in during the vacancy and—and I've been sent to replace *him*."

Larsen bobbed her head in agreement. "There's no quarrel between Lilymead and the Free State of Venus," she said. "The ships that were, ah, detained, they've all been released. The two here and the others elsewhere, I'm told, a week ago. Mister Kansuale here will verify that. He's, he's from Venus too."

"Won't you have some fruit?" said another Fed official. He was a gangling lad who seemed to have outgrown his uniform tunic. He gestured the Molt behind him to come forward with a basket of lemons the size of oranges. "Our Lilymead lemons are exceptionally large and sweet!"

He was more like a puppy than a puppy was. Stephen started to laugh. Everybody looked at him, but he was used to that. Holding his flashgun muzzle-up in one hand, he took a lemon, examined it, and bit one end off to suck some of the juice.

"He's right, Piet," Stephen said. To Prefect Larsen he added, "You know, you folks here ought to stick to agriculture and leave piracy to experts." He smiled. "Like us."

"There was confusion, but it's been resolved, truly," Larsen said, wiping her forehead with her cuff. "Kansuale, tell them. *Tell* them."

Kansuale was stocky, bald, and dressed in civilian clothes of dull blue with patches of electric green. The style had originated on Earth and been picked up by fops on Venus some three years since. Heaven knew how this trader came by it.

Kansuale bowed to Sal, then to Piet, and said, "Captain Blythe, gentlemen. I've been trading on Lilymead for seven years, but I was born and raised in a smallholding at the base of Mount Cypris."

"Can you identify him, Captain?" Piet asked Sal.

She nodded. "By communicator from orbit," she said. "He was my contact. I suppose he arranged for the lighter to transfer cargo." She sniffed. "The old screen wasn't very good, but the voice and the general features are right."

Sal looked uncomfortable in the helmet and breastplate of the hard suit Stephen had insisted she take as part of the *Gallant Sallie*'s refit. In the past, the vessel had carried a single hard suit for operations in heat or corrosive atmospheres. It was a shoddy piece of work as well as being larger than Sal could wear comfortably.

She needed better than that. Especially out beyond Pluto, where bullets were as likely a hazard as the natural ones.

Kansuale had been wary but not frightened the way the Fed officials were. When the trader saw that he wasn't being accepted as an unquestioned friend, his eyes drifted guardedly across the harsh faces before him.

"Yes . . ." he said. "The ships embargoed here, the *Clerambard* and the *Daniel III*, lifted off five days, Earth days,

ago. A courier had brought orders from Montreal counter-
manding the previous orders.''

"It was only a clarification," Dimetrio said. "Really, it—''

Dole, acting with the freedom of a man who'd served with
Piet Ricimer for fifteen years, tapped his carbine's muzzle
on the bridge of the fiscal's nose. "I hear liars' noses grow,''
Dole said. "I know sometimes they get shot off.''

Piet gestured his bosun back with a glance.

"However, the ships had been stripped of their weapons
and all spares and tools,'' Kansuale continued. He'd obviously decided that his safest course lay in telling the full truth
in as flat a tone as possible. "Also, three crewmen and the
captain of the *Daniel III* had been killed when the ships were
captured.''

Piet looked at Larsen and raised an eyebrow.

"I understand that's correct," the prefect said miserably.
"It was before my arrival, you realize.''

"The guns and gear was all sent off to Asunción before,''
said an official. The tag over the pocket of his blue tunic
read SUPERVISOR, but there was enough grease in the fabric
and under his fingernails to indicate that he actually worked
on ships as well as supervising a crew of Molts. "Then they
tell me to put the bitches back the way they were *tout le
suite* and send them home—and how am I going to do that,
I ask you, when they've taken the gear to Asunción, huh?''

"How much warning did you have that we were coming?" Stephen asked. There were more spies than honest
men in the Governor's Palace.

Stephen held the opened lemon to his lips, squeezing as
he sucked in more of the tart, luscious juice. He watched
Larsen over his hand and the fruit in it.

"Ten days," she said in a dead voice. She was looking in
his direction, but her eyes weren't focused on anything so
close. "Send the Venus ships back, get all the other shipping
off to Asunción or Racine where there's defenses. Everybody
to scatter from the settlements here and hide out until the,
the—''

The struggle in Larsen's mind brought her back to the
present. "Your squadron," she said simply, meeting Ste-

phen's gaze. "The pirates. We were to hide in the wild until you were gone and not give you any help. What would that have done? You'd have burned and blasted everything on Lilymead to a crater, that's what it would have done!"

The prefect had gone beyond fear to acceptance of the worst possible event. "Well, maybe you'll do that anyway," she said bitterly to Piet. "But I didn't come to Lilymead to be prefect of craters and burned fields, so you can just go ahead and shoot me before you start!"

Piet smiled and slung the double-barreled shotgun he carried as a personal weapon. "I don't think we'll need to do that," he said mildly. "Prefect Larsen, you'll supply provisions and reaction mass to my squadron at prices I will set after consultation with my officers."

He nodded to Sal Blythe.

"We will pay for these items—" Piet continued.

Fiscal Dimetrio blinked in surprise as great as that of seeing his life hang on Dole's 3-kilogram trigger pull.

"—in Venerian consols, after deductions for damages to the ships detained in violation of your government's safe conduct." His smile hardened momentarily as he added, "These damages will include death benefits for the men who were murdered. Do you understand?"

There was a stir in the crowd of civilians. Those near the front could hear Piet's clear voice. They repeated the words to their fellows farther back, whether or not they believed the statements.

"Yes sir," Prefect Larsen said, though that probably wasn't true. "We'll—may I radio my people? Quite a lot of them are hiding in the bush without proper shelter or provisions."

Piet nodded. "Go about your affairs, all of you. Major Castle," he said to the commander of the contingent of soldiers, "secure the west end of town. There's to be no looting or mistreatment of residents. Dole, you and your men cover the east. Confiscate weapons, but no trouble."

The troops dissolved into half squads under the bawled orders of their officers. Piet entered the Commandatura with the Fed officials. The flaccid remains of the lemon lay in the street. Stephen, his flashgun in ready position again, followed

Piet because he couldn't force his way to the front in time. The hallway was frescoed with scenes of the planet's settlement.

"I thought . . ." Sal Blythe said beside him. "I mean, if we're at war . . ."

Piet turned around and gave her his brilliant smile. "We're at war with President Pleyal," he said. "We're at war with a system that strips the Reaches of pre-Collapse remains without building anything new. A colony like Lilymead is just what mankind needs if we're to grow until we're so widely dispersed that there can't be another Collapse, not one that threatened *all* civilization."

"There's the problem with where their orders come from, of course," Stephen said. He instinctively looked in both directions along the corridor. The Commandatura appeared to be empty except for the officials who'd waited outside.

Brave folk. All those who'd stayed were brave folk.

"Oh, we'll take care of that the better way, Stephen," Piet said cheerfully. "You and I and Venus will, with the help of God. We'll cut off the tyranny at its head!"

And if you feel cheated of your chance to see real war, Captain Sarah Blythe, Stephen thought, *then wait till our next landfall on Racine.*

RACINE.

The *Gallant Sallie*, overfull though not overweighted by her cargo of soldiers, bobbed in the wake of the *Wrath*'s transsonic passage. "Don't touch those controls, you cunt brains!" Sal screamed to Harrigan and the two men with him at the attitude control panel.

The artificial intelligence—the new AI configured for atmospheric control, separate from the navigational unit—brought the ship steady with microburns from the attitude jets. Humans, even the picked men Sal had on the manual boards for backup, would have overcorrected and set the *Gallant Sallie* looping in a yo-yo pattern.

Though the new AI worked perfectly, the quick oscillation at 200 kph was too much for the stomachs of a dozen of the soldiers. One of them slammed his helmet visor closed to avoid spewing across the back of his neighbor; a kindly reflex, but one he was sure to regret until he got to a place where he could hose his suit out.

For that matter, the way the *Gallant Sallie* shuddered was frightening to anybody who knew the starship was roaring toward New Windsor, the planetary capital, at only a hundred meters above the ground. The soldiers packing the hold and too much of the cabin didn't realize the situation, thank God.

Several of the squadron's vessels fired from orbit. Plasma charges wobbled and dispersed in the kilometers of atmosphere. The bolts flickered like heat lightning rather than slashing cataclysmically, searing hectares without destroying any target of metal or masonry.

That sort of bombardment might keep the Feds' heads

49

down or at least draw their attention away from the ships coming in on the deck with companies of soldiers. It wouldn't seriously harm the defenses. The *Wrath* was designed to accept damage to her thrusters without corkscrewing out of control, so Piet Ricimer was taking her point-blank past the starport to deliver smashing blows.

Since the big warship's wake hadn't spun the *Gallant Sallie* into the ground, Sal was glad for the support.

The display Stephen had provided was crystal clear, amazingly clear to somebody who'd been used to optronics from the generation before her own. The AI projected digital information onto rushing terrain. The brown rock slashed with gullies of lush blue-tinged vegetation seemed too real to be an electronic image; but that's what it was, just like the map spread across the display's upper left quadrant.

Sal waited, her hands splayed and ready to take control from the guidance program. The *Gallant Sallie* had been chosen for the assault because of her state-of-the-art electronics, but Captain Ricimer had emphasized that in combat, events couldn't be preprogrammed. Sal's instincts were a necessary part of the operation.

She wondered where Stephen was. Aboard the *Wrath*, or in another of the assault vessels?

The horizon rippled with dazzling saffron brilliance, ten 20-cm plasma bolts fired within a microsecond. Piet Ricimer had to be just as good a pilot as his reputation to achieve what happened next: ten more rounds, nearly instantaneously. He'd let the recoil of the first broadside lift the *Wrath* from an axial tilt to port into a starboard tilt that aligned the other battery with ground targets.

The pulsing map cursor indicating the *Gallant Sallie*'s position slid past the ridgeline of the valley in which New Windsor lay. The city sprang into life on the main screen.

New Windsor was built of stone, dirty-looking volcanic tuff brightened by roofs of red, orange, and yellow sheeting. There were at least a thousand buildings plus corrals for the Molt slaves whose transshipment was a major part of the colony's commerce.

The town had a wall and fence with watchtowers containing plasma cannon and multitube lasers. "Setting down!"

Sal shouted as she rotated the thrusters to brake the *Gallant Sallie* fast.

The ship was stubbornly alive in Sal's hands, resisting the change from forward flight to hover the way a gyroscope fights a twisting force. She cued the attitude jets. The AI fired corresponding pairs from the bow and stern rings, swinging the *Gallant Sallie* broadside to her direction of flight.

One person with electronics like these could pilot a starship more precisely than the best-trained crew of a decade ago. Because of the microchips that Venerian raiders had wrenched from Federation hands in the Reaches, and because of the production lines set up on Venus with that loot, ships had become a hundred times safer than the cranky tubs in which mankind first returned to the stars.

The *Gallant Sallie* rotated 30° on her axis, raising her main thrusters to a part-forward attitude. Soldiers had toppled in clattering heaps when the vessel swung. Now they slid toward the starboard bulkhead. Sailors cursed and dodged the landsmen, dangerous weights in their hard suits festooned with weapons.

Sal doubled the thruster output momentarily. Precisely metered thrust balanced momentum. The *Gallant Sallie* halted fifty meters in the air.

The moment before the ship's vertical axis rotated back to normal was when the city defenses were most dangerous. The weapons on the guard towers were relatively light, intended for use against men and gangs of escaped Molts. They could damage a starship's hull badly enough to require later repairs, but they couldn't blast the *Gallant Sallie* out of the air. A hit on a thruster exposed as the vessel maneuvered, however, would shatter the nozzle. At this low altitude, the skewed thrust would drive the *Gallant Sallie* into the ground like the spud of a rototiller.

The Feds didn't fire. The starship settled gently against decreasing thrust, touching the volcanic soil so gently that Sal barely felt the outrigger struts compress.

That sort of control was possible because men like Piet Ricimer had a dream, and because men like Stephen Gregg were willing to pay the price of that dream.

Sal shut down the thrusters. She felt hydraulics whine as Rickalds in the hold raised the main hatch. Brantling beside her swung clear the outer cabin lock; the inner valve had been open since the *Gallant Sallie* had hit the atmosphere minutes before at the start of her low-level run toward New Windsor.

Heat from the rocks and wisps of the plasma exhaust that had seared those rocks to a glow entered the cabin. Soldiers trotted down the boarding ramp. Their hard suits protected them against the conditions of landing as against enemy fire that didn't come. The sailors were used to the heat and ozone, though Brantling sneezed and Sal's vision blurred as her eyes watered.

Another Venerian freighter screamed in low and disappeared into the smoke rising from north of the city. An explosion near the starport made the rocks quiver palpable seconds before the airborne shockwave reached the *Gallant Sallie*. A column of black debris twisted upward a thousand meters before it belled over and rained bits of itself over a wide area.

There was still no shooting from the walls six hundred meters way. Officers had sorted the soldiers from the *Gallant Sallie* into a line. They began to advance toward the city. Sal's crewmen were looking at her, but she didn't know any more than they did. Radio was useless for communications because the ions jumping from so many plasma engines were broadcasting across the RF spectrum. Nobody was bothering to direct a tight-beam commo laser toward the *Gallant Sallie*.

Sal rose from the console. "Clear our guns!" she ordered. The 10-cm cannon were in their traveling position. They couldn't have been used while the cabin was packed with soldiers. Run out there'd have been more room in the cabin, but opening the ports while the *Gallant Sallie* was making her approach would have created worse turbulence and an atmosphere sharp with exhaust ions.

As Sal spoke, the air began to shudder from the vibration of powerful thrusters. The *Wrath*, bathed in rainbow veils of her own exhaust, was settling into the starport. Her active thrusters were at full power, because half the warship's nozzles were cold and shrouded by blow-off screens. They would only be lit in case of damage to the operating units. The *Wrath*'s guns were out and ready to fire, but they remained silent.

"The city's been abandoned!" an unfamiliar voice announced from the console speaker. The *Gallant Sallie*'s contingent of soldiers had reached the walls. Some of them were waving their arms and one, standing on a guard tower, had thought to inform the ship with a modulated laser. "There's no troops, and there's nobody moving!"

"Tom, relay that to the ships in orbit," Sal ordered. Her legs trembled, and she had to grab the back of the seat to keep from falling.

"We've won!" Brantling cried loudly. "The Feds are too scared of us to even stand and fight! By God, we'll run them out of space before this voyage is over!"

Her men were cheering. *It was all so easy*, thought Sarah Blythe. *But so is falling, until you hit the ground.*

NEW WINDSOR, RACINE.

There were more than five hundred Molts in the pen. They pressed forward, making a groaning sound by rubbing their belly plates together. The noise was horrible, like that of rocks shearing in a landslip.

Soldiers with linked arms formed an aisle from the gate to troughs of water and tables of food overseen by Molts released earlier. The troops wore hard suits for protection. They didn't carry weapons, lest a Molt grab a gun or cutting bar and use it in starving desperation. Without the soldiers to stem and direct the flow of ravenous aliens, the feeding operation would turn into a feeding frenzy.

Guillermo and a Molt whose chitin showed the silvery patina of age stood near the gate, calling what Stephen assumed were words of calm and encouragement to the released slaves. There were humans who claimed to understand the aliens' own clicking speech, but Stephen wasn't one of them. There was usually at least one Molt in a group who spoke Trade English; and besides, diplomacy was somebody else's job.

One of the last of the squadron's ships was coming down with a great roar of thrusters on the city side of the field. New Windsor's port could comfortably handle a larger number of vessels than those comprising the Venerian squadron, but the later-landed crews were expected to walk some distance across the baked and blasted field. This captain—the ship was a large one of the old spherical style, so it was probably Captain Casson's *Freedom*—was setting down near the city, despite the danger to other vessels and people moving to and from them.

Starships weren't Stephen's area of responsibility either, but his face was hard behind his filtered visor as he watched the *Freedom* settle. Piet's lips pursed also, but if he said anything it would be to Casson in private. The first time, at least.

A soldier raised his armored fist to punch a Molt who'd shoved hard against him. Major Foster, commanding the company involved, rapped the back of the soldier's gauntlet with his swagger stick and shouted, "None of that! Move them on, that's all!"

Foster stepped back to Piet, with whom he'd been watching the proceedings. This was the last of the six pens, all of them full of slaves captured on worlds in which Molt culture survived though the human colonists vanished after the Collapse.

Racine, a Near Space planet with a relatively easy passage to the Reaches, was a convenient nexus for the slave trade. Most of the Molt-occupied planets were found in Near Space. The greatest need for slaves was on the planets of the Reaches where automated factories had built up huge stockpiles of microchips immediately after the Collapse, and where a few of the production lines were still operable, capable of turning out chips optimized for specialized needs. Because of the Molts' genetic memory, the Feds could use the superb ancient facilities without having the least understanding of them.

"Mind, I don't blame him," Foster said, shouting to be heard over the Molts' chitinous moans. "The way these filthy animals fight and shove when we're only trying to help them would try the patience of a saint, and I don't claim sainthood for my boys."

"The slaves were grabbed up from maybe twenty worlds," Stephen said, a fraction of a second before he consciously knew he was going to speak. "All their normal clan and rank gradations were erased with their capture. They were brought here, packed in the holds of freighters with no light and too little to eat, shifted into these pens—which broke up any status relationships that might have started to form during the voyage—''

Stephen was speaking loudly of necessity; but though he didn't really intend it, he knew his voice had a mocking lilt sure to put the back up of anybody toward whom it was directed.

''—and then not fed at all for three days,'' he continued, ''because the guards went haring off into the hills when they heard the pirates were coming. You know, if that happened to me, I might not be at my most civilized either.''

''The only thing I would add to that, Stephen,'' Piet said, stepping between his friend and Major Foster, ''is that the Molts are free now, not slaves. Before we leave Racine, they'll have weapons and a rudimentary social structure.''

Piet smiled. ''Quite apart from the justice of the matter,'' he added, ''I think this will prove a better way to disrupt an evil Federation commerce than burning the city down would be.''

The newly freed Molts spread to either side around the provisions. Most of them drank first, ducking their triangular heads into the troughs, then moved to the piles of foul-smelling yeast cakes to snatch food into their mouths. The aliens' metabolism was lower than that of similar-sized human beings, but their exoskeletal bodies didn't have a layer of subcutaneous fat for energy storage. Three days was very close to the point at which the slaves would have begun dying of hunger.

''I meant no disrespect to you, Mister Gregg,'' Major Foster said stiffly. His face was mottled with tight-held emotions. Like Piet, he wore only a helmet. Stephen's half armor increased his already considerable superiority in size. ''If you'd care to treat the matter as one requiring satisfaction between gentlemen, however—''

''I wouldn't,'' Stephen said. He stepped sideways so that he could take Foster's right hand without pushing Piet out of the way. ''I apologize, Major Foster. For my tone and for any negative implication that could have been drawn from my words.''

The Molts ate with a clicking buzz like a whispered version of their speech. The sound was much slighter than that of the moans that preceded it. The relative silence was equivalent to that of drips falling from trees in the minutes following the passage of a deafening rainstorm.

Foster let his breath out with a rush. "That's very handsome of you, Mister Gregg," he said. "But there's no need for an apology, none at all. I just wanted to be clear that I intended no offense."

Foster had obviously thought he was about to be challenged to a duel by Mister Stephen Gregg, an event Foster expected would be short and fatal for himself. That wouldn't have prevented the soldier from accepting the challenge—he was a gentleman, after all, one of the Fosters of Solange—but the relief he felt at being given his life back was as clear as a desert sunrise.

Stephen shook his head in irritation at his own behavior. "Piet," he said, "we'd better find some Feds who want to fight soon. Or you're going to have to lock me away until we do. I don't—"

He squeezed Foster's hand again and released it. "I haven't been sleeping well, Major," he said. "I'm irritable. But that's no cause to take it out on an officer controlling his men as ably as yourself."

"When we start making sweeps of the surrounding territory, Mister Gregg," Foster said in an attempt to be supportive, "then I'm sure we'll all find our fill of action."

"Have you been to see the *Gallant Sallie* since our landing, Stephen?" Piet asked. His eyes held a friend's concern.

"Thanks, Piet," Stephen said. "But I think if you don't need me here just now, I'll go get myself something to drink."

Quite a lot to drink. Possibly enough that he'd be able to sleep without being awakened every few minutes by the cries of people he'd killed over the years.

RACINE.

With Sal piloting, Brantling at the attitude-jet controls, and fifteen soldiers aboard, the cutter was packed and sluggish. Sal spotted the farm in the valley a thousand meters below and started a shallow turn to starboard. Her first concern was not to collide with Tom Harrigan's cutter; her second, not to lose control and spin into the ground. Cutters weren't ideal for use in an atmosphere; they were simply what the squadron had available for the purpose.

If telling the soldiers what was going on had a place in her calculations, it was as a bad third. She didn't need Lieutenant Pringle hammering on her shoulder and shouting over the roar of the thruster, "There! Go back now! There's one of their farms!"

"Get back, damn you!" Sal said as she spun the wheel to adjust the nozzle angle. A cutter couldn't hover on its single thruster, but an expert pilot could use a combination of thrust and momentum to bring the craft down in light fluttering circles like a leaf falling.

The farm was situated in a swale several kilometers long, narrow and steep-sided at the top but spreading wide at the shallow lower end. The farm buildings—house, barns, and the pentagonal Molt quarters, all within a stone-walled courtyard—were at the upper end. The sharp slope provided more shelter from the fierce winds that swept Racine in spring and fall.

Sal caught sunlight winking from Harrigan's cutter as it slanted toward the bare plains above the head of the swale.

She hauled her craft in the direction of the vegetated lower end.

Sal and Tom Harrigan had long experience maneuvering the bigger and equally cranky *Gallant Sallie* in atmospheres. As a result they were among the pilots chosen for raids beyond New Windsor, even though the boats and troops involved came from other, larger vessels of the squadron.

"They're shooting!" Pringle cried. If he'd jogged her shoulder again, she'd have taken a hand from the thruster's shuddering control wheel and elbowed him in the throat. "Christ's *blood*, they'll regret that!"

There were a dozen figures in the farm's courtyard. The cutter's optics weren't good enough to show weapons, but flashes indicated some of the Feds were indeed shooting at Harrigan's cutter as it circled down nearby.

Sal raised her craft's nose for aerodynamic lift as they thundered up the swale. Initially the vegetation was of crimson-leafed local varieties, stunted to the height of moss by the winds of the month before the squadron arrived. Closer to the buildings were fields of some thick-stemmed grass, corn or sorghum. The cutter's plasma exhaust shriveled the crop to either side and gouged a trench through the soil.

A line of junipers planted along the courtyard wall screened the buildings from the fields. Sal flared the thruster nozzle and brought her cutter down just short of the trees. It was a landing any pilot would have been proud of, given the load the cutter carried, but soldiers cursed as the impact slammed them into their fellows and the bulkheads.

The cutter's dorsal hatch had remained open throughout the flight. The soldiers piled out, chivied by their lieutenant. Pringle, in the far bow, couldn't reach the hatch until most of his men had exited. Because they didn't expect serious opposition on patrols like this, most of the troops wore only their helmets. Full armor would have made it nearly impossible to board and debark from a cutter's tight confinement.

Sal heard a soldier cry in pain; he'd probably fallen against a skid. A cutter's single small thruster didn't bake the ground to an oven the way a full-sized starship did, but the outriggers were exposed to the exhaust when the nozzle pivoted forward for landing. The bath of ions didn't damage the ceramic structure, but you didn't want to touch it till it had cooled for an hour, either.

Now that the thrusters were cold, Sal lifted the radio handset. "Cutter Blythe to base," she reported. She craned her neck to the side to shadow her navigational display so that she could read it. Daylight streaming through the open hatch washed out the self-luminous characters. "We and Cutter Harrigan have found Feds at vector three-three-one degrees, nineteen point three klicks from base."

She heard the faint popping of rifles at a distance, from or directed at Tom's men. "There's fighting going on. I don't know how serious it is."

She cleared her throat. Was that a proper report? She wasn't a soldier! "I don't think it's too serious. Out."

Brantling, holding a rifle from the *Gallant Sallie*'s arms locker, hopped to the cutter's upper deck. He shaded his eyes with his left hand to watch. The cutter's optical display showed a blurry image of Pringle and his men waddling toward the junipers.

Sal checked that her revolver was still in the flapped crossdraw holster along her left thigh. She swung herself to the deck just as Brantling jumped onto the ground well beyond the thruster's reach. Sal followed her crewman without letting herself think much about what she was doing.

Walking was harder than she'd expected. The soil was soft, and dark green leaves hid the furrows. Pringle called an order in a high-pitched voice. His soldiers pushed through the juniper hedge but halted at the waist-high wall beyond.

Most of the squadron's landsmen were combat veterans who'd fought against President Pleyal on Earth while serving in the Independent Coastal Republic. Only about half the troops were Venerians. Pringle was from Ishtar City, but from their accent and what she overheard of their conversation, most of the men under him were citizens of United Europe. A few of them shared the hatred of the Federation general among sailors from Venus, but for the most part the troops were fighting for pay and loot.

That was all right, so long as they fought.

Sal reached the wall and knelt between a pair of soldiers. One man rested his rifle on the cement coping; the other carried a cutting bar and had a short-barreled shotgun dangling on a lanyard looped through his right epaulet. He gave Sal a gap-toothed grin.

She peered over the wall, breathing hard. Juniper branches had scratched her face, and her low-sided shipboard slippers were full of sticky black dirt.

The stone house was forty meters away. A bullet ricocheted from its roof, passing high overhead with a nervous *bwee-bwee-bwee*. An unarmed man ran out the back door, followed by half a dozen women and children. Four men with guns left the building last.

The Feds were looking over their shoulders toward where Harrigan's cutter had landed. They were nearly to the stone wall before one of the women looked up, saw the waiting Venerians, and screamed. Pringle's order was drowned in the blast of shots.

All the Fed males went down, along with several women. Pellets from the edge of a shotgun's pattern clawed the face of a 6-year-old. He ran in circles, shrieking and spraying blood.

Pringle and his soldiers jumped over the wall and charged the buildings. A Molt came out of the nearer barn. Brantling, running with the troops, shot and spun the alien. A shotgun blast from one of the other cutter's men knocked the Molt sprawling.

Sal was alone in a haze of sweetish smoke. Ceramic cartridge cases gleamed in the sunlight. The troops hadn't bothered to pick the hulls up for reloading as they would during target practice.

Someone inside the farther barn screamed, but there were no more shots. Soldiers from both cutters ran into the buildings. Sal could glimpse them through the windows of the house.

The survivors of the Feds who'd run toward Pringle's men lay flat among their dead and wounded. Two soldiers with cutting bars guarded them. One of the troops had caught the wounded boy and was applying a pressure bandage; the victim kicked and flailed his arms in blind terror. Sal stepped over the wall to help. As she did so, the boy went as flaccid as a half-filled bladder. He'd fainted, or . . .

Sal jogged past the prisoners and into the house, so that she wouldn't have to consider the other possibility for the moment. The holstered revolver slapped her thigh as she moved.

There was a dead man in the kitchen, decapitated by a cutting bar. Wisps of his white beard, sawn by the same stroke, drifted in the air. There was blood over everything.

The living room beyond was a tangle of bedding and over-turned furniture that several soldiers were searching with their cutting bars. The farm had obviously taken in refugees from New Windsor; maybe relatives, maybe not.

A whining bar slashed a cushion to fuzz. The stroke continued toward Sal's head. She ducked. It looked like simple vandalism to her, but perhaps the soldiers knew what they were doing.

She started up the stairs to get away from the troops' enthusiasm. A plasma thruster blatted unexpectedly. A cutter hopped the wall at low level and landed in the courtyard. Reinforcements sent because of her report, she supposed. There was room for a good pilot to land without hurting anybody on the ground, but he'd better have been good.

A woman screamed in the room at the top of the stairs. The door was ajar. Sal flung it open with her left hand. The panel bounced back from Lieutenant Pringle's shoulder. He stepped aside so that Sal could enter.

She'd tried to draw her revolver. She only managed to get the holster flap unbuttoned before she saw that there was no danger.

Two soldiers held the fully clothed woman they'd dragged from piled bedding in which she'd tried to conceal herself. The captive was about Sal's age, swarthy and terrified. "Not a treasure in chips," Pringle said cheerfully, "but she should provide some entertainment."

The woman's dress was a shiny orange synthetic fabric. One of the soldiers tried to rip it at the neckline and only managed to jerk the captive's head forward. She continued to scream.

"Let her go!" Sal said. She looked at Pringle. "Make them let her go at once!"

The second soldier put his free hand beside his comrade's.

They pulled in opposite directions. The dress tore all the way down the front. The bandeau beneath was so loose that one of the woman's full breasts flopped out.

"You needn't watch," Pringle said coolly. "They shot at us, so they ought to know what to expect."

One soldier caught both the woman's wrists in one hand. He flung her backward onto the bed when his partner kicked her legs from beneath her.

"Stop that!" Sal said. Pringle stepped in front of her. She backed and drew the revolver.

"Listen, you whore!" Pringle shouted. "If you don't want to find yourself spread-eagled beside her, you'd better—"

He moved forward. Sal couldn't shoot him in cold blood.

"Tom!" she screamed. She raised the revolver's muzzle and fired three shots into the ceiling as fast as she could pull the trigger. The blasts were deafening in the enclosure. Bits of shattered lath from the ceiling exploded across the room. One of the bullets bounced back from the roof slates and buried itself in the window ledge.

The two soldiers jumped up from their captive. Pringle grabbed Sal's wrist. He punched her in the jaw with his free hand. "Stupid whore!" he shouted.

Sal's world went white and buzzing. She sagged until Pringle let go of her wrist; then she fell to the floor. She could hear voices, but they were ten decibels weaker than they'd been a moment before.

Stephen Gregg stepped into the bedroom. He held his flashgun to his shoulder. Pringle dropped the revolver he'd twisted from Sal's grip.

More men followed Stephen, too many for the available space. "I gave orders against rape," said Piet Ricimer as he knelt beside Sal. "Mister Dole, all three of these men are to be confined in close arrest. I'll try them later this evening."

"Sir, I . . ." Pringle said. "We . . ."

Ricimer put an arm under Sal's shoulders. "Can you move?" he asked.

She could hear normally. When she raised her torso with Ricimer's help, her eyes focused again also. "I'm all right," she said, hating the wobble in her voice.

Stephen said, "Dole? Hold this." He handed his heavy flashgun to the bosun.

"Look!" Pringle said. "This is—"

Stephen slapped him with his open hand. The sound was as loud as a revolver shot. Pringle flew across the room, hit the far wall, and fell onto the bed from which the Fed woman had just risen.

Pringle's cheek was a mass of blood where his teeth had cut him from the inside. His lower jaw hung loose.

Stephen's face was as white as old bone. He took the flashgun back from Dole without looking away from the bleeding officer.

NEW WINDSOR, RACINE.

November 25, year 26.
0811 hours, Venus Time.

The thousands of soldiers and sailors were too many for Commandatura Square in the center of New Windsor, so Piet had decided to use the gate arch of a Molt pen for the gibbet. Stephen stood at Piet's side, looking out at the expressions of the assembled men: some angry, some worried, some obviously drunk. All of them grim, as grim as the task itself.

"We'll make our landfall in the Reaches at Castalia," Piet said quietly. At the other gate support, Pringle was kneeling in prayer with the flagship's chaplain. "It's a Molt world, but the Molts are organized in small bands of migratory hunters, very unusual for them. They're too sparsely settled and too dangerous for the Feds to make slaving expeditions there. I'm not worried about us being discovered, though we'll keep a guardship in orbit at all times."

Dole and a detail of armed sailors guarded the two men taken with Pringle. One of the soldiers had a greenish pallor and looked as though he might faint.

"Rather than directly to Arles?" Stephen said. He didn't really care where they went next. The future was a gray blur, punctuated by flashes of screaming red.

"I'd like to have a base to reconnoiter before we hit Arles," Piet explained. "Besides, it'll be a long voyage. We have to expect it to take twenty days since there's so many ships to keep together, and we certainly won't make it in less than fifteen. The soldiers won't have much stomach left after so many transits."

"The soldiers won't be alone," Stephen said with a wan smile. He could no more learn to be comfortable when his whole body seemed to turn inside out during transit than he could have learned to be comfortable with a sunburn. The experience was simply one to be borne for however long was necessary.

Pringle stood up. His face was pale but composed. Dole looked at Piet. Piet nodded, and the crowd gave a collective sigh.

"Several of the warehouses here are full of the metal ingots the Feds use for trade with the Molts," Piet murmured. He was talking about the future to avoid thinking about the immediate present. "We'll carry a sufficiency of them to buy peace with the Castalian tribes for the short time we'll be staying."

Dole tossed a rope with an ordinary slipknot in the end over the crossbar of the gate. Two of his squad were fitting a canvas hood over Pringle's head. They walked the officer over to Dole. The bosun snugged the loop around Pringle's neck and handed the free end of the rope to the soldiers convicted of attempted rape—and sentenced to execute judgment on the officer who'd egged them on.

Piet took the bullhorn from Guillermo, who stood on his other side. "Men of my command," he said. "Soldiers of God."

He paused. The ships in the spaceport beyond reflected faint echoes of his words.

"We are here to defeat the tyrant Pleyal who sets himself up as a rival to God," Piet said. His voice had the full, rich tone he used to lead assemblies in prayer. "If we act like beasts, then our Lord, in Whose sole help we trust, will desert us and leave us to die like beasts of the field."

The breath of the crowd soughed like a low, sad breeze. Sal Blythe was there somewhere. Stephen couldn't make out her face, and he didn't really want to. Not here, not now.

"I would rather undergo any torture myself than to permit that to happen by my own inaction!" Piet shouted. He threw down the bullhorn and said crisply to the pair of soldiers, "Carry out your duties."

The soldiers pulled on the rope, grunting to lift Pringle hand over hand. Dole hadn't bothered to hang a pulley, so the crossbar's friction was added to the weight of the man gurgling under the hood. A sailor in the front rank of the assembly fell on his face before his neighbors could grab him.

One of the executioners wept as he staggered forward, trying to haul briskly. Both of them had their backs to the man they were strangling. Pringle's legs kicked out wildly. His arms were tied behind his back to prevent him from climbing up the noose.

Dole judged height and distance, shrugged, and tied the rope off to the support beside Piet, Stephen, and Guillermo. "All right," the bosun said gruffly to the executioners. "You two have done your job. Go put something on your hands before the rope burns get infected."

Pringle thrashed. His body spun on the single strand like a fly caught by a jumping spider. Occasionally he was able to draw enough breath to make the hood flutter.

"For *Christ's* sake!" Stephen said. "Doesn't he have any friends? Are they going to leave him to choke for the next five minutes?"

"If he had any friends, Stephen," Piet said in a voice as gray as a millstone, "they'd be afraid of what you might do if they ended this."

"*Christ,*" said Stephen Gregg. The word was as close to a prayer as he'd spoken since he first voyaged to the Reaches.

He stepped forward, caught the hanging man's leg at the knee, and jerked down with all his strength.

Pringle's neck popped like a twig breaking, severing the spinal cord and finishing him without further pain.

CASTALIA.

The truck Sal had borrowed from the *Wrath* was more of a powered bed frame with an open cab. It lurched as one or more of the six driven wheels dropped into a hole concealed by vegetation matted by earlier traffic. The jolts weren't dangerous; the truck was designed to carry heavy loads under much worse conditions. If a starship had bounced around that way, though, it would be on the verge of crashing or disintegration. Sal's jaw had been set and her knuckles white within a minute of when she started driving toward the *Sandringham* and the guarded trading station on the edge of the forest beside the vessel.

The savannah's yellowish vegetation grew in flat stems forming coils up to two meters off the ground. The mass looked like a tangle of razor ribbon, but the stems weren't any stronger than grass blades. A vehicle crushed them down, and a man could force his way through without a machete or cutting bar if he had to.

Four similar trucks were parked in the clearing that plasma had seared to the red soil when the starship landed. Sal still couldn't see the guard post. She stopped beside the *Sandringham* and shut off her loudly ringing ceramic diesel so that she could hear. Three sailors who'd watched Sal approach from the starship's hatch said nothing.

"Is Mister Gregg here?" Sal called. "Stephen!"

Captain Wohlman had landed the *Sandringham* on the edge of the forest, almost a klick from the site the general commander designated and several hundred meters from the nearest of the squadron's other vessels. Wohlman wasn't exceptionally skillful even during his intervals of sobriety, and the *Sandringham*'s electronics were in a class with those of the *Gallant Sallie* before her refit.

Piet Ricimer had made virtue of necessity by establishing the *Sandringham* as the contact point with the local Molts. The trading post protected the outlying vessel and made it clear to the aliens that they weren't to approach the rest of the squadron.

Ricimer hadn't chewed Wohlman out for his bad landing, but the captain was by his own action isolated in a dangerous spot. So, of course, were his men. Sal figured they had a right to be surly, but they didn't need to take it out on her.

"I said—" she said, rising in the open cab. Yellow-gray foliage quivered at the corner of her eye. She reached for her revolver. Stephen stepped out, cradling the flashgun he favored.

"Stephen!" Sal cried. "Ah, Mister Gregg."

"Stephen," he said with a smile. He reached into the cab and spun the large wing nut securing the wheel to the steering column. "I don't want this to wander away," he said, pulling the wheel off one-handed. The trucks didn't have starter locks, but there were other basic security arrangements.

Stephen looked up at the three sullen crewmen. He smiled again, a very different expression from the one with which he greeted Sal.

"I wanted to see the forest," she said as she jumped from the truck.

"We've got a party of Molts," Stephen said. He handed her the steering wheel so that he was free to use the flashgun. "You can see them and the forest. And me."

The guard post was a long shed with roof and walls— rolled up, since it wasn't raining—of plastic sheeting, hung on a frame of local wood. The post was only twenty meters from the edge of the oval the *Sandringham*'s exhaust had cleared, but the vegetation had sprung back to hide the path completely.

Fifty or so troops stood nearby. They wore half armor and had their weapons ready, but they didn't appear nervous. Three more landsmen, technicians rather than line soldiers, sat at a humming console beneath the shed. They looked up from their screens, nodded to Stephen—one looked at Sal with speculation—and went back to their duties.

"We can pick up a Molt's footfalls a thousand meters out," Stephen explained in a quiet voice. "Closer in we can vector on airborne noise as well, though—"

He grinned. She didn't remember having seen Stephen so . . . relaxed wasn't the word, but perhaps cheerful.

"—if they come hand over hand through the tree branches, there could be a problem before we sort things out."

Stephen was genuinely glad to see her.

Captain Casson and two of his officers squatted with Guillermo at the tree line, facing four of the local Molts. The locals' exoskeletons were cloudy gray. The color looked sickly to a human, but the soft sheen of wax over the chitin indicated the creatures were in good health. Three-kilo ingots of aluminum and rust-streaked iron were stacked on a pallet behind Casson.

"There's twenty more of them in the forest," Stephen said. "They've got bows with arrows nearly two meters long. I wouldn't think that was practical. According to what the Feds who've landed here report—the survivors report—the Molts know what they're doing well enough."

One of the four Molts visible was easily twice the size of his fellows and weighed at least 150 kilos. The giant held a mace with a triangular stone head, the only weapon visible among the delegation.

"The big one's the chief?" Sal said.

"The chief's companion," Stephen said. "Just a tool, really. I wouldn't want to meet him hand to hand. Though I don't suppose he'd like that either."

His tone was soft. Sal expected his lips to twist into the terrible grin she'd seen there before, but instead Stephen gave the Molt bodyguard a wry but honest smile. "I wonder if they're friends, he and his chief," he said.

Casson handed an ingot to a Molt. The Molt scraped a chitinous fingertip across the soft aluminum, then passed the ingot to one of his fellows.

Trees rose like giant bristles from the margin of the savannah. Instead of rounded surfaces, the trunks were sharply triangular in cross section as if their growth had been crystalline rather than organic. Limbs spiked out in clusters of three. The boles and branches were gray. The foliage that flared like a pattern of giant fans a hundred meters in the air was a yellow similar to that of the ground cover.

"You slapped Lieutenant Pringle," Sal said in a voice no one but the pair of them could have heard. "Instead of . . ."

Stephen snorted. He wasn't looking at her. "I have better things to do than break my knuckles," he said in a tone as thin as a knifeblade. "Shooting him . . . shooting him would have been murder. You have to have control."

His face was frozen, horrible. "Control is what sets human beings apart from the beasts, you know."

The Molt tribesmen were now examining an iron ingot. Three of them were, that is. The giant's lidless eyes were fixed on Stephen. Just watching.

"Stephen," Sal said. "If there wasn't a war, what would you do?"

In a bleak voice Stephen said, "If I had *no* purpose in life, you mean? Well, I don't think I need to worry about that. There'll never be a time that men exist and there's no war."

"There's more to you than that!" Sal said. Casson looked back with a scowl. She hadn't meant to shout.

She tugged Stephen a few steps down the path to where the vegetation screened them. Soldiers watched sidelong, but none of them were willing to look directly at Stephen at this moment.

"Listen to me!" Sal said in an angry whisper. "You're still human. Just as human as the ones who haven't faced what you've faced. You've got a soul!"

When the muscles of Stephen's cheeks relaxed, he looked like a wholly different person. "You know, Sal," he said liltingly. It was the first time he'd called her "Sal." "Late at night, I believe in God. A just God would put a person who'd done the things I've done in Hell."

Sal wanted to look away from his eyes, but she forced herself to meet them.

"And that's just what He's done," said Stephen Gregg.

CASTALIA.

Sunrise on Castalia sent streaks of purple and violet streaming out of the clouds on the eastern horizon. Flying creatures mounted in vast spirals from communal burrows in the savannah. The scales on their wings caught light in jeweled splendor as they rose.

Already most of the captains of the twenty vessels on the ground stood with specialists in the flagship's ample portside boarding hold. Wohlman, red-faced and puffing with exertion, was jogging the last hundred meters to the open hatch.

Stephen had never known Piet to miss consulting his officers on matters of general importance. Neither did he recall a time when Piet failed to make the final decision himself, whatever the sense of the assembly.

"Please, you aren't going to leave me here, are you?" whimpered Bowersock, the captain of the local-area freighter that a squadron featherboat had captured above Arles. "The bugs here are cannibals; they *eat* men."

"Shut up, you!" Dole said. He jerked up on the prisoner's hands, tied behind his back.

Piet, Guillermo, and a technician knelt on the pair of cargo pallets that formed a low dais for the council of war. They were making adjustments to the hologram projector that the Molt would operate while Piet spoke.

"It's no more cannibalism for a Molt to eat you, Bowersock," Stephen said quietly, "than it is for me to eat a crayfish. But if you keep your mouth shut like the bosun says, you'll probably be released in your own ship."

"That slopbucket's not worth us taking, that's for sure, Mister Gregg," Dole agreed with a nod.

Bowersock was present as window dressing. Though he was the titular captain of the prize, he didn't know the landing codes for Arles or the other planets among which his vessel shuttled. Bowersock left that and everything else involved in running the ship to the three Molts of his crew.

One of the Molts spoke Trade English. She'd been more than happy to give the Venerians the information they needed—after Guillermo assured her that she wouldn't be left on Castalia either. Bowersock was right about one thing: the local tribes *were* cannibals. Very likely they were also willing to eat humans they happened to catch.

Sal Blythe sat cross-legged on one of the pistons that raised and lowered the hatch/ramp. She smiled at Stephen in friendly awareness, nothing unprofessional. Sal hadn't come forward to chat when she arrived for the council, the way he'd thought she might.

Stephen smiled back.

Captain Wohlman clomped up the ramp. He'd slept in his uniform, perhaps for several days. Piet turned from the projector and said, "Captain Wohlman, captains all. The featherboat *Praisegod* has returned from Arles with current images and a vessel captured above the planet. I've called you to discuss what these developments mean for our plans."

"Doesn't that mean we've already put the wind up the Feds?" Captain Kotzwinkle demanded. He was one of Casson's cronies, though a generation younger and not nearly so experienced. Not a bad navigator, Piet said; and Piet wasn't a charitable judge of such things.

Salomon of the *Praisegod* bent forward to glare at Kotzwinkle. Before either man could speak, Piet said, "The prize's linear amp is burned out. The Fed captain"—Piet nodded to call attention to Bowersock—"confirms that they hadn't been able to reach port control in three orbits and were about to land without making contact."

Stephen stared over the head of the Fed captain at Kotzwinkle. Salomon had sailed with Piet and Stephen before; had saved their lives and an expedition at least once by his quick action. Kotzwinkle was a pimple to be popped if he became troublesome. . . .

"However, he also says the Feds throughout the Reaches have been warned to expect our squadron," Piet said. Guillermo projected into the air beside Piet a holographic view of a city of several thousand buildings and the adjacent spaceport.

"This is Savoy, the capital of Arles," he continued. "According to Captain Salomon's prisoners, the news had been received three weeks ago when their vessel last touched down there."

"There's treachery on Venus for that to happen!" said a military officer with a guttural European accent.

"Very likely," Piet said, "but that's a matter for the governor and such as Councilor Duneen to attend to. What concerns us is merely the immediate situation."

Guillermo expanded the image of the port, crowding all but the margin of Savoy City out of the frame. Stephen watched intently, though he'd gone over the imagery with Piet in private as soon as the *Praisegod* landed.

For the most part, featherboats had optics as rudimentary as those of cutters. Piet himself owned and had equipped the *Praisegod*, with the plan of using her to scout target sites. This view was as sharp as any image taken through twenty klicks of air could be, and the projector's enhancement program ironed out atmospheric ripples and distortions.

There were forty-three vessels in the port area, none of them large or heavily armed. Piet guessed the assembly was regional shipping, collected here under the guns of the port for protection from the Venerian squadron.

The guns were the main focus of Stephen's consideration. Savoy's Commandatura was on the west side of the port, adjacent to the berm surrounding the reservation. Each of the building's four corners had a turret containing a heavy plasma cannon, 15-cm or better. A second four-gun position stood on the east side of the port, two kilometers from the Commandatura.

All eight guns were run out and elevated when Salomon took the images. That didn't absolutely prove that the weapons were loaded and their crews alert, but any sane attack plan would have to presume so.

"The crew of the prize has provided us with the identification codes for Arles," Piet continued. "God willing, there shouldn't be serious difficulty in landing one of our smaller vessels with troops aboard. We'll have to come in near daybreak or sunset, where the ceramic construction of a Venerian craft won't be evident."

"That's a terrible plan," Captain Casson said bluntly. "It's not a plan at all. There's two forts, don't you see?"

"We can't land two ships together; that'd alert them surer than blowing a siren," Kotzwinkle said.

"This is a job for guns, not men!" Casson said. "For good Venerian ordnance. Land the whole squadron together before they know what's happening, then blow them to splinters with point-blank gunfire!"

"The fighting ships, you mean, Captain Casson," Bowersock said in hopeful clarification.

"The fighting *captains*, Bowersock," Casson thundered. "I wouldn't expect to see the *Sandringham* land till the fight was over."

The council dissolved into a blur of discussions between neighbors and simultaneous attempts to gain the floor. The walls of the boarding hold weren't baffled, so echoes magnified the chaos.

Piet gestured to Guillermo. The Molt's console emitted a *bleep-whoop* attention signal not quite loud enough to be painful. Conversation stopped.

"Mister Gregg," said Piet formally, "would you care to give your view, as the expedition's military chief?"

"Yes, I would," Stephen said, stepping onto the dais. He'd also have liked to see how far he could stuff Casson and Kotzwinkle's heads up one another's ass, but there would be no sign of that in his voice. He would be calm.

"If you'll expand the view of the Commandatura, Guillermo . . ." he said. Before the request was complete, the image of the building's roof and four turrets increased tenfold.

"The defenses are intended for use against ships in the air or in orbit above Savoy," Stephen said. He used his left index finger as a pointer. The air-formed hologram shimmered as his hand interrupted the line of one of the projectors. "The other position is the same. Only the two inner gun turrets can bear on vessels actually on the ground within the port reservation. The inner turrets and the mass of the building itself block the other pairs of guns until a ship is above, say, two hundred meters."

"Just what I said!" Casson said. "When we're on the ground, only half their guns can even bear on us!"

"I don't recall you saying anything so foolish, Captain," Stephen said, his voice an octave lighter and snapping like a whip. "My point, of course, is that we can't fire on four of the Fed guns once we're on the ground. *Those* positions would have to be carried by ground assault. Otherwise they'd quite certainly destroy any ship attempting to take off again."

Stephen tapped the air over the western pair of turrets. The image dissolved, then re-formed as he stepped away. "If I'm going to attack a fortress, I'd rather do it by surprise than after an hour or so of fireworks have alerted the defenders."

Stephen stared at Captain Casson without expression. "I hope nobody feels that makes me a coward."

Casson's face went blotchy red. He took a step forward. Kotzwinkle and two other nearby officers grabbed the old man and dragged him back by main force.

"Hellfire!" Stephen whispered. He shivered in self-loathing for what he'd just tried to precipitate. He'd promised himself that he wouldn't lose control . . .

He hadn't lost control. He coldly and with consideration had done a thing that endangered the expedition more than any action of President Pleyal.

"Casson, I apologize," Stephen said. He looked at Piet. "I apologize," he repeated. "Piet, just put me close to the enemy."

"Captain Casson put his finger on the problem," Piet said smoothly. His voice was slightly louder than before, to drown the heavy breathing of Casson and his fellows. "We can only land one ship without causing alarm, and the forts are widely separated."

Piet and Guillermo had choreographed this part of the

presentation. "I believe the way around the problem is to land here," Piet continued, extending an index finger. The eastern edge of the reservation, including the berm and gun tower, appeared just beyond the fingertip.

"We'll use a small freighter, a vessel that won't arouse concern," Piet said. The scale of the image rose to encompass the entire port area again. "The cabin will be packed with troops. The hold will contain a landing barge that's also full of troops. As soon as the freighter touches down, the barge will launch under full power, cross the reservation, and land on the roof of the Commandatura."

The council broke into at least a dozen animated discussions. Stephen heard a military officer say to Captain Salomon, "How many men does a barge hold, anyway? Will that be—"

"I'll be in command of the barge's contingent," Stephen said in a loud, calm voice. "I'm expecting a team of eighteen men in half armor. I believe that will be ample for the purpose."

"May I request to lead the cabin party!" shouted Major Cardiff. He was young for his rank at 25, but from reports he'd seen almost continuous action for the past ten years. Cardiff bowed to Stephen. "Under your overall command, of course, sir," he said.

Stephen looked at Piet and raised an eyebrow in interrogation.

Piet shrugged. "I wouldn't think of interfering with your choice of troops for the operation, Stephen," he said.

"I'd be glad to have you, Major," Stephen said, returning Cardiff's bow. What was it about men that made them crave chances to die?

Sal Blythe dropped her feet firmly to the deck. "The *Gallant Sallie* has a full-length hatch," she said over the buzz of general conversation starting to pick up again. "I'll take the assault force down with her."

There was dead silence.

"Thank you for the offer, Captain," Piet said. "I'd like to discuss the matter with your co-owner before I make a decision, though."

"I am the vessel's captain, with full authority to determine her usage!'' Sal said. ''Under your overall command, of course, sir.''

''Stephen?'' Piet said.

Stephen Gregg shook his head in amusement, not denial. He chuckled. The world, the universe, was all mad. ''Piet, I don't have anything to tell you about how to deploy ships. Nobody in this room does.''

Piet nodded crisply. ''Captain Blythe, I have full confidence in your piloting skills. The *Gallant Sallie* is a perfectly suitable choice for the mission.''

He bowed to the assembly. ''Gentlemen, thank you for your attention and advice. The council is dismissed for now. I expect to summon you in the near future to discuss specific assignments.''

Piet waited two beats and added, ''Will the three officers directly involved in the assault please join me in my cabin for a moment now?''

Talk and the tramp of boots on the hold's hard deck raised a screen of noise. Kotzwinkle threw a glance over his shoulder as he accompanied Casson out the hatchway, but the old captain himself walked stiff-backed in anger.

Sal and Major Cardiff were making their way forward. Stephen leaned close to Piet's ear and said, ''Are you learning to delegate?''

''About not taking the *Gallant Sallie* in myself, you mean?'' Piet said with an elfin smile. ''Well, I'm an able pilot, Stephen; but I can't very well pilot the freighter and the barge both, can I?''

APPROACHING SAVOY PORT, ARLES.

Federation vessels tended to land fast and hard. Their thrusters and attitude jets weren't in condition to make the sort of perfectly balanced set-downs a Venus skipper strove for. That was especially true of the shoddy, locally built ships that carried the Feds' cargoes within the Reaches.

"There's no danger," Sal warned, "but stand by for a rough ride!" She signaled Brantling, in the hold wearing a hard suit, by turning the light above his hatch control panel from red to green. After Brantling started the hatch cycle, he'd step into the passage between hold and cabin.

The *Gallant Sallie*'s crew had rigged a pair of loudspeakers in the cabin's back corners. Without amplification, the desperately nervous infantry couldn't have heard Sal's reassurance from the navigation console because of the thrusters and atmospheric hammering.

There were twenty-eight troops in their armor, clinging to heavy fiberglass ropes rigged as temporary stanchions. The interior of the cabin had been gutted to hold the men. The normal stores, gear, and plasma cannon had been transferred to the *Mount Ida* along with most of Sal's crew.

This one was neck or nothing.

To look like local traffic, Sal had to drop the *Gallant Sallie* faster through the dawn than she wanted to do. The slamming deceleration that would come two hundred meters up would flatten the troops, ropes or no. There was always the possibility that somebody would flail his armored fist through the attitude controls for all that Harrigan and his men could do to stop it.

"There's no danger!" Sal repeated. The *Gallant Sallie* bobbled like a float in a waterjet as the cargo hatch started to open.

The hatch had to be raised during approach so that the barge could exit the instant the *Gallant Sallie* touched ground. Sal, Tom Harrigan, and Captain Ricimer himself had viewed the ship, discussed stresses, and designed a thruster program for the AI. They'd made sure the maneuver wouldn't either tear off the hatch in the airstream or flip the ship into the ground upside down.

Stephen had then brought up something that none of the spacers would have thought of: when the hatch opened, the infantry would think the ship was about to come apart.

The troops were all brave men, volunteers for the expedition and picked volunteers to be in this forlorn hope under Major Cardiff; but they were landsmen, and the courage to charge a battery of plasma cannon doesn't necessarily prevent panic at the idea of dropping kilometers after a ceramic ball shatters around you. If the men weren't kept informed, there could be a wild-eyed berserk in the cabin at a delicate time.

Thus the prebriefings, the loudspeakers, and the reassurance. Eventually everything breaks, and it isn't as easy to calculate the stresses on a mind as on a hinge joint.

"We're nearing the ground!" Sal said. "There'll be heavy braking in a moment, but we'll set down gently!"

There were no other ships near the gun tower. Half a dozen vessels—probably scrapped hulls—were clustered in the northeast corner some distance away.

Over the years, several Federation freighters had come down east of the berm and the stabilized soil of the port reservation. Only the upper curves of their hulls were now visible, like whales broaching from the bog. The crew of the gun tower wouldn't like seeing a ship wobble down so close to them, wreathed in the flaring brilliance of her exhaust, but neither would they be surprised.

The Commandatura was three stories high, the tallest

building in Savoy. The vertical tubes of the four big guns on its roof gleamed in the dawn like stellite smokestacks.

Full-bore thrust roared from the *Gallant Sallie*'s nozzles. The soldiers remained standing for a moment, braced against one another and the bulkheads as well gripping the cables. Exhaust reflected from the approaching ground caught the hatch like an open flap and jerked the ship violently around its bow-to-stern axis. Everybody went down in a clatter of weapons and ceramic armor.

The *Gallant Sallie*'s outriggers touched raggedly. Her thrust had pitted the ground into dimpled mounds. "We're—" Sal shouted.

Rickalds (who'd fallen also; anybody standing would have fallen) was opening the outer cabin hatch. Armored soldiers got to their feet, aware that they'd reached the ground and now everything was up to them.

The *Gallant Sallie* lurched, her port outrigger coming a handsbreadth off the ground as the blast of a thruster from within her hold lifted her. The barge was away, a blaze of iridescence crosshatched on Sal's screen to save the eyes of the viewer.

Go with God, Stephen.

SAVOY, ARLES.

The barge wasn't a handy craft, but its full-span dorsal hatch could be removed—had been removed before they shipped the little vessel aboard the *Gallant Sallie*—and both sides flopped down to ease unloading on the ground.

Stephen crouched slightly against the buffeting airstream at the starboard front of the cargo compartment, watching the Commandatura loom over the bow. He'd lowered his helmet visor, and he carried the flashgun beneath the compartment's lip. The wind catching the broad muzzle would try to snatch the weapon out of his hands.

Stephen could have fired his flashgun through the turbulence if he'd had to; fired and hit his target, as he'd done more times than he could remember when he was awake. He'd known for a decade, now, that whatever controlled his muscles when he was killing wasn't human.

They were dropping toward the Commandatura. A long plume of glowing ions and dust lifting from the ground marked their course across the spaceport. The barge's low arc from the freighter's hold peaked fifty meters in the air, halfway to their objective. Officers on the ships below would be screaming at what they thought was a dangerous stunt . . .

A Molt stood on the building's roof watching them. In a moment the alien would cry an alarm; in another moment the barge would crash down among the gun turrets and it would be too late for any alarm.

The Molt was as good as dead. He'd be shot if he survived the flare of the barge's exhaust. Stephen wouldn't kill him, but one of the men beside him would.

Stephen wouldn't kill the Molt because there was no need. There would be plenty of other killing in the next moments, fully justified by the circumstances.

The barge bucked, lifted. For an instant Stephen thought they'd been hit by some preternaturally alert guard, but it was only Piet raising the bow for aerodynamic braking. A huge doughnut of plasma flared about the lower hull, momentarily concealing the roof to the level of the cannon muzzles. The landing skids hit with a crash—speed over delicacy, and barges *did* handle like pigs, even with Piet Ricimer at the controls.

"Get 'em!" Dole bawled as he dropped the sides of the cargo compartment. The assault force, Mister Stephen Gregg and seventeen members of the *Wrath*'s B Watch close-combat team, were out before the side panels had bounced.

Stephen hit the roof running. His repeating carbine, despite its tight sling, clashed against the left side of his breastplate. The trap door in the middle of the roof was open; so were the side hatches of the three gun positions Stephen could see as he ran for the stairs.

Dole was in command on the roof. There were three men for each gun position, to take them *now* because the first ships of the squadron would be landing within a minute. The job of Mister Stephen Gregg, with Giddings and Lewis to load for him and three men more as a security detail, was to find the fire director somewhere within the building and destroy it. To destroy everything that got in their way.

A man—a human being in white with some gold braid on his shoulders—started out of the trap door just as Stephen reached it. The flashgun wasn't the choice for point-blank, but it was in Stephen's hands and he fired. The laser bolt drained the battery in the gun butt in a single pulse. The Fed's torso absorbed the enormous energy and exploded in the steam of his own blood.

He'd been a young man with a delicate mustache.

Stephen tossed the flashgun behind him. Giddings should be there with a satchel of batteries. If not, there was no time to worry about empty weapons now.

The stairs were steep. Stephen unslung the carbine and was throwing up the visor that had darkened to save his vision from the flashgun's intense glare. He didn't have a hand free for the balustrade. His boots slipped midway in fluids spewed from the corpse, and he bounced down the remainder of the steps on his buttocks, backplate, and helmet.

He didn't lose the carbine, didn't even lose his rough point of aim. A Molt stood in the middle of the hallway, blinking his side-moving eyelids at the sudden events. Stephen shot the creature through the center of the chest by reflex. He didn't have time for decisions now, only points of aim.

There were half a dozen small offices on the left side of the hallway. None of their lights were on. Several doors were ajar the way the staff had left them at the close of the previous workday.

The three offices on the right side were larger. Two were closed and dark save for the warmth of dawn blushing from their outside windows onto the frosted glass doors. The Molt had come from the third, near the main stairs at the far end of the hall.

Shots and the scream of a bar cutting something harder than bone sounded from the roof. Stephen's squad came down the stairs as he had, slipping and crashing. Lightbody fired his shotgun into the hallway ceiling. On a bad day, your own people could be more dangerous than the Feds.

A female Molt—female, because her ovipositor was half extended—stepped from the office doorway and knelt over the stiff body of the male. Stephen grabbed her by the hard-shelled neck and shouted, "Where's the fire director?"

"What is a fire director, master?" the Molt said. Her fingers delicately caressed the bullet hole in the dead alien's carapace.

"The gun controls!" Stephen said. "The guns on the roof!"

Lightbody leaned over the stairwell and fired the second barrel of his shotgun toward a lower floor. Calwell and Brody were knocking open office doors, though what they expected to find there was beyond Stephen.

"Master, the data lines to the cannon on the roof come from the port operations room in the basement of the building," the Molt said.

"Basement!" Stephen shouted as he let her go.

A bullet from below blew splinters and plaster out of the railing where Lightbody'd fired a moment before. Stephen pivoted onto the top tread. Three white-jacketed Feds stood at the base of the stairs. Two pointed weapons; the third was reloading her rifle.

Stephen shot the man with the shotgun. The second man fired into the railing to Stephen's left and Stephen killed him also, head shots out of habit though these targets weren't wearing body armor; most Feds didn't.

Stephen pumped the lever to shuck another round into his chamber. The head of the empty case cracked, and the carbine jammed. Lightbody smashed the third Fed to the floor with a charge of buckshot, then shot her again as she twitched.

"Rifle!" Stephen shouted as he tossed the carbine back. Lewis thrust forward a loaded weapon. Stephen gripped it like a pistol as he took the stairs three at a time, controlling his descent with his left hand on the balustrade. He couldn't afford to fall on his ass now.

The building's second floor was a bullpen of slanted desks and narrow benches designed for the utility if not comfort of Molt clerks. Several of the aliens stood against the wall at the far end of the room, as motionless as painted targets. Stephen ignored them.

Did Molts cry? Surely they grieved. The Molt he'd killed on the third floor was a motion in a hostile building. There'd been no time for a Stephen Gregg to do other than shoot.

The Commandatura had a small barracks on the ground floor, facing the arched street entrance. The guards were probably more for ceremony than function, but the three who'd run upstairs at the sound of gunfire had been alert if not particularly skillful.

Two rifles fired at Stephen midway down the last flight of stairs. The staircase here was real stone, not paint on lath and plaster. One bullet shattered a bannister into pebbles and dust. The other ricocheted from Stephen's breastplate, knocking him back a step and tearing his left biceps with a spray of impact-melted lead.

"Flashgun!" he shouted, but he had the powerful repeater to his shoulder and was firing already when the bullet hit him. The repeater was a lovely weapon with a slide working a glass-smooth European action, but when Stephen emptied the rotary magazine he tossed the weapon behind him to be caught or to fall.

There was no time for tools, only for killing. He took the reloaded flashgun.

A dead guard lay half out the barracks doorway. The door itself was metal and thick enough to bounce Lightbody's buckshot off in a bright smear against the panel. It would probably turn rifle bullets also, but Calwell and Brody were shooting through the high ground-floor windows at civilians in the street, and Stephen's own rounds had all gone through the crack in the door.

Somebody out of sight in the barracks was tugging the corpse out of the way to close the panel. Stephen flopped down his visor and fired the flashgun through the opening into the Charge-of-Quarters' wooden desk.

The desk exploded in a fireball that would have hurled blazing fragments twenty meters in every direction if there'd been enough open space around it. A Fed ran out of the room screaming. Lightbody killed her before Giddings could slap the carbine, cleared and reloaded, into Stephen's palm. No one else came out.

As soon as the port defenses were out of action, six transports would brake from orbit. The squadron's initial wave contained nearly a thousand troops, enough to secure Savoy no matter how many of the citizens were willing to die to protect their city. First, though, the port defenses . . .

The door to the basement was set into the well of the main stairs and labeled AUTHORIZED PERSONNEL ONLY. It was closed and locked. Stephen reached for the cutting bar clipped to a stud on his breastplate. A bullet came *in* through a front window and knocked bits from a ceiling molding.

"I've got it!" said Piet Ricimer, switching on his bar. He leaned into the tool as its tip howled against the lock plate. Piet didn't like to wear armor while piloting a vessel. He'd tossed on his back-and-breast plates before leaving the barge, but he hadn't buckled them properly. The armor flopped open on the right side in a gap through which a bullet or stone-sliver could fly.

The lock was sturdy. Sparks flew as the cutting bar ripped metal, but the bolt didn't part.

A projectile whanged off the staircase a meter above Stephen's head. He turned. Twenty-odd armed Molts were getting out of a bus marked PORT CONTROL in big white letters. Brody, Calwell, and Lightbody were banging away at them. The Molts with guns—most of the aliens carried cutting bars or spiked clubs—were shooting back.

Giddings and Lewis had ducked into the shelter of the stone bannisters instead of firing the weapons they carried for Stephen. It was because he could depend on the pair to carry out his directions *exactly* that he'd detailed them for this dangerous and thankless task.

"Flashgun!" Stephen said. A Molt rose with a rifle from behind the engine compartment of the bus. Stephen punched a carbine bullet through the center of the triangular skull, then traded the light weapon for his flashgun.

"Ready!" Piet said.

"Giddings!" Stephen cried as he shot, closing his eyes against the glare. The vehicle's fuel tank was under the cab, cut out in a step to help the driver enter. The laser bolt struck the black-painted metal at a seam. The tank ruptured in a fountain of blazing fuel. Fire engulfed much of the street. Stephen traded weapons.

Piet pulled the door wide. Stephen went through the opening first by using his bulk and strength to shoulder his friend aside. Somebody'd turned off the lights in the room beneath, but the holographic screens of the three control consoles showed movement—huddling, ghostly figures.

Maybe the flashgun would have been a better choice.

Stephen walked down the steps deliberately, firing as quickly as he could work the lever of his carbine. His muzzle flashes were a continuous red throbbing. A human screamed and a Molt gave a loud, rasping cry of agony.

All eight rounds cycled perfectly through the carbine's action. Stephen saved the final three shots for the consoles themselves. The last shorted into arclight as bright as a flashgun pulse, though nearly as brief.

The overhead lights went on. Piet had found a switch at the top of the stairs. Three Molts and a human female lay dead under the consoles where they'd tried to shelter. Where blood mixed with the pools of ichor leaking from the Molts, it reacted to form a purple colloid.

None of the control room crew was armed. If they'd left the lights on, they might all still be alive.

"Stephen, let's get up to the roof," Piet ordered in a crisp tone. "You've taken care of things here."

He set one of the side latches of his armor and added, "I think it'll be the easiest place to defend until the squadron arrives."

Stephen nodded and turned. He was thumbing cartridges into the carbine's loading tube himself, since Piet was between him and his loaders.

Behind the men a console melted down with a sullen hiss. The corpses sprawled beneath it burned with the mingled odors of pork and shrimp cooking.

SAVOY, ARLES.

JANUARY 1, YEAR 27.
1042 HOURS, VENUS TIME.

A bright blue rocket streaked from the roof of the Commandatura, signaling that the guns had been put out of action. Smoke rose from a ground-floor window. Sal thought she could see an occasional wink of flame in the room beyond.

"*Gallant Sallie* to *Spirit of Ashdod*," she said into the microphone, watching the fancied flame and wondering what it implied for the men in the Commandatura. The *Ashdod* was in geosynchronous orbit above Savoy, from where it could relay Sal's straight-line laser communications to the rest of the squadron. "The guns have all been captured. You can bring the fleet in."

There *were* flames. "Bring the fleet in fast! Over."

Sal still heard occasional shots from the adjacent gun tower, but Major Cardiff had sent up his green rocket three minutes before. The assault force couldn't trust radio within the port area, nor for communication with the rest of the squadron in orbit where any number of ships might be firing plasma thrusters to hold station.

"Acknowledged, *Gallant Sallie*," replied the *Ashdod*'s communications officer. The light-borne signal was clear, though it wobbled in the lower registers. "I'm relaying your message to the *Freedom*. Out."

Captain Casson was in command of the first landing wave. Sal frowned at the thought, remembering the hostility she'd heard—she'd approved—in Old Port taverns in the years before she dreamed she'd ever meet Piet Ricimer herself.

"*To hear that puppy Ricimer talk, nobody ever conned a*

*ship before he came along.'' A shot of slash down Casson's
throat, then a long draught of beer.*

*''Well, a lot of that's said of him, not by him, you know.''
Marcus Blythe, not as quick to move as he'd been a decade
before, but still a spacer and a man. ''The Betaport crowd,
they know they're second best. It makes them boast when
they've the least excuse.''*

*''What other people are saying are the lies they heard
from Ricimer's lips first!'' Casson glaring around the booth;
all spacers, but none of them his equal. All nodding agreement.*

Nobody'd ever suggested Willem Casson was likely to
hang back in a fight, though. He was a good choice to lead
the transports in, as well as a diplomatic one. Casson would
have his ships down as soon as orbital dynamics permitted.
Half an hour. Even less with luck.

Rickalds had closed the cockpit hatch when the last of the
soldiers lumbered out. The soil, heated white by the *Gallant
Sallie*'s exhaust, radiated unpleasantly into the cabin otherwise. The troops were in full hard suits not as protection
against the defenders' small arms (half armor would have
been a better compromise for that purpose) but rather so that
they could attack immediately across the plasma-seared terrain.

The area had cooled by now. Sal rose from the navigation
console and reopened the hatch so that she could look at the
Commandatura directly instead of on the *Gallant Sallie*'s
screen. While Harrigan and the other men examined damage
the barge had caused to the hold, Brantling was alone with
her in the cabin. He watched Sal but didn't speak.

Humming like a swarm of hornets, a large aircar driven
by pairs of ducted fans bow and stern rose into view beyond
the Commandatura. The car mounted a squat weapon behind
the pilot's hatch. Troops, most of them Molts, looked out
from both sides of the central cargo compartment. There
must have been forty of them.

The weapon in the car's bow was a multitube laser. It fired
three strobing pulses at the Commandatura. Fed troops in the
aircar were shooting also.

The laser disintegrated like a bubble popping with a violet

flash. The *snickWhack/snickWhack/snickWhack* of the pulses' slapping impacts on the building arrived a measurable second after the laser's destruction.

Sal couldn't see what was happening on the roof of the Commandatura from her angle. Her heart surged at what the event implied, however: Stephen Gregg was alive, and he still had his flashgun.

The aircar banked, circling a stone's throw from the Commandatura at thirty meters altitude. The roof coping would have protected the Venerians against troops shooting from the ground, but it was less use against rifles fired from above.

Rock dust danced from the side of the building. This time Sal saw the spark of Stephen's flashgun, a saffron needle that ripped a puff of metal from the aircar's bow. The vehicle continued its circle unhindered. Guns banged from the cargo compartment. Distance dulled the reports.

The aircar was a military vehicle. The pilot used remote viewing rather than a clear windscreen, and the polished skin was resistant to if not entirely proof against a flashgun's bolt. The fans and the motors driving them were buried deep in the hull, shielded unless the pilot overflew the shooter.

The troops in the cargo compartment could be hit—one of the Feds dropped in the instant the situation formed in Sal's mind. But there were a lot of them, and the vehicle gave them better protection than Stephen and his fellows had. The squadron wouldn't be down before—

"*Brantling, help me—*" Sal shouted as she turned from the hatch and realized the guns weren't there. The *Gallant Sallie*'s plasma cannon were still in orbit, so Sal couldn't blast the Fed vehicle from the air with them after all.

Sal jumped from the hatch. The ground was still too hot for slippers, but she was three steps around the vessel before she noticed the heat. It wouldn't have mattered anyway.

"Captain?" Brantling called from the hatch with nervous concern in his voice.

"Mind the console!" she shouted back.

The revolver holster slapped her left thigh as she ran for the gun tower. The tower platform was ten meters off the ground, supported on four squat concrete legs. Spiral steps were cast into each leg. There was a hatch into the platform at the top of the helix. Halfway up Sal realized she was mounting the northwest leg while Major Cardiff had led his troops up the southwest stairs.

I should have brought a cutting bar in case the hatch was locked. Sal drew her revolver, though the chance of shooting a metal door open was a lot slimmer than the chance of killing herself with a ricochet.

Harrigan shouted from the ground. Sal ignored him. Gunfire from the Commandatura was a constant muffled rattle, and she tried to ignore that as well. She grabbed the latch lever and turned it. There wasn't a lock mechanism.

Sal jerked the door open. The Fed hiding in the compartment beyond screamed, "*Mother of God!*" and swung a crowbar at her. He hit the low ceiling instead.

Sal shot him in the face. The muzzle flash was a saturated red-orange, so vivid in the dimness that she almost didn't notice the thunderous report.

The Fed flopped backward. His forelock was burning. Sal stepped over the body and lifted the trap door to the gun platform beyond.

A Venerian soldier with his faceshield raised saw her, jumped back, and tried to aim his shotgun. Major Cardiff knocked the weapon aside with a shout of fear and anger.

"Where's the fire director?" Sal demanded as she clambered out. There were a dozen corpses on the platform, most of them Molts. Cardiff's men were dragging more bodies from the four metal turrets. The cannon still pointed skyward.

"Mistress Blythe, you shouldn't have come here!" Cardiff said. "You could have been killed!"

"Where's the fire director, you stupid whoreson?" Sal shouted. "There's men dying at the Commandatura now, and there'll be more unless we get our fingers out of our butts and help them!"

Cardiff's head jerked as he looked toward the Commandatura. He'd been too involved with his own operation to consider what was happening across the spaceport. "Yes, I see," he said.

He glanced across his visible troops. "Davis, Podgorny!" he shouted. "Let's get these guns working!"

The northeast turret was the same diameter as the others

but was taller by two meters to add space for equipment.
Cardiff ran toward it, sluggish in his hard suit. "They've
been gunners," the major added as he saw Sal was keeping
pace with him.

The fire director was a Janus-faced console in the center
of the room beneath the turret. On one side was a narrow
Molt-style bench; integral to the other side was a cushioned
human chair. The walls and equipment were splashed with
ichor, already crusting in the heat, but the bodies had been
removed.

"Get one of these guns to bear on the car that's attacking
the Commandatura!" Cardiff said to his men. "Can you do
it? And don't on your souls hit the building!"

The major stepped back. Davis and Podgorny—Sal didn't
know which was which—stepped gingerly to the console.
They took off their gauntlets and tossed them clashing to the
floor.

"Tubes are loaded, at least," muttered the soldier with a
black mustache flowing into his sideburns. He squinted at
the screen's pastel images. "Standard gear, but it's not going
to track a car flitting like that."

"Just get moving, wormshit!" Sal said. "If you put a
twenty-centimeter bolt through the air beside that car, they
aren't going to stick around to see where the next shot goes."

The soldier looked up, startled at the words in a woman's
voice. The other man said, "Here, I think I've got a solution.
I'm not sure which—"

Gear motors whined in the roof of the control room. A
soldier outside shouted, "Hey! The turret's moving!"

"It's all right!" Major Cardiff shouted out the hatchway.
"Everybody put your visors down, though!"

Cardiff noticed the forearm of a Molt, severed by a cutting
bar. He half scraped, half kicked the limb out onto the platform. Sal heard a nearby rifleshot.

"The concrete's a honeycomb, not solid," Cardiff explained. He raised his voice to be heard over the rumble of
the turret mechanism. Tonnes of metal were turning in perfect balance. "The gun crews were living up here. The bugs
in the crews, at least. The boys are still flushing some of
them out."

Sal nodded to indicate she understood. Her face felt stiff. She moved behind the mustached soldier so that she could view his display. He had to lean over the chair to reach the keyboard, since his hard suit was too bulky for him to sit normally at the console.

The upper left corner of the display read ARMED in scarlet letters and MANUAL below them in blue. At the bottom of the screen was a bar with a mass of data regarding temperature, atmospheric conditions, and other matters of no significance at what was point-blank range for the big cannon.

Four green radial lines at 90° to one another midway on the display implied a centerpoint above the right edge of the Commandatura. A similar set of radii trembled slowly down and across the display from the upper right corner, indicating the cannon's true current boresight.

The fire director was capable of zeroing onto a target through the full depth of a planet's roiling atmosphere. The screen's image of the nearby Commandatura was as sharp as a miniature in a glass case. Sal could see the bodies, one sprawled beside the landing barge and the other at the doorway down to the interior of the building. If she dialed up the magnification, she could probably identify the members of the assault force who'd been killed.

The soldier glanced over his shoulder at her. "The guns won't depress enough to bear on the city," he explained. "There's a lockout in the gun mechanism itself. Fuckers in that car aren't quite so low, though."

He grinned. His front teeth were missing.

Sal noticed she was still holding her revolver. She tried twice unsuccessfully to slide it into the holster. After the second attempt, she glanced down and realized she needed to lift the holster flap.

The Fed's crowbar had showered sparks as it clanged against the concrete. If it had struck her head . . .

The orange radii crawled toward congruence with the green point of aim. "I have the controls!" warned the soldier on the other side of the console.

The man on Sal's side raised his hands to indicate he wouldn't interfere in his enthusiasm. His armored forearm jolted her.

The radii mated. The paired set became orange and began to pulse. The turret mechanism stopped its rumbling movement.

In the sudden silence, Sal heard three shots and a howling ricochet from the platform. Men shouted together in triumph.

The image of the aircar curved slowly around that of the Commandatura. The pilot was holding his speed and attitude steady to help the gunmen in the cargo compartment. Five muzzle flashes, as regular as metronome strokes, winked from one corner of the roof coping.

The aircar slid into the indicated point of aim. For a moment, the vehicle's motion relative to the plasma cannon was almost nil. The soldier controlling the gun touched a control.

The crash of the cannon made the world jump. A miniature thermonuclear explosion flung the forged stellite gun tube back in recoil. Solid-seeming pearly radiance reflected through the open hatch of the director room.

Sal had never seen so large a plasma cannon before, nor had she ever been around a gun when it was fired in an atmosphere. The shock of light and sound crushed her inward like a mass of bricks. Major Cardiff gasped, ''Christ Jesus!'' and jumped back from the hatch.

Sal stepped outside, staring across the starport. A cloud of scintillant vapor hung in the air to the right of the Commandatura. Fragments of blazing metal traced arcs of smoke out of the center of the glow. The aircar's thunderous destruction would have been deafening had her ears not already been stunned by the cannon's discharge.

Sal felt a low-pitched rumbling through the soles of her shoes. She looked at the turret to see if it was traversing again. The gun, its muzzle white from the plasma it had channeled downrange, was still. Pastel iridescence quivered on the tube and the turret dome.

Sal turned and looked higher, into the western horizon. Six globs of light, starships gleaming from atmospheric friction and the plasma roaring from their thrusters as they braked, thundered toward Savoy.

''Make the remaining guns safe!'' Sal called into the director's room. ''We don't want any accidents now that our relief's arrived!''

SAVOY, ARLES.

"By God, sir, look at them run!" said Lieutenant Lemkin, standing on the roof coping in his hard suit to watch the refugees through an electronic magnifier. The soldier's perch looked dangerous to Stephen, but that wasn't anything for Stephen Gregg to get worked up about. "Say, can't one of your ships lift a company west of the city to cut them off? By *God*, we could cut them off!"

"To what end, Mister Lemkin?" Piet said. "To force them to stand and fight? And I'll thank you not to take so lightly the name of God Who gave us this victory."

Suppressed pain wrung Piet's voice dry. Weicker, the *Wrath*'s surgeon, was cleaning the burns on Piet's leg while an assistant probed bits of metal from Stephen's left arm.

"You should have come sooner, Lemkin," Stephen said. "There was plenty of fighting for everybody half an hour ago."

He was sick with anger at himself. Giddings was dead. So were Blaise and Portillo, from Dole's contingent, and there were half a dozen serious wounds.

Plus the little stuff. Piet had made it all the way through the fighting uninjured, then been burned by flaming debris from the aircar. Cheap at the price.

It all was, Stephen supposed.

Lemkin hopped down from the coping and faced Stephen in a stiff brace. "Sir!" he said. "My company relieved the Commandatura as ordered, within three minutes of the time the hatches of the *Freedom* transporting us opened. Are you commenting on my courage?"

"I'm not commenting on anything, soldier," Stephen said. "I'm too tired."

Piet lowered his visor to watch the corkscrew descent of a 300-tonne armed freighter. "Four square kilometers of field and we'll have a collision yet," he muttered. "It was a lot simpler when we had one seventy-tonne ship to worry about."

After the first wave, the ships of the squadron were coming down one at a time. They were supposed to land on the east side of the field where there was more space, but through sheer incompetence several had dropped close enough to the Commandatura that their exhaust wash warmed the command group on the roof.

"I think that's the last of the fragments, sir," the surgeon's assistant said.

He stepped back from Stephen and wiped nervous sweat from his brow. Had the fellow been afraid he was going to poke a nerve and have his head blown off for his mistake?

Stephen stood and shrugged off his back-and-breast armor now that his arm was free. He raised the hem of his sweat-soaked tunic and examined the fist-sized bruise where a bullet had slammed the lower edge of his breastplate into the flesh over his hipbone.

"Let me see that," Weicker said sharply. He knelt before Stephen.

Piet frowned as he watched. He looked uncommonly odd with one pant leg cut off at the knee and the calf below smeared with ointment after it had been debrided.

Weicker drew Stephen's waistband down, then up again. "No penetration," he said, straightening.

Stephen tapped the lip of his breastplate. Lead was a bright splash on the black-finished ceramic.

The surgeon shook his head. "If that bullet had hit lower by as little as half its diameter," he said, "pieces of it would certainly have torn your femoral artery. You're very lucky to be alive, sir!"

Stephen looked at Weicker. "Do you really think so?" he asked in a voice he hadn't meant to use.

Weicker frowned in surprise.

Piet laid a hand on Stephen's shoulder. "I'm lucky you're

alive," he said. "Let's go downstairs for a moment. There's something in the foyer that you may not have noticed."

Stephen stared at Savoy City. "Sure," he said.

The squadron's troops were moving cautiously into the city under their own officers. In theory, ground operations were conducted under Stephen's control, but the officers had been fully briefed. Besides, they were more experienced at ordinary military operations than Stephen. This wasn't a one-ship, smash-and-grab raid of the sort that had made Piet Ricimer a byword on Venus and a nightmare to President Pleyal.

Stephen Gregg's real job had been to clear the Commandatura. Stephen Gregg's job was to kill, not to command.

Two soldiers came up through the trap door. They'd discarded the arm pieces and lower-body portions of their armor. "Colonel Gregg?" the first of them said.

"Report to Lieutenant Lemkin," Piet said, pointing to that officer.

The soldier recognized the smaller figure shadowed by Stephen's bulk. "Oh!" he said. "Yes sir, Factor Ricimer!"

"Your leg all right?" Stephen asked as he led the way down the stairs.

Dole had put the Molts captured alive in the gun turrets—the five uninjured ones—to cleaning up the building. The corpses were gone from the hallway, but the hundreds of bullets fired during repeated Fed assaults had knocked the office partitions to splinters.

"Stiff, nothing serious," Piet said. "I was running for the barge's cockpit when the car blew up. I wasn't expecting that."

The bodies on the second floor had been removed also, along with the grass pads that had cushioned the floor. Blood had soaked through the matting and into the porous concrete.

Four Venerian soldiers were posted at windows from which they could watch the boulevard and the buildings across from the Commandatura. They noticed the squadron's commanders and turned. "Sir?" one asked.

"Carry on with your duties, gentlemen," Piet said.

The soles of Stephen's boots were tacky for the next several steps down to the ground floor.

"It surprised me too, Piet," Stephen said. Conversationally, as if it meant no more to him than the color of the sunrise, he went on, "You know, if I hadn't wrecked the fire director in the basement here, we'd have been able to use our own roof guns to bring down that car. I figure that decision of mine cost us most of our casualties."

The steel door to the guard quarters was now shut, but the foyer's marble floor slopped with water on which floated ash and bits of charred wood. Dole and several sailors watched Molts coil hoses. Savoy's fire company was housed in the building adjacent to the Commandatura. The human officers had fled, but the alien crew had managed to put out the blaze in the guard quarters before it spread to the rest of the building. Stephen hadn't thought that would be possible.

Piet gestured around the sides and front of the entrance hallway in which they stood. Sixty percent of the surface was floor to ceiling windows. Most of the small individual panes had been shot or blown out.

"We couldn't have held the ground floor from so many armed Feds," Piet said. "It was difficult enough with them continuing to charge the roof stairs. And we couldn't *possibly* have hit so maneuverable a craft from one of the turrets here. The only way Cardiff managed it—and I bless him for it—was because the Fed pilot wasn't paying attention to what was happening on the other side of the field."

He's right, but I should have thought *of using the guns.* "It's done now," Stephen said aloud.

The Commandatura's front entrance was a pair of double archways. Piet stopped in front of them. The alcove set between the doors held an idealized holographic portrait of President Pleyal clad in gold robes of state: stern, black-haired, standing arms akimbo. Behind Pleyal was a starscape. The motto below the display read *Non sufficit mundus.*

"I've heard of these shrines, but I'd never seen one before with my own eyes," Piet said.

Stephen noted the delicacy of the holographic resolution and calculated the expense. "Rather a waste of good microchips," he said mildly. "But I suppose we'll find something better to do with them back on Venus."

"Do you see the legend?" Piet said. "That means, 'The

universe is not enough'! That's what we're fighting against, Stephen! *That's* why we have to fight.''

The bodies carried from the Commandatura had been stacked like cordwood in the street outside. There were about a hundred of them, a score of humans and the rest Molts.

''I'm not fighting against anything, Piet,'' Stephen said softly. ''I'm just fighting.''

They stared at the splendid, shimmering portrait of a man who confused himself with God. Piet whispered to Stephen, ''I should have taken the barge up to ram the aircar as soon as it appeared. The exhaust wash wasn't as great a danger as the gunmen. . . .''

SAVOY, ARLES.

JANUARY 3, YEAR 27.
1514 HOURS, VENUS TIME.

Sal heard the thump of an explosion from somewhere in Savoy City. She and several other officers turned around. None of them reacted more quickly than Piet Ricimer himself. There was nothing to see over the spaceport berm.

"It can't be too serious," the general commander said with a faint smile. "Probably somebody blowing up a statue of President Pleyal."

Sal returned her attention to the ship the party of officers was examining. At one time the vessel had been named, perhaps *Maria*. Takeoffs and landings had flaked the letters into ghosts of themselves. Nickel-iron hull, eight thrusters with about half the life span left to their nozzles. A hundred and fifty tonnes burden, or perhaps a trifle more.

"Has the government said anything about ransoming the city, sir?" asked Jankowich. He'd probably started thinking along the same lines Sal had when she heard the explosion. "A place that's built of rock the way this one is won't be a snap to blow up if they refuse to pay."

"I didn't send the envoys out till this morning," Ricimer said. "Three Molt officials from the city administration. They'd have been shot out of sheer jumpiness by one side or the other if they'd gone while it was still dark."

"The streets here don't seem to be paved with microchips, Ricimer," Captain Casson said with gloomy relish. "Let's hope they took the loot with them when they ran."

"Yes, I hope that, Captain," Piet Ricimer said. "But as I warned everyone in Betaport, and again in Venus orbit: we're here for God and for Venus, not simply to line our pockets. Now, this ship would seem to me to be worth taking as a prize instead of destroying."

"Can you trust Molts to deal straight with us?" Captain Boler asked, reverting to the previous subject. "I mean, they were fighting us. Mostly the Feds ran, but their bugs sure didn't."

"Yes, they can be trusted," Guillermo said.

The group surveying the vessels captured in the port consisted of Captain Ricimer, six chosen captains (Sal attributed her inclusion among them to Stephen's influence), and Ricimer's Molt servant. According to Stephen, the alien was a quick, skillful navigator. Guillermo might lack Piet's feel for a ship, but he didn't make mistakes at the controls.

The other captains clearly thought of the Molt as furniture. They were shocked when Guillermo spoke.

"Molts form clans with a strongly hierarchical structure, Captain," Ricimer said. He smiled faintly. "Even more hierarchical than our own. They'll treat humans, no matter how brutal, as clan superiors until the structure is smashed."

"Which you certainly did here, sir," Sal said in a loud voice. Stephen was on the city perimeter, setting up defenses in case the Feds tried to retake Savoy. His presence in the survey group would have changed the tone, not entirely in a bad direction.

"The hull's heavier than ceramic and no stronger," Captain Salomon said. "The navigational AI is all right, but the attitude controls are as basic as a stone axe."

"The controls can be upgraded easily enough if the hull's worth it," Sal said. She'd seen Salomon take off and land often enough to understand why Ricimer had given the man a ship.

"A proper spacer doesn't need a machine to do his thinking for him," Casson rumbled. He glared at Sal. "Or her thinking either."

Ricimer and Salomon both opened their mouths to speak. Sal, feeling suddenly cold inside, spread her left hand to silence them. She said, "I'd think that those of us who learned our skills on older ships, Captain, would be the quickest to appreciate how much better and safer the new electronics are than what we were used to. Certainly I'd feel

more comfortable in a fleet this size if I were sure that an
AI was landing the ship beside me. Instead of some ham-
fisted incompetent who couldn't be trusted to hit the whole
of Ishtar City, let alone the dock.''

Sal had grown up respecting Willem Casson; first because
her father did, then because she'd grown old enough to appreciate the old man's exploits herself. Now—

What Casson had done was still impressive. But he didn't
like female captains any better than he liked youths from
Betaport who'd been brilliant while Willem Casson had
merely been courageous; and for all Casson's skill and experience, the expedition would be better off if he'd stayed
on Venus.

Three red signal rockets shot up from the doubly baffled
entrance through the berm. The gateway was designed to
prevent exhaust wash from flaring beyond the port reservation. A three-axle Venerian truck negotiated it and accelerated toward the group conducting the survey.

"I believe that's Stephen driving," Piet Ricimer said.
Then he added, "We'll take up the survey another time, gentlemen and Mistress. Stephen doesn't react at nothing."

The vehicle pulled up beside the survey group. Lightbody,
a religious sailor who glowered whenever he saw Sal, was
in the open cab with Stephen. In back, three Molts kept a
fourth prostrate on a blanket from sliding off the open sides.

Captain Ricimer and three of the younger captains hopped
onto the truck bed. Sal stood on the cab's running board,
looking into the back. Stephen turned in the seat beside her,
face remote.

"These are the envoys, Piet," Stephen said. "I brought
them directly to you because there wasn't a lot of time."

Piet knelt by the injured Molt, then looked at Stephen in
white fury. "This man should never have been moved!" he
said.

"I couldn't hurt him now, Piet," Stephen said. "You
needed to see him while he was still alive." Piet's anger
streamed through as if Stephen's soul was transparent to it.

"Master," said a Molt who'd earlier been working on casualties from the city's capture, humans and aliens as well.

"Kletch-han knows he is dying, but he begs to speak with you first."

Ricimer nodded curtly. He touched the upper carapace of the injured Molt with his fingertips and said, "Kletch-han, how did this happen?"

The Molt's chitinous exoskeleton had a pearly translucence that Sal had never before noticed. Kletch-han wore a sash-of-office with blue chevrons on white. The fabric had been driven into one of his lower belly plates and left embedded in the blunt puncture wound.

"We drove out the west road in the vehicle you provided us, Master," Kletch-han said. Sal could understand the words, but there was more of a clicking crispness to them than was normal in the speech of Molts in high positions. The three envoys had been principal clerks in the Savoy administration.

"We met a group of soldiers three kilometers from the city," the Molt continued. The brown stain was spreading on his sash. "They were in a brush-filled gully beside the road. The officer wore a naval uniform. I didn't recognize him. I got out of the vehicle, holding the white flag you gave me."

Another of the Molts from the embassy raised the flag to show it to the humans. It was a pillowcase tied to the end of a threaded steel rod a meter and a half long and about a centimeter thick. It had been assembled from what happened to be available when Ricimer sent the envoys out.

The base of the rod a handsbreadth deep was smeared with brown ichor.

"I explained that Captain Ricimer had sent us to Director Eliahu to set up a meeting regarding the ransom of Savoy," Kletch-han said. "The officer said to his men, 'Do they think we're going to treat with bug slaves?' He took the flag from me and struck me as you see. He and his troops took the vehicle and drove westward with it. That is all."

"We ran into the brush when Kletch-han was attacked," the third envoy said. "When the soldiers left, we carried Kletch-han back to the city. Master Gregg summoned Dirksahla to treat Kletch-han though we told him that was unnecessary. Then Mister Gregg brought us here."

Stephen's face and whole body were quiescent, waiting for emotion to fill them. He had no more expression than the trigger of his flashgun did.

Captain Ricimer nodded. "Captain Blythe," he said crisply. "Are the reaction mass tanks of your vessel topped off?"

"Yes," Sal said, "and the air tanks have been dumped and refilled."

"We won't be high enough to pressurize," Ricimer said. "Gentlemen, help our Molt friends here lift Kletch-han down gently."

Boler and Salomon slid their arms under the chitinous body. Molts massed somewhat less than humans on average, and both captains were powerful men. As they handed the dying envoy to Jankowich and Casson on the ground, Ricimer said, "Stephen, who's our highest-ranking human captive from Savoy?"

"We've got the head of the Merchants' Guild, Madame Dumesnil," Stephen said in a voice that could have been a machine's. "She was trying to load her whole warehouse onto a truck when some sailors from the *Wrath* arrived."

"Fine; have her at the port entrance on my return," Ricimer said. "She'll take the next message to Director Eliahu. Stephen, swing by the *Wrath* on our way to the *Gallant Sallie*. With full AI controls, Guillermo can handle the attitude board alone, but I'll want a second man with Lightbody watching the water flow to the thrusters."

"I'll take care of that," Sal said. She lifted herself into the back of the vehicle, though she supposed she could have ridden on the running board as easily.

"Mistress Blythe, you will do as I command you!" the general commander said with the same shocking rage that had flared at Stephen a moment before.

"Captain Ricimer," Sal replied, "you will not order me off my own vessel! Besides which, you don't have a man better able to monitor the *Gallant Sallie*'s fuel feeds!"

Stephen put the truck in gear, accelerating smoothly. He made small steering corrections to miss the worst of the craters starships had blasted in the field's surface. It was still a bone-jarring ride.

"She's a stubborn lady, Piet," Stephen called over the rattle of the truck.

"She's also correct," Ricimer said. He reached his right hand across the truck bed, swaying with the vehicle's motion. Guillermo put an arm around Ricimer's waist to brace him. "I've noted your shiphandling with pleasure, Captain Blythe. I'm fortunate to have you in this squadron."

The general commander's handshake was firm and dry. Sal swallowed, stunned at the memory of what she'd just done. "Factor Ricimer," she said. "I—"

"And if you'll call me 'Piet' in private, Mistress, I'll feel a little less like one of the Federation's saints' idols," Ricimer continued. He smiled wanly. "Too many of the people I respect seem to be afraid of me."

"They're confusing you with me," Stephen said. The truck was nearing the *Gallant Sallie* against the eastern berm. The surface on this side of the reservation was less pitted, and he was getting as much speed from the vehicle as the diesel's governor allowed.

"Do you think that's it?" Ricimer—*Piet*—said. He looked at Sal and, in a voice that neither man in the cab could have heard, said, "I sometimes think Stephen and I are halves of the same soul, Sal. But the division was very unjust to him."

They stopped beside the *Gallant Sallie*, casting a spray of sand in front of the cab. Rickalds and Kubelick, the anchor watch, stared from the cockpit hatch in surprise.

Piet jumped from the vehicle. "Stephen," he said, "drive these men back to the port entrance. Make sure Madame Dumesnil is waiting for me."

Stephen got out, slinging his flashgun. "They can drive themselves," he said. "And Salomon will make sure the lady arrives where you want her. I'm going along."

Sal climbed the three steps extended from the cabin airlock when the *Gallant Sallie* was on the ground. "Kubelick," she said, "drive Rickalds back to the gate. Find Captain Salomon and tell him he's responsible for the general commander's orders regarding the head of the Merchants' Guild."

"Stephen, I'm taking a minimum crew on this," Piet said

sharply. "You know absolutely nothing about operating a starship!"

"I know about defending them if they come down some place they shouldn't," Stephen said in the same detached tone he'd used since he arrived with the dying envoy. "Besides, you'll have to shoot me to keep me off."

"Captain?" Rickalds murmured with a worried expression.

"Get this damned truck out of here!" Sal shouted as she bent to switch on the vessel's electronics. "We're lifting as soon as you're clear."

Her men obeyed instantly, though Rickalds frowned and muttered a question to Kubelick. Lightbody, carrying a shotgun, was already aboard. Guillermo followed the sailor and sat at one of the three places around the attitude-control boards. The Molt seemed comfortable on a seat designed for humans.

Sal took the starboard motor panel, across the cabin from Lightbody. Piet settled himself at the navigation console and made adjustments to the couch. Stephen cycled the outer hatch closed and squatted in the lock, his boots and shoulders braced against opposite sides of the chamber.

"Then again," Piet said as he waited for the hydraulics to build up pressure, "perhaps my trouble is that not enough people are afraid of me."

In a different voice he added, "Crew, prepare for liftoff."

Piet lit the thrusters, then brought the *Gallant Sallie* to a roaring hover about a meter above the ground. His left hand made minuscule adjustments in the flow rate of individual motors. The visual display throbbed with plasma, and the hull shook with the hammering of exhaust reflected from the ground.

Sal gripped the stanchion beside her flop-down seat. She expected the general commander to boost thrust to lift out of the port as soon as he'd dialed in the motors to his own satisfaction. Instead, Piet ran up the flow of reaction mass while simultaneously flaring the nozzles with consequent loss of efficiency. The *Gallant Sallie* continued to bobble in place, rising and falling only a few centimeters despite the variation in control settings.

"Lifting," Piet called. He reduced the nozzle irises to three-quarters power. The *Gallant Sallie* sprang a hundred meters in the air. Piet shifted into forward flight, vectoring the nozzles as smoothly as Sal could have done herself after being raised on the vessel.

Stephen smiled from the airlock in her direction. It was a cool expression, the sort of look a statue might have worn. She wasn't sure it had anything to do with her.

The *Gallant Sallie* left the port reservation to the north and curved around Savoy in a shallow bank instead of over-flying the city. The newly installed optics gave Sal a better view from the middle of the cabin than she'd have had in past years from the navigation console itself. Arles in the vicinity of Savoy was covered in tawny shrubbery against which the green of introduced vegetation made a vivid contrast.

The line of the main western highway out of Savoy came into view ahead of them. Piet swung the *Gallant Sallie* par-allel to the road and about half a kilometer out from it. He flared the thruster nozzles. The ship dropped mushily and slowed to 50 kph of forward motion. Plasma roiled out to either side and behind the vessel, billowing as far as the highway to port and an equal distance to starboard. The *Gallant Sallie* advanced in a hissing roar, burning the country-side around her as bare as a sheet of fresh lava.

Arles had been a major administrative center early in the Federation's recolonization efforts. Now it was a backwater, a source of grain and oil seed for the Reaches and a center of local trade because of the excellent port facilities remain-ing from the planet's former glory. Many of the villas along the road had been abandoned a generation before, though refugees from Savoy might have been sheltering in the ruins.

Everything died beneath the plasma scourge. Foliage wilted, then blazed in a faint challenge to the seething iri-descence. Tile shattered and stone walls crumbled to gravel as moisture within the pores of the rock flashed to steam.

Flesh would explode and burn also, if there were flesh in the sun-hot plasma below. Perhaps there was no one in the *Gallant Sallie*'s path.

Piet swung the vessel five kilometers from the western

edge of the city, crossed the highway, and brought the *Gallant Sallie* back on the south side of the road. With the nozzles flared, the motors consumed reaction mass at more than ten times the normal rate to achieve this modest level of thrust. The waste ions spread in a glowing fog, hiding the *Gallant Sallie* from anyone outside the curtain of death.

And hiding from the humans aboard the sight of just what they were doing.

None of them spoke. Lightbody took a small New Testament from a pocket in his tunic and held it, the metal covers closed, as he watched the feed gauges.

As the *Gallant Sallie* approached Savoy, Piet sphinctered down the nozzles and lifted the vessel a safe hundred meters in the air to curve back to the port. As the *Gallant Sallie* rotated at altitude, Sal glanced at the screen's view of what they'd accomplished. The countryside west of Savoy was a steaming, smoking wasteland. Everything in that broad swath was gray.

It had been a brilliant piece of piloting. Sal knew that with the thrusters operating at low efficiency, the controls felt as if they were rubber. Nothing you did at the console seemed to affect the ship. Piet had followed the terrain, rising and falling to achieve the maximum effect without ever endangering the vessel.

They landed very close to the entrance, searing the finish of a Federation freighter and Captain Casson's *Freedom* as they did so. Sal cleared her throat. "There's a hard suit aboard, sir," she said. "If you'd like to leave before the ground cools."

Piet looked back at her from the console. "Thank you, Captain," he said quietly. "I can wait five minutes."

When Stephen finally opened the cockpit hatch, the sunlight was a relief to Sal. She'd spent what seemed a lifetime in silence with only her thoughts for company.

All five of them were experienced spacers, but they ran to clear the surface immediately surrounding the vessel. Five minutes wasn't really enough for the plasma-heated ground to cool. . . .

The ends of the berm overlapped at the entrance to the reservation. Smaller mounds on both port and city sides increased the protection. Nearly a hundred Venerian officers and men waited for Piet within the baffles.

Between Captains Casson and Salomon stood an angry, frightened woman in her sixties. She was tall and muscular as well as fat; but fat certainly. She eyed Piet as a rat eyes a ferret.

"This is Madame Dumesnil, sir," Salomon said. Casson prodded the woman a step forward.

"Madame," Piet said with a cold anger very different from the blasts he'd directed at Stephen and Sal in the immediate past. "You will be given a vehicle and sent out the highway to the west. You will find Director Eliahu. You will inform him that at local noon every day I will conduct a similar operation until the man who murdered my previous envoy is surrendered to me."

"What sort of—" Dumesnil said.

"You will see as you drive out of the city," Piet said, "and the director will know very well. Make it clear to him, Madame, that unless he complies every village, every farm, every field on Arles will be burned to the bare rock! If there are any men surviving, they'll hide in the ditches like Rabbits after the Collapse and the Molts will hunt them for food. Tell him!"

Piet's body trembled. He gestured to Salomon and muttered, "Put her on a truck and get her out of here."

Dumesnil didn't understand what she'd been told, but Piet's tone shocked her to silence. Salomon bundled her quickly through the crowd to the vehicle that had brought her.

Casson scowled uncomfortably. "You know, Ricimer," he said, "if a Fed managed to shoot out one of your thruster nozzles while you were mooching along at low altitude, you'd likely dive right into the ground."

"I always appreciate my subordinates' concern for my safety, Captain Casson," Piet said so loudly that most of those watching from the sides and top of the berm could hear him. "No matter how inappropriate that concern might be!"

Piet turned sharply to Sal. His eyes were a brown as hard as agate. "Captain Blythe, please have your vessel refueled immediately. I like the way she handles, and I may need her again tomorrow noon."

SAVOY, ARLES.

Dawn of the short Arlesian day hinted from the east, but the truck coming up the western highway was in complete darkness. The vehicle proceeded at a walking pace. Its headlights were on, and the Klaxon on the driver's side of the cab sounded constantly. The cab's passenger waved a flag.

"Somebody who appreciates the risk he's taking," Stephen Gregg said. He smiled faintly to Sal, who stood beside him.

Stephen hitched his breastplate a little higher. When it hung in its normal position, the ceramic lip pressed the bruise above his pelvis.

"They also appreciate the risk if they wait and Captain Ricimer decides to make another demonstration earlier than he'd said," Sal said.

Stephen shrugged. "Piet'll keep his word to them," he said. "Either way, he'll keep his word."

This side of the city was given over to human residences. Molts who weren't owned by individual Feds—slaves in the municipal and port administration—had housing adjacent to the noise and drifting ions of the port reservation.

Thousands of Molts, seemingly all those who'd remained in Savoy after the human residents fled, now sat or stood where they could watch the oncoming vehicle. The Molts were careful not to crowd the fifty-man Venerian guard post, and they opened lanes quickly for humans coming from elsewhere in the city. Nonetheless, the heavily armed troops eyed the massed aliens with disquiet.

Sal looked at the Molt faces, as surely expectant as if they were muscle under skin instead of hard chitin. "How do you suppose they knew?" she asked. "They're not telepathic, are they?"

"Not that I've heard," Stephen said. Piet was two meters away, talking quietly to Guillermo and the pair of surviving Molt envoys at the gate in the barricade blocking the road. Piet wore half armor for show, but he wasn't carrying a weapon. This wasn't going to be a battle . . . and besides, he had Stephen.

Lewis stood in back of Sal and Stephen, holding a repeater. He wore bandoliers of ammunition and flashgun batteries. Stephen needed to find a replacement for Giddings. He'd never understood why men would volunteer for the job, but they did.

"Maybe Beverly," he murmured.

"Sorry?" Sal said.

"Didn't realize I'd spoken aloud," he said. "I was wondering who I'd get for a second loader." He nodded to Lewis to show that he wasn't treating the man as a piece of furniture.

"There's going to be fighting now?" Sal asked. Her tone was tense, not anxious.

"I don't think so," Stephen said.

The slowly moving truck entered the pool of light cast by the banks of floods mounted on roofs to either side of the barricade. There were five people on the vehicle: all human, all male, and all wearing Federation uniforms of either military or civil style.

None of them was armed. Stephen felt himself relax, though he hadn't been consciously aware of his tension.

The truck stopped. The man beside the driver stepped down. He still carried the white flag he'd been waving from the open cab. Two of the men in back wrestled out the third, whose arms were pinioned behind his back. All four of them approached the barricade. After a moment, the driver got out and stood beside the cab.

"I'm John McKensie, the Fiscal of Arles," said the man with the flag of truce. He was within the penumbra of the floodlights, blinking and angry with fear. "I've brought Navigator Jenks to the Venerian commander."

Piet opened the gate. Stephen was through it behind him. Sal, Lewis, and—unexpectedly—the surviving Molt envoys followed.

"I'm General Commander Ricimer," Piet said. "Kal-cha, is this man Jenks the one who killed your colleague?"

"Are you questioning the word of a gentleman, Mister Ricimer?" McKensie shouted tremblingly.

"Gentlemen don't need to be told it's wrong to murder an envoy under a flag of truce!" Sal said in a voice of harsh authority.

"This is the man, Master," the Molt wearing the yellow sash said.

Jenks was young, probably still in his teens. He had flowing black hair and a beard that partially hid the bruises on his face.

He was beyond fighting now. Jenks' eyes were dull and he looked ready to faint in the hands of the Feds holding his elbows.

Piet nodded. "Very well, then," he said. "I need to confer for a moment."

He turned his back on the fiscal to talk intently with the Molts. Guillermo and Kal-cha fell into a side discussion of clicks and chittering.

Stephen looked around. More Venerians appeared, on foot or driving. Some of them seemed to think there'd been an attack. Nobody started shooting; not yet, at least. Stephen was half smiling as he returned his attention to McKensie.

"I don't know how God can let people like you exist!" the fiscal said in a hoarse whisper. "You slaughtered innocent women and children, *infants*. You burned them alive!"

Stephen felt his mind sinking into the cold, gray place where only the view through a gunsight had reality. He heard his voice lilt as he said, "You know, it takes a lot to set Piet Ricimer off. He's as kindly a man as ever shipped beyond Pluto."

Stephen smiled. He knew he was smiling because he could feel the muscles of his face shift and could see the horror in McKensie's eyes. "But some of Piet's subordinates aren't like that at all. Some of us could line up every man, woman, and child on this planet and cut their throats, and sleep none the worse for it. Do you understand?''

McKensie said nothing. One of the men holding Jenks turned his head away.

Looking grim, Piet stepped aside so that several Molts could come through the gate. One of the aliens was a squat giant with torso and limbs half again the thickness of the others'. He wore a leather bandolier from which dangled a dozen knives in loops.

Jenks stared at the Molt. ''He's the butcher!'' he shouted in a cracking voice. ''He butchers pigs at the port, I've *seen* him. He's a *butcher*!''

''Are you empowered by Director Eliahu to negotiate a ransom for Savoy, Mister McKensie?'' Piet asked.

Jenks tried to kick free. The butcher's two assistants gripped the prisoner's arms. The Fed guards backed away. One of them wiped his hands. Stephen felt Sal stiffen at his side.

''We can't afford much,'' McKensie said. His face was frozen. He kept his eyes on Piet to avoid looking at anything else. ''This is a poor planet, a very poor planet.''

''We'll discuss that in due course,'' Piet said. He gripped the fiscal by the shoulder and forced him to turn.

Jenks was crying in the grip of the two assistants. The hulking butcher stepped behind him. The Molt held a knife with a broad 30-centimeter blade in his right hand. He grabbed a handful of Jenks' long hair with his left hand and drew the man's head back.

The watching Molts gave a collective sigh.

The butcher drew his blade across the prisoner's throat in a long, clean stroke, severing everything but the spinal column. Blood spurted a handsbreadth into the air, drowning Jenks' shout in a gurgle.

The butcher stepped back. His assistants upended the thrashing body so that it would drain properly. As Jenks himself had said, their training had been with hogs.

The Molt spectators began to leave. The sun was fully up. Somebody switched off the floodlights, though Stephen didn't hear the order given.

''We'll take your vehicle to the Commandatura, Mister

McKensie," Piet said conversationally, "and perhaps your men should come with us. I want it to be clear to my people that you're all under my protection." He gave the envoy a very hard smile. "So that I don't have to hang any of my own men."

"Dole, take two of our people and ride along with them," Stephen ordered. The bosun nodded to a pair of men from the *Wrath*.

"You're staying here?" Sal asked.

Stephen nodded. "For a while," he said. "If I were running the show for the Federation, this is just when I'd counterattack. Of course, that's if I had troops that were worth piss. Which Eliahu doesn't."

Together they looked out at the bleak landscape the *Gallant Sallie* had scoured. The truck with Piet and the Fed envoys drove past them into the city.

"I'm glad you're not working for President Pleyal," Sal said quietly.

He laughed. "Oh, so am I. I hate to be on the losing side, and nobody's going to beat Piet Ricimer."

Jenks lay on ground black with his blood. The Molts had almost completely dispersed. One of the butcher's assistants finished cleaning the knife with a wad of raw fiber, then handed it back to his master. They left also.

"You were lying when you said ... what you said to McKensie," Sal said.

"There's lies and lies," Stephen said. For a moment he thought he was going back to that place. He felt someone clutch his hand; Sal touched him, held his hand firmly.

"If they thought doing something like that would bother me," Stephen said, "they might think I wouldn't really do it, and that would be worse than a lie. Piet wouldn't order anything like that. Not unless he really had to."

Sal whispered something. He couldn't be sure of the words. He thought they were, "Oh dear God."

"And anyway," Stephen added, "I don't think I could sleep much worse than I do already."

SAVOY, ARLES.

JANUARY 10, YEAR 27.
1808 HOURS, VENUS TIME.

The *Gallant Sallie*'s crew had the two lower floors of what had been a rich man's residence in the north suburb of Savoy, but Sal kept the two-room suite and garden on the roof for herself. She and Stephen had just finished dinner—Rickalds had cooked it with surprising talent—in the shade of a potted palm tree when they heard boots on the outside staircase. Stephen lifted and pointed the flashgun waiting muzzle down beside his chair.

"Hello the house!" called Piet Ricimer. "May I come up, or would you rather I check back another time?"

"There's never a time I'd regret seeing you, Piet," Stephen called as he settled the flashgun back. "Though it's not my—"

He glanced at Sal.

"Honored, sir, deeply honored," Sal said as she rose and walked to the stairs. The outside facility was little more than a ladder. There was a more comfortable staircase within the suite, but the owner had obviously wanted a means of private access for himself and his guests.

The general commander, resplendent in maroon velvet with a chain and medallion of massive gold, hopped up and over the waist-high wall into the garden. He looked at Sal, in a black-and-silver dress she'd found here in a closet, looked at Stephen, and gestured to the garden. "You have excellent taste, Sal. In all things."

She forced a smile.

"Stephen," Piet said. He sat near the table, on a bench built around a stand of four-meter-high bamboo. "I think

116

we've achieved all we're going to here, and I'm ready to move on. I'm comfortable with the status of the ships and captains. . . .

He grinned at Sal. His face lit like a plasma thruster when he wanted it too ". . . some more than others, of course. But I'd like your opinion of the troops."

Stephen nodded twice while he marshaled his thoughts. "They fought well during the initial assault," he said. "I'd have been surprised if they didn't, of course. What's of more importance is that they've kept good watch during the past week when the danger receded. Discipline's been good in general. The men obey their officers, and the officers carry out your orders."

"I haven't noticed the friction between soldiers and sailors that I'd feared," Piet said. "Is that your observation also?"

Stephen nodded. "Healthy arrogance on both sides," he said, "but nothing worse. Seven gunshot wounds since the fighting ended, and one fellow managed to lop off his foot with a cutting bar. But it's all been accidental."

He gave his friend a tight smile. "You'd better get us back into action, Piet," he said, "or drunken foolishness is going to eat us down to a nub."

Piet squeezed the back of Stephen's hand and released it. "I think we can expect action on Berryhill," he said. "There's a military garrison there, and the defenses of St. Mary's Port are too dispersed for us to hope to slip in the way we did here."

"The men hired on to fight, Piet," Stephen said. "They'll do that. And Pleyal doesn't have any force in the Reaches that can stand against us."

It was odd to watch the pair of them this way, acting as if they were the only two people in the universe. No bluster, no hesitation, no beating around the bush. The truth as they saw it, analyzed by minds as fine as Stephen's marksmanship and Piet's touch on a starship's controls.

"Then I'll leave you two to your dinner," Piet said, rising. "I'll have a draft of an operational plan tomorrow for us to go over. Mistress Blythe—Sal—your pardon for the interruption."

He was gone over the wall even as he spoke. His boots clacked on the wooden steps.

"People think Piet takes risks," Stephen said as the footsteps faded. "And he does, of course. But they don't understand that he makes plans that keep the risks to a minimum."

"You take risks," Sal said. "With him."

Stephen gave her a wan smile. "What do I have to lose?" he said softly.

She walked to his chair, knelt, and put her arms around him. His body was as tense as a trigger-spring. It was long seconds before he responded.

She felt Stephen get out of bed at close to local midnight. Arles had three moons, but they were too small to cast noticeable illumination.

She didn't speak until she realized that he was putting his clothes on. "Don't go," she whispered.

He bent and kissed her. Then he was gone, and she heard the outside stairs creak with his solid weight.

Somebody on the ground floor was singing, "*From this valley they say you are leaving . . .*" She thought the voice was Tom Harrigan's pleasant baritone.

Sal slept fitfully till dawn. Whenever her eyes closed, she saw the face of the Fed in the tower, lighted by the red flash of her revolver.

BERRYHILL.

The last of the four transports that had carried the ground forces was the *Mount Maat*, a sphere-built 400-tonner even older than Whitey Wister, her captain. Stephen visored his eyes against the glare as she lifted with a delicacy the operation's two new vessels might have envied.

The *Mount Maat* swept south with less than ten meters between her thrusters and the tidal flats. Her exhaust blasted a trench in the mud, flinging up sand fused into gossamer sheets so fragile that they shattered again before they touched the ground.

The tracks of the other transports were clouds fading above the ocean as the steam of their passage cooled. Liftoffs—and the previous landing approaches—so close to horizontal were dangerous for any but the most skilled pilots. Such maneuvers were less risky than rising high enough for the plasma cannon of St. Mary's Port to bear on the ships, though.

The roar of the *Mount Maat*'s motors faded. The transport began to climb into a sky that retained some color from a sun that had just set at ground level. The *Mount Maat* was still vectored away from the port's guns. Her exhaust licked pearly highlights onto the sullen rollers.

"I shipped with Whitey once," Lewis said to Beverly beside him. "Crackerjack pilot, but he's a bugger. Him and his navigator, they're at it every night in their cabin."

"Bit old for that, I'd think," Beverly replied. "Both of them could be my granddad."

"Don't you believe it," Lewis insisted. "Them buggers,

119

they don't never lose pressure in their hoses the way decent folks does.''

Stephen's aide for the operation was a European lieutenant named Vanderdrekkan. When the transport was far enough away that the recombining ions of her exhaust no longer completely smothered the RF spectrum, the delicate-looking blond man resumed his conversation on a portable radio.

Major Cardiff had recommended Vanderdrekkan for the job, saying that he was careful and precise. Brave as well, though that went without saying. Vanderdrekkan's only flaw was that he'd take all night to plan an assault when a quick rush would have been cheaper.

The *Gallant Sallie* had been the first of the four transports to land on Berryhill. Piet had planned to use a larger ship, but he'd accepted Sal's offer when she volunteered. Stephen hadn't said anything. He hadn't known what to wish for, and he knew life too well to want responsibility for unpredictable results.

When Stephen Gregg pulled a trigger, he knew exactly what to expect. That was responsibility enough for anyone.

Vanderdrekkan lowered the radio and said, ''Colonel? Seibel says they're making progress, but he's going to have to replace the men clearing the path soon.''

Troops filed by in a ragged double column. All of them were in half armor. Besides personal weapons, these men from the *Mount Maat* carried cases of ammunition and replacement batteries slung on poles between each pair of them.

''We've got six hundred men,'' Beverly muttered, more or less to Lewis. ''Guess we can wear out a few cutting trail and still whip Pleyal's ass.''

Maybe I should put my loaders in charge of the advance company, Stephen thought.

Lieutenant Vanderdrekkan cleared his throat and looked embarrassed. ''Seibel also says he can see a paved road on the other side of the river.''

''Tell Seibel . . .'' Stephen said. He paused and smiled grimly. He considered waiting till he saw Seibel. No. ''Tell Seibel over the radio that it's only a little less likely that the Feds have defended the highway from the obvious landing spot than that they've defended the spaceport itself. Tell him also that if he has further stupid suggestions, I'll be up with him in a few minutes and he can make them to my face.''

Lewis grinned and winked at Beverly. The sailors claimed Mister Gregg as one of theirs when they boasted to the squadron's landsmen. Stephen knew very well that he wasn't anybody's, least of all his own; but it was small enough reward for men willing to walk into Hell at his back.

The tremble as of heat lightning to the north was the squadron in orbit exchanging plasma bolts with the defenses of St. Mary's Port. The demonstration might make the Feds nervous, but they wouldn't neglect the ground defenses. ''Let's go,'' Stephen said to Vanderdrekkan. ''All Seibel has to do is keep the river on his left, but that may be beyond his competence.''

The aide trotted a few paces ahead, muttering, ''Make way for the colonel,'' to heavily laden troops as he passed them. Stephen swung along the muddy track with his loaders following him closely.

Major Cardiff was in charge of the rear guard. He'd wanted to lead the advance, but Stephen needed somebody he trusted to chivy stragglers forward and make sure none of the inevitable minor casualties were abandoned in the brush. Seibel wouldn't have another significant position in any force Stephen was involved with, but his dithering didn't matter now. Stephen didn't have a high opinion of himself as a commander, but he knew how to lead; and you only lead from the front.

The vegetation covering the thick silt along the river was woody, thumb-thick, and branched into whips reaching as far as five meters in the air. In a few hundred meters the troops would reach the limestone bluff on which St. Mary's Port was built. After the climb, they'd be in the local equivalent of short grass and the going would be easier.

There'd be a realistic danger of ambush too, of course. The Feds had been given more than a month to prepare.

Besides Stephen and his immediate staff, the *Gallant Sallie* had landed fifty sailors and a 10-cm plasma cannon on a ground carriage. The gun was in the care of Stampfer, who'd followed Piet as master gunner through a series of commands. Dole was in charge of the men who dragged the weapon and its attendant paraphernalia along the rugged trail. Most of Dole's party was from his close-combat team. There was no risk of a Fed sortie overrunning the gun.

"That's right, boys, put your backs in it," the bosun called from just ahead in the darkness. "If they don't get out in front better, we'll roll some of these soldiers into the ground, seeing they like dirt so well."

Dole was bantering, not snarling at his men. He knew as Stephen did that pride would take the sailors farther and faster than threats ever could.

The plasma cannon was a dense mass filling the track. Stephen heard cutting bars whine up ahead. Sailors were widening the gap opened by the infantry pioneers now leading the column. The cut brush went to corduroy the muddy surface for the gun's balloon tires.

Stephen touched his aide on the shoulder and said, "I'll lead for a moment, Vanderdrekkan." He broke trail through resisting brush to avoid getting in the way of the crew pushing and pulling the massive cannon.

Dole stepped aside to wait for him. "Going up to sort out these landsmen, sir?" he asked.

"Going to make sure we're pointed in the right direction, at least," Stephen said. "Everything under control here?"

The bosun was a stocky man whose bald spot gleamed on a head of coarse black hair. He carried a carbine and wore back-and-breast armor, though the sailors with the gun had been specifically exempted from the orders requiring half armor for the landing force. At least a third of the sailors sweated in ceramic cuirasses as they dragged their tonnes of ordnance forward.

The armor was bravado. *There's nobody on this planet as tough as we are.* And when veteran troops felt that way, they were very generally correct.

"I sent Lightbody and Tiempro forward to set pulleys for the block and tackle at the top of the rise," Dole said. "We'll have the gun sited and ready before you're halfway to town."

Stampfer came back to join them. He and the six men of his crew each wore a canvas vest holding four dense 10-cm shells. The gunner had decided that was a better way to carry munitions on this trail than a wheeled cart.

"Remember, don't get overanxious," Stephen said. He raised his voice enough to be heard by sailors shuffling past on the drag ropes. There was no chance of Stampfer—or Dole—disclosing the gun position before time, but the common sailors might mutter and complain unless they knew the orders came directly from Mister Gregg. "We won't need you unless they come at us with ships. Then we'll need you bad, and I want your first shot to count."

"Don't bloody fear, sir," Stampfer said in a low rumble. He was a squat troll of a man. Instead of a firearm or a cutting bar, the gunner carried a meter-long trunnion adjustment wrench. He was quite capable of using it on anyone jostling him as he laid a plasma cannon.

"Wish I was going with you, Mister Gregg," Dole said. "But I suppose there'll be another time, won't there?"

Stephen nodded. "There always is," he said. *If you live*; but Stephen didn't have to warn the bosun about danger. It was amazing that Dole had survived after following Captain Ricimer and Mister Gregg so long.

The gun had staggered past as the officers talked. "Well, carry on and don't be greedy," Stephen said to Dole and Stampfer. "These soldiers aren't any more use on a ship than I am, so don't grudge them and me a chance to pretend we're good for something."

He pushed into the brush again. "Let's see what Major Seibel's about, Vanderdrekkan. We're certainly not needed here."

ABOVE BERRYHILL.

Sarah Blythe's new hard suit fitted so well that in weightless conditions she sometimes forgot she had it on. The extra thirty kilos of mass were still there. She strained her shoulder when she caught a stanchion to halt behind Piet Ricimer's console.

The *Wrath* was under combat regulations: all personnel in armor, and internal pressure low to limit air loss during gunnery. A gunner's mate shrieked in a voice made pale by the thin air, "Mister Stampfer's going to *cry* when he comes back if you fucking whoresons don't train your guns better on the next firing pass! I could piss out a port and hurt the Feds worse!"

Piet wore all but the gauntlets of a gilded hard suit. He was talking into a handset against his left cheek while his right hand manipulated a display filled with numbers. After a decent interval, Sal said, "Captain Blythe reporting as ordered, General Commander!"

"At the very least, Captain Holmberg," Piet said, "your ship may draw a bolt that would otherwise have damaged a useful element of the squadron. Take your place in the rotation, or expect to answer for your cowardice as soon as we're on the ground. Out!"

Piet turned to Sal. The *Wrath* had five navigational consoles—the pair to starboard separated from the other three by a splinterproof bulkhead of clear glass. Guillermo was in the seat beside Piet, and a Betaport navigator Sal recognized but couldn't name was at the remaining console of the main triad.

"Holmberg thinks that because the *Zephyr*'s popguns won't do any damage from orbit, he ought to keep her out of the bombardment chain," Piet said. "He doesn't appreciate that the sheer number of ships involved affects Fed morale."

"Holmberg owns the *Zephyr*," Sal said. She hoped she was offering the statement as information rather than seeming to take the part of an Ishtar City man she knew well enough to detest.

"His heirs will own the *Zephyr* if he plays the coward with me," Piet said in a voice as emotionless as the one Stephen used when he discussed similar things.

Piet wiped his face with a bandanna, said, "Sorry," and then went on. "First, how did the landing go?"

He manipulated the keyboard with his right index finger without bothering to look at it. The numbers vanished like a coin spinning and were replaced by an image of Berryhill. Sal wasn't sure whether the vast turquoise globe was a real-time view or summoned from memory.

"No problems, sir," Sal said. The *Queen of Sheba* had come down too close to the river's edge and flooded her boarding holds when the hatches opened, but Captain Gruen had redeemed himself by rocking the transport free with his attitude jets before lighting his thrusters. Nothing Piet had to learn about officially. "The ground forces were proceeding ahead of schedule when I lifted for orbit."

Piet grinned tightly. "Stephen and I discussed the possibility that the river delta would be defended," he said. "I'm glad it wasn't."

The *Wrath* had just completed a firing pass when Sal came aboard in obedience to the general commander's summons. All the squadron's armed vessels—the four transports had been stripped of guns for the landing—were in a gigantic rotation that took them dipping one at a time into the atmosphere above St. Mary's Port. The Venerian bombardment wasn't likely to damage the defenses, but it was all the ships could safely do to support the ground force.

Under Piet's control, the display focused down in a series of x10 steps. After the last jump, an image of St. Mary's Port filled the holographic screen.

There were six gun positions sited around the large rhomboidal field. The tower holding the four heaviest guns was ten meters high, commanding much of the surrounding countryside.

The city south of the port area had originally been protected against marauding Rabbits by a ditch and berm. As the Federation colony grew, danger from the savage remnants of pre-Collapse society receded. Buildings now spilled beyond the berm to the south and west. The holographic image was sharp enough that Sal could see that alleys and the highway south, crossing the St. Mary's River, were barricaded against the expected Venerian assault.

Piet rolled the ball switch controlling the display's scale and focus and clicked up the scale. As the center of the image area slid upward, the port reservation expanded to fill the screen.

"This is what concerns me," Piet said, "and why I called you here."

There were nearly a hundred ships on the vast field, most of them Reaches-built trash with flimsy hulls and too few thrusters for their mass. Half a dozen had the presence of solider vessels, though these weren't of any great size either.

At the time the image was recorded, probably during a firing pass before nightfall, a pair of cylindrical 200-tonne ships were testing their thrusters. Wisps of iridescence glimmered downwind of the hulls, obvious to a spacer's eye.

Piet increased the scale once more. Guns projected from the side ports of both vessels; ten total on one ship, twelve on the other. The tubes were a motley collection with evident variation in size between adjacent gunports.

"They can't hope to engage the squadron with a pair of merchant ships mounting whatever guns they had in inventory," Sal said. "So they're planning to use them on Stephen as mobile batteries. On the ground forces."

"Stampfer will give a good account of himself," Piet said, "but there's dead ground between where the gun is sited and the outskirts of the city. The Feds will drop into the swale as soon as the first bolt hits them."

Piet's mouth pursed as though he were sucking a lemon. "I thought of taking the *Wrath* in close where our fire could be significant," he said, "but the port defenses are well handled. The risk would be too high."

Piet's smile was cold. "Too high to a ship and crew which Venus will need in the real struggle which is coming soon. I intend instead to send down a pair of armed cutters to occupy the attention of the Fed warships until our troops can get into the town. Are you willing to pilot one of those cutters, Captain Blythe?"

"Yes, sir," Sal said.

She would have agreed to step into space in her underwear if Piet said it would help Stephen. The analytical part of her mind suggested that the one course was about as likely to be survivable as the other.

BERRYHILL.

Dawn winked on the fuselage and rotating wing of the autogyro in Stephen Gregg's sight picture. The Fed scouts flew over the southern edge of St. Mary's Port at a thousand meters altitude, high enough that they were safe from rifle fire from the Venerian ground troops for whom they were searching.

Stephen let his flashgun swing, tracking the glitter long enough to fall into a rhythm with his target. He didn't feel, he never felt, the gentle increase in the pressure the pad of his index finger was exerting on the trigger. The *whack* of the bolt and the blindness as his faceshield instantly darkened to save his retinas came as the usual surprise.

The six soldiers with flashguns in his lead company fired the moment after Stephen did, aiming at the second of the Federation's airborne scouts. Stephen's protective visor would take nearly a minute to fade to clear again. He flipped it up to survey the effectiveness of the laser pulses.

Stephen had hit the engine compartment of the autogyro he aimed at. The bolt had no penetration, even against an aircraft's light-alloy sheeting, but its enormous flux density converted the target surface into a plasma with a shattering acoustic pulse radiating from the back of the panel.

Steam blasted as the shock ripped away radiator hoses as well as the spark plug wires of the in-line engine. The two-seat autogyro staggered and curved downward, supported by the continuing self-rotation of its wing.

The Fed autogyros Stephen had seen in the past used radial

engines. He'd expected his bolt to rupture and ignite a fuel tank ahead of the cockpit. This result would do.

The first hundred Venerian troops moved out of the scrub and into the sorghum fields with a shout, though none of them was really running. The march, much of it uphill, had been brutal, and men so heavily laden with weapons and armor wouldn't have been able to run far even if they'd been fresh.

With the reflex of long practice, Stephen's fingers switched the battery in the butt of his weapon for a fresh one while his eyes scanned to find additional targets. Rifles flashed from the darkened fronts of buildings on the outskirts of St. Mary's Port, but small-arms projectiles were no danger at this range. The Feds rarely used flashguns, though they might have crew-served lasers in their defenses.

Stephen thought for a moment the second autogyro had escaped the volley his men had directed at it. The city was a good kilometer away, and slant distance to the aircraft was still farther; a long shot even for a marksman whose bolt didn't deviate from line of sight.

The autogyro was diving away northward. The pilot probably intended to land in the spaceport, out of the battle, but there was no reason to take chances. Stephen aligned the craft with the fat muzzle of his cassegrain laser. He had an almost zero-deflection shot, just a matter of taking account of the target's rapid descent. . . .

Before Stephen pulled the trigger, the advancing half of the autogyro's wing lifted vertical and flew away from the rest of the vehicle. A bolt had hit the wing near its rotor, and the stress of the dive had snapped the structure at the point of damage.

Tumbling over and over, the autogyro plunged five hundred meters into St. Mary's Port. A deep red fireball rose above the buildings three seconds before the thump of the fuel explosion.

"Let's go," Stephen muttered to his staff as he swung into a jog. His side throbbed when his left boot came down and his breastplate slapped against the bruise. Vanderdrekkan ran alongside him, trying to continue a conversation over the portable radio.

The sorghum was waist-high, completely hiding the ground beneath its broad, dark leaves. The furrows were perpendicular to the Venerians' advance, and you couldn't guess how you were going to step from one stride to the next.

The acreage was cultivated as a single expanse by Molts, to feed themselves and the other slaves of the region. There were no fences or hedgerows, but irrigation canals rising slightly above the tilth ran at fifty-meter intervals down the length of the field. Stephen had ordered the flashgunners—the other flashgunners—to crouch behind the northernmost canal mound to support the assault wave.

Midway across the field, six naked men with guns and bows rose from behind the nearest canal. They aimed at the backs of soldiers who'd just passed them without noticing the lurking enemies.

Stephen was still twenty meters behind the skirmish line proper. He fired at a figure by instinct, closing his eyes at the instant of trigger release. The bolt's intensity would leave purple afterimages drifting across his retinas despite his eyelid's shielding, but waiting to put his visor down first meant a soldier's life.

The attackers were Rabbits, remnants of Berryhill's pre-Collapse society. The Feds treated the savages they found on recolonized planets as vermin or slaves—and Molts made far better slaves. That obviously hadn't kept the government here from hiring or cajoling Rabbits to fight for them.

Die for them. The laser bolt caught a Rabbit in the small of the back. His shotgun fired skyward as his torso exploded in a mist of blood. Soldiers ahead of Stephen turned at the flash and muzzle blast.

An arrow struck a Venerian in the center of the chest, shattering on his ceramic cuirass. The Rabbit archer hadn't allowed for body armor. A charge of shotgun pellets ripped the leg of another soldier, but he stayed upright long enough to shoot his attacker three times in the chest with a pump carbine. Another Rabbit missed a rifleshot from two meters away because instead of aiming he waved his weapon wildly in the direction of his target before jerking the trigger.

All six Rabbits were down before Stephen could aim the repeater Lewis slapped into his hand in exchange for the flashgun. A mercenary from the Coastal Republic was finishing a wounded ambusher by holding his face in the canal with a cleated boot. The Rabbit's long hair and beard were as red as the blood on the soldier's left sleeve, torn by a bullet that had ricocheted from his titanium breastplate.

Powder smoke, ozone from the laser discharge, and the stink of opened body cavities hung in the air. Beverly picked up a satchel of batteries with a look of fascinated horror. A bullet fired by another member of the assault force had cut the strap without—quite—piercing Beverly's neck.

Vanderdrekkan had drawn but not fired one of his pair of long-barreled revolvers. "Three wounded, none of them seriously, sir," Vanderdrekkan said. "Holtsinger may not be able to accompany the rest of the force."

The Venerian with the shotgun wound looked up and snarled, "I can still fucking march anywhere a European pansy can!" Another soldier had cut Holtsinger's trousers open and was applying a field dressing.

Flashes and smoke marked where the Feds were firing from the city. None of the bullets came close enough to matter, though the attackers were within possible range by now.

"Keep them moving," Stephen said with a curt nod to his aide. He took the flashgun and jogged forward, trying to pull his skirmishers back into a straight line. Because the ambush had occurred in the center of the lead company, the ends had drawn forward like horns pointing toward St. Mary's Port. The second and third companies started to move out from the brush where they'd assembled.

With a roar that drowned the crash of occasional plasma bolts from the spaceport, a medium-sized starship rose into sight from the valley of the St. Mary's River. The ship moved with glacial slowness, a single maneuver at a time. Not until the vessel had reached its intended altitude of about fifty meters did its captain swing the bow to starboard so that his port broadside bore on the troops a kilometer away.

The ship seemed to float on a cloud of rainbow exhaust. The morning was quiet, poised between the land breeze of night and the wind that the river would funnel from the relatively cool ocean toward the city in a few hours.

Stephen lowered his visor. At this range, he couldn't

punch a flashgun bolt through the exhaust to shatter a thruster nozzle. The trick was possible—Stephen had done so more than once—but only if the pilot cooperated by bringing the vessel close enough or high enough to give the flashgunner an opportunity.

Stephen aimed at a gunport, a minuscule target and one where even a hit wouldn't change the course of battle. Still, a target.

He squeezed off. A flashgun bolt, not his, lit a stern panel. Vaporized metal combined with atmospheric oxygen in a harmless secondary flare. Many of the soldiers were firing, riflemen as well as flashgunners; even one desperate sod with a shotgun whose pellets couldn't *reach* the starship, much less harm it.

Stephen reloaded with his visor down and his head lowered. The starship fired six plasma cannon together.

The guns ranged from under 10-cm bore to 15-cm at least. They weren't especially well laid, but a single charge incinerated six soldiers as it gouged a long furrow across the field. Carbon in the soil and foliage burned red. A bolt that dug to bedrock blasted quicklime in white splendor.

Recoil from the simultaneous thermonuclear explosions rotated the vessel 20° upward on her axis, bringing the port thrusters into slightly better view. Stephen aimed again, seeing the blaze of the tungsten nozzles as a line of dashes through his darkened faceshield. Before he could fire, Stampfer's plasma cannon hit the forward quartet of thrusters squarely.

The thunder of the starship's guns was still echoing from the buildings of St. Mary's Port when the vessel nosed over and her stern motors drove her into the ground. She was nearly perpendicular when she hit. The bow stabbed meters through the soft limestone before strakes fractured and the rest of the ship crumpled like a melon in a drop forge.

Stephen knelt and covered the back of his neck with his hands. The groundshock threw him forward in a somersault fractionally before the sky-filling crash reached him through the air.

The sound went on for several seconds, punctuated by green flashes and the sharp cracking failure of the four stern thrusters. Normally the nozzles were cooled by reaction mass before it was converted to plasma. When the tanks ruptured, the coolant passages emptied and the thrusters exploded.

The ship excavated a crater fifty meters across and nearly half that in depth. Fragments of hull and shattered bedrock flew in parabolas from the impact. The scattered pieces knocked down buildings that the groundshock had spared, crushing Feds and attackers alike.

Stephen got to his feet. "Let's go!" he croaked. He couldn't see. It was a second or two before he remembered to raise his visor, smeared with dirt even though the filtering tint had started to clear.

Plumes of steam and dense black smoke twisted in a single rope from the crash site. Fires had broken out at a dozen places in the city. Despite the wreckage, a Molt fired from the rubble of a fallen wall. Stephen squinted and squeezed his trigger, flinging the alien back dead despite smoke and airborne debris that attenuated the laser's effect. He reloaded as he moved on.

A hundred meters of waste ground lay between the field and the nearest buildings. Plowed-up rocks were piled at the edge of the cultivated area. A few Fed marksmen had fired from rough stone hangars here. One of them was dead beneath a starship hatch that had tumbled like a flipped coin before pinning her to the ground; the rest had fled. Stephen strode past the body.

Lewis and Vanderdrekkan were still with him. Beverly wasn't. Stephen could see only a dozen other members of the lead company, but the casualties couldn't really be that high. Skirmishers who'd been thrown down or even stunned would get to their feet momentarily; the main body of the attack would follow in a matter of minutes or less, splitting the Fed defenses open from the lodgment Stephen and his handfuls tore in the immediate chaos.

"Rifle!" Stephen shouted, wondering if Lewis could hear him. He carried a cutting bar, but it wasn't his weapon. Even in a hand-to-hand fight at a barricade Stephen preferred a gun butt or the muzzle jabbing like a blunt spear to a bar's twitching edge.

For a moment he thought that the roar he heard was blood

racing in his ears. Pearly radiance blazed across the buildings, and he turned his head to the left.

Risen from the riverbed but barely brushing the surface of
the ground, a second Federation starship parted the pall
marking the destruction of its consort. The vessel was swinging to rake its broadside across the Venerian attack. Stephen
snatched back the flashgun from his loader. He aimed, because he had nothing better to do.

BERRYHILL.

Ditches the transports' exhaust had dug across the St. Mary's delta had filled with water and looked natural, but the amount of litter the ground force had left behind surprised Sal. Pallets, flexible sheeting, empty boxes, and containers of all kinds; clothing, pieces of body armor, scattered cartridges; even a rifle broken at the small of the stock.

A wrench pinged on the head of a bolt, rang from the gun mount, and dropped into a cutter's cabin to clang loudly on the deck. Tom Harrigan caught the wrench in the air as it started another bounce, this time toward the attitude-control panel. He blinked at the tool in pleased surprise.

"Sorry, sailor," muttered Godden, a gunner's mate from the *Wrath* and in charge of the weapon and two assistants. Over the intercom wired to Sal's helmet, Godden went on, "We've got this pig dogged down, ma'am. Ready any time you are."

It had taken fifteen minutes to mount the six-tube laser at the front edge of Cutter 725's dorsal hatch. The weapon and the 5-cm plasma cannon being fitted to Piet's Cutter 551 had to be carried within the little vessels during reentry. Though a cutter could fly at moderate speed through an atmosphere with the two-meter-by-one-meter hatch open, it couldn't survive braking from orbital velocity; neither could a weapon stuck out in the turbulent airstream.

"725 to 551," Sal said into her communications handset. The modulated laser was directed at the pickup antenna of the cutter eighty meters away, but she had to hope 551's console speaker was at full volume. Piet and his four sub-

ordinates were all visible on the hull or half out the cutter's
hatchway, wrestling with a mounting that obviously wasn't
going as planned. "We're ready to lift. Over."

725's optics were good for a cutter but not *good*. Piet,
recognizable only because of his gilded helmet, waved from
551. Sal heard him shout something but she couldn't make
out the words. She started to get up from her couch in the
far bow of the little vessel so that she could stick her head
out the central hatch.

"Captain says go on without him, ma'am," Godden relayed. "Says there's no time to lose."

"Understood," Sal said. "Prepare to lift." She lit 725's
thruster, lifted to balance a moment on a three-meter pillar
of flame, and roared north up the channel of the river at 50
kph. It would have been nice to fill the water tank, but the
small crew couldn't do that and mount the laser at the same
time.

The St. Mary's River drained through what had been a
fault in a limestone plate. Friction and acids from rotting
vegetation carried by the current had widened the crack to
half a kilometer, leaving bluffs a hundred meters high on
either side of the channel. Sal didn't have time to be im-
pressed, but she heard Godden mutter, "Holy Jesus!", forgetting the intercom was keyed.

She kept the cutter low, fighting the shockwaves reflected
from the surface of the water. The plume of steam behind
them warned anyone watching that they were coming, but
the thruster's snarl echoing up the channel would do that in
any case. They could only hope that the Feds were too busy
to worry about 725—or that their shots missed.

Steam was the first sign of their quarry as well. The bluffs
ten klicks up the river sloped and were only half the height
of those nearer the mouth. From side to side and spilling out
of the channel was a white pall from which slowly lifted a
starship with its guns run out. Vortices shot horizontally
through the fog. The captain was using his attitude jets to
bring his broadside to bear on the troops south of the city.

Godden bawled something on the intercom. Sal pulled
back her control yoke, lifting the cutter's bow and pointing

them more directly toward the Federation vessel; the six-tube laser had only 15° of traverse to either side of center.

"Aim for the attitude jets!" Sal shouted, hoping that Godden heard and understood. Harrigan kept 725 flat in the turn so that banking wouldn't introduce another variable in the gunner's calculations.

The laser fired, sequencing the tubes in microsecond pulses. 725 was flying ten or fifteen meters above the river when the first flash lit the channel and ripped a collop from the target's hull plating. The cutter lost all thrust for the duration of the burst, dropping like an anvil until its belly hit the water. Only the up-angle Sal had dialed in for aiming purposes kept them from drilling into the bottom muck to explode.

"*Holy Jesus!*" the gunner shouted, this time surely a prayer as his thumbs jerked back from the laser's butterfly trigger. The thruster nozzle boomed at full power, lifting the cutter on a huge bubble of live steam.

They—she, Piet, Godden, and Tom Harrigan—had worried about the laser's weight, bulk, and means of mounting. Sal had glanced at the weapon's power requirements, found they were within the excess of the fusion motor's output over what the cutter required to stay airborne, and dismissed the question. The others had probably done the same.

The figures were wrong, and the mistake had almost been fatal.

The laser was powered by a magnetohydrodynamic generator that in turn used the cutter's plasma motor as its prime mover. The generator, drawing from upstream of the thrust nozzle, had absorbed virtually all the motor's output. The trickle of plasma that remained wasn't sufficient to drive the cutter forward. Gravity and inertia took control.

Because the water bath enclosed the exhaust, 725 bounced forty meters into the air at a higher acceleration than Sal would have chosen for a craft so flimsy. The Fed starship had a ragged tear where the laser had struck it, so the weapon was a good choice—if they could use it without killing themselves.

"What happened?" Godden demanded. "What happened?"

"Godden, don't shoot till I tell you!" Sal ordered as she fought her control yoke. She brought the cutter around in a wide arc that took them over the city, climbing as she did.

Troops lay flat or dead on the open ground south of the city. The starship, though not seriously damaged by the laser bolts, grounded momentarily in a geyser of dirt because the clanging impacts startled the people at the controls. The thick hull paneling of another Fed vessel was strewn like tinsel around the hole its crash dug nearby.

"Get ready!" Sal warned. 725 was a kilometer high and a similar distance from the Federation vessel, a metallic cigar gleaming in a setting of iridescent exhaust. The cutter was a possible target for the guns of the port reservation, but if that happened at least it would be sudden.

Sal put the yoke over and dived on the target. "Get 'em, Godden!" she said.

The laser fired, ringing at high frequency through the fabric of the cutter. Sal's screen dulled the sparkle of the bolts, but metal burned from the starship's hull was an opaque white radiance wholly different from the wisps of steam still hanging in the river valley.

Again the thruster lost power, but Harrigan lifted 725's nose by increments, making up for frictional losses that steepened the glide angle. Godden traversed as he fired, drawing his stream of pulses along the target's hull at about the level of the open gunports.

When they'd dropped to a hundred meters above the ground, Sal shouted, "Cease fire!" Godden obeyed, and Sal used the thruster's resurgent power to hop 725 over the starship they couldn't have avoided in any other fashion.

The Feds fired a starboard plasma cannon at the cutter. The bolt came nowhere near a target angling past at more than 100 kph. An instant later the Feds fired their five-gun port broadside uselessly toward the eastern horizon. The vessel had yawed after it touched the ground, throwing the programmed plasma bolts wild.

A second cutter, Piet's 551, screamed past 725 on a nearly reciprocal course less than a hundred meters away. The light cannon mounted on 551's hatch fired a slug of ions into the

starship's hull, low enough to threaten the stern thruster nozzles. 551 twisted into a banking turn west of the river.

The Federation captain lifted his ship to gain control. He
swung the bow north to bring the remainder of his port
broadside to bear on the Venerian infantry. Stampfer center-
punched the vessel with a 10-cm bolt, powerful enough to
smash through both inner and outer hull.

The starship dipped back over the edge of the bluff. None
of the damage it had received was fatal; none of it would
have prevented a Venerian captain from continuing to fight.

This captain *wasn't* a Venerian. The vessel wallowed up
the river, accelerating from a walk to a run as it proceeded
northward. Steam boiled in the vessel's track, filtering the
hull to a ghostly outline and effectively armoring the Feds
against both laser light and plasma.

A bullet cracked on 725's belly. The projectile didn't—
couldn't—penetrate the ceramic plating, but the vicious
sound made Sal twitch at the controls. The cutter shuddered
under her unintended input.

She climbed to three hundred meters over the spaceport.
Sal threw the cutter into a hard, banking turn to head back
to the delta. 725 staggered and lost thrust as Godden's laser
ripped down into a Fed gun position.

"Hold your fire, you cack-handed fool!" Sal shouted.
"We're short on reaction mass and I don't want to waste it
fucking—"

The thruster burped and quit. Harrigan brought them level
with the attitude jets while Sal fought the yoke. The cutter
glided better than a brick, but only slightly better.

The motor found a little more water in the tank. Plasma
flared, bringing the nose up. Sal deliberately shut the thruster
down, husbanding the last of their reaction mass to cushion
the shock of landing. Air swept across the open hatch with
a *shoop-shoop-shoop* that sounded painfully loud in the near
silence.

There was no point in trying to maneuver. Sal aimed for
the largest open space in their direction of movement, the
park facing the Commandatura of St. Mary's Port. She'd
underestimated the flow when the motor was trying to power
both the laser and the thruster nozzle. . . .

At twenty meters she screamed, "Hang on!" and lit the thruster with the nozzle gimballed 60° forward. The water tank gave them a second and a half of burn. It was enough, if you didn't care what you said. Cutter 725 hit and slid forward through flowers and an ornamental hedge. The stern lifted, but they missed doing an endo by 10° and a prayer.

725 slammed back down on the skids. The instruments were black. Another bullet rang from the hull.

With a roar like that of a colossal beehive, Cutter 551 set down beside them under power. Sal felt a surge of relief. Whatever they'd gotten into, Piet Ricimer wasn't going to leave them there alone.

ST. MARY'S PORT, BERRYHILL.

Stephen Gregg saw movement behind the lace curtain blowing in the window across the street. He fired. A cat yowled briefly, despairingly. Stephen pumped a fresh cartridge into the chamber of his rifle, feeling as though the sky had fallen on him.

Somebody's pet. It could have been their child. It probably has been a child one or more times already today.

"Did you get one, sir?" Beverly asked. The loader wore a swatch from a cloth-of-gold altar hanging across his forehead and right eye. Blood had dried black against the fabric.

"Not this time," Stephen said.

A soldier backed out of a doorway down the street, circling his left thumb and forefinger to indicate all clear. Vanderdrekkan, breathing hard, trotted from the adjacent garden with a galvanized bucket. "Here you go, sir," he gasped. "It's water."

Stephen squatted, resting the rifle across his knees so that he could take the bucket in both hands to gulp from it. Beverly leaned forward and slipped a cartridge into the loading gate without disturbing the way the weapon lay. Lewis was three blocks back, his leg broken not by a bullet but when the stones of a crumpled wall turned under his boot.

Stephen thought the water had a chemical tinge, but that could as easily be the crap he'd been breathing in the past however long. He'd exhausted his four 2-liter canteens by the time he reached the city. Since then there'd been nothing but dust and powdersmoke and the stink of air burned by

141

flashgun discharges. He'd refused to take water from the troops he commanded.

Stephen lowered the bucket and checked the location of the dozen men with him on this street. "Odd numbers!" he ordered, his voice no longer the croak it had been during several previous leapfrog advances. He rose to his feet and jogged deliberately forward, scanning for motion.

Fed resistance had broken almost before Stephen and his troops reached the city proper. There'd been a short struggle among the houses barricaded on the edge of town, but the crash of the first starship had shaken down much of the prepared defense line. When the Feds saw the second vessel flee with its tail between its legs, they'd lost heart. Besides, though the Berryhill defenders were armed better than most Federation troops in the Reaches, they didn't have the body armor that protected the Venerians in a close-range slugfest.

At the head of the street was a park behind a waist-high brick wall. Three Molts and a human in a white jacket knelt on Stephen's side of the wall. They didn't see him coming. Cartridge cases around the Feds indicated they'd been firing through the plasma-seared hedge toward the pair of Venerian cutters in the park. A number of Molts with head wounds sprawled among the survivors.

Stephen fired four times. Some of the men who'd advanced with him, the odd numbers covered by the evens, fired also, but there wasn't need for more bullets than the one Stephen Gregg put through each Federation skull.

He swapped his rifle for the loaded carbine without needing to say anything to Beverly. "Coming through!" Stephen cried. "God for Venus! Coming through!"

He jumped over the wall. The Commandatura on the other side of the park was a mass of flames, as was what looked like a barracks block beside the administrative headquarters. Cutter 551's 5-cm plasma cannon wasn't a powerful weapon for space combat, but its slug of plasma could ignite virtually any structure on the ground.

Piet, wearing a helmet of plain off-white ceramic instead of his usual gilded piece, covered Stephen from the hatch of 551 until he was sure of the identification. More heads lifted from the cutters, two beside Piet and three from the farther vessel. Sal's mate, Harrigan his name was, and—

Sal. Captain Sarah Blythe. Her right cheek was bruised blue, but her eyes focused.

More Venerian troops entered the park from other radial streets. St. Mary's Port was built like the southern half of a wheel, with the Commandatura at the center of the chord and the spaceport directly north of the city. A heavy plasma cannon from a gun tower in the middle distance blasted its charge toward the orbiting squadron. There was no other sign of resistance.

Stephen halted by 551. Piet climbed down wearily, taking the hand his friend offered. "Piet," Stephen said, "the whole rest of the squadron could dive into the sun, and it wouldn't hurt Venus as much as if you'd gotten your head blown off here."

"I was going to pick up the crew of 725," Piet said, avoiding the question and Stephen's eyes. "But I had to use the exhaust to keep the Feds away, and then I didn't trust the reaction mass we had left would be enough to get us to a better spot."

"There's only been sniping since P-p-Captain Ricimer swept the north wall with his thruster," Sal said.

Stephen couldn't look at her. "The second ship, that would have been a problem," he said, facing Piet. "I suspect we'd still have gotten through the cannon fire, but not near so many of us. Thanks."

A plasma cannon fired. Only one gun tower seemed still to be operating. "Follow me!" Stephen said, shambling across the ruined park. It was better to act than to think about what might have happened, and might happen yet.

A brick arch beside the burning Commandatura marked the entrance through the port enclosure. A high-sided truck had driven onto the berm and overturned, blocking the passage for further vehicles trying to escape. They were abandoned in the entrance switchback.

Stephen climbed the sloped turf bank and lay down at the top to view the spaceport proper. Piet was on his left; someone else was on Stephen's right, but he refused to look to be sure.

The gun tower from which occasional bolts ripped skyward was half a klick away. The walls were sheer-sided with no rifle ports, even under examination through the electronic magnifier Piet handed Stephen without comment. The door at the base was metal and solid enough, but it wouldn't withstand more than a minute or two of surgery with cutting bars. The gun mounts were countersunk beneath a deep coping for protection, but that meant the tubes couldn't be depressed to bear on attacking infantry.

The tower had external loudspeakers. Through them blared harmonica music at distorting amplification.

"Let's go," Stephen said as he got to his feet. "But watch out for diehards in the ships on the field."

"Wait," said Piet, tugging Stephen's sleeve. "Listen to the music."

What had been puzzling noise suddenly clicked into place in Stephen's consciousness. His brain filled in the lyrics: . . . *where the dearest and best, for a world of lost sinners was slain.*

"*I will cling to the old rugged cross!*" Beverly sang in a hoarse roar. "Love of God, sir, what Fed would play *that* song?"

The harmonica music cut off. A voice, also distorted, called, "If the Venerian gentlemen would care to approach the fort, a European whom the Feds captured and enslaved on New Bayonne would be delighted to open it to them. And if the gentlemen have a way of opening a door which the Feds locked when they fled, they can shut off the noise of these cannon and their damnable automatic loaders."

"We've won," Sal said.

"In three weeks or a month we'll be back on Venus with all the loot the squadron can carry," Stephen said as he started down the inner slope, reaching for a cutting bar with his left hand.

He wondered if there'd ever been a time he'd believed that the survivors won a battle.

ISHTAR CITY, VENUS.

The footman swung the door of the private office inward and called, "Factor Ricimer and Mister Stephen Gregg to see you, sir!"

Uncle Ben—Factor Gregg of Weyston—rose behind a clear glass desk with nothing on its shimmering top. He'd redecorated the office since Stephen last saw it. The walls and ceiling were single-sheet mirrors, and there were no shelves nor cabinetry to interfere with the illusion of volume.

"Factor Ricimer, I'm honored," Benjamin Gregg said, extending his hand. "Stephen, I'm pleased you were able to come also. It's been too long."

It'd been longer than Stephen had realized. Uncle Ben looked old. His arm trembled, and there were liver spots on the backs of his hands.

Piet Ricimer had entered this office when he was a brash young space captain with a dream for Venus and mankind. In the decade since, Piet had gained experience and ten kilograms of flesh. The lines of his face were softer, but the spirit still burned as bright as it ever had. Piet hadn't lost his dream or his faith in God.

Stephen forced himself to view his own reflection. He was wearing a new set of court clothes in deference to Uncle Ben's sense of occasion. The fabric was a fine twill whose black-and-white striping looked gleamingly gray from any distance. Occasional silver threads added highlights to the perfectly tailored, obviously expensive ensemble.

Wearing the garments, Stephen Gregg looked like Death. The problem wasn't color. If he'd worn pink, he'd have

looked like Death. He was tall, gaunt, and blond, and he
looked like what he was.

"Gentlemen, please seat yourselves," Uncle Ben said. He
sank gratefully into his own chair. The seats were padded
and comfortable, the only elements of substance in the
room's design. Piet sat down, but Stephen balanced on the
arm of the other chair. He was nervous to have his own
reflection looking at him wherever he turned his eyes.

"I won't waste your time on chitchat, Factor Ricimer,"
Ben said. "You know I've invested in your previous expeditions. I didn't invest in this most recent one."

Piet glanced at Stephen and raised an eyebrow.

Stephen smiled faintly, amused to be Piet's business
spokesman again. "We made a paper loss, Uncle Ben," he
said. "In fact, none of the backers were really out of pocket,
but certainly the expedition wouldn't have repaid the risk. I
would have told you as much if you'd asked, but you're too
good a businessman to have needed the warning."

"We—Venus, myself, and my captains—gained experience in fleet operations, Factor Gregg," Piet said with quiet
intensity. "That was more important than the wealth we
brought back. Even more than the harm we did President
Pleyal!"

Uncle Ben sniffed in amusement. "You did harm there,
true enough," he said. "While your fleet was out, no ship-
ments of chips from the Reaches were sent back to Earth for
fear of being intercepted. The Federation's credit collapsed."

He looked at Stephen and went on with hard arrogance,
"I'm indeed a businessman, and successful enough at it that
I can afford to fund my whims. My pocketbook doesn't make
all my decisions. Particularly"—the old man's visage softened minusculely—"when the decision involves you, Stephen."

Stephen sucked in his lower lip in a grimace of apology.

"What I'm afraid of, Factor Ricimer," Uncle Ben said,
fully the trading magnate again, "is that if Venus doesn't
pull back now from this confrontation, matters will go over
the brink. The Federation won't make the first move toward
reconciliation. Venus has—*you* have, sir—the initiative. If

you keep pushing as in the past, the result will be the disaster of an all-out war that nobody can win.''

"Pleyal will never give anyone but those he owns the full access to the stars that all mankind needs to survive, sir,'' Piet said in growing animation. "Pleyal will die or be overthrown, certainly, but whoever replaces him will be the same sort of autocrat. If the Federation thinks Venus is weaker, they'll stifle us. If they think we're weak enough—and we *would* be weak without the opportunities men like your nephew and yes, myself, have wrenched from Pleyal's grip— then they'll crush us utterly. The only way the Pleyals know to live is with their boot on our neck or our boot on theirs.''

Piet stood, facing Uncle Ben stiffly. "And with the help of God, sir, I intend that it be Pleyal's face in the dust!''

Uncle Ben stood also. Ten years dropped away from him as he leaned across the desk. "Where will we be with the whole force of the Federation and the Southern Cross against us, Ricimer? Where will we be with hundreds of warships ringing Venus, bombing down through our clouds until every city has been ripped open to an atmosphere that corrodes and burns? During the Rebellion, Venus was a sideshow for the rebels attacking Earth. *We'll* be the focus the next time!''

"All the more reason to build and train a fleet so that we can not only stop Pleyal, we can forestall him!'' Piet replied. The two men weren't violent; there was no risk of a slap or one spitting on the other. They were passionate men, and passionate about the subject at issue.

"A stalemate that wrecks trade, that's your answer?'' Uncle Ben demanded. "Listen, boy, it was truly said that there was never a good war or a bad peace!''

Stephen got to his feet. "Gentlemen!'' he said. He rapped hard on the glass table with his knuckles. It rang like a jade gong. "Gentlemen.''

Piet and Uncle Ben eased back from their confrontation, breathing hard. Both of them looked embarrassed.

"Piet,'' Stephen said, gesturing his friend to his seat while keeping his eyes on Gregg of Weyston. Piet sat down.

"Uncle Ben,'' Stephen said, "the war's coming. Plan for it. There's always a way for a man who keeps his head in a crisis to make money.''

Uncle Ben opened his mouth to speak. Stephen chopped his right hand in a fierce cutting motion. "*No*. Let me finish. Piet will never let go till he's brought down the Federation. If he did, there'd be a hundred to take his place now that he's shown the way. Pushing until the war comes, no matter what you want or I want or Governor Halys herself wants. Depend on it."

Uncle Ben sighed and relaxed. "You could always see as far into a stone block as the next man, Stephen," he said. "And perhaps I can too. But I thought I ought to try."

He turned to Piet and said, "Factor Ricimer, could I prevail upon you for a moment alone with my nephew? My servants will outdo themselves getting you anything you want in the way of refreshment."

The old man smiled. "I directed them not to make pests of themselves, but I suppose as the most famous man on Venus you must be used to it by now."

"Sir," said Piet, "you're one of the men who've made Venus great. I'm honored to know you." He bowed low, then stepped out the door the footman peering through the crack pushed open for him.

The door closed. Uncle Ben looked at his nephew sadly. "When you first set out on a course of what I viewed as piracy, Stephen," he said, "I was worried that you might lose your life. I should have worried about your soul instead."

Stephen drew up sharply. "We Greggs have never been Bible pounders, Uncle Ben," he said.

The old man shook his head. "I don't care about your faith, Stephen," he said. "Fifty years of trade have scrubbed away any belief in God *I* ever had. But I do care about your soul."

Stephen stepped around the desk and put his arms around his uncle. Standing straight, Gregg of Weyston was the height of his nephew. They might have been father and son; as in a fashion they were.

"Somebody had to do it, Uncle Ben," Stephen said softly. "I'm better at it than most."

"No one ever had to tell a Gregg his duty, boy," Uncle Ben said. "But I wish . . ."

"What's done is done," Stephen said. Again, barely audible, "What's done is done."

BETAPORT, VENUS.

MARCH 12, YEAR 27.
0445 HOURS, VENUS TIME.

A rotary sander screamed as it polished a patch on the *Wrath*'s outer hull. The yard was working three shifts to put the big vessel right after the strains of her voyage to the Reaches. Though not so much as a rifle bullet had hit the *Wrath*, the repeated shocks of her own 20-cm plasma cannon firing had chipped gunports and even cracked some frame members.

"She was a little too taut for her own comfort when we left Venus," Piet said in near apology. "You mustn't think these repairs are anything against the design or construction. The *Wrath* handles beautifully. If Venus had fifty like her, we'd never have to fear from the Federation."

Captain Ricimer regularly visited the *Wrath* during the early hours of the morning with his friend Mister Gregg. This time they were accompanied by a middle-sized man in brown whose high collar obscured his face. None of the workmen was likely to recognize the third man as Councilor Duneen, who was having a private meeting in plain view on the bridge of the *Wrath*.

"We won't have fifty when Pleyal sends his fleet against us, as you well know," Duneen said. "Ten, I hope, but the rest of our strength in armed merchantmen as in the past."

For all the time Stephen had spent in the *Wrath* on the voyage just completed, he had no feeling for the vessel. That wouldn't come until he'd fought aboard her the first time.

At present the warship's twenty big guns were landed. Half the main-deck plates had been taken up so that the yard crew could work on the scantlings. Sternward, men with a hand kiln were recoating a beam that had been ground down to remove the surface crazing. The kiln nozzle hissed like an angry cat as it sprayed ceramic at just below the temperature of vaporization.

"We could gain more time if we raided Asunción and destroyed the Federation fleet before it's fitted out," Piet said, with the force of a man repeating an old argument.

"Ricimer, Governor Halys won't permit the fleet to leave the Solar System," the councilor said flatly. "That decision is between her and the three of us"—he nodded to Stephen—"but it's absolutely final. Not to put too fine a point on it, the governor doesn't want her fleet and her most able captains weeks and perhaps months away when the danger to Venus is so great."

"It's not 'months' to a Near Space world like Asunción, not even for Federation navigators," Piet said. "The way to scotch, to *end* this threat is—"

"*Final*, I said," Duneen repeated. "And I'm not going to claim that I think she's wrong. Asunción's orbital forts pose a risk that any sensible man would find daunting."

"I'll be given a squadron for operations within the Solar System?" Piet said with a grin of acquiescence. His expression sobered slightly. "That's how the orders will be phrased, 'within the Solar System'?"

Duneen nodded. "Yes. Much of the materiel with which the Feds are fitting out their fleet comes from Earth. You can interdict that trade."

"Winnipeg is the major port on Earth for supplies being sent to Asunción," Stephen said. They'd known the governor wouldn't permit a distant operation. The choice of an alternative target was Piet's, but the two of them together had roughed out the plan. All that remained was to sell Councilor Duneen on the idea.

"Good God, man!" the councilor said. "You can't just waltz into Winnipeg. The Feds know the risk, and they've surely increased their defenses over the past year!"

"We'll need current intelligence, that's true," Piet agreed.

Duneen shook his head. "The Feds are limiting the traffic that lands even on the commercial side of Winnipeg Port," he said. "Besides, since your last raid there's almost no direct Venus–Federation trade."

"Stephen here is the owner of a vessel in the regular Earth trade," Piet said. "With the right cargo, she'll be able to land in Winnipeg. Even now."

"What kind of cargo . . ." Duneen asked cautiously.

Piet nodded. "Venerian cannon, cast in Bahama. The arms trade from Venus to the Federation is at least as great as it ever was, because the prices Pleyal is willing to pay for first-quality guns is so high in the crisis. My father can get us a cargo from a firm who's supplied guns in the past."

"Look, Ricimer, you can't expect to spy out the port yourself," the councilor said, concern replacing shock on his face. "You'd be recognized!"

"Not as a common crewman," Piet said with a shrug. "The rest of the crew will be folk who've been with me for a decade, folk I know can keep their mouths shut. If I'm going to plan the operation, I can't trust any other eyes than my own."

"Good God," Duneen said softly. "Well, let's hope the governor doesn't hear about it. She'd flay me alive if she thought I'd let her favorite captain take a risk like that!"

Stephen Gregg thought about the risk to the *Gallant Sallie*'s captain, but he didn't speak. That didn't matter to anyone but himself; therefore it didn't matter at all.

EARTH ORBIT.

April 6, year 27.
0520 hours, Venus Time.

The Federation guardship was a blur with three distinct jags across it where the screen's raster skipped a line. Technicians had degraded the *Gallant Sallie*'s optronics by seventy percent for this part of the operation, so the image was even worse than what Sal would have had to make do with before the recent refit.

The four plasma cannon aimed at the *Gallant Sallie* were sufficiently clear. "Ten-centimeter?" Sal said to break the silence that had fallen over the cabin since suction clamps slapped the Fed boarding bridge over the cockpit hatch.

"About that," Stephen agreed in a tone of dreamy disinterest. He sat on a bunk, his hands in his lap and his eyes unfocused.

The outer airlock door squealed as the Federation inspector started to undog it manually from outside.

"Listen to me," Piet Ricimer said crisply from where he manned the attitude-control panel with Dole and Lightbody. "None of us need love the Feds, but anyone who causes an incident will answer to me afterwards. If we're both alive, that is. Understood?"

"Won't be a problem, sir," Dole said mildly. "Won't nobody make a problem."

"Tom, the hatch," Sal said to Harrigan. Harrigan threw the lever that retracted the dogs of the inner hatch hydraulically.

The hatch opened. The slightly higher pressure in the guardship and boarding tube popped the first of the three Fed inspectors into the cabin like a cork from a champagne bottle.

Harrigan tried to grab the man. The Fed batted Harrigan's hand away, spinning himself completely around before he fetched up against supply netting on the opposite bulkhead.

"Don't you stinkballers have a pressure system?" the Fed demanded. "And I'll tell you, if you'd taken one spin more before getting your rotation stopped, we'd have blown you to bits and inspected the pieces!"

All three inspectors were puffy-faced and run-down from too long in weightlessness. That probably accounted for some of their ill temper too, though Sal doubted the cream of the Federation military was assigned duty to the ships guarding the orbital entry windows for Winnipeg.

"Look, it's an old ship," she said in what she hoped was a reasonable tone. "First you make us do a slow three-sixty rotation to check for spy cameras, then you tell us to stand still for a boarding bridge. It's not that easy, you know!"

"Didn't say it was easy," said a second inspector. "Said the next trip back, you better learn to control this pig better or we get some target practice."

"Where's your fucking manifest?" the third inspector, the female, demanded. Tom Harrigan gave her a sheaf of hard copy on a clipboard.

The second inspector drifted over to the navigation console. Sal thought he intended to check the resolution of their screen. Instead the man reached down to pat her breast. She doubled her right leg, then kicked him across the cabin.

The Venerian crew grew very still. The Fed caught himself on a bunk, Stephen's bunk. He laughed. "You know, I thought it was funny you stinkballers would have a woman captain. Guess you're just a man with tits, huh, honey?"

"I own the ship, and I'm carrying you the cargo," Sal said tight-lipped. She had to assume that the inspectors lacked the authority to reject a vessel with a cargo like the *Gallant Sallie*'s, however they might bluster. If Sal didn't behave normally, she'd set off more alarm bells than if she did.

"So I see," said the woman with the manifest. "Six fifteen-centimeter plasma cannon. You know, some of you people would sell their mothers, wouldn't you?"

"Look, we're sailors, we're not politicians," Sal said. "If

President Pleyal doesn't want to do business, fine. There's a market for these, believe me."

The second inspector stared at Stephen beside him. "Hey," the Fed said. "You look like shit. Do you have something contagious, is that it?"

Stephen stared at his fingers interlaced on his lap. "I'm here to watch things for the seller," he said in a dead voice. "I'd never gone through transit, and I swear to God that once I'm back on Venus I never will again. Just do your job so I can stand on firm ground again. All right?"

The female inspector scrawled her initials on the bottom of the manifest. Instead of handing the clipboard back to Harrigan, she flipped it into a corner of the cabin. "Let's get out of this pigsty," she said. "The sulphur stink makes me want to puke."

The Feds bounced out the boarding tube. They moved in weightless conditions with the skill of experience, but there was a porcine sluggishness to them. Sal wondered how long Pleyal kept his guardship crews in orbit. Too long, certainly.

Harrigan shut the airlock hatches together. Probert, a motor specialist, said in an injured tone, "Where'd she get that stuff about sulphur? Our air's as clean as clean!"

Because Piet Ricimer was normally a flashy dresser, he stuck out like a sore thumb to his familiars now that he wore a common spacer's canvas jumpsuit. The Feds hadn't given him a second look, though.

He shrugged cheerfully. "If she hadn't made up a problem," he said, "she might have tried to find a real one. Give thanks for a small blessing, Probert."

The boarding bridge uncoupled from one edge to the other with a peevish squeal. Its asymmetrical pressure started a minute axial rotation in the *Gallant Sallie*.

Sal opened an access port in her console and reengaged the full electronics suite. Every stain on the guardship's plating sprang alive on the screen. An associated recorder was storing the images for later use. Though the Feds had made a production of searching the *Gallant Sallie* for external sensor packs, they hadn't bothered to consider that the vessel's normal electronics might be an order of magnitude better than what they expected of her type. Stephen's improvements to the *Gallant Sallie* had required a dockyard rebuild, not just a blister welded to the hull.

"*Gallant Sallie* requests permission to brake for Winnipeg landing," Sal said into the modulated laser directed at the guardship's communications antenna. "Over."

"Get your filthy scow out of our sky, stinkballers!" the Fed on commo duty replied.

Sal engaged the timing sequence on her AI. In the interval before the *Gallant Sallie* reached the reentry window, Sal looked over the back of her couch toward the men on the attitude controls. "Remember, we're going in manually so that we look the way the Feds expect us to. That means you guys need to make a few mistakes too. I know perfectly well we could between us set down as neatly as the new hardware could do it, but that's not what's called for today."

Piet laughed heartily. The AI gave a pleasant *bong*. Sal lit the eight thrusters, then ran the throttles forward to sixty percent power. The guardship vanished from the viewscreen. Earth, blue and cold-looking to eyes accustomed to the roiling earth tones of Venus, rotated slowly beneath them.

Atmosphere began to jar against the *Gallant Sallie*'s underside. Their exhaust streamed around them in the turbulence. Sal set the screen to discount the veiling and distortion of the plasma englobing the vessel. The planet sharpened in chilly majesty again.

"These guns we're delivering, Captain Ricimer?" Sal said, speaking carefully against the apparent weight of deceleration. "They're flawed, aren't they? They'd burst if the Feds fired them."

"Oh, I assure you, Captain," Piet said, "these are first-quality fifteen-centimeter guns. Nicholas Quintel may be a better merchant than patriot, but not even my father ever faulted the workmanship of the Quintel foundry. They have to be perfect. The Feds will certainly ultrasound the tubes, and they may well test-fire them before acceptance."

"Then we really *are* aiding the Feds?" Tom Harrigan asked, squatting with his back to the hatch and holding a stanchion. "This wasn't a trick?"

Stephen looked at him. "Don't worry, Mister Harrigan," he said. "We'll be paying another visit to Winnipeg before the Feds have a chance to mount or transship these guns. All they're doing is renting warehouse decorations for the next few days.''

Beneath the neutral tone of Stephen's words was an edge as stark as honed glass.

WINNIPEG, EARTH.

April 6, year 27.
0623 hours, Venus Time.

The *Gallant Sallie*'s plates pinged and clicked as they cooled nearby. The sky at local noon was a pale blue across which clouds moved at high altitude. In ten years, Stephen Gregg had learned to stand under open skies without cringing, but it wasn't a natural condition to him or to anyone raised in low corridors bored through the bedrock of Venus.

Piet, as though he were reading his friend's mind, said, "We're struggling so that men can live on worlds where they don't have to wear armor to go outside . . . but for myself, home is a room cut in the stone."

He gave Stephen his electric smile. "Or a ship's cabin, of course."

The civil port of Winnipeg didn't have a berm. The city whose houses grew like fungus on the ruins of the pre-Collapse foundations was several klicks to the west at the confluence of two rivers. Presumably the locals felt the distance was adequate protection.

There were seventy-odd ships in the civil port. Two of them were quite large, thousand-tonners in the regular trade to the Reaches. Piet eyed the monsters, far on the other side of the spacious field. "They're being refitted," he said. "The motors have been pulled from both of them."

"The gun towers are dangerous," Stephen said, standing with his hands in his pockets like a slovenly yokel from Venus viewing a real port for the first time. He didn't point or even nod toward the defenses. "The guns are on disappearing carriages. I'll give any odds that when the mounts are fully raised, they can bear on all parts of this field."

157

The military installations were north of the civil port. A concrete-faced berm enclosed a slightly trapezoidal field of a square kilometer. Towers mounting heavy plasma cannon, at least 20 cm in bore, stood at both south corners where they commanded the civil field as well.

Within the berm, glimpsed during the *Gallant Sallie*'s descent and recorded with crystalline precision for detailed planning, were six ships. Four were of the older spherical style; the domes of their upper decks were visible over the berm. The other two were new purpose-built warships that copied cylindrical Venerian design. A sphere is a more efficient way to enclose space, but the round-nosed cylinders were handier and could focus their guns on a point in a fashion the older vessels couldn't match.

"The gunpit is new," Piet said. "The civil port didn't have any defenses of its own at the last information we had."

The *Gallant Sallie*'s crew left Piet and Stephen alone on the starboard side of the vessel, standing twenty meters away to be clear of the surface recently heated by the exhaust. Ground personnel hadn't yet arrived to carry the cargo to one of the warehouses lining the south side of the port; in fact, there was no sign of customs officials. Winnipeg was fairly busy, but no ships had landed within the two hours before the *Gallant Sallie*. The delay in processing was as likely to be inefficiency as a deliberate insult to Venerians.

"Hey, you two!" Tom Harrigan bellowed. The mate gestured peremptorily from the main hatchway to Piet and Stephen. "Back here *now*!"

"A good actor," Stephen said as he started back to the *Gallant Sallie*. Deference or even Captain Blythe's direct interest would imply he and Piet weren't common sailors.

"It might be he's jealous," Piet suggested mildly.

"He . . ." Stephen said. He went on, "I really don't think he is. He doesn't understand; but then, neither do I."

"Captain needs you forward, sirs," Harrigan said as the two men sauntered up the ramp. He eyed them the way a child might view his first butterfly: something wondrous and strange, alien to his previous conceptions.

"I believe you're right," Piet murmured as he tramped through the passage behind his friend.

"There's a problem," Sal said crisply before Piet was wholly into the cabin. "The *Moll Dane* out of Ishtar City's on the ground here with a cargo like ours."

She looked grim and determined. Other crewmen held their tongues as they watched. "Which doesn't surprise me, since Dan Lasky's the owner and captain and he's wormshit."

Sal tapped the communications handset with her fingertip. "He's just called and said he'll be over for a visit, bringing a bottle. I told him not till we'd been through customs, but I can't just tell him to bugger himself or it'll look odd."

She made a moue of distaste. "Since we're both running guns to President Pleyal, you know."

"And he'd recognize Piet," Stephen said. "Well, we needed to talk to the troops at the gunpit in the middle of the field anyway."

Sal's eyes narrowed slightly. "Is that safe?" she asked.

Each man's personal gear was in a short duffel bag tied crossways to the end of a hammock netting: head end for the starboard watch, at the foot for the member of the port watch who shared the berth during alternate periods. Stephen opened his and removed a small parcel wrapped in burlap.

"It's safe if we're trading contraband with them," Stephen said. He tossed the package on the palm of his hand before dropping it into one of the bellows pockets on his tunic.

"That was Stephen's idea," Piet said affectionately. "He's the businessman of the partnership, you see."

"I do see," said Sal to the men's backs as they left the cabin more quickly than they'd come.

The Fed position was the better part of a kilometer away. Stephen felt naked outside the ship. There was nothing abnormal about a pair of sailors scuttling away from a vessel in port, but *he* knew that he was carrying out a military operation against the North American Federation. He had no weapon, no armor; nothing but coveralls and the floppy canvas hat that Venerians regularly wore under a naked sky.

A three-wheeled scooter pulled away from the port administration buildings south of the field. The vehicle carried two white-jacketed humans and a Molt driver.

"Customs is finally recognizing the *Gallant Sallie*," Piet

said. In a half-sneering, half-despairing tone he added, "Even on Earth the Feds are learning to depend on Molt slaves."

Because the field was so large, the vessels scattered across it looked as sparse as rocks on a Zen sand sculpture. A spherical 400-tonne merchantman took off from the port's left margin. Stephen felt first the tremble through his bootsoles as the thrusters ran up on static test. A plume of exhaust drifted eastward. Stephen's nose wrinkled with the familiar bite of ozone, though this far downwind the concentration was too slight to be dangerous.

The motors were an audible rumble at first, but when the ship managed to stagger its own height above the ground the blast became oppressively loud. Stephen kept his face turned down and away in what by now was a reflex to avoid damage to his sight. Piet bent their course to the other side of a freighter that showed no sign of life. The hull shadowed them until the rising vessel had reached a good thousand meters and her thruster nozzles no longer outglared the sun.

"There's a number of the ships here armed," Piet said, shouting over the roar of the liftoff. "I don't see that as a risk while we're making our landing approaches—the guns won't be run out, and firing up through the dorsal ports is difficult in a gravity well. But they may engage our ships after they've landed."

"You mean the latecomers may get to see some action too?" Stephen said. "I'd begun to think there was a rule that only the folks on your ship got to do any fighting."

"Captain Lasky would have recognized you too, Stephen," Piet said as if apropos nothing. "You're a more famous man on Venus than you might think."

"I'd trade fame for a night's sleep," Stephen said, marveling to hear himself speak the words. Not that the statement was news to Piet, or to others who'd shared the strait confines of a starship with Mister Stephen Gregg and his nightmares. He swallowed and went on, "They're watching us from the wicket. I'm going to wave."

At some time in the past year, the Winnipeg port authorities had installed two 20-cm plasma cannon on separate armored barbettes in the center of the civil field. To protect the gun position from starship plasma, they'd dug a pit several meters deep. The spoil was heaped in a berm that the Feds had faced with concrete to limit exhaust erosion.

The only entrance to the gunpit was through a steel gate with firing ports and a guard kiosk. The guard, a human, began talking into a handset when the Venerians approached within a hundred meters. One of the ports was initially bright from sunlight behind it, but it darkened like the other three a moment later. None of the watching Feds poked a gun out.

Stephen took the package from his pocket and made a quick gesture in the air with it. The guards wouldn't know what the contents were, but the display was communication enough: this pair of spacers had come to trade.

The gate was three meters wide. It squealed painfully outward, pivoting from the end opposite the kiosk, until there was barely room for a man to slip through the gap. "Come on, Christ's blood!" a woman snarled. "You want some prick in the control tower to report you?"

The gate was 1-cm steel plating on a frame of steel tubes. It was heavy and awkward to move by hand without rollers or frictionless bearings, but it wouldn't stop anything more energetic than a rifle bullet. A flashgun bolt would spall fragments from the back like a grenade going off, and a strong man with a cutting bar could slice through in a straight cut, plate and framework both.

The barbette bases were three meters below the original ground surface; even at 90° elevation, the muzzles of the powerful plasma cannon were protected by the berm around the gunpit. So long as the guns were operable, no hostile ship could safely land at Port Winnipeg. A single 20-cm bolt would do so much damage to thruster nozzles that even the largest vessel would lose control and crash.

Rather than stairs, a slope of earth stabilized with plasticizer ran from the gate to the barbette level. Eight humans and four Molts—the Molts had pushed the gate open; now they pulled it closed again—waited on the ramp head for the Venerians.

"What do you have?" asked the woman who'd ordered Piet and Stephen into the enclosure. She was young and plain. Her hair swirled to the right to conceal the fact she'd lost the lobe of that ear. The epaulets of her gray-blue jacket held gold stars crossed with a double line, but Stephen had never bothered to learn Federation rank insignia. Her name tag read PENGELLEY.

"What are you paying with?" he replied.

"You lot are from Venus," said a black-bearded Fed holding a single-shot rifle. Six humans and two Molts carried firearms, though the guns didn't look modern or particularly well maintained.

"So are the cannon they're unloading from our ship," Piet said, nodding in the direction of the *Gallant Sallie*. "Trade is trade, right?"

The doors to the gunhouses were open. Molts in the hatchways watched the proceedings at the gate. The turret armor was at least 15 centimeters thick, proof against penetration by anything except a heavy plasma charge at short range.

"We've got money, if that's what you mean," Pengelley said.

Stephen sniffed. "Mapleleafs? Right, we're going to try to pass Mapleleaf dollars in Ishtar City, the way they're beating the war drums there!"

"We figured," Piet said, "this being a port for the Reaches' trade, that a crate or two of microchips might have dropped out on the ground while a ship was being unloaded."

"Let's see what you've got to trade, stinkballers," the black-bearded man demanded.

Stephen looked at the fellow, smiled, and pulled the first of six 50-mm cubes from his packet. He handed it to Blackbeard.

"Our goods aren't for women," Piet told Pengelley with a smirk.

"What the hell's this?" Blackbeard said in irritation. He held the cube by the tips of all ten fingers, peering into its gray opacity.

"Warm it in your palms," another Fed soldier said. "I've heard of these."

Blackbeard scowled at his fellow, but he did as the man suggested. The gray suddenly cleared as the crystalline pattern of the cube's outer layer shifted to match polarity with the surface beneath.

"Mary, Mother of God!" Blackbeard said.

As well as being an idolator who worshipped saints' statues, President Pleyal was a sanctimonious prig. Under his rule, licentiousness and bawdiness were rigidly suppressed. Objects like these—cubes in which figures engaged in sexual acrobatics as layers changed state—were therefore worth their weight in microchips in the North American Federation.

"Pass it around, soldier," Piet said smugly. "Your pals want a look too."

Pengelley took the cube from Blackbeard. She watched for a moment, then closed her palms over it. "All right," she said. "What's your offer?"

"Three thousand consols apiece," Stephen said. "You pay in chips at the rate of a hundred and thirty consols per K2B, other chips valued in relation to that baseline."

"If you pay thirty thousand up front," Piet added, "you get the other six that we bring from the ship after we're paid. Deal?"

"That's a dirt poor price on K2Bs!" Blackbeard snapped.

"So?" Piet sneered. "Did you buy them out of Federation stores? Is that where you got your chips?"

"You can move these for five thousand apiece here in Winnipeg," Stephen said, removing the sample from Pengelley's hand after the slightest resistance. "Take them to West Montreal and the sky's the limit. Now, do you want to deal?"

Blackbeard clicked the safety of his rifle off, then on again. Stephen grinned at him. Blackbeard grimaced and looked down.

"All right," Pengelley said. She looked around the human members of her command to make it clear that she was speaking for all of them. "But you have to come back to Winnipeg with us to get paid. We'll be off duty in ten minutes. You can ride in with us on the truck. Understood?"

Stephen looked at Piet. "Understood," Piet said coolly.

The risk was obvious, but it was probably the only way the two of them were going to get out of the gunpit alive. Later . . . Well, somebody would become careless later.

And a close-up view of the gun installation had showed Stephen what he'd needed to know. The gunhouses were virtually impregnable if the hatches were closed, as they surely would be in event of an attack. But the turntables, though armored against fire from above, could very easily be jammed by troops who'd shot their way into the pit.

WINNIPEG, EARTH.

Dan Lasky was a red-haired man in his fifties: overweight, as many spacers became in the narrow tedium of voyages; flushed and defensive, even though he thought the *Gallant Sallie*'s crew was in the same disreputable trade as he was. He pinged a fingernail against the creamy ceramic muzzle of the 15-cm gun unswathed for inspection in the hold and said, "Well, that's the goods, all right."

He gave Sal a knowing glance. "Bet you had to give 'em your left leg for tubes like these, though, huh?"

"Bet you don't think I'm stupid enough to tell you my business so you can undercut me," she answered coldly.

Sal felt dirty every time Lasky looked at her. It was as though he'd found her working in a brothel. It was all very well to tell herself that she was doing it for the Free State of Venus. The feeling of degradation was still far worse than the undoubted danger.

Lasky chuckled breathily. "Let's go forward and open this," he said, waving the half-liter bottle he'd brought. It held some variety of amber Terran liquor. He looked at the grim-faced men in the hold with him and said, "Harrigan, you want a swig too? Guess it'll stretch that far."

"Don't lower yourself, Lasky," Harrigan said. "I'll make do with slash, I guess, and I'll do it in the company I choose."

The common sailors were Betaport men whom Lasky didn't recognize. Sal and her mate were familiar to him, and he was delighted to see their moral comedown.

"I'll have a drink with you," Sal said, leading the way to

the cabin, "and then you can take the rest of the bottle away. The quicker I get this cargo unloaded and me off-planet, the better I'll like it."

She was sure that the liquor was expensive. The mechanical uniformity of mass distillation wasn't a taste one learned on Venus, where most taverns brewed their own beer and every outlying hold distilled its own liquors.

She thought of herself and Stephen drinking slash at the first meeting a lifetime ago. It was hard to recognize the people they'd been as anyone she now knew.

"Christ's blood, I wish *I* was lifting soon," Lasky said. "I got people from the Navy, the Treasury, and the Bureau of the fucking Presidency and they're all arguing about whether they're going to pay my price."

Sal sat at the navigation console, rotating her chair to face her visitor on the end of the nearest bunk. Several of the crew were in the cabin—there was no privacy on a ship this size. Lightbody, seated in the airlock, glowered at Lasky as if considering whether to pull off his limbs one by one.

"You go where money takes you, boyo," Lasky said to him harshly. "You're no better than me!"

"Lightbody, go check nozzle wear," Sal ordered. "They should've cooled enough by now."

She'd been around Lightbody long enough to know that the man was in a way more dangerous than Stephen Gregg, because he didn't have Stephen's control. Lightbody's religion was as deep as that of Captain Ricimer, but the sailor's faith was a stark, gloomy thing instead of being the transfiguring love of God.

Lightbody viewed what they were doing as selling guns to Satan incarnate. Loathing at his own part in the transaction made him more, not less, prone to murderous violence against someone else in the same trade.

"What are you trying to pass off?" Sal asked Lasky. She took the bottle and drank. The liquor tasted thin with an undertone of smoke. "There's supposed to be a Navy agent here in an hour. If he takes our tubes at the customs evaluation, I won't have any complaint."

She'd been drinking a lot lately. Since Arles.

Lasky drank in turn without bothering to wipe the mouth

of the bottle. "I'm not asking more than fair," he complained. "Standard stellite poundage value with discounts for wear. Trouble is, the Treasury whoreson claims the Feds already own four of the ten tubes."

He took another, even longer, swallow. "Owns them all, by his lights, but he can't prove that."

"Where did you get stellite guns?" Sal asked sharply.

Venerian plasma cannon were invariably ceramic. After the Collapse, metal-poor Venus had been cut off from off-planet sources of metal. The ceramics technology developing from that necessity was now one of Venus' greatest industries. Other human cultures used tungsten and alloys like stellite from the heavy platinum triad for thruster nozzles and plasma cannon. Venerians were certain their ceramic equivalents wore longer as well as being appreciably lighter.

"Where the hell do you think I got them, lady?" Lasky sneered. He offered Sal the bottle again; the level was already below half. She waved it away curtly. "I bought in a lot of forty-seven tubes that came back from the Reaches with I-Walk-On-Water Ricimer, that's where I got them. For a song, too. Nobody on Venus thinks stellite guns are worth houseroom. But hell, the Feds don't know any better."

"And some of the guns come with Federation markings already," Sal said, understanding at last. "Well, I guess that's your problem, Lasky."

Lasky drank again morosely. "Oh, they'll come around," he muttered. "They will if they want the other thirty-seven tubes, they will. Only it may take a month before we get it all clear."

He thrust the bottle toward Sal. "Here," he said. "Go ahead and kill it. Good stuff, huh?"

Sal shook her head. "I've got paperwork to do even if the Navy assessor doesn't show up soon," she said. "Best you get off to your own people and leave me to it, Lasky."

Lasky stood up slowly, obviously unwilling to go back to the *Moll Dane* and a crew of the sort that would work for captains like him. He paused in the airlock. "Maybe I'll see you again in Winnipeg," he said.

Sal looked at the fat man. Wrapped in red tape, the *Moll Dane* could very well be on the ground in ten days when Piet Ricimer and his squadron called on Winnipeg.

"I hope so, Lasky," Sal said. "I really hope you do."

WINNIPEG, EARTH.

Stephen stared through the tavern's dingy window toward the twilit city beyond. The drink in his hand was fresh, so he tongued it carefully before he took a sip.

No drugs, no poisons; just cheap white liquor, served straight and warm. The Fed soldiers were buying. The bartender had offered mixers, but Stephen had waved them away. He doubted the Feds would add a Mickey Finn to his drink so long as he kept putting the liquor down at a rate they'd be sure would have him under the table in a few more hours, but there was no point in increasing their chances.

"And then he says, 'I don't know why you're complaining, we're on the ground, ain't we?' " Piet said, "like he couldn't see he was standing on the bulkhead because the ship was lying on her *side*!"

The Feds laughed heartily. Piet's stories of incompetent Venerian officers were all true, and they made him the life of the party. He never pumped the Feds for information, but his stories bred stories, and Piet listened.

Stephen Gregg listened too, as he sat halfway down the bar drinking morosely. The liquor wouldn't make him drunk. It just permitted him to view his life through thick windows that blocked the sharper pains and left him with only a dull, murderous ache.

Pengelley had made a call from the port administration building while the remainder of the gun crew waited with Piet and Stephen in a canvas-covered truck. When the truck dropped them all at a tavern in the heart of the city, a name-

168

less fat civilian was waiting with a briefcase of pre-Collapse microchips.

The civilian's bodyguard was broader than Stephen and almost as tall. Apart from those two and the bartender, no one else was present. The man who loitered outside the tavern door was obviously a guard.

The transaction had gone smoothly. The price for the porno cubes was fair, and the chips the civilian offered in payment were of the quality he claimed. There'd been a delay in getting transport back to the field after the deal was complete, though. The Fed soldiers offered to stand drinks; and more drinks; and more, as the slow spring evening shadowed the sky above the city.

"Freshen your drink, buddy?" the bartender offered. "The sergeant, she's paying." He nodded toward Pengelley.

"Sure," Stephen said. "I'm legless already, so another slug can't hurt. They'll have to carry me when the truck gets here."

He and Piet were going to have to make their move when they next went out the back to piss in the alley behind the tavern. The trouble wouldn't be making a break, but rather how they would get from central Winnipeg to the *Gallant Sallie* kilometers away. There was almost no motor transport in this dismal city. If he and Piet tried to hike up the sole road to the port, the locals—who surely had access to vehicles—would easily relocate them.

Piet and Stephen were perfectly willing to leave the Feds with the chips as well as the cubes, but if the Feds guessed that, they'd wonder what the pair of Venerians had really been up to.

If life were simple, then Venus wouldn't have needed a planner like Piet Ricimer. And Piet wouldn't have needed a killer like Stephen Gregg.

Winnipeg was less a city than a rubbish midden with dwellings on top. The community hadn't been bombed during the Outworld Rebellion a thousand years before. Rather, the walls had been pulled down stone by stone by the starving, desperate population during the ensuing Collapse. Occupation of the site had been continuous, reaching its nadir five hundred years in the past.

By the time technological civilization returned to the region under the guise of the North American Federation, the bricks, beams, and ashlars of pre-Collapse Winnipeg had been mined for multiple reuse. Now the city's tawdry present squatted on its ruined past.

Stephen looked down the bar, careful to avoid eye contact with the fat man's bodyguard. The fellow didn't seem smart enough to tie his own shoes, but he might be able to recognize a threat if one glared at him.

Piet was finishing a complicated story that involved a captain setting down in Betaport instead of Ishtar City, well across the planet, as he'd intended. Stephen waited for the last flourish and laughter, then called, "Hey, Janni! Give me a hand to the jakes. I can't walk by myself."

"Piet" wasn't an uncommon name, but it was the one Venerian name that had a connection for *every* Fed.

Piet looked around. As he did so, Sal, Harrigan, Dole, and three other sailors from the *Gallant Sallie* walked in the front door. The local who'd been posted outside to prevent interruption lay on the ground, moaning and clutching his groin.

"There you stupid scuts are!" Sal shouted. "By God, if I hadn't found you in the next five minutes, you could *swim* back to Venus!"

"Oh, ma'am, we weren't AWOL," Piet whined, snaking down beside his leg the case of microchips from the bartop.

The bodyguard stood in front of Sal. He held a meter-long crowbar across his chest. "This is a private party," he grated. "You buggers aren't wanted."

Stephen, moving before anyone but Piet knew he was going to move, stepped behind the bodyguard and gripped him by the belt and the back of the neck. Pengelley shouted and stumbled out of her chair.

The bodyguard managed only a startled grunt as Stephen half ran, half threw him into the wall at the end of the bar. The bodyguard went headfirst through the paneling and the two studs he hit on the way. Bits of plaster crumbled from the ceiling at the shock.

"Jesus, Mary, and Joseph!" Blackbeard cried as he stared at the destruction. The bartender reached beneath the bar.

Dole looked at him. The bartender brought his hands back into sight—empty.

"It's your own damned fault, feeding him booze like that!" Sal snarled at Blackbeard. "Christ's blood, he's not safe to be around sober. Harrigan, get them out of here. We're lifting in an hour."

The table had tipped when Stephen and the bodyguard went past. The fat civilian remained in his chair, sitting exactly as he had before the violence. He watched the Venerians leave, Piet still holding the microchips; but he said nothing and his hands, like the bartender's, were in plain sight.

Lightbody was driving a spaceport truck, obviously rented by means of a bribe to the right official. The guns and cutting bars that the rescue party hadn't wanted to display unless necessary were in the cab with him. Nobody came out of the tavern as the vehicle pulled away.

"Thanks, Sal," Stephen said softly.

"My pleasure," she replied in a neutral voice. "Much more pleasure than dealing with Dan Lasky this afternoon."

The truck jounced over potholes in the dirt street. At every corner hung one or more giant portraits of President Pleyal. Some of the pictures had been defaced with paint.

"Lasky's ship, the *Moll Dane*," Piet said, speaking over the rattle of the truck's suspension. "Is it a well-found vessel, Captain Blythe?"

Sal looked at him. Her face was shadowed, but puzzlement was evident in her voice as she said, "Not particularly. Why?"

"That's good," Piet said. "We don't have the authority to take a Venerian vessel prize when we return here. I certainly don't intend to leave the *Moll Dane* in the present hands, but I'd hate to destroy a really trim ship."

He smiled. For a moment, Stephen felt that he might have been looking into a mirror.

EARTH APPROACHES.

"God's love, that's a sharp image!" Tom Harrigan said as he hung in the air behind Sal at the navigation console, watching the remote display transmitted from the *New Year's Gift*. "If I was looking out the hatch, it wouldn't be that clear!"

The guardship at the orbital window for Winnipeg grew slowly on the screen as the *New Year's Gift* maneuvered carefully closer to the expectant Feds. The guardship's four cannon were run out, but her crew didn't go through the charade of aiming the guns at yet another intrasystem merchantman with a cargo for Winnipeg.

The squadron had captured the *New Year's Gift* at Berryhill on January 1. The vessel was metal and responded to the guardship's hail as the *Mary* of Vancouver with a cargo of forgings from the Asteroid Belt for Winnipeg. There was nothing about the ship or the situation to rouse the inspectors from their boredom.

"The imagery from when we scouted Winnipeg is still in the database," Sal explained. "The AI uses that data to sharpen the details we get from the *New Year's Gift*. Our optronics now are . . . We have as good a system as any ship in the squadron, the *Wrath* included."

She touched a control. The display switched from enhanced visuals of the guardship to a scene including both the guardship and the *New Year's Gift* as the latter approached for inspection. The image of the Venerian vessel was entirely computer-modeled from the *Gallant Sallie*'s database.

Sal's whole crew hung in the cabin, using the freedom of

172

weightlessness to position themselves so that everybody had a view of the display. They could get to their duty stations within five seconds. Unless and until the *New Year's Gift* carried out her mission, the rest of the squadron *had* no duty to perform.

Piet had divided his vessels between the thirteen that would stay in Earth orbit to prevent the Feds from reinforcing Winnipeg from space, and the twelve ships that would actually land in the port. The *Gallant Sallie* was in the latter group, but because of her excellent controls, she would land last.

Piet knew Sal would set down within meters of the planned landing spot—not on top of a ship that had landed a few minutes earlier. Some of the larger freighters might in the confusion come down almost anywhere.

"Amazing," Harrigan whispered.

"Cost more than the hull, I shouldn't doubt," said Godden. He'd been assigned to serve as the *Gallant Sallie*'s gunner during the operation. All the ships landing at Winnipeg carried their regular batteries, despite the fact the guns diminished space that could be given over to loot. Even more than the recent voyage to the Reaches, this raid was a military rather than commercial operation.

"Too right it did," Brantling said. "My cousin's the assistant manager at Torrington's Chandlery. He says because it was Mister Gregg buying, Old Man Torrington did the work at cost. Even then it was more than he'd ever heard being spent on a ship this old."

Sal looked back at Brantling. She hadn't known the details. Stephen had listed the equipment at invoice price rather than at its much higher fair market value.

"Keep your fingers crossed," Tom Harrigan said softly.

The images of the guardship and the *New Year's Gift* were almost touching as they prepared for external inspection. The two oversized gunports in the *Gift*'s cargo bay swung open on the side opposite the guardship.

"The scantlings of a tin can like that'll never take the shock of twenty-centimeter guns," Godden muttered disapprovingly. "They'll shake her apart."

Steam puffed from the attitude jets of the *New Year's Gift*. The vessel began to rotate slowly on her axis.

"She doesn't have to survive any longer than it takes to fire two shots," Sal said. She gripped the edge of her keyboard as if it were all that prevented her from dropping over a chasm. "Or even one, if things work out as they ought."

She touched a control. She'd been tempted to display the view that the guardship's crew would have in their last moments of life: the merchantman turning with a slight wobble on her axis; the meter-square hatches open, nonstandard and puzzling, but not a sign of danger. At the final instant, the devouring flash of a 20-cm plasma charge ripping into the guardship before anyone could send a warning to Earth.

Instead, Sal returned the image to the *Gift*-transmitted realtime view of the guardship. Every seam, every rust stain was evident in the enhanced image.

"Firing without running the guns out . . ." Godden said. The gunner was speaking aloud but to himself. "I know, so the Feds don't see what's coming, but the side-scatter'll blow plates off the hull."

The central half of the guardship exploded in rainbow coruscance. An instant later another heavy plasma bolt vanished into the swelling chaos created by the first. The extreme bow and stern of the guardship spun away from the glowing gas cloud. There could be no one alive in either section.

"Prepare for transit," Sal said in a cool, gray voice. Her crew was already taking its stations.

The *Wrath* transited into the orbital window under Piet Ricimer's usual flawless navigation. The big warship began braking for reentry at once. If all went well, in a matter of minutes Stephen Gregg would be leading his band against the Fed guns.

Sal watched the *Wrath* shrink as the warship dropped away from the *New Year's Gift*. Her heart shrank with the image.

WINNIPEG SPACEPORT, EARTH.

Because the *Wrath* was designed by men who'd done all the jobs on starships in war and peace, the vessel had visual displays in its boarding holds. On merchant ships used for war service, men waiting in the holds in hard suits to attack were as blind as sausages in a can. They had to guess the ship's status from the shocks and bumps: braking thrust, atmospheric turbulence because the guns had been run out; and always at the backs of their minds was the fear that any particular jolt might have been the plasma bolt that would cause the overstressed hull to crumble about them.

Nobody who'd experienced that blind helplessness thought it was beneficial to men preparing for combat, so the *Wrath* had a medium-resolution visual display in both of her boarding holds. Stephen Gregg, twenty-five soldiers under Major Cardiff as second in command, and half the men of the B Watch close-combat team could watch flat prairie galloping closer through a veil of exhaust plasma and the friction-heated glare of the warship's rapid descent.

Piet brought them down out of the east, just above the risen sun. The guardship hadn't flashed the port a warning, so the ground staff wasn't afraid of hostile forces, but the *Wrath*'s display was thunderous and colorful. It was sure to draw eyes in a port where excitement generally meant that a ship had lost control during her landing approach.

"Bet they're waking the crash crews right now, boys," Stephen shouted over the roaring descent. Sailors laughed and catcalled; soldiers relaxed minusculely in their shells of ceramic or metal.

By choice, Stephen would have been silent before action, but this time he had the responsibilities of command. Few if any of the soldiers had experienced a combat descent. Most of them thought the *Wrath* really was about to crash. Hearing the sailors laugh at the thought was the best tonic Colonel Gregg could offer.

Stephen checked the Fed defenses as their images grew. The gun tower batteries were lowered into their cradles. The guns in the pit were vertical in their equivalent rest position. The tubes were dim blurs at the display's modest resolution because they projected only two meters above the gunhouses, but the long shadows the sun threw from them were clear to a trained eye.

The port's scarred gray surface filled the screen. The *Wrath* sailed at a steep angle past a pair of vessels undergoing maintenance on the ground.

"Get a good grip, boys," Dole bellowed. "Captain Ricimer's the best there is, but inertia's still inertia!"

All sixteen thrusters cut in at full output, slowing the big vessel to the speed of a dropping feather in the last two hundred meters before she touched down. Despite the warning and the stanchions planted thickly in a hold designed for combat, not cargo operations, half the landsmen crashed to the deck under the braking thrust.

Dole had wanted to use only sailors for the operation; but the soldiers had more experience in ground operations, and half a dozen of the landsmen were reasonably expert with the heavy, dangerous flashguns that few sailors cared to use. Life is a trade-off. . . .

Touchdown was so delicate that Stephen noticed not the contact but the cessation of the thrusters' roaring vibration. The hold was configured for rapid assaults: instead of a single hatch across the entire frontage, worked by a screw jack, the hold had six paired clamshell doors that sprang open under the action of powerful hydraulic rams.

Ideally they sprang open. This time the lower trio worked properly, but the center door of the upper tier jammed half raised to hang like the sole tooth in a gaffer's mouth. Men in the middle of the assault force lurched right or left, fouling their fellows as they charged into the seething hell beyond.

The last of the *Wrath*'s exhaust lifted in a superheated doughnut as the hatches opened. A blast of incoming cooler air ripped trash and pebbles from the ground. It slammed the troops and staggered them, even the sailors who knew more or less what to expect. The flashgun tugged in Stephen's grasp, though he was barely conscious of the fact.

If Stephen Gregg had an article of faith, it was that his weapon would point where he wanted it to point and would fire when it bore on a target, no matter what the universe did to obstruct him. Other men had warmer, brighter gods; but as the veil of plasma lifted and the enemy's gunpit came in sight—this faith would serve. This would serve very well.

Stephen took three paces forward, breathing bottled air in his sealed hard suit. He couldn't see anything until the roiling air settled, but he knew from the display in the boarding hold and a decade of working with Piet that the *Wrath* had set down where planned, twenty meters or so from the gate to the gunpit. There were men to Stephen's immediate right and left. Major Cardiff in armor yellow-striped for identification pressed forward on the left flank of the assault force.

Rocks and debris pattered from the sky on Stephen and his fellows. He saw the gate clearing from the turbulence. The morning sun backlit the firing slits. One of the horizontal bars darkened. Stephen fired without needing to give a conscious order to his trigger finger.

The laser bolt struck just below the slit. It flash-heated the nickel steel in a yellow patch the size of a soup plate with a blazing white heart. The surface facing Stephen blistered outward, while the back of the plate exploded in ragged flakes. The slit brightened as the Fed who'd stood behind it fell.

Stephen reloaded as he ran forward. He paused at the gate to snatch at the cutting bar clipped to the right hip of his suit. Dole beside him already had his bar ready. The bosun cut down in a single powerful stroke. The blade's hornet whine became momentarily deeper where it sheared frame as well as plating. To the left, soldiers were mounting the steep berm. Pairs of armored men knelt to form a stirrup of their hands for a third who vaulted to the top.

A sailor fired both barrels of his shotgun down through

the slotted opening of the guard kiosk. That probably wasn't necessary, because the Fed guard hadn't worn a hard suit. It was barely possible that the fellow on duty this morning had survived the *Wrath*'s exhaust, but he certainly wasn't in shape to resist. Better to make sure, though. Always better to kill.

Dole's bar cut to the ground in a last spray of burning steel. Stephen and a dozen sailors hit the gate with their armored shoulders, ramming it backward faster than a Fed crew had ever opened it. The body of a Molt lay where Stephen's bolt had spalled supersonic fragments of steel from the plate to disembowel her.

The hatch of the farther gunhouse was closed. The hatch of the nearer gunhouse was closing. Stephen fired into the crack, blowing a divot of metal from the jamb and perhaps reflecting some of the laser's energy into the gunhouse.

The hatch slammed shut anyway. A dozen Fed crewmen, humans and Molts, were trapped in the pit but closed out of the gunhouses. The humans screamed, raising their hands or dodging to shelter on the other side of the armored houses.

A Molt fired his rifle. The bullet hit Stephen in the center of the chest, knocking him back a pace. Scores of bullets and shotgun charges ripped the trapped Feds, killing all of them.

Stephen strode down the ramp. His chest tingled. He didn't think the bullet had penetrated his hard suit, but he couldn't worry about that now. The gun crew wasn't prepared to fight men in full armor, though they'd reacted pretty well to what must have been a complete surprise.

The nearer barbette began to rotate to face the eastern sky. The gunners were preparing for a target to approach from orbit.

Stephen dropped flat on his belly with his head cocked to the side so that he could see from that position despite the limited width of his faceshield. The gunhouse shaded the barbette's gear train, but he could see the quiver of motion. He aimed the flashgun and fired.

The flash of coherent light ignited an explosive secondary glare as metal burned white. The welded gear bound. The barbette stopped with a squeal.

Soldiers with flashguns knelt or sprawled to fire into the workings of the other barbette. Bubbles of vaporized metal spurted explosively from beneath the gunhouse. A man stepped past Stephen and held his flashgun almost in contact with the nearer gunhouse's hatch.

"Don't!" Stephen bellowed though his hard suit's external speakers.

The soldier didn't hear or didn't care. His bolt blasted a fist-sized divot of steel from the heavy door, making the gunhouse ring but doing no harm whatever to the Feds within. The vaporized metal blew outward, knocking the shooter across the pit. The shock wave staggered Stephen even though he'd braced himself on all fours when he saw what the foolish whoreson was about to do.

Stephen had lowered his face to the ground. If he'd been turned in the direction of the blast, metal would have redeposited on his visor in an opaque coating.

"Throw something in those gun muzzles!" Stephen ordered as he got up. He tossed his discharged flashgun battery toward the nearer plasma cannon, several meters above him. The battery, a 20-by-6-by-4-centimeter prism, bounced back from the stellite tube.

Other men tried their luck with pebbles and debris; a sailor succeeded in lobbing the broken buttstock of a shotgun up and into the gun tube. Major Cardiff was climbing a ladder welded to the side of the farther gunhouse with a Fed's white jacket in his hand to drape over the muzzle.

What looked like a game was nothing of the sort. A plasma cannon's shell was a spherical array of miniature lasers that, when tripped, compressed a bead of tritium from all points but the one in line with the bore. Plasma propagated from the resulting thermonuclear explosion at light speed, but the ions were themselves of slight mass. The least obstruction within the gun tube would disrupt the stream and reflect enough of the enormous energy backward to destroy the weapon itself.

"Vanderdrekkan!" Stephen called, looking around for his aide with the laser communicator. "Van—"

The European lieutenant was at Stephen's elbow. Their

suits clashed together as Stephen turned quickly. "Oh! Get up the ramp—"

Major Cardiff stood on the roof of the gunhouse and tossed the wadded jacket into the 20-centimeter hole.

"—and tell Piet that these guns are—"

The *Wrath*'s main battery let loose in a rippling string. Ten bolts, her port broadside—tearing the sky, shocking the assault force as much by the intensity of light as the crashing thunder of air filling each track superheated to near vacuum by the plasma.

A moment later the starboard guns fired. This time the *Wrath*'s hull muffled the havoc somewhat. The targets, hidden from the assault force by the gunpit and berm, fountained in white coruscance a kilometer high.

Piet had landed the *Wrath* so that Hatch 3 was adjacent to the gunpit gate, *and* so that the vessel's guns (trained as far forward as the ports allowed) bore on the towers of the military port. The gun towers were of sturdy construction with sloped concrete copings to shield the guns at the rest position. It would have required several broadsides to hammer through their protection.

Instead of that, Piet had waited till the Feds raised the guns to engage the invaders who had landed in the civil port. As soon as the Fed weapons appeared over the coping, the *Wrath*'s waiting gunners blew them to shimmering plasma.

The Feds didn't get off a shot. Their own ammunition added to the towers' scintillating destruction.

Stephen cleared his throat. The port-side guns had fired directly over the gunpit. "Tell Piet—" he repeated.

The world went white. Every sensory impression vanished.

Stephen Gregg was lying halfway up the gunpit ramp. He was on his belly, his head pointed toward where the gate had been.

The gate was gone. Stephen didn't have his flashgun, and the two satchels of batteries he'd worn over his shoulders on crossed straps were missing also. The cutting bar was still clipped to his left hip.

Stephen levered himself upright and looked back into the pit. The base of the farther gunhouse was stamped down as if drop-forged over the gearing below. The structure's armor had been 15 centimeters thick on the sides, 20 on the front and probably the top. The lower meter or so of the walls was now splayed out from the base. Everything above that height—the height of the plasma cannon's breech when the weapon fired—had been eroded into the iridescent cloud towering from the blast site into a dumbbell thousands of meters high.

The Feds in the gunhouse had fired their cannon. Either they didn't know the bore was plugged or they'd preferred to die in a blaze of glory rather than surrender to pirates from Venus. Major Cardiff had been on top of the thermonuclear explosion. He no longer existed. Several of his nearer men had been blown to fragments despite their sturdy hard suits. The nearer gunhouse had shielded Stephen, but if he hadn't moved slightly to give an order it could have—

It could have meant that he'd have gone to whatever eternity God keeps for men like Stephen Gregg.

The hatch of the nearer gunhouse unsealed. A Fed officer, waving his white jacket on a pry bar, babbled, "Don't blow us up! Don't blow us up! We surrender!"

Several Molts crouched behind him, fear in their carriage though their exoskeletal faces were impassive. The Feds thought Stephen's men had vaporized the other gunhouse.

"Vanderdrekkan?" Stephen croaked. His aide was one of the armored men picking themselves up nearby, but he'd lost his laser communicator just as Stephen had lost the flashgun in the shock wave.

Stephen had been close to death before, many times before; but generally he'd known the danger was present. This time—

The fighting wasn't over, not by hours or maybe days, but the initial assault was complete. Stephen's troops had carried their objective without casualties and almost without fighting.

And then the blast that Major Lucas Cardiff hadn't felt, and Colonel Stephen Gregg wouldn't have felt either if he'd been standing one pace to his right. God's will, Stephen supposed; and therefore unfathomable by human beings, Piet would add. But . . .

Why Cardiff and not me? Why so many others over so many years, and not me?

Stephen started up the ramp to carry the message of success since he couldn't send it to the *Wrath*. Piet Ricimer in gilded half-armor, carrying a shotgun and a laser communicator, stepped though the opening from which the gate and gateposts had both been blown by the explosion.

"Bring the squadron in, Guillermo," Piet ordered into the communicator's mouthpiece. "The guns have been eliminated."

Stephen flipped up his faceshield. Piet's eyes flicked from the Fed gun position to the man climbing toward him in a hard suit blurred by the frosty gray of recondensed metal vapor. "Stephen? Stephen, are you all right?"

"For *God's* sake, Piet," Stephen Gregg whispered as he embraced his friend. "For God's sake."

All Stephen could think of in that moment was that if Piet had leaped from the *Wrath*'s cockpit hatch a few seconds sooner, the general commander in his half armor would have been ripped to atoms as surely as the gate itself.

And Stephen Gregg would still have been alive with the memory.

WINNIPEG SPACEPORT, EARTH.

Steam, smoke, or sometimes flame flared from every opening of the 400-tonne Federation freighter across the field from the *Gallant Sallie*. While Sal was still in orbit, she'd watched the destruction on a signal from the *Wrath*.

The Fed crew had run out eight of their moderate-sized plasma cannon as Captain Casson brought the *Freedom* down. The Feds fired three bolts at the *Freedom*. They hit twice but didn't penetrate the big armed merchantman's hull. Before the other Fed guns could fire, the *Wrath* and the *Freedom* together put a dozen rounds of 17-, 20-, and 25-cm cannonfire into the metal-built vessel, turning it into a blazing white inferno.

"I'm going to open the hatches now," Sal said.

"We ought to give the ground another minute—" Tom Harrigan said.

Brantling stepped past the mate and threw the controls for the cockpit hatch. Harrigan grimaced but didn't object. Air, throbbing with the heat of the ground and scores of fires across the spaceport, entered the cabin.

Sal stood up and adjusted her pistol holster to the side now that the navigation console's bucket seat no longer squeezed her hips. She thought of taking a respirator from the locker near the hatch, but she didn't bother. She'd breathed hotter, fiercer air every time she crossed to or from a starship in a transfer dock on Venus. She could take this.

A Venerian 6x6 with fiberglass wheels drove toward the *Gallant Sallie*. The vehicle was moving as fast as the load, two heavy plasma cannon, allowed.

Only one Fed ship had attempted to resist the Venerian assault on Winnipeg. The crews—mostly just anchor watches—of the others abandoned their vessels on foot, trudging toward the edge of the reservation. The risk of another ship landing close by in a crown of lethal exhaust seemed less serious than that of being used for target practice by the invaders.

Sal stood a meter back from the hatch so that the angle through the airlock chamber would trap heat radiating from the ground. There was a good deal of activity around the warehouses and administrative buildings on the port's southern edge. The fighting seemed to be over, though Sal couldn't be sure from a klick away.

She wondered where Stephen was.

"Ma'am?" Godden called. "Captain Blythe, sir?"

Sal turned. "Ma'am?" the gunner repeated. "Can I fire into that freighter that's burning? I'd like to see—"

"Christ's blood, man!" Harrigan shouted. "What d'ye want to be wasting ammunition for? Aren't there fireworks enough for you?"

Godden stiffened. "I'd like to see how a gun handles before I use it for serious, sir," he said. Godden was a rated specialist, not a common sailor, and he'd been posted to the *Gallant Sallie* from the general commander's own ship. "And as for blasphemy—your soul's in your own keeping, Mister Harrigan, but I don't care to be party to terms such as you just used."

The remainder of the crew watched the gunner and their officers. Their faces were in general studiously blank, but Brantling wore a broad grin.

"Tom, see what the truck's doing here," Sal ordered crisply. "Godden, one round, and make damned sure that you don't hit somebody driving past!"

She stepped to the hatch to join Harrigan. She'd extricated the mate from a situation he shouldn't have gotten involved with in the first place. Tom wasn't the *Gallant Sallie*'s captain; but everyone aboard was tense and uncertain right now, in a chaotic, dangerous place and out of communication with the other Venerian ships.

When the truck stopped, the driver in the open cab was

only two meters from the airlock hatch. The man wore a full
hard suit. He'd thrown open his faceshield, but Sal didn't
recognize him.

"*Gallant Sallie*?" the driver called. He jerked an armored
thumb toward the two 15-cm plasma cannon in the truck bed.
"Captain Ricimer said to bring you these to load soonest,
then for me to get back. There's more where these come
from, if they can just get them out before the whole warehouse burns."

Sal jumped to the truck bed. "Tom, unlimber the winch
and get these aboard!" To the driver she added, "You! Pull
around to the main hatch."

The truck's torque converter built to a peevish whine as
inertia fought the diesel's rattling surge. The vehicle eased
forward to halt again by the hatch as it lowered.

Sal rubbed her hands together. Her throat was dry. She
should have grabbed a water bottle.

"Is Mister Gregg with the general commander, then?" she
asked the driver. She wished she knew the man's name.
She'd seen him aboard the *Wrath*, she was sure.

"Oh, yeah," the driver said cheerfully. He gave Sal a
slight smile as he eyed her. "The Feds tried to start
something at the arms warehouse, so he was there to sort
them out."

"He's all right, though?" Sal asked, her heart as parched
as her mouth.

"You needn't worry about him, ma'am," the driver said.
"Our Mister Gregg—he's the Angel of Death, he is."

The *Gallant Sallie*'s crane squealed as Brantling ran the
hook out the beam positioned over a gun tube. Four crewmen
were lifting the fiberglass sashes tied around the heavy
weapon.

"Harrigan!" Sal called. "When we've got these guns
loaded, take charge of the ship. I'm going back on the truck
to—to see what's going on."

WINNIPEG SPACEPORT, EARTH.

APRIL 16, YEAR 27.
0345 HOURS, VENUS TIME.

The casters clacked like gunshots at every irregularity in the warehouse floor. The manual dolly tracked straight enough, but as the entrance neared Stephen saw that they weren't going to clear the door, which had jammed only three-quarters open.

Piet, across the dolly from Stephen, leaned hard against the muzzle of the 15-cm gun tube. The dolly continued along an unchanged line. The concrete was sloped, slightly but enough to give the tonnes of plasma cannon a will of its own.

"I'm changing sides," Stephen shouted. The fire at the rear of the big warehouse was bursting containers—clangs, not explosions, but they reverberated loudly within the structure.

The hot, smoky air made Stephen's eyes water and his lungs burn. He'd raised his faceshield because he wanted to save the remaining contents of his air bottle for a real emergency, but he was beginning to think he'd need it before they got out of this *damned* building.

The hard suit chafed Stephen's neck, his hipbone, and his knees. Maybe he should have taken the suit off, but when they entered the warehouse they hadn't been sure how quickly the fire would spread. The armor would have been their only chance of survival if the roof had collapsed . . .

"We'll be all right," Piet gasped. The rhythm of the casters slowed slightly. The four men with Piet and Stephen slacked their efforts as they saw the problem ahead.

Stephen let the dolly rumble past, then walked behind it

and around to take his position directly in back of Piet. He'd thought of trotting in front of the gun—and thought of slipping on the concrete, exhausted, and having the dolly upset its load onto him. His hard suit might or might not withstand the shock, but they'd certainly lose the gun tube.

"Easy, now," Piet warned. Stephen settled his weight against the weapon, then put a little more of his strength into the side thrust with every pace. The dolly hesitated, then slanted 15° to the right; enough to miss the door wedged open by a corpse that had fallen into the track. Stephen stepped back, made sure the dolly would hold its new line, and trekked around to the right side again.

The sunlight beyond was a beckoning dazzle. Smoke rising from the fires in the rear of the building filtered the overhead lights into ruddy glows. The ventilation fans in the roof peaks prevented the haze from filling the warehouse, but they also stirred the flames to greater enthusiasm. The Feds hadn't stored fuel or munitions here, but the packing materials themselves were combustible.

"Watch the lip!" Piet warned. The metal threshold plate was a half-centimeter higher than the concrete to which it was bolted. The front casters hit the plate at a skew angle. The dolly rocked, then righted, and rolled out onto the stabilized earth of the spaceport proper.

A dozen Venerians, several of them gentlemen wearing enameled and polished half armor, were arguing around the 15-cm gun Piet's team had dumped in front of the warehouse before going back for the next one.

"Well, let me tell you, Blassingame!" an officer shouted. "Even if it had been my men responsible for the fire, I don't have to answer to you about it!"

"Let the whole bloody—" another officer said. The sound of the dolly banging over the threshold made him turn.

"God and His saints!" a sailor who'd sailed with Piet in the past blurted. "It's the captain!"

The truck that had carried the first two guns to the *Gallant Sallie* was coming toward the warehouse again. Because of fatigue and the sweat in his eyes, Stephen at first saw only that there was someone in the cab with Tsarev, the driver.

His vision cleared suddenly; he recognized Sal. He wished

she was—home on Venus, in orbit; anywhere but in this dangerous mare's nest. But he was very glad to see her.

"All right," Piet said in a hoarse voice. He loosened the turnbuckles clamping the gun to the dolly. "Everyone on the right side and push."

"The truck's coming back, sir," Vanderdrekkan said. He took his place beside the other five men of Piet's team, however, his gauntlets against the plasma cannon.

"It has the winch and sheerlegs," Stephen rasped. "It'll lift as well from the ground as from this dolly."

"Together," Piet said. "Push . . ."

The men who'd been gathered in front of the warehouse stepped clear when they saw what was about to happen. A pair of sailors moved to join Piet's team, but they were too late to help and unnecessary anyway. The gun tube rolled off the dolly and crashed to the ground like a meteor impact.

Tsarev pulled the truck around in a U-turn, then backed close to the pair of 15-cm guns. Sal stepped out onto the running board to guide him. She was wearing a helmet but no other protective garb.

"Blassingame," Piet ordered. "Take five of these men and get the remaining gun tubes. They're midway down Aisle Three."

A plasma cannon spoke from far across the field. One of the Venerian ships was shooting at Feds peering over the berm of the military port.

"But it's burning, sir!" Blassingame said in surprise. His family had a small hold in the Maxwell Range, not dissimilar to Eryx where Stephen had been born.

"Then you'd better work fast, hadn't you, man?" Piet said. His tone was even rougher than his throat, very unusual for him. "The Feds will have time to sift the ashes for anything we miss, so I don't intend to leave them guns that won't be harmed by a fire."

Blassingame nodded in puzzled agreement. "Whatever you say, sir," he said.

Blassingame wasn't one of the squadron's brighter lights, but now as in the past he'd proved himself dependable within his capacities. He pointed to a group of men and said, "You five, come along now!" He suited his actions to his words by personally wheeling the dolly around to return.

Vanderdrekkan had hopped into the cab. He was trying to raise someone on the truck's radio. He didn't seem to be having any luck because of the varied forms of interference.

Tsarev, Sal, and the three sailors who'd helped push the guns out of the warehouse were looping sashes beneath a tube for the truck's winch to hook. Stephen checked the sling of the rifle that had replaced the flashgun he lost in the gun-pit, then knelt to join them.

"Cherwell," Piet ordered sharply. "You and the rest of these men load the guns. When you've done that, go into the warehouse and help Blassingame."

"At once, sir!" Cherwell said, bracing himself to attention. He glared at the men with him and said, "You heard Factor Ricimer. Get to work!"

"Were your arms amputated, Cherwell?" Stephen heard himself demand in a high, liquid voice. "Or is it that you don't think anyone who works with his hands can be a gentleman?"

The plain finish of Stephen's hard suit was now dirty gray from condensed metal. Save for his size, he was anonymous at a quick glance. Cherwell, a young gentleman, hadn't noticed Stephen until he spoke.

Cherwell bent to put his weight with the others rolling the plasma cannon over the fiberglass sash. "I'm not too proud to serve Venus in whatever fashion Factor Ricimer orders," he said with a simple dignity that raised him several steps in Stephen's estimation.

A party of ten or a dozen sailors trotted by a hundred meters away. They carried cutting bars and firearms, but only a few of them were wearing body armor. Piet shouted to the men—whatever they thought they were doing was less important than getting the last pair of guns out of the warehouse. They couldn't hear over the gunfire and engine noise pulsing across the spaceport like chop on a pond.

Stephen looked at Sal, who'd stepped out of the way when Cherwell's men took over from Piet's team. She was fresh, but handling tonnes of dense ceramic was a job for bulk and peak strength, not endurance and good will.

"Any trouble landing?" he asked inanely. As he spoke, his eyes continued to check his surroundings, and he shifted on his left heel to scan through the helmet locked to the gorget of his hard suit.

"We—" Sal said. She lifted her helmet to wipe her forehead with a bandanna. A roar building within the military port smothered the rest of her sentence.

Plasma billowed over the berm. A cylindrical starship—a moderate-sized freighter, two or three hundred tonnes burden—lifted into sight some distance within the enclosure. The vessel wobbled a little, but it had no forward way on.

A midships hatch was lifted like a wing. There would be a cutter in the hold, ready to take the skeleton crew to safety once the Feds had locked their controls on course for one of the larger Venerian vessels.

"We're going to have to do something about the military port," Piet said. His voice was clear and calm. Sight of the next task had done more than the few moments of rest to cleanse his body of fatigue.

The featherboat and three large cutters Piet had set to watch for just such an eventuality lifted from the field. Bulging cargo nets on the bows of all four boats were filled with spun-glass matting that would resist the wash of ionized exhaust. The 5-cm cannon in the featherboat's nose was covered by the cushion.

A starship was a potential missile with enormous kinetic energy, even at the relatively low speeds possible immediately after takeoff. Concentrated cannonfire could destroy a ship—the freighter blazing in the middle of the field was proof of that—but jolts of ions wouldn't in themselves counteract the momentum of hundreds of tonnes of steel. The Fed vessel's bow might be a white glowing mass when it hit a Venerian ship, but that wouldn't keep the impact from being wholly devastating to the target.

A Venerian cutter, then the other two cutters and the featherboat, edged forward at a walking pace. The small vessels kept as low as possible: Fed vessels within the military port would have their cannon trained over the berm to smash anything that rose high enough to be visible. A ship the size of the Fed freighter could absorb punishment for a minute or two, but a boat of less than 50 tonnes would disintegrate at the first plasma bolt.

The freighter porpoised as it started toward the civil port, dipping and then rising again enough to clear the berm. The featherboat and cutters swung wide, still keeping close to the surface of the field.

The Venerian small craft had expert pilots, briefed for this task. Piet had calculated that by butting gently against the freighter's starboard bow and then boosting their thrusters to maximum output, they could swing the bigger vessel harmlessly off its line and send it off over the hectares of wasteland and farms. If the Feds stayed aboard they could perhaps maneuver into the *Wrath* or another important ship despite the picket boats, but that would be literal suicide for the crew. President Pleyal didn't inspire that degree of loyalty.

"I'll take a company into the military port," Stephen decided aloud. "Fifty or a hundred men ought to be enough to sort things out. I don't imagine the Feds will hold after the first volley."

Vanderdrekkan was at Stephen's side again. "I believe all the troops have been committed, sir," he said. "Do you want me to gather men at random, or did you have a particular contingent in mind?"

"Belay that, Cherwell," Piet ordered, gesturing to the half-raised gun tube. "The guns can stay here for the time being. I'm going to need the truck myself."

The Fed merchantman dipped again as it gathered forward speed. If the Venerian pickets hit the Fed too hard, the freighter's thicker hull would shatter the boats and brush the fragments away. The small craft pogoed nervously as they maneuvered toward contact. The featherboat was slightly larger than the cutters, but it too depended on a single thruster. Not even the most skillful pilot and crew could keep a one-nozzle vessel perfectly stable in a hover.

"The A Watch close-combat team is still aboard the *Wrath* for emergencies," Stephen said to his aide. "The Feds getting their act together across the berm is as close to an emergency as we're likely to have. I want men in full armor because the ships inside'll fire when we cross. The splash from plasma cannon is going to be too hot for anything but hard suits.''

He was planning against near misses by the Federation cannoneers. Armor didn't make any difference for the inevitable direct hits, since the heaviest suit a man could carry would burn like a cotton wisp in the direct path of a slug of ions.

The Fed freighter nosed over the berm. Two guns fired from the *Freedom*, against Piet Ricimer's direct orders.

The shock wave from the bolts hitting the freighter rocked the picket vessels violently. The nearest cutter spun a full 360°, touched the ground, and bounded a hundred meters in the air. The pilot got control just in time to dive to safety as a bolt from the military port slashed the air where the cutter had been.

A rainbow fireball engulfed the freighter's bow. The *Freedom* mounted several 25-cm smashers as part of its heterogeneous battery. Stampfer, the expert on plasma cannon so far as Stephen was concerned, said that 20-cm guns were superior to the big guns because they cooled much faster between shots and because 25-cm shells were so heavy that they led to dangerous accidents as the crews handled them under the stress of combat.

For all that, 25-cm plasma bolts made an impressive show when they hit a metal hull in an oxidizing atmosphere. The first round punched the lower curve of the vessel's bow and vaporized a square meter of hull plating. The bubble of gaseous steel used the top of the berm as a fulcrum to lift the freighter.

The second bolt, fired a half-second later—and it was probably pure chance, but Stephen had known for a decade that in war it was better to be lucky than skillful—hit the nest of four thrusters under the bow. The tungsten nozzles exploded in green radiance, destroyed as much by the ions they were channeling as by the cannon bolt that overloaded their outer surfaces.

Inertia kept the vessel moving forward even after the bow thrusters were destroyed, but the nose dipped as gravity pulled it down. The freighter hit the berm, quenching the white-hot metal as it plowed through a hundred cubic meters of earth. Sparks flew from rocks in the dirt. The noise was overwhelming, even in comparison to the *clang* of cannonfire a moment before.

The Fed captain reacted instantly and as well as was possible under the circumstances. He (or not unlikely she, in Federation service) chopped the throttles to the quartet of thrusters in the stern. Their continued thrust would have lifted the freighter onto its ruined nose, then flipped the vessel over the berm on its back.

With the power off and the bow supported three meters above the ground by the berm, the stern dropped and hit with a crash. The freighter bounced, hopped several meters forward, and came down again to break its back on the berm.

The wreckage lay steaming in a haze of dirt. The vessel's crumpled bow lay in the civil field, but the stern remained in the military port.

Almost as an afterthought, the final impact flung the prepared escape boat out of the hold. It hit something within the military port. An orange flash brightened the morning momentarily, followed by the thud of an explosion.

"I'm very glad none of our people were injured by those bolts," Piet said in a voice as neutral as possible, given the need to shout to be heard over the continuing clangor. His face was hard.

Stephen regarded casualties as a fact of war, and it didn't particularly matter to him whether they were caused by the enemy or by a friendly mistake. Dead was dead. But for Piet, a victory had to be without friendly loss to be complete. If Casson had killed Venerian sailors when he disobeyed the general commander's orders, he might have found that Piet Ricimer in a rage was as fearful a thing as his friend Stephen Gregg.

Piet looked at Stephen, smiled slightly, and went on, "We won't cross the berm on foot, Stephen. We'll take the *Moll Dane* in. She's sturdy enough to survive a few shots. The loss among unprotected troops would be higher than I'd care to accept."

The guns of the *Freedom* and several other Venerian ships battered the wreckage of the Fed vessel. Plasma bolts were quick darts of iridescence across the field, followed by

balls of opaque white fire as collops of steel burned under
the ions' impact. The shots hit like hammers on a huge anvil.
Shock waves caused each hull plate to slam against its neighbors, flinging heavy fragments into the air.

"All right," Stephen said. His mind worked in several
directions at once. Part of him was planning the operation,
pulling up information on how the Fed ships had been arranged within the military port when the *Wrath* descended;
part of him noted that he'd be able to get another flashgun
from the flagship's armory when he returned to gather the
close-combat team.

But Stephen Gregg's main concern at this moment—

"That's a good idea, Piet," he said aloud. Cherwell's crew
had loosed the gun tube from the winch; the truck was ready
to take Stephen to the *Wrath*. "But you're not coming yourself. You won't wear a hard suit while you're piloting in an
atmosphere, and you won't take the time to put one on after
we've landed."

"I—" Piet said.

"No!" Stephen said. "You scared me too much at the
gunpit, Piet. Half the Fed ships across the berm have probably got their thrusters lit. I'm not going to carry your ashes
home, and I'm not going to trust you to put your suit on
when I know you'd be lying if you told me you would. I
won't!"

"Guillermo will pilot the ship," Piet said. He slapped his
trouser leg with a bare hand. "I'll put on the rest of my
armor on the *Wrath*."

"I'll pilot the *Moll Dane*," Sal said in a voice as clear
and strong as those of the men. "Guillermo can work the
attitude-control board with Harrigan and Brantling from my
ship. They're current on manual systems, and people from a
new warship probably wouldn't be."

Stephen looked at Piet. Piet raised an eyebrow. Stephen
nodded, although he felt as if the ground had opened beneath
his feet.

*Sal wouldn't have any use for him if he didn't treat her
as a person in her own right; and he wouldn't have any use
for her if she weren't a person.*

"Right," Piet said, walking to the truck. Stephen boosted

his friend into the back of the vehicle, then stepped onto the middle tire and let Piet's wiry strength help lift his own armored weight.

Sal, settling herself in the cab beside Tsarev, ordered, "Swing by the *Gallant Sallie* on the way to the *Wrath*, sailor. And step on it!"

Stephen felt his lips smile, but his mind was a thousand light-years away.

WINNIPEG SPACEPORT, EARTH.

APRIL 16, YEAR 27.
0433 HOURS, VENUS TIME.

The interior of the *Moll Dane* was a pigsty, which neither surprised Sal nor mattered to her. There was also up to 10 millimeters' play in the controls. That was no more surprising than the other, but it could matter very much indeed.

"Ready at the attitude controls?" Sal called. A dozen men in hard suits packed the freighter's cabin. When the armored sailors moved, their suits clashed loudly together. The forty or so in the hold had cleared space for themselves by dumping the *Moll Dane*'s stores and cargo onto the field.

"I hope to God that they work better than they look like they work," Tom Harrigan replied. "But yeah, we're as ready here as we can be."

"The bastard responsible for maintaining these won't leave Earth alive if I catch him!" Brantling added.

In fact, Captain Lasky and his crew had very little chance of surviving if men of the Venerian squadron caught them. Technically, selling cannon to President Pleyal wasn't a violation of Venerian law. The men risking their lives in this attack weren't lawyers but rather patriots; and killers already, the most of them. The gunrunners knew that. They'd abandoned the *Moll Dane* so quickly that half-eaten rations littered the deck.

The lower two-thirds of the *Moll Dane*'s console display was adequate. The images weren't razor sharp, but they were about as clear as those of the *Gallant Sallie*'s screen before the recent upgrade. The top third of the screen was a murky purple sea in which shadowed objects moved like fish swim-

196

ming at great depths. Thank God that for this hop, the lower portion was all Sal needed.

Sal lit the thrusters. As the vessel shuddered beneath her, she monitored the fuel flow. All eight motors were within comfortable parameters. A slight taste of burned air made her sneeze.

The *Moll Dane*'s layout was similar to that of the *Gallant Sallie*, but Lasky's ship lacked a separate cabin airlock. All entry and exit was through the hold. The passage through the central water tank acted as the only lock for operations in vacuum or a hostile atmosphere.

At the moment, the outer hatch and passage were both open. The assault force breathed bottled oxygen within its hard suits, enduring the wash of exhaust. Sal and her operational crew were old hands, too hardened to be seriously inconvenienced by the amount of plasma that trailed into the cabin.

"Prepare to lift!" Sal warned. She doubted whether the armored men in the cabin could hear her, but they were veteran sailors who didn't need coddling. She slid the two linked quartets of throttle controls forward, then twisted a separate knob to shrink the nozzle irises.

The *Moll Dane* wobbled nervously as the skids unloaded. The stern lifted first and crawled 10° to starboard. Brantling shouted a curse. Attitude jets fired, and the ship steadied.

Stephen and Piet Ricimer were in the vessel's hold. They would be among the first men out of the *Moll Dane*.

The military port was more than a klick from the *Moll Dane*'s berth near the warehouses. Sal found, somewhat to her surprise, that Lasky's vessel handled well in ground-effect mode; a meter or so above the ground, buoyed on a cushion of exhaust reflected onto the belly plates. Sal kept the *Moll Dane* there instead of rising to twenty meters and sailing toward the berm as she'd intended. She had to hold their forward speed to 10 kph to avoid outrunning the effect, but the loss of a minute or two in transit time was a cheap price to pay for the relative safety and control.

Sal corrected twice to avoid ships studding the big field, first a Fed craft and then the *Cyprian*, an armed merchantman from Betaport. Sailors on the *Cyprian*'s loading ramps waved enthusiastically to the *Moll Dane* scudding past in a cloud of dust and plasma.

Sal guided their course toward a point on the berm a hundred meters to the left of the wrecked Fed freighter. She couldn't see any Feds watching from the top of the concrete-surfaced slope—gunners on grounded Venerian ships were looking for any excuse to fire their cannon—but defenders within the military port would be able to track the approaching vessel by its exhaust plume.

The *Moll Dane*'s hatch was to starboard. Sal came to a halt ten meters from the scarred berm, then swung the *Moll Dane* cautiously on its vertical axis to put the berm on the port side. The skids touched twice, port side and then starboard, as the *Moll Dane* rocked queasily. Thanks to luck and skilled hands at the attitude-control console, the vessel didn't overset.

The guns of the Venerian squadron had fallen silent, *God be praised*! The bolt of a friendly gunner who misjudged Sal's intended course could do worse damage in the open hold than the Feds' fire concentrated on the solid hull.

Sal tightened the nozzle irises with the throttles on sixty percent power. The *Moll Dane* lifted, slightly nose-down, and slid forty meters forward, parallel to the berm. If the Feds had aimed their cannon at the center of the previous exhaust plume, they were going to get a surprise.

When she'd brought her vessel its own length beyond its previous location, Sal touched her skids to the ground again to kill her forward motion. She cocked the nozzles a hair to starboard, then slid the thruster controls up to full output. Roaring like an avalanche, the *Moll Dane* rose over the berm at an angle that became a catenary arc when Sal eased back on the throttles again.

At least twenty plasma cannon fired within the two seconds of the *Moll Dane*'s rise and fall. Most of the Fed guns blasted into the berm or ripped the air just above it at the point where the Venerian ship had first paused.

Three bolts struck the vessel. Two of the impacts were sternward. They made the hull ring and may have penetrated the hold full of assault troops, but they didn't affect Sal's control of the *Moll Dane*.

The third round slammed the hull at midline forward. The plasma itself didn't penetrate the cabin, but it blew a high-voltage power line in the ceiling. The *bang* of the explosion was sharper than lightning. Molten metal gouted through the light headliner, spraying the armored assault party and the crewmen in cabin clothes at the attitude controls.

Sal heard Brantling scream. The vessel twisted as Sal lost half the power to her nozzle-alignment motors. She fought her controls. The cabin was bitterly gray with ozone and burned insulation.

The *Moll Dane*'s roll to port slowed, then reversed. Brantling was batting bare-handed at his smoldering tunic, but Harrigan and Piet's Molt navigator were still at the attitude board despite their burns.

Using both hands on the control yoke, Sal kicked the *Moll Dane*'s stern out to cross the bow of the purpose-built Fed warship they'd otherwise crash into. The Fed vessel—the *Holy Office*, according to the osmium letters inlaid onto the bow—had moved parallel to the berm and within twenty meters of it since the *Gallant Sallie* had viewed the military port during landing.

A collision between the *Moll Dane* and the *Holy Office* would have killed everyone aboard both vessels. No amount of damage to a ship of the North American Federation could have repaid the death of Piet Ricimer.

Because of the violent maneuver, the *Moll Dane* hit so hard that the left landing skid shattered. The cabin lights, normally on whenever the vessel was under way, blew out. The navigation console and apparently the attitude controls still had power.

Sal made as swift and skillful an instinctive decision as she'd ever managed in her life: she chopped one starboard and both port thrusters in each quartet simultaneously, but she didn't shut off the remaining motor to bow and stern for another fraction of a second. The momentary additional output eased the *Moll Dane* down on the starboard skid instead of dropping the ship like 200 tonnes of old junk.

The men in the hold were sailors. They fell down at the shock, but a moment later they were on their feet and clumping out of the hold to attack.

In the middle of the enclosure three hundred meters away, a freighter much like the one the *Freedom*'s guns destroyed was being readied for another ramming attack on the Venerian squadron. Ionized exhaust bathed the vessel; she was already light on her skids.

When the *Moll Dane* hopped over the berm, the ramship's captain shut down his thrusters. The hatches were already open. The crew spilled out of the vessel, abandoning ship in a panic greater than their fear of the throbbing hot ground onto which they were jumping.

There were three Fed warships in the military port with their gunports open, as well as a number of freighters that either were unarmed or didn't have crews aboard to work the guns. The warships' guns weren't visible; they'd recoiled back within the vessel when they salvoed at the *Moll Dane*.

Members of the assault force were still jostling their way out of the cabin through the narrow passage. Sal set her console display for a 360° panorama. Men of the first wave from the hold trotted around the *Moll Dane*'s bow and stern, their weapons ready. A score of Fed soldiers stood in the loading ramp of the spherical warship two hundred meters away, shooting as the Venerians appeared.

Stephen, identifiable from the piebald condition of his hard suit, halted at the *Moll Dane*'s bow. He fired five times. Each time his rifle lifted in recoil, his left hand pumped the slide to chamber a fresh round; and each time, a white-uniformed soldier toppled backward. The Feds were wearing body armor, so Stephen must have been aiming for heads—and hitting them.

Stephen tossed the emptied rifle behind him and took a carbine from one of his loaders. Other members of the assault force jogged by like boulders with limbs. Once Sal saw a Venerian stagger when a Fed bullet ricocheted from his armor, but the man caught his step and continued on.

Sal got up from her console when the cabin emptied enough to give the flight crew some room. She opened the first-aid kit on her belt and took out the jar of salve. Tom Harrigan was daubing Brantling's burns. A huge blister was rising on the mate's bald spot. The fringe of hair still smoldered.

There were just the four of them in the flight crew: motormen to watch the plasma thrusters weren't necessary for a quick up and down, and their presence would have meant one fewer man in the assault force. The odds were in the order of ten to one as it was, though the Venerians were in full armor and further strengthened by absolute certainty that they would win. Captain Ricimer and Mister Gregg always won. . . .

"Guillermo, are you all right?" she asked the Molt. The alien's carapace was normally a smooth brownish mauve. His exoskeleton didn't blister like human skin, but spattering copper had burned off the waxy coat and pitted the chitin beneath.

Guillermo took a wad of tarry substance out of his mouth where he'd been masticating it. "Yes, Captain," he said. He smeared the softened goo onto his burns with a three-fingered hand.

Harrigan turned his head at the touch of Sal's fingers on his scalp. His eyes caught the display behind her. "God help us, Sal!" he shouted. "We've got to get out of the ship!"

Sal looked around. Unusual for a Federation warship, the *Holy Office* was of cylindrical rather than spherical layout. During the past two years, Pleyal's naval architects had started to copy the latest Venerian design philosophy. A port in the vessel's extreme bow had opened.

Despite the *Moll Dane*'s fuzzy optics, Sal could see members of the Fed crew swinging a heavy gun on a traveling mount to bear on the Venerian ship. At point-blank range, the bolt would turn the interior of the *Moll Dane*'s weakened hull into an inferno.

"Right, we'll—" Sal started to say.

Stephen Gregg took the flashgun one of his loaders carried for him. He leaned against the *Moll Dane*'s bow, aiming up at the *Holy Office*. The laser pulse momentarily lit the muzzle of the big plasma cannon.

Because of the angle, Stephen couldn't fire directly along the barrel's axis. The gun bore was highly polished to direct the stream of plasma with minimum erosion, however. The smooth surface worked equally well to reflect the bolt down to the shell loaded in the cannon's breech.

Dirty red smoke engulfed the gunport as the shell detonated in a low-order explosion. Stephen traded the cassegrain
laser for his slide-action rifle. With his loaders behind him,
he stalked up the forward boarding ramp of the *Holy Office*.

WINNIPEG SPACEPORT, EARTH.

The *Holy Office* was boarded via through-holds, chambers the width of the vessel with no internal partitions, fore and aft on the lowest level. When both the port and starboard hatches were lowered, as they were now, you could see through the ship to the northern berm of the military port.

A human and a pair of Molts lay beside the hatch control panel set into an alcove in the front of the hold. They'd been shot dead by Venerians who'd rounded the *Moll Dane*'s stern with Piet while Stephen led the other contingent by way of the bow.

The bulkhead separating the bow and stern holds was armored and thick. It contained a separate companionway for either hold. As a safety feature, there was no direct connection between the two holds; though that didn't help now, since the aft hatches were open also. The Feds hadn't expected a shipload of Venerian infantry to be lofted over the berm.

The first troops aboard the *Holy Office* had already fought their way up the companionway. A Fed officer in half armor dangled from the railing, his foot caught between a tread and a stanchion. A shotgun blast had nearly decapitated him. A Venerian lay at the foot of the companionway, his breastplate starred by a bullet that had punched through the center of it. A Fed sailor and the ichor-leaking arm of a Molt littered the steps, crushed by the armored weight of men who'd charged up to the main deck.

Stephen's nasal passages were dry from breathing pure

bottled oxygen. As he started for the companionway, he touched his left hand to his helmet to raise his faceshield.

The through-hold exploded in a cataclysm of sparks and clangor. Beverly's body caromed into Stephen and knocked him down. The dangling Fed corpse flew out the starboard hatchway in a mist of blood and pureed flesh, all but the leg that still hung from the railing.

Without rising, Stephen turned his head and torso to see where the shots had come from. His rifle fire had killed or dispersed the troops surprised in the lower hold of the spherical Federation warship two hundred meters away. The crew of that vessel had set up a defensive position on the midline deck with hatches intended for loading in vacuum. Men in armor and Molts in protective suits of quilted rock-wool knelt behind a barricade of crated cargo.

At this range, riflefire wasn't particularly dangerous to troops in ceramic hard suits, but the Feds also had an antiboarding weapon—a hand-cranked rotary cannon. The five 2-cm rounds the gun spit out before it jammed—solid steel shot with no bursting charge—ricocheted lethally from the bulkhead of the *Holy Office* and penetrated everything else they hit.

Beverly was carrying the flashgun. Stephen grabbed the weapon. The sling was caught on the loader's suit. A shot from the rotary cannon had struck Beverly's left shoulder, crushing the backplate and gorget. The ceramic shards were slippery with blood, but there was no time to worry about that now.

"Philips!" Stephen called. He tugged the flashgun. Beverly thrashed, but the weapon didn't come loose. Stephen tugged again. The fiberglass sling parted, and the universe settled into the glassy calm that Stephen Gregg knew so well.

It was the only time he was at peace.

The rotary cannon stood out in sharp relief in Stephen's mind. Three crewmen bent over the weapon, prying at a burst cartridge case. An officer in polished armor shouted orders as she leaned on the hand crank, backing the barrel cluster to give her crewmen's tools more room.

The marksmen, eight or ten of them rising to fire and then vanishing again behind the barricade to reload, didn't really

figure in Stephen's calculations. They were motions in black
and white, while in his mind the cannon and its crew had
color and detail richer than human eyes could possibly make
out at this distance.

Bullets whanged across the boarding hold. They didn't
impinge on Stephen's consciousness, any more than did the
back muscle he'd pulled when Beverly cannoned into him.

A Fed crewman, a Molt, stepped back from the gun, waving a ruptured case triumphantly in the jaws of his pliers.
Stephen's index finger took up the last pressure on the flashgun's electronic trigger. The bolt hit one of the gun's six
barrels at the crank assembly. Ionized steel flashed in a white
shock wave that knocked down the gun captain and the two
crewmen standing on the near side of the weapon.

Stephen reached for the satchel holding fresh batteries. It
was gone, his whole equipment belt shot away by the same
burst of fire that wounded Beverly. He started to turn Beverly
over to search for the spares the loader carried.

Philips, kneeling, waved the battery in his right hand.
There were four more batteries fanned upward from Philips'
left gauntlet, ready for Stephen to snatch as he fired.

Violent fighting was taking place on the gun deck of the
Holy Office, directly above the boarding hold. Maybe Piet
could use help there, but the crew of the spherical warship
was too alert to be ignored.

The Fed riflemen had ducked to cover when the rotary
cannon exploded beside them, but now one took a chance of
rising to shoot. Smoke drifted from where the blazing steel
had sprayed the barricade. Without being fully conscious of
his decision until he'd made it, Stephen fired into a wooden
packing crate instead of the face of the Molt rifleman.

The crate erupted as it absorbed the energy of the monopulse laser. The metal food cans inside were nonflammable,
but they were packed in extruded cellulose that ignited in a
red fireball.

Feds jumped up, batting at themselves instinctively even
though most of them wore protective garb. Rifleshots from
Venerians still arriving from the *Moll Dane* knocked several
of them over. When the box of cannon cartridges went off

in smoky, rippling flashes a moment later, the surviving Feds abandoned the position to the flames.

Stephen got to his feet. "Do what you can for Beverly," he said to Philips in a voice that seemed half human even to his own ears. He'd have slung the flashgun if the sling were whole, but he probably wouldn't need the laser in the tight constraints of a starship's compartments. He dropped the flashgun on the deck and took the pump gun lying beside Philips. He liked the feel of the slide working, and the rifle's powerful cartridges were a better choice than the lighter carbine when so many of the Feds wore armor.

Stephen walked up the companionway, taking the last six steps in three. He burst onto the chaotic gun deck like a float bobbing from the deep sea. As he appeared, a Venerian sailor fired at a Molt near the stern and hit instead the 17-cm plasma cannon behind which the target was sheltering. The bullet ricocheted, clipped the left-side latch of Stephen's faceshield, and fell to the deck without actually harming anyone.

The Molt rose with a flechette gun whose four heavy barrels were welded together into a unit that looked massive enough to be part of a ship's landing gear. Stephen and the alien fired simultaneously.

Stephen's bullet slammed the Molt backward with a hole near the top of the plastron. The flechette gun emitted an orange-red, bottle-shaped muzzleflash and a *crack* so loud that it forged compression bands in the smoky cabin air. The hypervelocity projectile struck the lower lip of the Venerian sailor's breastplate, shattered it, and was deflected straight up the inside of the backplate. Battered but still moving, the flechette exited through the neck opening of the armor and tipped off the sailor's helmet as he fell forward.

A Fed grabbed the flechette gun as it fell from the Molt's hands. Stephen shot the man, then shot the fellow again in the head since he refused to fall to a bullet placed perfectly to wreck the knot of blood vessels above the heart.

A red needle sprang up beside Stephen's rear sight, indicating that the round just fired was the last one in his rifle. Beverly hadn't managed to fully load the weapon before Stephen snatched it back from him the last time.

The shot that carried away his battery satchel hadn't touched his bandolier of rifle and carbine ammunition. He took out a fan of five bottle-necked cartridges and began to load.

The *Holy Office*'s crew still held the sternmost third of the gun deck. Gunsmoke and smudge fires ignited by the battle screened the parties from one another, though there were probably eighty or a hundred men and Molts locked in combat in the confined space.

Most shots were fired by men who poked a weapon up from cover one-handed and loosed blindly in the general direction of the enemy. Venerians advanced crabwise, hopping back and forth across the central aisle because the lines of plasma cannon were offset to give them a greater distance to recoil.

Occasionally somebody would bellow forward with a cutting bar. As shots flashed in both directions along the cabin, sparks and the shriek of teeth shearing armor spewed from a gun bay.

Stampfer, who shouldn't have been in the assault party at all, was ignoring the battle. Piet's gunner struggled alone with a 17-cm cannon of the starboard battery. The gun's power assist was either damaged or disabled from the bridge, so Stampfer was running the massive weapon to firing position by cranking the manual capstan with a come-along. The gunner's backplate was cracked and a charge of buckshot had smeared the side of his helmet, but he kept to his self-appointed task.

"Stephen, help me!" Piet Ricimer called from forward. Even in the present noise and carnage, that voice reached Stephen's directing mind. As he turned, his gauntleted fingers continued to feed cartridges up the loading gate in the rifle's receiver.

The battle for the forward portion of the gun deck was over. At least a score of bodies and partial bodies littered the deck or were draped over the guns. Most of the casualties were from the Fed crew, but the Venerian sprawled on his back with a hole through his thigh armor was certainly dead by now if the femoral artery had been nicked.

There were two more bodies in Venerian hard suits at the

head of the cabin. The helmet of one had been topped like
a soft-boiled egg; brains were leaking out. Piet, holding a
cutting bar, stood between the corpses of his companions.

The situation was easy to read. The control room in the
nose of the *Holy Office* was separated from the gun deck by
an airlock passage similar to but much wider than that between the *Gallant Sallie*'s hold and cabin. Piet had headed
for the control room with the two nearest men, leaving the
rest of the assault force to deal with the crew of the *Holy
Office*. The Venerians had cut through the hinges of the out-
ward-opening hatch and pried it away from the opening.

A Fed in full armor waited in the passage with a pair of
cutting bars. The man was a giant. The surface of his hard
suit was silvered to reflect laser beams. Judging by the fresh
scars—from bullets and cutting bars both—the plates beneath were exceptionally thick as well.

The Venerians were expecting an empty passage when
they cleared the hatch. The Fed guardian fell on them, hack-
ing with both hands and rightly confident that his armor was
proof against their panicked response.

Piet had dodged back in time—Stephen had never seen
his friend completely surprised by any event—but the sailors
with him died beneath the paired cutting bars. The giant then
backed up and waited for the next assault, knowing that the
passage protected his flanks from the numbers that could
otherwise be brought against him.

"Don't bother shooting, Stephen," Piet called without taking his eyes off the giant. "If you block the right-hand bar
with your own, I'll block the left and—"

Stephen closed to two meters and tossed his rifle in the
giant's face. As the weapon clanged harmlessly off the helmet, Stephen lunged forward like a missile himself. Their
breastplates crashed together. Stephen caught the Fed's armored wrists before the bars could scissor together on his
helmet.

The howling edges pressed toward Stephen's face despite
anything he could do. "Christ Jesus bugger you, you Federation whoreson!" he screamed as he butted the Fed's faceplate. He'd always known there were men stronger than he
was, but he didn't meet them often.

This man was strong enough to hand Stephen Gregg his head, literally.

For a moment, Stephen thought the vibration and screaming refractories came from the giant's bars cutting into his helmet. The Fed threw himself backward, pulling Stephen with him. They smashed into the hatch between the passage and the control room. The cutting bar fell from the giant's right hand.

Piet Ricimer gripped the Fed's shoulder with his left gauntlet while he drove the tip of his cutting bar into the man's faceplate. The blade suddenly lurched 15 centimeters inward till the tip shrieked on the back of the giant's helmet from the inside. The giant slumped down against the hatch he'd defended as long as life was in him.

"Stephen, are you all right?" Piet demanded. The bar spun itself clear of bits of bone as he withdrew it. "Did he cut you? Are you all right?"

"I'm not hurt!" Stephen said. "Why do you think—"

As he heard himself speak, he realized for the first time that he was on the floor of the passageway, sprawled across the body of the Fed giant. He'd put every bit of his strength into the fight, and the Fed was still stronger.

"I'm not hurt," Stephen repeated more softly. In a whisper he added, "It's better to have friends than be strong, Piet."

"Venus forward!" Piet shouted. "Wraths to me *now*!"

He took a cutting bar the giant had dropped; the battery of Piet's own must be nearly exhausted from cutting at the airlock, then through the giant's thick faceshield. Piet set the tip of the fresh tool against the 10-by-4-centimeter nickel-steel crossbar that locked the hatch. Leaning his whole weight on the hilt, he worried the cutting bar through in geysers of sparks blazing as the blade flung them into the air.

Stephen got to his feet and unclipped his own bar. It wasn't his weapon of choice, but the rifle was somewhere beneath the giant's body. The bar might do better than a gun in the confined space anyway.

The crossbar fell in pieces. The hatch pivoted inward. Stephen crashed into the control room a step behind Piet.

A Fed sailor threw down her rifle as the armored Venerians burst from the hatchway. An officer struggled up from a console, tangled in the cord of a communications handset while he tried to reach his holstered revolver. He screamed in abject terror as Stephen took two long strides toward him.

Stephen slashed with a skill he probably couldn't have equaled in practice. The cutting bar's tip skidded across the surface of the Fed's breastplate and severed the pistol belt. It didn't touch the man.

The holster clunked to the deck. The Fed leaned forward and began blubbering into his hands.

The bridge crew, six humans and three Molts, made no resistance. The man Stephen had disarmed was the only officer. The Molts were curled into mauve lumps as if preparing to go into suspended animation. Piet, Stephen, and the six men shouldering into the control room behind them looked as out of place as guns among table settings of silver and crystal.

Piet shoved the Fed officer aside, hastily but without brutality, and seated himself at the command console. The sound of fighting on the gun deck had died away; Fed resistance must have broken suddenly. Piet took his gauntlets off and called up an alphanumeric sidebar on the console's panoramic display. Stephen noticed his friend seemed perfectly comfortable working controls in a hard suit when circumstances demanded it.

Stephen picked up the rifle on the deck, then took the sailor's ammunition too by breaking the buckle of her belt. He stepped to the control room's starboard airlock and activated the control. While he waited for the hatches to cycle, he watched the panoramic display.

Until very recently, Federation optronics had been an order of magnitude better than the best available on Venus. That was no longer true at the high end, because Venerian microchip production—and loot—was catching up with the huge pre-Collapse stockpiles the Feds brought back from the Reaches. Nonetheless, the *Holy Office*'s screens gave a crisp, ground-level view of what was happening in Winnipeg's military port.

The administrative offices and barracks were built into the

north wall of the berm. A pole stood before the concrete-pillared entrance, but the flag was a red-and-white tangle on this windless day.

The gunports of the warships that had joined the *Holy Office* in firing on the *Moll Dane* were open but empty at present. Plasma cannon had to cool for several minutes between shots—the interval becoming longer as the bore of the weapon increased. Reloading too quickly risked a detonation of the shell that, because the tritium core wasn't compressed in a programmed sequence, was almost certain to rupture the cannon and kill the crew.

Federation plasma cannon were large-crystal castings of tungsten, stellite, or other heavy metals, and they almost invariably had to be loaded from the muzzle. Venus built ceramic breechloaders that cooled more quickly, particularly in an atmosphere. Although the fighting aboard the *Holy Office* seemed to have gone on forever, the minutes that had actually passed weren't long enough for the Feds to reload their pieces.

In common with most spherical-design vessels, this Fed ship carried the tanks for its reaction mass—water—along the vertical axis. Instead of putting a bolt into the ship's thick hull, Stampfer had aimed the powerful 17-cm gun at the midline hatch the Feds had opened as a fighting position. Smoke and sparks erupted from the hatchway, but the water tank took the bolt's main impact. Steam pistoned the incompressible remaining liquid through ruptured seams, then flooded every deck with searing fog.

Piet lit the *Holy Office*'s thrusters. Exhaust curled in through the airlock. Stephen snapped down the faceshield he didn't remember lifting and stepped to the outer hatchway, searching for targets.

Another of the *Holy Office*'s big guns fired. When the assault force no longer had Fed crewmen to fight, they'd joined Stampfer in running out the starboard battery. The high entrance doors of the headquarters bunker exploded in a rainbow flash. The shock wave shattered the pillars, which bowed outward and collapsed, dragging the triangular pediment with them.

Piet's voice snarled from the vessel's PA system, "Abandon ship! This is Captain Ricimer speaking. All men off the vessel now!''

Crewmen staggered out of the steam wreathing the vessel Stampfer hit first. Stephen aimed at a figure who still carried a weapon. His shot blasted concrete dust ten meters beyond the Fed. This rifle shot 20 centimeters wide to the left at this range, but because of the downward angle Stephen could adjust his aim.

He reloaded the turn-bolt single-shot and fired again. The Fed skidded facedown on the concrete.

The Fed warship near the east berm, six hundred meters from the *Holy Office*, fired a pair of light plasma cannon. One of the bolts struck the stern of the *Holy Office*. Three 17-cm guns answered it, their crackling discharges ringing at four-second intervals through the fabric of the captured warship. Stampfer must have laid all the guns himself. Common sailors couldn't have hammered the same point with such precision.

The flash of the first bolt hitting was white and prismatic; superheated hull metal blazed in the atmosphere. The second bolt, striking an instant after the initial fireball had lifted from a basin-sized hole in the hull, spent its energy inside the vessel. Flames—red, orange, and streaked with plumes of white smoke at high pressure—engulfed the warship's second deck level.

If the Feds had had the time and the inclination to set up their vessel's internal compartmentalization, the third round wouldn't have added anything to the damage the immediately previous bolt had caused. People act hastily in crises. Not all the companionway hatches were dogged shut, and few of the floor-to-ceiling baffles had been raised to prevent an explosion from involving an entire deck.

Plasma from the third round blew flaming gas and debris into every chamber of the Federation vessel. Gunports flapped outward, spewing black smoke and occasionally parts of Fed crewmen. A ready-use magazine of plasma shells went off on the midline deck. Iridescent flame gouged away the sides of the openings through which it streamed. The vessel settled slightly as white-hot structural members lost strength.

"Abandon ship!" Piet's voice ordered. "Abandon ship! All Wraths out of the military port *now*!"

A *fourth running figure*. Stephen killed him. It was a Molt and unarmed when the hot fog cleared momentarily about the body an instant after the shot. Stephen stepped back from the hatch to draw another cartridge from the ammo belt.

He and Piet were the only Venerians still in the control room. The Fed officer and the three Molts—upright now but motionless—stood against the port bulkhead. Stephen glanced through the passageway aft. As far as he could tell, Stampfer and the rest of the assault force had abandoned ship as ordered.

The thrusters roared at full output, though the flared nozzles spread the ions in a billowing sheet across the ground instead of lifting the *Holy Office*. Exhaust puffed through the open airlock, blinding Stephen momentarily with its brilliance. He backed another step from the hatch.

Piet keyed in a complex series of commands, then rose from the console and drew on his gauntlets. The port airlock started to open, forcing two of the Molts to move.

"Stephen!" Piet said in surprise. "Come on, we've got to get out before the ship lifts. I programmed it to crash into the freighters on the west berm!"

"And them?" Stephen said, waving to the prisoners who hadn't fled aft with their fellows.

"Get out!" Piet shouted. "We're going to crash!"

The three Molts turned and leaped into the sea of radiance, one at a time. Though they jumped as far as they could, they were well within the bath of ions when they hit the ground. The bodies shriveled and burned like figures of straw.

"I'll follow you, Piet," Stephen said. He dropped the rifle and grabbed the Fed officer around the waist.

Piet looked momentarily doubtful, but he latched down his visor and jumped from the hatch. The *Holy Office* shook itself like a dog just risen from the water. The nozzle irises were closing, restricting the flow to boost thrust.

Stephen, clasping the screaming officer tightly, took three running steps and leaped from the lip of the outer hatch. Exhaust pulsed around him. His boots hit the concrete two meters below. He skidded but kept his footing, thrusting the

Fed out as a balance weight. He kept running until he hit the inner face of the berm.

The Fed's uniform smoldered and his exposed skin was already beginning to blister, but he was alive. For the moment, he was alive.

Which was the most anyone could say, after all.

WINNIPEG SPACEPORT, EARTH.

Sal grasped a wrist-thick tree growing between a pair of the concrete slabs covering the berm. She reached down to take Brantling's good hand, his left, while Tom Harrigan pushed the injured sailor from below.

The berm sloped at 45°, a steeper climb than Brantling could handle at the moment. There was a flight of broad steps fifty meters away, but they were crowded with exhausted men in hard suits carrying their weapons and their casualties. Sal and her flight crew would have risked jostling and worse if they'd tried to leave the military port by that route. The assault force had expended too much physical and emotional energy in its brief fight to be careful now.

"Thanks, Cap'n Blythe," Brantling muttered as Sal half helped, half dragged him past her to get a grip and then a foothold on the tree. Her breath rasped. Four meters of 1:1 slope didn't seem especially difficult until you tried to climb it when you were wrung-out emotionally.

Guillermo perched like a gargoyle on the berm's broad top. He took Brantling's hand for what help he could offer.

The flight crew had been forgotten as soon as the *Moll Dane* landed. Nobody informed them of what was happening, nobody even thought about Sal and her men aboard the crumpled freighter. The assault preparations had been sudden and *ad hoc*. Even Sal hadn't thought about what she was supposed to do when and if she survived landing.

Sal had never before felt so completely abandoned.

The note of the *Holy Office*'s thrusters changed, sharpened. Sal looked over her shoulder as the vessel lifted min-

215

usculely from the concrete. The nozzle irises were tightening down. An armored figure leaped from the cockpit airlock, stumbled in the iridescent hellfire, and trotted out of the exhaust corona. A second, heavier figure followed. The *Holy Office* began to skitter forward like a chunk of sodium dropped on a still pond.

"I've got it," Harrigan said, ignoring Sal's offered hand to zigzag leftward instead. His toes had found purchase between two of the facing slabs. Sal got a foot against the tree trunk and flopped belly-down on top of the berm.

The *Holy Office* gained speed gradually as it crossed the military port in hops of ten, twenty, fifty meters. Each time the unmanned vessel tilted enough to lose ground effect, the skid on the lower side brushed sparklingly along the concrete. The ship lifted again, tacking slightly toward that contact, and touched on the opposite skid. Sarah Blythe had no false modesty regarding her own piloting skills, but she could never have programmed an artificial intelligence to carry out the maneuver she was watching.

Harrigan, thinking the same thing, said, "There's somebody at the controls."

"Captain Ricimer *was* at the controls, Mister Harrigan," Guillermo responded with quiet pride.

Three great spherical freighters from the Reaches trade stood three hundred meters apart along the west edge of the port. The *Holy Office* struck the nearest, an 800-tonner, a glancing blow low on the starboard side. The shrieking contact continued deafeningly for several seconds. The warship caromed off the larger merchantman and swapped ends twice before it smashed broadside into the 1,200-tonne giant north of the initial target.

This time the noise was like that of planets colliding. Both the *Holy Office* and the merchantman had thick hulls, but the kinetic energy of the impact was of astronomical level. The surfaces of nickel-steel plates vaporized and the frame members behind them compressed like putty.

A plasma motor, its nozzle sealed by the 20 centimeters of tough plating rammed into it, became a fusion bomb. The flash seemed to transfuse solid metal. Remnants of the *Holy Office*, half the stern to one side and fragments that had been part of the bow to the other, blew back in a ravening white glare. The four upper decks of the exploding freighter lifted as a piece, flattening as they rose.

A munitions explosion, slighter than the first but cataclysmic nonetheless, gushed red flame from the center of the inferno. The top of the vessel flipped sideways. It struck the ground and carved a trench twenty meters deep through the concrete, then sheared into the remaining freighter.

The third vessel was pinned between the anvil of the berm and the upper half of the 1,200-tonner, a hammer more massive than the *Holy Office* had been when complete. Steam and fire engulfed the site. Slabs shook from the berm hundreds of meters away, and a pall of dust lifted from the surface of the port.

No skill could have planned a result so destructive. "Maybe God does fight for Venus," Sal whispered, though her mind couldn't find much of God in what she had just watched. She'd spent her life carrying cargoes, and shipwreck was the greatest disaster she could imagine.

Below Sal, two men in hard suits staggered toward the stairway. The gilded armor, now scoured and defaced by the plasma bath, was Piet Ricimer's.

Piet kept his right gauntlet against the berm to guide him where he didn't trust his eyes. His left hand gripped the right gauntlet of the bigger man, who held what looked like a bindle of smoking fabric.

Stephen was still alive, but at this moment Sal had only intellect left to be glad of the fact. The earthshaking thumps of further destruction blurred even that.

"That'll teach them not to mess with Venus, won't it, Mister Harrigan?" Brantling crowed. "We fed them the sharp end this time!"

"Aye, by God we did," Tom Harrigan said in guttural triumph. "We've singed President Pleyal's beard, we have!"

Across the port, three ships that could have supplied a large colony for a year blazed in devouring glory.

ISHTAR CITY, VENUS.

JUNE 6, YEAR 27.
0331 HOURS, VENUS TIME.

Sal opened the door with exaggerated care, stepped into the front room of the apartment she shared with her father, and closed the door on her fingers. "Christ's bleeding wounds!" she shouted before she remembered she was trying not to disturb Marcus.

Marcus Blythe lurched upright on the divan where he'd been dozing. "Sal?" he called. He turned up the table lamp from a vague glow to full brightness.

"Sorry, Dad," Sal said. "I didn't mean to . . ."

She shook her head in puzzlement, trying to remember what it was she'd meant to say. "Look, why don't you go off to bed now, Dad?"

"Here, you sit down," Marcus said. He tossed off the sheet covering him, then rose from the divan by shifting his torso forward and catching himself with his cane before he fell back. "I'll scramble some eggs for you. You always liked my eggs, didn't you, Sallie?"

"Dad, I'm not . . ." Sal muttered. *Maybe I'm hungry after all.* Her legs weren't working right, certainly. She flopped into the straight-backed chair by the little table. She teetered for a moment but didn't fall over.

"Some food will be good, Sallie," Marcus said as he shuffled into the kitchenette adjacent to the front room. "Don't I know it. I've had my nights out partying too, you know."

Sal moved the lamp, certain that Marcus' bottle was on the other side of it. There was no bottle on the table. She frowned and bent over to see if the liquor was on the floor

218

beside the divan. There wouldn't be much left, of course,
but . . .

No bottle on the floor either.

"Ferlinghetti at the Fiddler's Green was saying the Southern ship your squadron captured was as rich a prize as any
Captain Ricimer ever brought back," Marcus said. Eggs
spattered on hot grease.

"Richer than that," Sal said absently. "Where's your bottle, Dad?"

They'd stumbled into the *Mae do Deus* on Callisto, where
the crew had attempted to conceal their 2,000-tonne monster
when they heard Piet Ricimer was out with a squadron. The
vessel had been one of the largest merchantmen of the Southern Cross before President Pleyal's coup de main six years
before absorbed what had been a separate nation into the
North American Federation.

"Ah, you know, Sallie dearest, I'm not sure there *is* a
bottle in the apartment," her father said in brittle cheeriness.
"I'll have to pick something up, won't I?"

"What d'ye mean, there's no bottle?" Sal shouted. She
stood halfway up, lost her balance, and sat back down with
a crash that jolted her spine all the way to the base of her
skull.

Marcus' fork clinked busily against the pan, stirring in the
spices and pepper sauce. "Fullerenes from the Mirrorside,"
he said as if he hadn't heard his daughter. "Worth more than
microchips are, Ferlinghetti says."

"You bet," Sal agreed morosely. "A captain's share of
what we took from the *Mae* . . . I'm a rich girl, Daddy. Your
little Sal is rich, rich, rich."

She reached into the right-hand pocket of her loose tunic
and brought out a liter bottle of amber Terran whiskey. It
was nearly full. She couldn't remember how it had gotten
there.

"*Sing praises to our God and king . . .*" Sal warbled, trying to open the bottle. After three failures, she squinted carefully and saw that the bottle had a screw cap instead of the
plug stopper she was used to.

Marcus lifted the pan and scraped eggs onto a serving
plate. "Ah, Sal?" he said nervously. "I thought that tonight

you might, you know, have something to eat and go to bed. Instead of stay—''

"Who the hell are you to think anything, you damned old drunk?" Sal shouted. She stood up. The chair overset in one direction and the table in another. "I'll go to sleep when I'm damned—''

The lamp with a bubble-thin shade the color of a monarch butterfly's wing was Venerian ceramic. It hit the floor and bounced, chiming in several keys but undamaged. The glass bottle from Earth shattered in a spray of liquor.

"Oh, the bastards," Sal said. Her body swayed. "Oh, the dirty bastards."

Marcus scuffled across the room and embraced her. "Let's have a little something to eat, Sallie my love," he said. "You like my eggs, don't you, dear?"

"It'd be all right if I'd seen his face before I shot him," Sal whispered as she hugged her father.

"Sallie?" Marcus said.

"On Arles," she said, thinking she was explaining. "Every night he comes to me and he's a different face. I could take one, that'd be, that'd be . . . But he's different every night, and then *mush*. Red mush, dad. One after another and then they die."

"Oh, Sallie," Marcus said. "Oh, my little baby girl."

Sal shuddered and drew herself upright. "That's all right, Dad," she said. "I appreciate the trouble you took, but I'm going out for a bit, I think. I'll be back, you know, later."

"Sal, *please* don't go out again tonight," Marcus pleaded.

Captain Sarah Blythe, heroine of Venus' struggle against Federation tyranny, closed the door behind her. The night clerk at the baths usually had a bottle under his counter.

BETAPORT, VENUS.

"What do you think of them, Gregg?" said Alexi Mostert, gesturing as he shouted over the echoing racket of the New Dock. "All three of them as handy as the *Wrath*, and their scantlings just as sturdy."

"We've spread the nozzle clusters," Siddons Mostert added from Stephen's other side. "Another ten centimeters between adjacent thrusters to improve hover performance."

The vessels in the three nearest cradles were purpose-built warships; like the *Wrath*, as even Stephen could see, but the finer points of construction were as much beyond his capacity to judge as they were outside his interests. It was inconceivable that the Mostert brothers had invited him here to talk about scantlings and hover performance.

"Ships are things that I ride on, gentlemen," Stephen said dryly. "I'm sure Piet would be delighted to discuss the way the *Wrath* handled, if you want to talk with him."

The twenty-odd ships fitting out in the gigantic New Dock were either state-owned or under contract to the governor's forces. Access to the dock was limited for fear of sabotage. A platoon of black-armored Governor's Guards at the entrance checked the sailors, workmen, and carters flowing into New Dock at all hours, and there were parties of armed men aboard each vessel.

Stephen suspected that the guards were a psychological exercise thought up by Councilor Duneen or another of the governor's close advisors rather than a response to real concerns. Through the guards' presence, Governor Halys said to the people of Venus, "The Federation threat is real and im-

221

minent, and the sacrifices you will shortly be called on to make are justified."

The governor was right about the threat, at least. Stephen Gregg, who knew as much about sacrifice as the next person, would have been uncomfortable urging it on anyone else.

"Yes, Factor Ricimer is a marvelous sailor, isn't he?" Siddons said. "And marvelously lucky as well. Snapping up the *Mae do Deus* like that!"

Siddons was a tall, slightly hunched man with the solemn mien of a preacher. He was the elder brother by two years and looked considerably older than that, although the close-coupled Alexi had spent far more of his life in the hardships and deprivations of long voyages. Alexi Mostert continued to lead an occasional argosy even now that he'd been appointed Chief Constructor of the Fleet.

"If you call that luck," Stephen said with a cold smile. "Piet interviewed prisoners at Winnipeg and learned the ship was already overdue. He calculated her back-course and plotted the locations where her captain might lay up if he learned the Earth Approaches were too risky."

"Ah," Alexi said, nodding in understanding.

"Very simple in hindsight, isn't it, gentlemen?" Stephen said. "Good preparation often makes a task look easy."

"I think back to the days we were shipmates, Piet and I," Alexi said with forced heartiness. "And you too, Gregg. We paid a price, we did, but it was worth it for Venus' sake! There's bigger things than any one man."

Stephen looked at Mostert and shrugged. Alexi Mostert had lost all his teeth while starving on a hellish voyage back from the Reaches, where the Feds had ambushed what was meant to be a peaceful trading expedition. There'd been fifteen survivors out of more than a hundred men crammed aboard a ship that was damaged escaping.

"I don't know what anything's worth, Mostert," Stephen said.

He realized the statement wasn't true even as the words came out of his mouth. Things were worth what somebody was willing to pay for them. That was the first rule of business. Though . . . Stephen wasn't sure that he, or Alexi, or even Piet had paid the prices they did for anything as abstract as "Venus."

"I was wondering," Siddons Mostert said, pausing to clear his throat. "I was wondering who Factor Ricimer thinks the governor should appoint commander of our fleet when Pleyal attacks. Eh, Gregg?"

"I think you ought to ask Piet about that, Mostert," Stephen said. "If you really think it's any of your business."

He heard the edge in his voice. That shouldn't bother anyone who knew him, though it might worry the Mosterts. Friends knew that Stephen Gregg spoke in a musical lilt when he was determining who to kill first.

An electric-powered tractor, its transmission whining in compound low as it dragged three wagons filled with cannon shells, would pass close enough to brush the trio of men. Stephen walked forward, toward the warship looming in its cradle overhead. The legend inlaid in violet porcelain on her bow was GOVERNOR HALYS. There were at least six state or state-hired vessels named that or simply *Halys*, which would be at best confusing in the fleet actions everyone expected.

"Ah, it could be rather awkward, Gregg," Siddons said. He stood looking up at the *Governor Halys*, his neck at the same angle as Stephen's. "It's possible that the governor might feel that she had to appoint someone of a, an older factorial family to the position. Factor Ricimer might think his merits should overcome any question of his birth. Eh?"

"If the governor wants to know Piet's opinion . . ." Stephen said. His words were ordered as precisely as cartridges in a repeater's magazine. ". . . then she should ask him the next time he visits the mansion. I gather he's invited at least once a week when he's on Venus."

"Yes, but—" Alexi said.

"Listen to me, Mostert," Stephen interrupted. "If you brought me here to ask what Piet's opinion on this thing or that thing might be, then I'm going to go off and get a drink and we can all stop wasting our time."

Alexi Mostert turned sideways to face Stephen squarely. He crossed his hands behind his back and said, "All right, Gregg. What's your opinion of someone other than Factor Ricimer being appointed Commander of the Fleet?"

Stephen looked at the burly older man. He'd known Alexi Mostert for more than a decade. Stephen had shipped out to the Reaches for the first time aboard a vessel of the Mostert Trading Company. Though acquaintances rather than friends, they'd been through harsh times together just as Alexi said, in battle and in its aftermath.

"This is official business, isn't it?" Stephen said. "Somebody's afraid that I might kill anybody who was put in charge of the fleet over Piet's head? Yes?"

Behind him, Siddons Mostert choked. Alexi, standing with as much stiff dignity as his build and years allowed, said, "Well, since the question's come up, Gregg—how would you answer it?"

Stephen stared at Mostert. The older man, though obviously frightened, met his gaze. On all Venus, there were only a few men—and one woman—who could have ordered the Mostert brothers to ask the question that Alexi had just put.

"Since I'm being consulted as an expert," Stephen said in a cool, businesslike tone, "let's consider the general situation first. The governor *has* to appoint someone whose ancestors were factors back to before the Collapse. Otherwise every gentleman in the fleet will be squabbling over precedence. We'll kill more of ourselves in duels than we will Feds in battle."

Alexi let out a deep breath, nodding approvingly.

"I'm aware of that, and I'm sure Piet's aware of it," Stephen continued. "And I assure you, Piet wants Federation tyranny broken more than he wants honors for himself"— Stephen grinned coldly—"much though he wants honors for himself."

"And has earned them, nobody more," Siddons Mostert said effusively. "I think there may have been concern that political necessities might have been viewed as an insult to Factor Ricimer, when nothing could be farther from the truth."

A crane traveling in a trackway built into the dock's ceiling rumbled slowly past, carrying a tank of reaction mass. Drops of condensate fell from the outside of the tank like a linear rain shower. One of them plucked Stephen's right cuff.

"You asked me here to have this meeting," Stephen said,

looking up at the huge water tank, "because of the armed guards, isn't that right? In case I flew hot and decided to kill you."

"It was my idea," Siddons admitted miserably. "Alexi said it wouldn't make any difference if, if you . . ."

Stephen laughed. "Oh, that's true enough to take to the bank, yes," he said.

Ten meters away, an officer in half armor looked bored. Two sailors chatted with their shotguns leaning against a pile of crates in a cargo net beside them. Stephen could have both guns before the guards realized he was taking them; though it would be much easier to grip a Mostert by the throat in either hand and batter their heads together until there was nothing left to break.

Stephen smiled.

"I've never been unwilling to do my duty to Venus and the governor, Gregg," Alexi Mostert said, standing stiff again. For all the words were as pompous as the old spacer looked in his present pose, they were basically the truth. There'd never been a lack of folk on Venus willing to sacrifice themselves for a cause they thought worthy.

"For what it's worth," Stephen said, nodding to Siddons, "I've never killed anybody just because I was angry. I've killed them for less reason, killed them because they were available and I was putting the fear of God into my general surroundings at the time. But never because I was angry."

"You've always been a loyal citizen of Venus, Mister Gregg," Siddons Mostert said. "Nobody doubts your patriotism."

"I'm not a patriot, Mostert," Stephen said. "Sometimes I've been a friend, though. It can amount to the same thing."

He bowed formally to the brothers. "I'm going to get a drink, since I believe we've covered our business, yes?"

"Yes, that's right," Alexi said. "Ah—we're heading for dinner, Siddons and I. If you'd like to come . . ."

Stephen shook his head, smiling. "Just a drink," he said. His expression shifted, though it would have been hard to say precisely which muscles tensed or slackened to make such a horrible change. "You know," he said, "sometimes

I think the only time I'm alive is when I'm killing somebody. Funny, isn't it?''

Siddons Mostert stood with a frozen smile. Alexi, very slowly, shook his head.

HELDENSBURG.

The wind across the starport was gusty and strong, but it blew directly from Sal, leaning out of the cabin airlock, to the nearest of the forts. The flag of United Europe, sixteen stars on a green field, was only an occasional flap of bunting from behind the pole.

The fort and the three others like it on the margins of the field each had firing slits and a garrison of fifty or so human soldiers as well as heavy, ship-smashing plasma cannon. The troops looked bored as they watched starships from the walls of the position, but their personal weapons were always nearby.

Those were the sorts of details Sal had learned to consider since she started voyaging beyond Pluto.

"All right, lift her, but *easy*!" Tom Harrigan ordered.

Winches on the *Gallant Sallie* and the port operations lowboy took the first strain together. The ceramic turbine for a city-sized plasma power plant would have been a marginal load for either crane alone, especially at the full extension necessary to transfer it from hold to trailer. When the cables took the weight, the turbine skidded toward the hatchway. Brantling slowly let out slack while the Heldensburg operator reeled the load toward the lowboy at the same rate.

Wueppertal, the operations manager assigned to the *Gallant Sallie*, nodded approvingly from beside Harrigan. "Wueppertal?" Sal called. "What's the word on our return cargo?"

The Heldensburg official looked around and walked closer to the hatch. The turbine was balanced now. Brantling paid

227

out more cable, allowing the other operator to draw the load over the bed of the lowboy.

Wueppertal patted the two-way radio hooked to his belt. "They've located the rest of the chips, Captain," he said. "It was an inventory error, somebody entering two crates when it should have been eleven. We'll have them out to you yet this evening, after we've off-loaded the rest of your cargo."

The microchips Sal was contracted to carry back to Paris-Ouest on Earth were newly manufactured on a Near Space colony of the Independent Coastal Republic. Heldensburg produced very little itself, but in the past ten years it had become a major transit point for Near Space trade.

Heldensburg's powerful defenses were an important attraction, but it wasn't only captains concerned about Pleyal's claimed monopoly on trade beyond Pluto who called here. The ship nearest to the *Gallant Sallie* was a Federation vessel. Molt crew members had pulled several attitude jets and were polishing them on a workbench under the desultory supervision of a boyish-looking human officer.

"Do you have many Feds here?" Sal asked, trying to keep the disapproval out of her voice.

Wueppertal waved a hand. "About a third of our traffic," he said. "Look, their credit drafts spend just the same as yours. If we didn't have those guns"—a nod toward the nearby fort—"then I'd worry, sure. But we do."

"Yes . . ." Sal said. She might have let the subject drop, but she hadn't been sleeping well for too long. "Heldensburg's too tough a nut for Pleyal to crack, now. But if it weren't for the trouble Venus has been causing him these past ten years, he'd have crushed you all like bugs before you got properly settled."

The turbine settled onto the lowboy. The trailer's suspension compressed a good 10 centimeters before the winch cables slackened.

A spherical 600-tonne merchantman was discharging grain into a series of hopper cars. From details of its design, Sal guessed the vessel was from the Federation. The Feds were drawn here by the variety of available cargoes, just as the other traders were. The fact that those cargoes depended on plasma cannon to keep President Pleyal's warships away was an irony of human existence.

"Oh, there's something to be said for a guy like Pleyal," Wueppertal said with the same tone of almost-challenge that Sal had heard in her own voice. "He knows what order is and he's not afraid to enforce it. Commandant La Fouche said just last week in staff meeting that there's other places that could use a little discipline of the sort."

"We'll give Pleyal discipline, all right," Tom Harrigan said, wandering over to the forward hatch now that the loading operation was complete. "He'll try to clamp down on Venus, and we'll go through his fleet like shit through a goose."

"You think that?" Wueppertal said. He was a smallish man, dark-haired but with brilliant blue eyes.

"I know that," the mate said. "Why, the man who owns this ship, Mister Gregg—that's *Stephen* Gregg, Wueppertal—"

"*Co*-owns the *Gallant Sallie*, Harrigan," Sal said in a crisp voice.

"Sure, co-owns," Harrigan agreed. "I've seen him clear a Fed warship single-handed—and that in a Fed port! And brought us back rich, too. Why, there's Dock Street ladies who bought country seats from what they made off sailors come back from Winnipeg and Callisto!"

Sal thought of the slaughter, of the columns of smoke rising from Winnipeg Spaceport as the *Gallant Sallie* lifted. She didn't say anything to the men standing below her.

Wueppertal's eyes narrowed. "You know Colonel Gregg?" he said.

Tom Harrigan nodded. "Let me tell you," he said. "When we hopped the *Moll Dane* into the military port at Winnipeg, Mister Gregg was as close to me as you are now. Captain Blythe was piloting"—Wueppertal's eyes followed Tom's nod under a frown of disbelief—"and Mister Gregg was right there with us, and Factor Ricimer too. Don't I have the scars?"

Harrigan bent his head and ran an index finger over the ridged pink-and-white keloid on his scalp. He straightened and continued forcefully, "Listen! When it comes to real war, we'll whip the Feds right back to Montreal, and we'll do it because God's on our side. Factor Ricimer preaches God like nobody you've heard in chapel of a Sunday, and Mister Gregg—he's the Wrath of God, he is!''

Sal thought of the Stephen Gregg she knew. Her eyes were on the distant horizon, and her expression was as hard as cast iron.

The stevedores had completed tying the turbine firmly onto the trailer bed. One of the men called, ''Hey, Hymie!'' and waved to Wueppertal. ''You want us to go on back now?''

Wueppertal said, ''Hang on, I'll ride with you!'' To Harrigan and Sal he added, ''I'll make sure they've got the chips ready to go. The sort of screwups they got running Warehouse Four, they're as likely to be piling more crates on top of yours as they are to be loading them onto trucks.''

Harrigan sat on the topmost of the three steps from the hatch to the ground, watching the tractor and lowboy head toward the complex of low warehouses west of the field. ''Paris and then home, Sal?'' he asked.

Sal shrugged. The gesture was pointless since the mate wasn't looking at her. ''Maybe home,'' she said. ''There may be a load of desalinization equipment ready for carriage to Drottingholm. Europe and the Coasties have set up a joint colony there.''

A starship was landing almost precisely in line with the morning sun. Harrigan took a filter from his breast pocket and used it to view the ship through the double glare. ''A big one,'' he remarked idly. ''Shouldn't wonder if it was another Fed.''

He turned his head to look up at Sal. ''We've been lucky with cargoes, you know,'' he said. ''Short layovers and almost never lifting empty. Sure a change from the old days.''

''It's a change, but it's not luck,'' Sal replied sharply. ''Mister Gregg's making the arrangements. Balancing cargoes, setting up credit lines—judging who'll need something and who can pay for it.''

She flicked an index finger in the direction of the lowboy, now halfway to the warehouses. ''These power plants. Stephen—Mister Gregg—he set up the whole deal. All the principals had to do was sign the agreement he offered them! We're getting the haulage fees, but buyer and seller both are gaining a lot more from the deal than we are.''

"Who'd have thought it?" Harrigan said. "A man like Mister Gregg, and he's a merchant besides!"

The thrusters of the ship in its landing approach braked at maximum output, bellowing across the starport at a level that forbade speech.

Who would have thought it? Gregg of Weyston was one of the largest intrasystem shippers on Venus. It shouldn't surprise anyone that his nephew would have an equal flair for the complexities of trade.

It wouldn't have surprised those who knew Stephen Gregg before he first voyaged to the Reaches and defeated everything he found there except his own human soul.

And very nearly his soul as well.

BETAPORT, VENUS.

JULY 12, YEAR 27.
1658 HOURS, VENUS TIME.

Originally Dock Street had been the route by which starships were hauled between the transfer docks, whose domes slid open for takeoffs and landings, and the storage docks where vessels were refitted between voyages. New routes and docks had been built to suit the ever-larger ships operating from Betaport, but Dock Street remained a broad, high-roofed corridor and the center of nautical affairs in a city built on star travel.

Guild marshals were trying to keep the crowd back from the red carpet laid for the occasion. They had their work cut out for them, especially here near the train station where the dignitaries were gathered. The station itself was ringed by men who were something more than an "honor" guard: the *Wrath*'s B Watch close-combat team. Today the Wraths carried batons rather than shotguns and cutting bars, but Dole had told them what they could expect if anybody jostled Commander Bruckshaw.

Dole saw Stephen blocked by a press of citizens who'd overwhelmed the guild marshals. "Make a path for Mister Gregg, you whoresons!" the bosun shouted.

Stephen forced a smile. He was as tense as a trigger with only the last gram of take-up remaining. He'd been raised in Eryx, his family's small keep on the Atalanta Plains. Space was at a premium, but there weren't enough people in the entire community to constitute a crowd by Betaport standards.

Stephen's instincts were all wrong for a mob of people like this. Unless of course the folk around him had been hostile, in which case he could have cleared a path very quickly indeed.

The sailors in the crowd were already dodging away when the *Wrath*'s men strode forward. Some countrymen from the surrounding region, come to town for the event, would be lucky if nothing was dislocated; and the wife of one got a baton where she probably hadn't expected it. Dole waggled a horny fist in salute to Stephen as he passed the gentleman through.

Piet Ricimer had turned from the group of town and guild officials inside the station when he heard the shout. "Stephen?" he said. He blinked in pleased wonder. "Stephen!"

"I went to the tailor my uncle recommended in Ishtar City," Stephen said in embarrassment. "He decided brighter colors would 'soften the image,' as he put it. I feel like an idiot."

Piet laughed melodiously. "Nothing in this world or the next is going to make you look soft, my friend," he said. "But you look very striking indeed."

When Stephen Gregg consulted an expert, he abided by the expert's advice; a courtesy he expected from others when they asked *his* advice. Today he wore crimson tights with canary yellow sleeves, matching yellow boots, and a helmet and breastplate of copper/uranium alloy that shimmered purple.

The only part of the outfit he'd refused was the holstered pistol. "Just for show," the court tailor had explained.

Stephen didn't wear weapons just for show.

Piet squeezed his elbow. "Glad you made it," he said. "I'd hate to greet Councilor Bruckshaw without my right arm present."

Air rammed hissing through the station ahead of the train warned of the Councilor's arrival. Intercommunity travel on Venus had been by subsurface electric trains as far back as the first pre-Collapse colonies.

Within communities—even Ishtar City, the largest by far, with a population climbing above 200,000 souls in the past decade—people walked. Corridors cut with difficulty through the planetary crust were too narrow for vehicular traffic. Wealthy folk who thought to ignore the laws as a form of ostentation found themselves overturned within minutes. The mob accepted class distinctions, but it had a firm grasp also of the distinction between citizen and slave.

The train sighed to a halt, then settled with a *clackclack-clack* onto the rail as power to the suspension magnets was cut. The double doors sprang open for Councilor Duneen and Councilor Bruckshaw, Commander of the Fleet, to step onto the platform together.

Staff members, ordered by precedence, walked behind their chiefs in more-than-military order. Each councilor had a good dozen folk in his entourage. The first man out of the train behind Duneen was Jeremy Moore, Factor Moore of Rhadicund, and an old shipmate of Piet and Stephen.

Piet strode forward and made a full bow. "Councilors," he said, "you honor Betaport with your presence. Please permit me and the chief men of our community to guide you to your destination."

With Stephen to his right and the Betaport magnates falling in behind, Piet Ricimer walked out of the train station. Four of the *Wrath*'s men led the procession. Dole and the remainder of the team walked along beside the dignitaries, enfolding them the way a magazine follower does the spring that drives it.

A cheer greeted Piet and Stephen. When the councilors came out of the station a moment later, a claque of carefully briefed sailors bellowed, "*Long life to Commander Bruckshaw! Long life to Commander Bruckshaw!*"

Piet leaned close to Stephen's ear and whispered, "After this, I don't think the commander will doubt the loyal willingness of Betaport to accept the decisions of Governor Halys."

"I don't think he'll doubt the loyalty of Betaport's first citizen, either," Stephen whispered in reply. "How do you like the red carpet?"

"*Long life to Commander Bruckshaw!*" The whole crowd had taken up the chant. The guards from the *Wrath* made sure that each new blockful of spectators knew what to shout as the honored visitors approached.

"Excellent quality," Piet said. "I wasn't expecting anything more than a roll of cloth. How much do I owe you?"

Stephen chuckled. "I pointed out to Haskins of Haskins
Furnishings that he could double the new price to every social climber in Beta Regio—and *I* wasn't going to make sure
he didn't sell somebody a piece that the governor's closest
advisors hadn't really stepped on. The use is free, Piet."

"Where would I be without you, Stephen?" Piet murmured. His smile drooped slightly, unintentionally.

"Long life to Commander Bruckshaw!"

It was seven blocks from the train station to the Blue Rose
Tavern across from the transfer docks. The tavern had been
Piet Ricimer's unofficial headquarters since the days he was
an ambitious teenager, mate on an intrasystem trader.

The first wealth from Piet's successful voyages had bought
him a ship of his own, but the next stage of his climb was
Betaport real estate. He'd bought the ground lease of the
Blue Rose before even buying a house for himself. The front
room was still a working tavern, but the back and upper floor
of the building had become the center of Betaport's operations against President Pleyal and those who would support
his tyranny.

Piet had raised a meter-high temporary dais in front of the
Blue Rose. He paused at the steps, bowed again, and gestured
the governor's councilors to precede him onto it. The Wraths
made sure that none of the Betaport magnates tried to increase their dignity by hopping up with the three principals.
As for the councilors' staff members—many of them courtiers of high rank themselves—Stephen Gregg stood at the
base of the steps, grinning, and no one at all tried to push
past him.

"People of Betaport!" Commander Bruckshaw said. He
had a high, reedy voice, which nonetheless carried well
across the packed street. "Free citizens of Venus!"

The immediate crowd quieted. The sough of folk more
distant, chopped to verbal silage by the twists and corners of
the corridors, continued as it always did in the cities of Venus.

"I appreciate the honor her excellency the governor did
in appointing me commander of her fleet," Bruckshaw continued, "as I appreciate the honor you have done me on my
arrival. I know as well as you do that there's a great deal I

have yet to learn about crushing the tyrant Pleyal's minions in space, however.''

Bruckshaw had an ascetically handsome face. The commander didn't look to be a terribly dynamic personality, but there was no lack of firmness and authority in his countenance. Not only was he a cousin to Governor Halys, members of Bruckshaw's direct lineage had in their own right been powerful figures on Venus for all the thousand years since the Collapse.

''I know also that there are no folk better able to teach me how to pay out the Federation than the sailors of Betaport can,'' Bruckshaw said, ''and the—''

The roar of bloodthirsty triumph from the crowd drowned even the thought of intelligible speech. Bruckshaw and Duneen smiled; Piet Ricimer beamed like a floodlight on the people of the community that raised him.

Bruckshaw raised both hands for silence, still smiling. When the cheers muted to a dull rumble he resumed. ''The sailors of Betaport, and the greatest space captain of all time, Factor Ricimer of Porcelain!''

The roar this time made even the previous cheers seem puny. Only the hoarseness of minutes of unrestrained shouting brought the silence for which the commander gestured again.

''In appreciation of Factor Ricimer's unequaled skills and his former services to the Free State of Venus...'' Bruckshaw said.

He paused. Councilor Duneen stepped forward, holding a box inlaid with wood and nacre imported to Venus at obvious expense. Duneen opened the case. Bruckshaw removed a necklace from which depended a porcelain medallion in the form of Venus seen in partial eclipse: Governor Halys' crest.

''... I have appointed Factor Ricimer as my deputy commander,'' Bruckshaw said, draping the necklace over Piet's head. ''He will be my closest advisor, as he has been for so many years the greatest enemy of Federation tyranny!''

The three men on the dais raised their hands together, Piet between the two councilors. They ducked quickly and slipped into the Blue Rose to plan the defeat of the Federation armada that would surely destroy Venus as a free society if they failed.

As Stephen Gregg followed the chiefs through the familiar door of the Blue Rose, he wondered if President Pleyal's officers had ever heard a sound to compare with the cheering. The walls of living rock trembled to the roar.

BETAPORT, VENUS.

JULY 12, YEAR 27.
1741 HOURS, VENUS TIME.

The upper floor of the Blue Rose had originally been four two-room apartments whose tenants sublet space to sailors in port who could afford better accommodation than a flophouse. Folk on Venus lived tightly together, and starship crews were used to living tighter still.

Piet had knocked out the internal divisions, save for two pillars of living rock where the load-bearing crosswall had been. The area had become working quarters for the part of the Ricimer household whose duties involved the still-undeclared war against President Pleyal, with the desks, files, and communications equipment necessary for that task.

Normally Piet conducted business, including conferences, in the back room of the tavern's lower floor. That comfortable, familiar chamber was full when a dozen men were present and packed by twenty. For this meeting, bringing together Governor Halys' representatives with the most experienced of the captains who would command her fleet, Piet needed the volume of the tavern's upper floor.

Stephen looked around the room with a critical eye and decided that Piet's staff had done a creditable job with the makeover. There hadn't been time to tile the bare rock walls. Instead, tapestries covered the scars and scribbles of centuries of occupation by spacers and leaseholders who were themselves only a handsbreadth above poverty.

The hangings were eclectic in style and materials. Batiks and thickly woven wools imported from Earth hung beside Venerian synthetics, and there were even a few Molt designs identifiable by odd color contrasts and recurrent pentagonal motifs. Piet had scoured the wealthy households of Betaport to meet the sudden requirement for wall coverings.

The mélange shouldn't have worked together, but it somehow did. The chamber had a barbaric power that well symbolized the strength of Venus against the imposed uniformity of President Pleyal and his North American Federation.

There were many assembly rooms in Ishtar City that could have contained the gathering without difficulty. Commander Bruckshaw had chosen the Blue Rose Tavern to underline implicitly what he had said from the dais: it was due to Betaport sailors that Venus could claim to be a rival to the North American Federation, rather than merely a backwater to be overwhelmed (as the Southern Cross had been) when it suited Pleyal's whim to extend his tyranny.

Bruckshaw's ability to see and willingness to state that fact spoke well of the governor's choice of a commander for her fleet. Stephen Gregg didn't worry about the possibility of losing—he'd be dead before that happened, so it didn't figure in his personal considerations—but he knew the Free State of Venus couldn't afford internal bickering if it were to survive the Federation onslaught.

The delegation of captains from Ishtar City and the few from lesser ports scattered across the wind-scoured face of Venus were already present in the meeting room. They'd had no part in the arrival ceremony. That was between Betaport and the governor's representatives. Some of the outsiders had been drinking downstairs in the tavern. They watched with a palpable air of dogs in another pack's territory as Betaport captains trooped in behind the high dignitaries.

Alexi Mostert caught Stephen's eye and nodded friendly awareness. Captain Casson was present also, but Stephen noted that he and his clique of three younger men stood separate from most of the Ishtar City captains.

The meeting room's only furniture was a small desk holding a holographic projector beside which Guillermo waited, his face chitinously bland. Chairs and a table would have meant formal order and decisions about precedence. There would have been immediate scuffles and perhaps a dozen duels fought in the next days following. So long as the fifty-odd participants could move around freely, no one need feel honor-bound to claim redress for a slight.

Stephen positioned himself in a corner behind where Piet and the two councilors faced the bulk of the gathering. This assembly was for senior captains to give their opinions. Decisions would be made later by a much smaller group, in which Stephen would be present. He'd gain more by watching the interplays than he could by becoming involved at this stage.

To Stephen's amusement though not surprise, Jeremy Moore was in the opposite corner behind Councilor Duneen. Jeremy caught Stephen's eye and winked. He wore a cream suit trimmed with black lace—handsome, verging on the pudgy, every finger's breadth the courtier.

You had to look carefully to notice that Jeremy's left arm was withered and his hand tucked into the bodice of his blouse. At the back of Jeremy's eyes was another sign that didn't come from his time as Councilor Duneen's brother-in-law and trusted assistant; but you had to know to look for that and to recognize what you saw.

"Gentlemen," Commander Bruckshaw said. "Captains of Venus. We all know that the tyrant Pleyal is on the verge of making a direct attack on Venus. He's failed to choke off our trade, he's failed to defend *his* trade against us. His only remaining option is to put his troops in every community on Venus, enforcing his will, under the threat of blowing those communities open to the atmosphere. I've come before you on behalf of the governor to get expert opinions on how Pleyal may be stopped."

Stephen smiled slightly. The Federation also had the option of making peace with Venus; opening its trade, founding joint colonies, and advancing the cause of all mankind instead of the portion of humanity that bowed to President Pleyal.

Piet presumably believed that someday the lion would lie down with the lamb, though it was hard to see signs of that belief in Piet's actions.

"Stop him before he gets started," said Quigley before other mouths had opened. He was a competent, middle-aged Betaport man who'd captained one of the ships that landed

during the Winnipeg raid. "Hit Nuevo Asunción while the
Fed fleet is still on the ground there. Blast it the way we
blasted Winnipeg and it'll be ten years before Pleyal *could*
gather enough ships to mount a real threat again."

"You're forgetting about the orbital forts guarding Asunción," Groener said from Captain Casson's flank. "Thirty-
centimeter guns that'd turn any of our ships inside out if we
were stupid enough to come within range."

"Well, I'm talking about a surprise attack, aren't I?"
Quigley snapped. "I know Betaport men can navigate well
enough to—"

"Gentlemen!" Piet Ricimer said. His shout cut through
the babble an instant before it degenerated into a brawl. A
run-up of only thirty seconds to a riot would have been quick
work even for Venerian space captains, Stephen thought sardonically.

The courtiers seemed to be taken aback. Meetings of the
Governor's Council were acrimonious enough by all reports,
but the veneer of civilized discourse was a trifle thicker.

"The skills of the men present are witnessed by the fact
the men *are* present," Commander Bruckshaw said in the
tense hush. "I do not choose to listen to empty comments
on the subject."

"But I'll say," Piet said, eyeing Quigley stiffly, "that I
personally don't trust my navigation to the point that I'd
transit a ship close enough to an orbital fort to be sure of an
instantaneous kill. There are three forts orbiting Nuevo Asunción."

Quigley scowled at his feet in embarrassment. Despite the
sparks, it was a good thing the first man to get out of line
was from Betaport. By stepping on Quigley hard, Piet had
gained the authority to do the same to Ishtar City captains.

"We could blockade Asunción, though," Salomon suggested. "Cut the Feds off from the supplies they need to
complete outfitting their fleet and let them rust on the
ground."

Half a dozen men boomed simultaneous responses. Bruckshaw raised his left hand for silence, then said, "Captain
Casson, you had a comment to that suggestion?"

"Sure I've got a comment," Casson growled. "It's crazy,

that's my comment. We wear our ships out transiting. Use up our reaction mass so when the Feds do come up, they'll be able to run clear of us. Our men spending weeks, months, maybe years weightless—what are they going to be worth in a fight?''

The buzz of agreement following Casson's remarks was by no means limited to the Ishtar City contingent.

"And I might add, there's the governor's problem of how to pay the wages of a large fleet for an indefinite period," Councilor Duneen added. "Though the suggestion clearly has merit."

"If we're all off to Asunción," Captain Luzanne said, "then what's to keep the Feds from shipping an army to Venus on intrasystem hulls? They don't need a fleet if our fighting ships are buggering themselves off in Near Space."

"They wouldn't dare do that!" a Betaport man shouted.

The friend beside him said, "I don't know why they wouldn't! We did it at Winnipeg, didn't we?"

The chaotic conversation of the next moments was a discussion, not a series of arguments. Bruckshaw let it go on for more than a minute before he raised his hand and said, "Gentlemen. Gentlemen!" Eyes focused on him.

In the hush, Salomon went on, "The Fed strategy will be to englobe Venus and threaten to bomb through the clouds unless we let them land and plant garrisons in our towns. They don't have good maps of Venus and it's not easy to hit anything through the winds of our upper atmosphere, but they'll do real damage. We've got to stop them, break up their formation, before they reach the Solar System."

"Why, if they sit in Venus orbit, we'll eat them like pieces of popcorn!" Groener said. Even Captain Casson scowled and shook his head at his acolyte.

A single bomb could rupture the covering of any community on Venus, letting in the planet's searing, corrosive atmosphere. No responsible Venerian leader could contemplate a battle fought in Venus orbit, when even a victory could cost higher civilian casualties than the ninety-five percent of the population that had died during the Collapse.

Alexi Mostert strode verbally across the gloom with which the gathering reacted to the truth belying Groener's bravado.

"While Pleyal will have more ships than we do," he said in a loud voice, "the best of them won't be able to maneuver with the least of ours. The new ships that our yards are turning out for the governor will dance circles around anything wearing a mapleleaf!"

"The *Wrath* came closer to her programmed positions than any other vessel I've handled," Piet agreed. "That's both in sidereal space and during transit."

"Fads are well enough for those that like them," Casson said, showing nearly the truculence of Quigley at the start of the conference. "All I see nowadays are cylindrical ships that're twice as big as anybody in *my* day would think of building so inefficient a design. Give me a round ship with a thick hull, and you can hang me if she doesn't maneuver well enough to pay out the Feds."

"It's gunnery that'll pay them out," said Blassingame, a young fire-eater from a community near Cybebe so small that it had only a single dock. Ships were stored in the town center in the rare event of a second vessel docking while the first was still on the ground. "Maneuvering just lets us keep off and blast them from where they can't board us."

"That's so," Mostert agreed. "I think we can all agree about that: our hope, the hope of Venus, is to stand back and let our guns do the job for us."

"The Federation vessels will be carrying soldiers," said a courtier Stephen didn't recognize, a member of Duneen's entourage. "Over ten thousand troops have been gathered on Nuevo Asunción, and our expectation is that most or all of them will embark with the fleet."

The speaker was a man in his sixties, wizened and wearing a beaded cap over what was clearly a bald scalp. It was the first time a member of a councilor's staff had entered the discussion.

"The primary purpose of the troops is to provide initial garrisons for Venus if we open our cities due to the threat of bombing," Councilor Duneen added. "But they'll certainly be prepared to fight in a boarding battle between ships as well."

"There's no need to board," Mostert said. "Not for any

of our vessels, certainly not for the new-design ships, which can concentrate their fire as—''

He paused a half-beat to glance, not glare, at Captain Casson.

''—geometry prevents old-style spheres like the *Freedom* from doing, though God Himself were at the controls.''

''We've smashed Fed ships to gas and fragments plenty of times,'' Captain Salomon said. ''Because they can't maneuver with us, we'll run past them like they were on the ground. Our big guns will chew them away like files eating down an aluminum bar!''

The assembly growled murderous agreement.

Stephen Gregg's expression looked like a slight smile: approving, to an onlooker eager for approval; neutral, to a neutral observer. Jeremy Moore pursed his lips in Stephen's direction, then raised an eyebrow. Stephen shrugged.

The size of the Federation fleet frightened them all, though few in this room would admit it. No one knew exactly how many ships President Pleyal would be able to gather, but everyone was aware that the resources of the Federation were many times greater than those of Venus. Venus was better able to concentrate what ships and men she had, but when the fleets met, the disparity in numbers as well as in the size of individual ships was certain to be great.

The men here wanted desperately to believe that gunnery was the answer to the Federation threat. Maybe they were right, but Stephen as a matter of policy distrusted ''certainties'' when the folk proclaiming them thought nothing else stood between them and the abyss. The vision of a Federation fleet melting like salt under a hose as plasma bolts washed their ships was attractive, but that didn't make it true.

The next dozen speakers trampled over the same ground. Stephen waited, his face intent but only the surface level of his mind listening. Venerian ships had better fire control, better guns, more *big* guns, ship-smashing guns. Venerian crews reloaded faster, and their ceramic tubes increased the rate of fire by a good thirty percent over that of the Feds' stellite weapons, even when the Feds were crack personnel.

Each statement was true in itself. Stephen had seen the truth repeatedly demonstrated in blood and flame from Win-

nipeg to the Reaches. But there was a greater question: "Is
this enough to destroy the fleet that will otherwise destroy
Venus?" Every one of the captains speaking begged the truth
of that question, but for Stephen Gregg it had yet to be
proved.

Eventually Piet cleared his throat. Councilor Duneen
caught Bruckshaw's eye and nodded.

Commander Bruckshaw said, "Gentlemen? As you know,
my final plans will be drawn up in close consultation with
Factor Ricimer. I think it might be useful at this juncture for
all of us to hear what his current thinking on the matter may
be. Sir?"

Piet nodded twice and crossed his hands behind his back.
"Commander, gentlemen," he said. "I don't believe Governor Halys will permit any significant portion of her fleet
to leave the Solar System at the present juncture—"

He glanced in the direction of Councilor Duneen. Duneen
smiled dryly and nodded agreement. What had been true before the Winnipeg raid was even more certain now that full-
scale war was inevitable.

"Therefore we'll have to rely on picket vessels to inform
us when the Feds leave Asunción," Piet resumed. "I hope
and expect, with God's blessing, that we'll still be able to
meet the Feds many days' transit from Venus."

"Nuevo Asunción *is* only eight days from Venus," Casson interrupted.

Bruckshaw looked at the Ishtar City captain with a gaze
Stephen wouldn't have wanted turned on himself. Piet
merely smiled agreement and said, "Yes, for us; and probably no more than ten days for an ordinarily well-found Federation ship with a Federation crew. But we're not to forget
that the Feds will be traveling as a fleet, a very large fleet.
Further, they'll know that their only chance of safety against
us will be to hold a tight formation at all times. They'll have
to make very short transit series."

Casson shrugged with a black expression. Most of the
other captains nodded or murmured assent. Everybody knew
that not only did a company of vessels travel at the rate of
the one least able to navigate accurately, the difficulties in-

creased almost as the logarithm of the number of ships involved.

Practical interstellar travel required that a vessel transfer from the sidereal universe to a series of other bubble universes. Each cell of the hyperuniversal sponge-space matrix had its own different constants of time and distance. The ship retained momentum from the sidereal universe and from thrust expended within each cell that it transited, but the effect of motion within a cell could exceed by thousands of times that of motion within the sidereal universe.

Distances within the sidereal universe were of no practical significance, because even the stars nearest to the Solar System were too far for trade through normal space. The concepts of Near Space and the Reaches referred to the relative length of voyages to those locations through the enormously complex patterns of sponge space.

The artificial intelligences that calculated transit series were the most sophisticated electronics in the human universe. Because of constant slight changes in the association of bubble universes and in the energy gradients separating one cell from the next, no sidereal distance longer than those within the core of a planetary system could be encompassed by a single transit series.

Ships made a number of gut-wrenching hops back and forth from normal space to cells of sponge space, then paused for hours or days while their AIs compared sidereal reality with the navigators' programmed intent. The process was time-consuming and uncomfortable even for hardened spacers, but it made the stars and their multiplicity of Earthlike planets available to mankind. If transit had been developed ten generations sooner, there would not have been a network of colonies burrowing through the crust of Venus—

And surviving, even when the Outer Planets Rebellion brought human civilization down in crashing horror through a handful of pinprick attacks that a less centralized, less homogeneous, society could have ignored.

No two ships metered thrust or judged angles in quite the same fashion. Since differences were multiplied by scores or thousands during every transit, it was obvious that a large fleet that was required to stay in close formation would have to proceed by brief series with correspondingly long delays to recalibrate for the next hop.

The Federation force would certainly be huge, and neither President Pleyal's vessels nor his captains were of Venerian standard. Normally ships in company proceeded each at its own pace and rendezvoused at the end of each day's voyaging. The Grand Fleet of Retribution had to keep much closer contact, or the individual ships would be gobbled up by Venerians in concert. Bruckshaw would have his own problems, since Venerian ships and navigators were of varying capacities too; but the average capacity was very much higher.

"We can easily calculate the Fed course to Venus from the time they rise from Asunción," Piet continued. "I would recommend that we meet them at the earliest point along that route in which our force can be complete."

He swept the room with his fiery, brilliant smile. Even after so many years, that smile had the ability to warm Stephen. It wasn't a pretense with Piet: it was his real spirit blazing out on those around him.

"Some of you may remember times I've rushed in when others, wiser folk perhaps, would have waited for more support to arrive," Piet said. "Not this time. If we attack the Feds in penny packets while they keep an ordered formation, we'll waste ammunition that we can't afford as well as the moral advantage we have until they see us fail."

No one understood morale effects better than Piet Ricimer. The Feds who knew *Captain Ricimer* was coming down on them with his undefeated pack of killers would think themselves half beaten no matter how great their numbers in ships and men.

Captain Ricimer and his killers. Stephen rubbed his forehead hard, so that the pain drew him back to the present.

"The Feds will take far longer than us to recalibrate in sidereal space for the next transit series," Piet said. "Their ships will be scattered, with the help of God. Our forces can cruise past Fed ships, always staying under power, and hit them with our heavy guns. They won't be able to reply effectively so long as we stand off and keep under way. And if we always remain at the correct point relative to them in sidereal space, they won't be able to transit directly toward Venus.''

"We can keep them wandering like Israel in the wilderness!'' Salomon said.

Piet nodded assent as solemn as "Amen'' to close a prayer. He faced toward Commander Bruckshaw and bowed, turning the meeting back to him.

Bruckshaw cleared his throat. His visage hardened very slightly, an unconscious preparation for his next words. He said, "Gentlemen and captains, you've heard Factor Ricimer's opinion based on his own experience and what has been said in this room. Under God and Governor Halys, I and no other command the fleet of Venus.''

He looked around the room, his eyes lighting last of all on Stephen Gregg. Stephen nodded acknowledgment.

"However,'' the commander continued in a lighter tone, "I'm not a man to overrule experts for the sake of proving my authority. If anyone questions that authority, I'll remove him as I would swat a fly; but with that understood, I will tell you here and now that Factor Ricimer can expect my fullest cooperation in the ordering of the fleet according to expert judgment. My cooperation will extend to the corridors of the palace where perhaps the recommendations of a space captain, even the greatest of space captains, haven't till now been accepted as quickly as the present crisis requires.''

Bruckshaw turned and clasped Piet by both hands, raising them into the air as he looked at the assembled captains. The cheering was general and heartfelt; even, Stephen thought, the grudging nod of Captain Casson.

But would it be enough?

BETAPORT, VENUS.

When the cheers died away, Piet Ricimer rang a ceramic bell shaped like a rose blooming from the end of a baton. The outer doors opened; servants hired for the purpose carried in narrow tables already set with covered dishes and an array of liquors.

"I hope you'll all be able to join me in a buffet," Piet said, "where we can discuss details informally."

The manners of men who lived no more than arm's length from their fellows during long voyages were less fastidious than those of the governor's court. Space captains began lifting lids and—especially—snatching bottles before the tables were even in place against the back wall. Members of the councilors' staffs gaped in horrified surprise, though Bruckshaw's expression was politely bland and Councilor Duneen seemed rather amused.

Stephen wanted a drink, but not particularly in this company. As he considered alternatives, Jeremy Moore walked over to him and said, "I was thinking of taking a turn down Dock Street for old times' sake, Stephen. Care to come?"

Stephen chuckled. "With me looking like the biggest parrot on Venus, and you not exactly dressed like a sailor yourself? The mob's had its entertainment today. Why don't you and I go below, pick up a bottle in the tavern, and chat in Piet's office? It'll be empty, or we can empty it."

"You country boys," Jeremy said with a smile that shimmered over tension. He and Stephen had been shipmates on one voyage, a very long voyage. They'd gotten to know and respect one another; and between them, they'd killed more people than anyone around had time to count. "Afraid of a few people bumping you. But sure, let's do that."

Piet and Councilor Duneen had already gathered clots of people offering ideas or making requests. Stephen made a slight gesture when Piet's eye brushed him; Piet nodded minusculely. To Stephen's amusement, he noticed that Jeremy took leave of Councilor Duneen in precisely the same way.

Jeremy slipped between the servants coming up the narrow stairs before they were fully aware that he was moving past them. He'd always been good at finding paths to a destination, Jeremy had. Stephen followed swiftly, because servants flattened against the stairwell wall at his presence. They would have done the same for any guest; but perhaps without the slight glint of fear at being so close to Colonel Gregg, the killer.

They should have seen Jeremy Moore with a cutting bar on the blood-splashed bridge of the *Keys to the Kingdom*.

Moore was Factor of Rhadicund, a title his ancestors in direct line had held ever since the Collapse. His grandfather had sold up the small keep and moved to Ishtar City to swim—and promptly sink—in the politics of the Governor's Palace.

Jeremy had survived, barely, through his status as a gentleman, on his wizardry with electronics—and because he liked women almost as much as women liked him. He'd joined Captain Ricimer to escape what he was as well as to make himself something better.

"Better" was a word that depended on what you saw to judge; but certainly the Jeremy Moore who returned to Venus had become Councilor Duneen's top aide.

The Blue Rose was crowded with locals who elbowed sightseers hoping for another glimpse of the dignitaries meeting upstairs. Jeremy worked through them with surprisingly little contact. He'd grown up in Ishtar City's Old Town, where the corridors were rarely less crowded than this tavern at present.

"Todd, a bottle of slash," Stephen called through the clamor. His path to the bar cleared when other drinkers recognized his voice. "What would you like, Jeremy? Todd has most anything you'd care for nowadays."

The folk visiting Piet Ricimer's headquarters were a cosmopolitan lot. Todd, who sublet the Blue Rose from Piet and ran the tavern with his family, had found the profit in exotic liquors far exceeded the trouble of keeping them on hand; though for lack of storage space, tuns of beer were delivered every half hour at busy times.

"A carafe of citrus juice if you've got it," Jeremy said, "because I'm really dry. But ice water would be fine."

"Always glad to oblige a gentleman, sir," Todd said. He handed Stephen a square-faced bottle of Eryx slash and the pitcher of orange juice from the refrigerator beneath the bar. He whispered to a child, probably his granddaughter since she couldn't have been older than eight. She scuttled out of the tavern and down the corridor in search of more juice.

Jeremy opened the door to the office, what had been the tavern's private room before Piet acquired the leasehold, and bowed Stephen inside. Stephen glanced at the electronic lock and said, "Was that open?"

Jeremy displayed the little device he wore on his right index finger like a downturned ring. He grinned. "Just to keep my hand in," he said. He closed the door behind them.

Stephen set the pitcher and bottle on the black glass table in the center of the room. The bases rocked slightly because the tabletop was a sheet of obsidian left in its natural state, rather than something cast and polished in a foundry.

"So, Jeremy . . ." Stephen said as he took tumblers from the cabinet in the corner. "Will you be coming out with us this time?"

Jeremy snorted. He lifted the pitcher in his good hand and drank from the side of it. "You won't need a crippled close-combat man, Stephen," he said. "It's going to be a gunnery battle. I heard all those experienced captains say so, one after the other."

Stephen took a swig straight from the bottle of slash. The algal liquor was harsh and warming. "Yeah," he said, his voice deeper than it had been a moment earlier. "I'm worried about the same thing. Maybe they're right, though. Maybe it's just that nobody likes to believe that what he does isn't needed any more."

"What I used to do," Jeremy said softly. The juice trembled in his hand. He slurped more, then put the pitcher down.

Stephen settled himself onto a chair. Jeremy took another on the same side of the table, turning so that he faced Stephen.

"I hear it's you we have to thank for the fact Venus has a single communications net," Stephen said. "Identical codes and everything tied together. I never thought I'd live long enough to see that."

"Ninety-eight percent of Venus tied together," Jeremy said with a reminiscent smile. "You and I may *not* be alive by the time the rest gets linked. But it's really due to Councilor Duneen—and President Pleyal, believe it or not. We need the net for trade, but the council would have bickered till the equator froze except that the councilor convinced Governor Halys that universal communications were a defense necessity."

"I don't doubt your patron's political skill," Stephen said as he savored the cloying, half-rotted aftertaste of slash from his family's keep. "But in my own life, I haven't noticed that a job magically does itself because the man on top gives an order."

Jeremy laughed heartily. "Oh, Stephen," he said, "I've been called names the Feds never thought of! By people who thought there was money to be made and too little of it was coming their way, and by other folks who thought, quite correctly, that I was trampling the right of themselves and their community to be pointlessly unique. I don't know how many times somebody shouted, 'Moore, you don't understand!' When the problem was that I did understand, and that absolutely nothing was going to stop me from doing what was necessary for Venus."

Stephen drank. He saw in his mind's eye the Jeremy Moore of a few years earlier, swinging a cutting bar for as long as there was an enemy standing; and when the last Fed had fallen, he'd hacked corpses in his unslaked bloodlust.

Jeremy chuckled. "Mind," he said, "there *was* a lot of money to be made. But not by pricks. I believe Weyston Trading was the prime contractor for the Atalanta Plains?"

"My uncle thanks you," Stephen agreed. "And I don't

think my brother Augustus ever really looked up to me before he learned that the assessment on Eryx Keep had been waived because he was my relative. It's funny. I could have paid the charges easily enough, but that just would have meant I was rich. That Factor Moore had the charges waived—that made me somebody.''

He drank again. The level in the bottle had gone down more than he felt as if it should have.

Jeremy stared at his fist on the table and said, very softly, ''I'd rather die than wrap my hand around the grip of a cutting bar again.''

He looked at his friend and went on. ''How are you sleeping, Stephen?''

Stephen shrugged. ''Hasn't been a lot of change there,'' he said with a slight smile directed at the liquor bottle. ''It's not the thing I do best.''

He looked up. ''How about you, Jeremy?''

''Better than it was,'' Jeremy said. ''I don't scare my wife anymore.''

He forced a smile, but the expression died on the underlying tension. ''It was my own fault, Stephen. I kept trying to explain things that Melinda didn't have the vocabulary to understand. She tried, she really did, but she could only hear words. They didn't mean what they did to me. To us.''

Jeremy drained all the juice from the pitcher. Staring at the empty container as he set it on the table, he went on, ''And I had to stop drinking. I thought it helped—and it did, it helped me sleep, *you* know what I mean.''

Stephen nodded. His big hands were laced around the slash bottle. ''More juice?'' he asked. ''Todd will have some by now.''

''I'm all right,'' Jeremy said. He took a deep breath. ''It helped me sleep,'' he went on, ''but I don't have your control, Stephen. I was at a party. It was more of a family thing than politics, though of course with the councilor everything is politics. I'd had a few, no more than usual. Talk got around to our heroes out in the Reaches.''

He grimaced. ''I shouldn't have—you can't explain, *you* know that. But I said it wasn't heroes out beyond Pluto, it was nothing but blood and waste. And somebody I hadn't met. He told me I ought to keep my mouth shut. When I didn't know what I was talking about. He knew what it was like. His nephew had sailed with Captain Ricimer.''

Jeremy's voice quivered. He'd pressed his palm flat against the tabletop, but his forearm trembled. "*Christ*, this is stupid!'' he said. "No control, Stephen. No control at all.''

"More control than I've got,'' Stephen said, laying his right hand over Jeremy's. "You got out.''

"Stephen, I almost killed him,'' Jeremy said with his eyes bright. "It took four men to pull me off.'' He smiled wanly. "They say it did. God knows I don't remember.''

"I decided a long time ago that there were too many fools for me to kill them all,'' Stephen said. "But it's a temptation, I know.''

"There wasn't any problem about it,'' Jeremy said, his voice stronger and nearly normal again. "Turned out the fellow was a second cousin who'd barely scraped onto the guest list. He came to my office the next afternoon and apologized on his knees. He hadn't known he was speaking to the Factor of Rhadicund.''

Stephen laughed with as much humor as his laugh usually held. "He *wasn't* speaking to the Factor of Rhadicund,'' he said. "He was talking to the fellow who led Piet Ricimer's boarding crew.''

Stephen stood up. He looked at the bottle in his hands, then flung it with all his strength at the wall. A tile shattered, but the bottle bounced spraying liquor three times before it caught an angle wrong and disintegrated into tiny crystal shards. Good Venerian material, able to withstand enormous stresses before at last it broke.

"*Christ*, I'm glad you got out, Jeremy,'' Stephen said to the wall in a husky voice.

Jeremy was standing beside him. "I'm told you've formed a partnership with a Captain Blythe, Stephen,'' he said mildly.

Stephen looked at him in amazement.

"Well, my job's communications, Stephen,'' Jeremy said with a tinge of embarrassment. "I don't spy on my friends, but if I hear something, I . . .''

Stephen nodded and turned his head again. "She's a good person, Jeremy. Too good a person to—"

He looked at the table and didn't slam his fist against it after all. Throwing the bottle had reminded him that he didn't dare blame things outside himself for problems that were solely in his mind.

"You know what I'm like, Jeremy," he said. "It's not fair to use a decent person to keep from . . . Anyway, there's slash. Sal and I own a ship together, but there's no need for us to meet. I'd decided that before Winnipeg."

Stephen attempted a smile, decided it worked, and faced his friend again.

"Stephen," Jeremy said softly. "It's none of my business, but listen anyway. She's not a thing, she's a person. If she's willing, then don't keep away from her for her sake. That's *her* choice. All the liquor does is put another shovel of dirt on what's down there. There's not enough liquor in all the world to keep it down forever, so you may as well have a woman help you face it."

Jeremy laughed suddenly. He wiped his sweaty palm on a handkerchief he snaked from the opening in his jacket that held his left forearm, withered by a Federation bullet in the shoulder joint. "Women are," he said in a light tone, "one of my areas of expertise."

Stephen sighed. "Oh, I'll be all right, Jeremy," he said. "Seeing an old friend . . ."

He paused. "You give me hope, Jeremy. Maybe that's what I'm really afraid of. Hope."

"We'd best get back upstairs," Jeremy said. "Making our principals look important is part of the job too, after all."

He swallowed, touched his tongue to his lips, and said, "Stephen? Do you think Piet really will need boarding crews when the Feds come this time?"

Stephen shrugged. Jeremy gripped the bigger man's arm and turned him so that they were face to face. "*Tell* me, Stephen," he said.

"Not as much as Venus needs heroes on the ground here, Jeremy," Stephen said. "War's easy. *You* know that. Making life worth something—that's a lot harder."

Factor Moore of Rhadicund nodded and opened the door to the excited bustle of the Blue Rose Tavern.

BETAPORT, VENUS.

Hergesheimer Dock was one of Betaport's oldest storage docks. The vessel nearest the entrance was dollied up for movement but the tractor operator, the ship's officers, and an official or two representing the dock were arguing beside the tractor. Everyone involved shouted at the top of his voice, but the volume drank all but a susurrus of echoes.

"There we go," Sal said. "Cradle Eight, not Cradle Three. I got out in the transfer dock when we brought her from Ishtar City, and handwriting isn't Harrigan's strong suit. The *Clarence*, formerly the *Maid of Bellemont*, formerly the *Grace*. Not a new ship, but I've gone up and down in her and she's well-found at the core."

Stephen crossed his hands behind the small of his back and wondered what it was he was supposed to be seeing in the utterly nondescript vessel before them. From any distance the *Clarence* could have passed as a twin to the *Gallant Sallie*.

Sal had asked Stephen to come here with her. He'd been planning to see her ever since he talked to Jeremy Moore, but he hadn't been sure how he was going to make the contact.

He didn't have a clue as to why Sal had brought him here, though.

"The main thing was that she could be had for a song," Sal continued. "The widow wasn't interested in keeping anything that reminded her of her husband—he died in a brothel, not a shipping accident—and the electronics were going to

256

have to be replaced. That doesn't matter for our purposes, of course.''

"You bought her?'' Stephen said, a light dawning. Sal needed a loan to—

"*You* bought her,'' Sal said crisply. "To be precise, I bought her on your behalf, using the commercial letter of credit with which you'd provided me.''

Stephen grew very still. "The letter of credit was to cover trading opportunities for the *Gallant Sallie* at times when I was unavailable,'' he said without affect.

"Was it?'' Sal said, her chin sticking out in determination. "That's not what the document says. You can rescind it, but the purchase transaction is valid.''

"I accept that,'' said Stephen. He hadn't seen Sarah Blythe in person since the squadron lifted from Winnipeg. . . . "Go on.''

"I have a list of captains who I think will work the *Clarence* for quarter shares,'' Sal said. "That's after you upgrade the electronics to *Gallant Sallie* standards, of course. They're all solid men, but I haven't discussed the matter in case you might have a personal problem with one of them.''

She handed Stephen a list printed on flimsy paper. He crumpled it into his palm. "I don't have personal problems with people,'' he said. He smiled like black ice over lava. "Not long term.''

Sal nodded, her face tightly emotionless. "Actually, I think you'll be able to hire—take as partners—all six of them before too long. There are a lot of ships like the *Clarence*, like the *Gallant Sallie* was. They need upgrades. Most people haven't appreciated that the expansion of trade going on right now makes it cost-effective to upgrade even hulls as old as these.''

"Sal,'' Stephen said, "if I wanted to be in the shipping business, I'd be managing Weyston Trading for my uncle right now. I—''

"No!'' Sal said. She turned abruptly away and wiped her eyes. "No, Stephen,'' she said. "Weyston Trading's an established intrasystem operation. I could run it, Tom *Harrigan* could run it. What Venus needs—''

She looked at Stephen fiercely again, pretending to ignore

the tears on her cheeks. "What Venus needs is trade, *real* trade, to Near Space and the Reaches. That's going to take somebody with imagination to lead the way, to show other people how much profit there is to be made there. *Everybody* will gain."

"I'm not—" Stephen said.

"You are!" Sal said. "You owe it to Venus and you owe it to yourself!"

Stephen looked at her for some moments without speaking. At last he said, "A strictly business operation, I take it?"

She blinked. "Of course."

He nodded. "All right," he said. "We'll incorporate as Blythe Spirits. You'll be managing director with a fifty percent share of the profits. Oh, and put yourself down for a five percent finder's fee on ships bought for the corporation."

"I—" Sal said. "That isn't . . ."

Stephen smoothed the piece of flimsy so that he could read the names. He squinted. The illumination of Hergesheimer Dock had been marginal even when twice as many of the overhead lights worked. "Tell me about Captain Lou Montrose," he said.

"Stephen, I'm not a manager," Sal whispered.

"We're all learning new things, aren't we?" Stephen Gregg replied with a crooked smile. "We owe it to Venus or some such thing, I'm told."

Looking toward the flimsy, he went on, "What are you doing for dinner tonight?"

The tractor operator finally put his vehicle into gear. The joints of the dolly clanged, echoing through the dock like the bells of a great temple.

BETAPORT, VENUS.

Sal heard the commotion outside the Blue Rose, but because she wasn't a Betaport native she couldn't judge how unusual it was. Nobody else in the tavern seemed to care.

Stephen threw his last dart into the rim. The ships' officers crowding the taproom groaned or hooted, depending on how their side bets lay.

Sal put her hand on Stephen's shoulder and said, "Some marksman you are!"

"Find me a board that throws back and see how I do," Stephen called, loud enough to be heard generally.

Guillermo stepped from Piet's office behind the taproom. At the same instant the door to Dock Street flew open and a sailor shouted, "Sir! Captain Ricimer! The *Oriflamme*'s in from Asunción and the Feds are coming out!"

Sal felt her rib muscles tighten. Her mind wasn't ready to consider what the news meant, but her body was already reacting.

All the light went out of Stephen Gregg's expression. He folded his retrieved darts into a strip of soft leather with the economical motions of a man whose fingers had reloaded any number of weapons, and who would shortly be reloading more.

Sound erupted, then ceased like a bubble that rose to the surface of a swamp and plopped into nonexistence. Faces turned toward the messenger in the doorway rotated as suddenly toward Piet Ricimer.

"Guillermo?" Piet said. He sounded nonchalant.

"Ishtar City and the other defense ports have been alerted,

259

Captain," the Molt said. One of Piet's trusted subordinates had been on communications watch in the office every day for the past six. Because ships couldn't communicate with the ground through the charged, turbulent Venerian atmosphere, information would have been carried by land line from the transfer dock to the office at the same time as the dock's external speakers shouted the news to those passing by in the street. "Ships in Betaport intended for the squadron have been informed also."

Sal had seen Guillermo's three-fingered hands working a keyboard intended for humans. The Molt was at least as quick as a human operator because he never, absolutely never, made a false movement. He'd transmitted the alert to all necessary recipients of the information, and he'd still entered the taproom in no more time than it had taken a sailor to run across the street.

Men shoved toward the door in a group just short of a mob. Virtually everyone in the Blue Rose had duties on one of Venus' fighting ships.

"One moment, gentlemen!" Piet Ricimer said, slicing the chaos like a shovel through gravel. Everyone stopped and turned again.

"Guillermo, what is the status of the transfer docks?" Piet asked.

"There are six vessels in orbit queued to land, Captain," Guillermo said. "The docks won't be clear for another three hours at best."

"Much as I thought," Piet said. He beamed to the men around him. "I believe the *Wrath*'s duty officer and anchor watch can receive the reporting crewmen for the next ten minutes without me. That should give us time to finish our game. Captain Salomon, I recall it being your throw."

Stephen Gregg began to laugh the way he had on Lilymead, great, booming gusts of laughter. He bent over, supporting himself in part by resting his empty right hand on his thigh. Men looked at the big man as if he were a ticking bomb.

"Your throw, Mister Salomon," Piet prodded gently.

Salomon swallowed and stepped to the scratch. His darts flew wild, in sharp contrast to earlier in the evening when his mechanical precision had put him and Todarov, his partner, well ahead.

More men entered from Dock Street. Each newcomer started to shout the news, then was hushed by those in the taproom already.

"May God bless our enterprise," said Piet Ricimer in a calm voice. He threw. Each of his darts landed within a millimeter of his point of aim, putting the game to bed.

Stephen enfolded Sal in his arms, squeezed and released her, and strode to the door ahead of Piet; Colonel Gregg preceded Deputy Commander Ricimer through a crowd of their subordinates.

But Stephen was still laughing.

BETAPORT, VENUS.

"*There were ninety and nine—*" sang six crewmen near Stephen as they gripped the stanchions around the *Wrath*'s Number One gun. They were supernumeraries for takeoff and landing, as were most members of the vessel's complement. "*—who safely lay—*"

"The dome is opening, Captain," Guillermo reported from the leftmost of the three primary navigation consoles. The Molt always sounded prim. His enunciation was perfect, but the hard edges of his triangular jaws clipped words as a matter of physical necessity.

"*—in the* shel-*ter of the fold*," the singers continued. Perhaps it was their way of dealing with the nervousness on takeoff that was normal even among spacers. Perhaps they just liked to sing hymns.

The great screen before Piet at the center console boiled a smoky yellow-red. The Venerian atmosphere poured down on the *Wrath* as soon as the clamshell lids of the transfer dock began to draw back.

At ground level the air was almost still, but in the topmost of the three bands of convection cells, sulphurous winds of over 400 kph buffeted vessels. The atmosphere had been the Venus colony's greatest protection from out-planet raiders during the Rebellion, but it had devoured a thousand ships and their unskillful or unlucky crews in the millennium since.

"*But one was out on the—*"

"Will you shut the bloody noise off, you bloody widdiful!" Philips said in a shout that was nearly a scream.

The leader of the singers, a gunner's mate, looked around

with a sneer on his lips and a snarl on the tip of his tongue. His face cleared and he swallowed the words when he saw that Philips squatted beside Mister Gregg in back of the navigation consoles. Philips might have been speaking on the gentleman's behalf; and anyway, the men who loaded for Mister Gregg had a certain status on the *Wrath*.

"Sorry, sir," the gunner's mate muttered to Stephen, hushing his fellows with a hand.

"You may light the thrusters, Mister Simms," Piet said to the navigator at the console to his immediate right. Simms touched a key.

The vessel came alive. Even on minimum flow the plasma motors gave the *Wrath* a vibrant feel far different from the solemn throb of the auxiliary power unit and the varied shrillness of pumps and fans throughout the hull.

"Sorry, sir," Philips muttered to Stephen. "Seems to me they're singing for fun, not like it was a Christian thing to do now. And it's not right, with our people back home and only us to stop the Feds."

The *Wrath* had thirty-two separate plasma motors, giving the warship a greater delicacy of maneuver than a freighter of similar size could achieve with thrust channeled through eight or perhaps a dozen nozzles. Piet ran their power up and down, four thrusters at a time, as the dock's lid continued to edge sideways above them. On the screen, exhaust added brilliance to an atmosphere lit by a bloody, sullen sun.

"Sir?" Philips asked. He was a solid sailor, a motorman's mate of 25. He retained his ordinary shipboard duties after he volunteered to load for Stephen, though Mister Gregg's convenience became paramount. "What will happen if we don't . . . What if the Feds do reach Venus, sir?"

"The dock is fully open, Captain," Guillermo said. Desire to get the entire squadron into Venus orbit wouldn't affect Piet's normal—nonemergency—start-up routine.

"They'll orbit," Stephen said with deliberate calm. Philips' first child, a girl, had been born three days before. She and the mother were in Betaport, sure to be the second target of Pleyal's forces if not their first. "They'll demand landing clearance under threat of bombing, and they'll get it. Nobody on Venus is going to have cities ripped open."

"They'll put down soldiers, then?" Philips said.

"Garrisons, yes," Stephen agreed. "Enough to show that they're in charge, but not a fighting army it wouldn't be. Maybe five or ten thousand troops, spread out all over the planet. It won't be pleasant. They'll desecrate churches, putting up their idols. And I'm sure folk in the government will be arrested. But not so very terrible for ordinary people, I shouldn't think."

"I guess with their own soldiers in cities, it'll be safer," Philips suggested hopefully. "They won't blow the roof in with their own people there."

"Prepare for liftoff!" Piet announced, his voice ringing through the *Wrath*'s tannoys. The thrusters ran up to full output, their irises still dilated.

Stephen thumped his loader in friendly fashion with his left hand; his right gripped the stanchion against which both men braced themselves. "I don't expect to lose, though, Philips," he shouted over the roar as thruster nozzles shrank down.

Nor did Stephen Gregg expect to survive a defeat himself. But Philips was very naive if he thought President Pleyal would bomb a riotous city any less quickly for the fact a few hundred Federation troops would burn in the corrosive atmosphere with the tens of thousands of Venerian civilians—like Philips' wife and child.

ABOARD THE *WRATH*.

"Holy Jesus Christ our lord and savior," somebody said in a hushed voice. Stephen realized his eyes were closed. He opened them carefully and saw the fleet of the North American Federation.

The *Wrath* was four days out from Venus. The transit series just concluded had been of twenty-seven separate exits from and reentries to the sidereal universe. Each one had hooked a needle through Stephen's soul and drawn another stitch stranglingly tight.

For ten years, transit had been a regular part of Stephen Gregg's existence. Each new experience was exactly like the last. Sometimes his eyes welled tears; always the pain in his skull made his stomach try to turn itself inside out.

Stephen would rather have had his teeth pulled without anesthetic than undergo transit. Dentistry wouldn't take him across interstellar space to where he had a job to do, so transit it was.

He understood why first sight of the enemy had brought the amazed prayer—it really had been a prayer—from Simms, who'd recovered fractionally quicker than Stephen had. The navigator's pride at meeting the enemy across trackless light-years was muted by realization of what they'd caught.

The Federation fleet was awesome. The number of ships, well over a hundred, wasn't unexpected, though seeing them had an emotional impact on even a prepared mind. What Stephen found shocking was the regularity of the Feds' formation.

He rose to his feet. The *Wrath* was under power, a standard 1-g acceleration for comfort's sake. Piet felt or saw the movement at the back of his console and turned. "That was the last transit series for some hours, I think, Stephen," he said. "How do you feel?"

"I'll live," Stephen said. He quirked a smile, knowing that between them "whether I like it or not" was understood to close the sentence. "I don't want to bother you if you . . ." He shrugged and flicked a finger toward the display.

"Nothing until the commander and the rest of the fleet arrives," Piet said. Ninety percent of Simms' screen was given over to alphanumeric data, but a visual sidebar in the lower right corner showed Venerian dispositions. Three more beads winked into sight simultaneously, bringing the total to ten.

"They're doing a good job of holding together," Stephen said, his eyes on the Federation fleet. The Feds were in a tight globe. Most of the ships were large, and some were very large. The vessels in the interior of the formation, like the stone in a peach, didn't have guns to run out when the Venerians appeared. Those would be the stores ships and probably troopers; not fighting vessels, though their size and added numbers couldn't fail to have a morale effect on their opponents.

The outer sphere was of warships, arrayed with fields of fire interlocked like the spines of a bramble bush. There were at least eighty of them, twice as many as the heavy vessels of the Venerian fleet.

"They've got more experience in fleet operations than we do," Piet said simply. "I'm surprised to see how well they're keeping formation, though. Their captains and commander are both smarter and more skillful than I'd thought they would be."

Guillermo turned from his adjacent console. "I have been listening to the talk within the Federation fleet, Captain," he said.

"How are you doing that?" Stephen asked in surprise. Modulated laser was the only practical means of communication between starships, since plasma thrusters acted as omniband radio-frequency transmitters. Unlike radio, laser communicators were tight-beam devices that had to be carefully aimed to be heard even by the intended recipient.

Guillermo made a grating motion with his belly plates, the Molt equivalent of laughter. "Their communication beams reflect from their hulls, Colonel," he said. "I directed the *Wrath's* fine sensors to pick up the reflected light, and her fine computers to analyze and enhance the glimmers. As no doubt an ancestor of mine was taught to do before the Collapse."

There were folk who denied that Molts had real intelligence. They claimed the aliens were merely bundles of genetic memory, operating like machines according to programmed pathways. Those folk—bigots, fools, and very often grasping pinchfarts to whom the profit in trading Molt slaves was all the justification necessary—hadn't worked *with* Molts the way Piet and Stephen had done in the past decade.

The navigator's sidebar now showed nearly forty ships, though there was no way of telling from the schematic how many of them were the fleet's accompanying light vessels—couriers and rescue craft—without combat value.

"What are they saying, Guillermo?" Simms demanded. "Are they going to attack us?"

"The Federation officers are terrified, Navigator Simms," Guillermo said. "They thought it was impossible that we would locate them before they had reached the Solar System."

Stephen chuckled. The prospect of action was doing more for his transit-induced queasiness than the solid deck alone could have managed. "The other guy's always three meters tall," he said. "We need to remember that to the Feds, we're the other guy."

An attention signal chimed through the *Wrath*. An image of Commander Bruckshaw formed on the upper left corner of the main display. Piet touched a control, reversing the images so that the enemy fleet was a miniature and the commander's huge visage looked sternly across the cockpit and from all the flagship's displays slaved to the main screen.

Stephen straightened to parade rest, feet spread and his hands crossed behind his back. Bruckshaw's screen displayed a montage of images from all the vessels linked to his flagship, the *Venus*—probably all the vessels in the fleet at this moment. The view transmitted from the optronics of some of the older ships would be at best a fuzzy blur, but Bruckshaw would be well able to see Stephen if he cared to look. It didn't matter, but the principle of disciplined readiness mattered.

"Gentlemen and sailors of Venus," Bruckshaw said. "This is the day we have prayed for: the day that God may, with His blessing, give the Federation into our hands and free Venus from the threat of tyranny forever."

He gestured. Transmission parameters shrank and stripped the commander's voice, but the *Wrath*'s AI swelled it again to more than fullness. Bruckshaw had a good oral style, and to his words' enhanced majesty he added the bedrock of utter sincerity.

"Our foes are numerous, as we knew they would be," Bruckshaw continued. "The formation they keep looks impressive, but a formation doesn't fight battles—men fight battles, and the men with courage and God on their side win those battles! We will take thirty minutes to prepare ourselves. Then we will all attack. Captains, ready your ships for action!"

The shrilling Action Stations alert stepped on the chime closing the transmission over the command channel. A view of the Federation fleet against an alien starscape replaced Commander Bruckshaw's face again.

"Let's get our suits on, Philips," Stephen said. "I'll want you and Hadley each carrying an extra flashgun as well as rifles this time, I think."

ABOARD THE *WRATH*.

Piet Ricimer raised a gauntlet to pat Stephen's, gripping the stanchion behind Piet's console. Then he said, "Prepare for action," in a calm, clear voice through the *Wrath*'s PA system.

Piet pressed a key with an index finger, enabling the manual controls. His touch on the yoke was smooth and delicate despite his hard suit. Stephen felt angled thrust send the *Wrath* toward the Federation's defensive globe like a shark easing toward prey.

Stephen's faceshield was raised. Pumps had lowered the *Wrath*'s internal air pressure to half Earth normal at sea level before the ventilation system shut down as a preliminary to action, but the crew wouldn't need to switch to their suits' air bottles until the guns began firing.

The worst disadvantage of operations in near vacuum was that ordinary speech required an atmosphere to carry sound. Stephen's helmet, like those of other key personnel—gunner's mates, damage control teams, motormen—was equipped with a modulated infrared intercom, but for many of the *Wrath*'s crew the later stages of the battle would be fought in silence save for terrifying shocks ringing through their bootsoles.

Flexible gaiters sealed the cannon barrels to the inner hull so that air didn't escape—quickly—when the gunports opened; the temporary splinter shields erected like transparent booths around each gun position were nominally airtight also. The recoil and backblast of the first plasma discharge would start seams in both protective devices, draining the

269

vessel's atmosphere within the minutes of even a short action.

Aboard the *Wrath* everyone wore his hard suit, Guillermo included. The Molt looked odd because the armor was relatively bulky on his narrow limbs. The officers of Federation vessels wore hard suits, but the most part of even the gunnery crews made do with breathing apparatus and quilted asbestos clothing. Many of those aboard, especially the soldiers embarked for this expedition, would have no protection but sealed compartments and a prayer that no Venerian bolt would puncture their section of the hull.

But the Feds had a very great number of ships. President Pleyal wouldn't notice personnel casualties, particularly among Molt slaves, if his fleet crushed or brushed aside the ships defending Venus this day.

"Starboard guns are prepared to fire," Stampfer said. The master gunner made no pretense of aristocratic coolness. If his crews and equipment weren't perfect on the verge of action—and what human endeavor was perfect?—those around him knew it. At the moment Stampfer sounded angry enough to chew a hole through the *Wrath*'s double hull. "Port guns are on twenty-second standby."

The *Wrath*'s gunners manned half the plasma cannon at a time. Because of the time gun tubes took to cool before they could be safely reloaded, full crews for all the guns would have been a waste of the space the men and their subsistence required. Besides the savings in volume, by rotating on her long axis the *Wrath* displayed a fresh expanse of hull to an enemy whose return fire might have damaged the surface initially exposed.

Stampfer was at a mobile fire director plugged into jacks on the gun deck, not at the position provided for him here on the bridge. He wanted—needed—to be in position to aim his cannon by eye if the fire-direction optronics failed in action. Stephen had seen Stampfer running from tube to tube in the past, his crews poised to act exactly as their master gunner ordered. If all the ships in the present fleet hit as hard and as accurately as Stampfer's guns had done in those less sophisticated days, the Feds were in for a long day and a short war.

The main display before Piet was a maze of colored jack-straws—the courses, past and calculated, of all vessels in both fleets. Each ship was a different hue, though with over a hundred and fifty individuals to track some variations were extremely slight. Simms' screen was a mass of alphanumeric data, while Guillermo viewed the fleets as beads rather than vectors and had a numeric sidebar.

None of the navigation displays meant a lot to Stephen, but he could see through the transparent blast wall to the gunnery console. Though the position was unmanned, its screen was slaved to the mobile director Stampfer was using on the gun deck.

A spherical Federation warship swelled on the display, rotating slowly around its axis of motion. Stephen had no certain scale to judge by, but the ship's nine full decks implied it was large—probably upward of a ,1,000 tonnes' burden.

The Fed vessel's gunports were open and the guns already run out. She carried more than thirty tubes, but as the image grew Stephen saw to his amazement that the weapons on the midline weren't plasma cannon. The Feds had welded projectile weapons on ground carriages to the deck of the hold.

Given the speeds at which starships traveled, projectiles fired at only a thousand meters per second were unlikely to hit any target that wasn't matching velocities alongside. Projectile cannon had some use in a boarding battle, but not enough to justify their weight and bulk. The Feds must be desperately short of naval ordnance if they were arming vessels with ground weapons.

For safety, the *Wrath*'s ports opened to receive the guns only moments before the weapons fired. A bolt that struck the warship's thick hull might not penetrate, but even a small slug of plasma lucky enough to enter through an open port could wreak terrible damage in the interior.

"Fire as you bear!" Piet ordered.

The *Wrath* shuddered as hydraulic rams slid her ten starboard guns to battery. Internal pressure dropped noticeably. Stephen slapped his faceshield down.

The 20-cm cannon fired a rippling salvo at the Fed a kilometer distant. The gun across the blast wall from Stephen recoiled violently in a haze of plasma. The muzzle and the

whole bore glowed white as the gunner's mate opened the
breech. The six men of the crew sprang out the rear hatch
of their splinter shield, ran around the end of the blast wall,
and took their station at the port-side gun.

The shock of the discharges vibrated through the warship's
fabric for thirty seconds before it finally damped to a mere
lively trembling. Piet gripped a T-handled lever with his left
hand, drew it to its lower stop, and then centered it again. A
third of the *Wrath*'s attitude jets fired. Another third fired
seconds later to balance the initial impulse. The ship rotated
180° on its long axis, bringing its port battery toward the
enemy.

The image on the gunnery display didn't change during
the *Wrath*'s maneuvers. Four and maybe a fifth of Stampfer's
bolts had slammed the Fed's hull. Vaporized metal streamed
back like spindrift. Because the Fed was rotating at a meter
per second at its midline, no two of the *Wrath*'s bolts struck
exactly the same point. One round nonetheless pierced the
Fed's hull. A plume of air vented a large compartment.

Sparks flashed across the image; Fed guns recoiled into
their ports. They were firing also, but Stephen didn't feel an
impact. The spinning vessel was difficult to damage, but it
made an almost impossible aiming platform for its own gunners.

"Fire as you bear!" Piet ordered. The port-side guns
skreeled forward, blasted back from their ports at one-second
intervals bow to stern, and stood in a mist of glowing ions
as their crews scampered to the starboard battery again.

Three bolts from the second broadside struck the Federation vessel. One blew gas and fragments in a perfect circle
from the midline deck where the shell guns were mounted.
The vessel was a converted merchantman. The central hold,
intended for easy cargo operations in orbit, was completely
open. The 20-cm bolt had struck the deck at a flat angle,
disintegrating the partition walls the Feds had erected to sub-
divide the hold.

The *Wrath*'s shooting had been remarkably accurate, causing casualties and discomfort aboard one of the Feds' larger
vessels. Despite that, the damage wasn't serious. Stephen,
balancing the hits against the *Wrath*'s load of twenty-five

shells per 20-cm gun at the start of the action, didn't believe
Stampfer *could* do serious damage to the Fed ship at this
rate.

The Fed vanished from the targeting display. Stephen
turned—at the waist, because the gorget locked his helmet
to his thorax armor—and saw that the entire Federation fleet
had transited. Most of the vectors calculated on Piet's display
were truncated at point of transit, though the predicted
courses of Venerian ships still wove wildly across the screen.
The attack had been as uncoordinated as that of bees swarm-
ing at a hive robber.

The *Wrath* transited, a sickening lurch from reality that
bothered Stephen less than it would have if he'd been expecting it. Navigational parameters were so extraordinarily
complex that there was effectively only one solution to a
given problem. The *Wrath*'s AI and the artificial intelligences
of the other Venerian ships reached the same navigational
result as their Federation prey by virtue of knowing the precise instant at which the Fed fleet transited.

Flop. Back to the sidereal universe, a microsecond of
ship's time after exit and untold light-years distant from the
previous location. The Fed formation hung on the display,
distorted like a smoke ring starting to drift. The Feds were
gone and the *Wrath* was gone, plunged into a bubble universe with no light or life or existence in human terms,
then—

Flop. Stephen's soul turning inside out, but it wasn't really
so very terrible, not as bad as it usually was for him. There
was an enemy in sight, and it if wasn't a target for the flashgun slung from his right shoulder—that would come. That
would surely come.

The Fed formation looked like a melon rupturing at the
impact of a high-velocity bullet. Some ships had scattered a
considerable distance from the defensive array while others
clumped too closely together for safety.

Transit *in* to gray Hell. Moments alone with only the past,
with only the dead, and in a blaze of white light Sal with
her hand outstretched and a smile.

Flop. The Fed fleet straggled like froth on a beer mug.
The captain of the bridge gun crew sprayed the bore of his

gun with compressed gas to allow convection cooling. The
loader waited with the chunky near-sphere of the shell in his
hands, ready to ease it into the breech on command.

Stephen's guts tightened for another transit. The Feds remained in normal space. Had Pleyal's forces not been under
pressure by the Venerian fleet, they might have extended the
series farther, but already the outlying ships were in danger
of being enveloped by their enemy.

A large vessel could accept a great deal of hull damage
and remain a fighting unit, but a bolt or two in the thruster
nozzles would leave it helpless. The Feds had to reform their
defensive array, or the more maneuverable Venerian ships
would attack from "below" and disable them one by one.

"Mister Stampfer?" Piet's voice demanded through the
excited shouts cluttering the intercom system.

"Gunners, load your fucking tubes!" Stampfer roared.
"And if they fucking blow, it's too fucking bad! Load your
tubes!"

The loader of the bridge crew handed his shell into the
breech with his captain watching intently. The munition's
narrow flats fit the bore with a mirror's precision. The captain
closed and locked the breechblock home.

"Prepare for action!"

A pair of Federation vessels collided. Stephen didn't notice the vectors merge, but Piet keyed in a series of quick
left-handed commands. An image of the collision filled half
of his display.

The ships were both of spherical plan. One was good-sized
but the other was much larger—easily 1,200 tonnes. The
Wrath's optronics were so sharp that Stephen could read the
name inlaid around the seated figure on the giant's extreme
bow: SAVIOR ENTHRONED.

The contact had been glancing, but considerable debris
sprayed from the point of intersection. The smaller vessel
had torn away at least half of the *Savior Enthroned*'s thruster
nozzles.

Piet switched back to a full navigational display. With the
control yoke he varied the angle and, very slightly, the
amount of thrust from the *Wrath*'s nozzles.

Stephen half expected the *Savior Enthroned* to flash onto the gunnery screen. Instead, a cylindrical Federation warship appeared and began to grow. The damaged vessel was in the heart of the Fed formation, protected by the same crush that had caused the collision. Piet had chosen a more practical target.

"Mister Stampfer," Piet ordered, "fire as you—"

A plasma bolt struck the *Wrath*. The lights, already flat because they lacked air to scatter their illumination normally, flickered, then returned.

"—bear."

The 20-cm guns rumbled forward on their tracks, then recoiled in quick succession. The slam of the *Wrath*'s own guns firing was greater than that of the bolt that had hit her.

Three iridescent flashes lit the hull of the Fed vessel. One round may have penetrated: in addition to the plumes of hull metal, Stephen thought he saw light flicker simultaneously from a line of gunports shocked open by a 20-cm bolt. The Fed vessel continued under power, rotating slowly as it drew away.

"Attitude jet S14's running thirty percent down!" reported a voice Stephen didn't recognize. "I think the throat's choked by trash, not damaged. Do you want us to clear it?"

"Absolutely not!" Piet snapped in reply. "No one is to go out onto the hull unless I tell you that the safety of the ship depends on it!"

Piet adjusted his intercom's filter to narrow his next words to a single recipient. "Stephen," he said without turning his armored body to face his friend, "what do you think of the battle?"

Stephen eyed the navigation display as he coded his IR sender to Piet alone. Lines marking the course of Venerian ships curved toward and away from the stolid Federation fleet. For all that, the Feds were reforming the globe from which they'd begun their transit series. In a little while, an hour or so, their AIs would have calculated the next series; then the next, and the next.

The present Venerian attack was less frantic than the first. The most aggressive captains had fired all their heavy guns on the first pass. Gas cooling could speed the recovery of half the battery, albeit at the risk of cracked tubes, but the rate of fire even in the best-conducted vessels was relatively low.

The only Federation ship in serious difficulties was the *Savior Enthroned*—which had not, so far as Stephen could tell, been touched by hostile gunfire. Three featherboats had gone to the big vessel's aid, and a medium-sized freighter was standing by. The damaged ship would be under way by the time the navigational computers had recalibrated, though it was possible that the smaller freighter would attach tow cables to aid maneuvering.

"They can't hurt us, Piet," Stephen said. Piet switched the left half of his display to a close-up of the *Savior Enthroned*. The image looked glossy because computer enhancement invented details that increasing distance prevented the actual optics from viewing.

Stephen shrugged inside his hard suit and continued, "There isn't much better of a chance that we'll hurt them bad enough that they'll really feel. Not if they hold their formation, and especially not if we stand off the way we're doing."

"I'm concerned somewhat about morale," Piet said. "Ours and theirs both, if we're seen to be unable to destroy their ships."

"Can you put the *Wrath* alongside the damaged ship?" Stephen asked.

On the display, the ragged Venerian attacks had almost ceased while ships cooled their guns. The Fed formation was nearly perfect again. At this rate of travel it would take them a month to reach Venus; but they *would* reach Venus.

"Yes," said Piet. "That was my thought also. Both broadsides at very short range might be enough. With the help of God I can transit the *Wrath* into the formation, though we'll be hammered getting off again in normal space."

"No, not that," said Stephen with a faint smile. His mind stared at alternate futures, events that might or might not happen. "They've got their hatches open for repair crews. Get me close enough with fifty men and we'll board and take her."

"That's . . ." Piet said. "Very risky."

"The risk's in getting close, Piet," Stephen said. "I don't know what twenty rounds will do to a ship that big. Remember, we don't have an atmosphere to ignite the interior even if the hull's pierced. I do know what me and a close-combat team will do."

He laughed harshly. "It's all I'm good for, Piet," he added. "You may as well use me."

"It's not all you're good for, Stephen," Piet said. "But God gave us all skills to use in His service, and no one could question your skills. I'll program the transit."

Stephen rotated the dial of his intercom to the *Wrath*'s general command coding. "This is Mister Gregg speaking," he said. "B Watch close-combat team to Hold One. Make sure you've got lots of ammunition, boys, because there'll be God's own plenty of targets where we're going next!"

ABOARD THE *WRATH*.

Stephen Gregg had never before faced raw vacuum during transit. The clamshell hatches of Hold 1 were open to save fifteen seconds. Stephen, his loaders, and the B Watch close-combat team gripped stanchions and waited.

The starscape vanished. All that existed were random purple flares as a few of Stephen's own optical nerves fired.

Starlight again, though the edge of a different galaxy and both of them indescribably far from the Milky Way in the sidereal universe. For a fraction of a second, Stephen's being regrouped, took stock of itself. The sensation of transit in nothingness was oddly—

Transit. Instead of being locked in his own soul, Stephen was momentarily a part of a universe that was alien but not hostile.

—less disquieting than what engulfed him while traveling in a ship's cabin under normal conditions.

The stars were back but against them was a tiara too dense for a star cluster, too regular for a random distribution of gases. He was seeing the Federation fleet, its nearest components only a few kilometers away—so close that they had shape rather than merely glinting reflection.

Transit. Unexpected, slicing short a calculation of what a flashgun bolt could be expected to do to a Federation warship across three klicks of vacuum. Stephen Gregg merged with a universe as warped and alien as his image of his own soul.

The sidereal universe was a starship's hatch gaping twenty meters away. The *Wrath* and the *Savior Enthroned* both

278

coasted weightless. In the Fed vessel's midships through-hold, a team of Molts in flexible vacuum suits maneuvered a three-head laser cutter and the MHD generator that powered it. Other workmen, most of them aliens, were bringing tools and materials from elevators in the center of the hold.

A featherboat stood a hundred meters off. Four humans, one of them wearing a hard suit, smoothed kinks from a safety net that the featherboat was stretching from the top edge of the *Savior Enthroned*'s hatch.

None of the Feds was armed. Dole sprang for the *Savior Enthroned*, carrying a magnetic grapnel. He didn't bother to use the hydrogen peroxide motor in the grapnel's head. Half a dozen other veteran spacers jumped only fractionally later, each carrying his own line and grapnel.

Before following Dole, Stephen shot the Molt at the controls of the nearer elevator. The laser pierced the Molt's rubberized suit, flinging the body against the back of the cage on the pressure of escaping gases and the creature's ruptured internal organs.

Stephen thrust the flashgun behind him with his index finger raised. Philips exchanged it for the pump-action rifle as Stephen pushed off, the boarding line in the crook of his left arm.

Dole clamped the grapnel to the deck of the vast hold. A Molt swung awkwardly at the bosun with a massive hydraulic wrench. Dole stuck the muzzle of his shotgun against the Molt's chest and fired.

Though Dole gripped the line to keep from being hurled back through the hatchway, recoil spun his body around the grapnel like an armored pinwheel. The shot charge folded the alien's corpse into the appearance of a squid jetting away, leaving a bloom of bodily fluids behind to confuse pursuit.

Dole launched himself toward the elevator with the expertise of a man who had spent almost thirty years in space. Stephen's hard suit clanged hard against the deck and grapnel: he *wasn't* a spacer, not really, and the flat illumination between the stars made it difficult to judge distance. He snubbed the line around his left forearm and fired five times at the Feds in the elevator cage. He hit each of the four Molts in the chest. The human might have been wearing armor so

Stephen aimed at her hip joint, a weak point and almost as disabling as a heart shot anyway.

Bodies tumbled wildly, spun by the projectiles' momentum and gases voiding the suits through bullet holes. Materials being brought from other decks for the repair work bounced and floated with the Fed corpses.

Light and shadows shifted. Stephen traded the rifle for Hadley's—two fingers raised—flashgun. Now that Hold 1 was empty, the *Wrath*'s loadmasters had cast off the boarding lines and the warship was moving away under the impulse of her attitude jets only. Her gunports were closed and the protective shutters sealed all thirty-two thruster nozzles.

A plasma bolt bathed the *Wrath* with brilliant coruscation. The *Savior Enthroned* wasn't firing. She was a transport, and the few light guns she carried hadn't even been run out of their ports. The gunners of a Fed warship that had come within half a klick of the damaged vessel reacted swiftly and accurately, though accuracy was easier because there was no relative motion between ships coasting on stored momentum.

Slugs of ions missing to punch through vacuum forever at light speed flickered at the edge of Stephen's vision. Two more rounds hit, lighting the *Wrath*'s hull. A third bolt made the fabric of the *Savior Enthroned* ring like a gong through Stephen's bootsoles.

The *Wrath* shrank without apparently moving. Several more bolts dazzlingly lit her. Ships on all sides of the tight Federation array were firing at the intruder. A Fed passed so close to the glint marking the *Wrath* that Stephen thought the two would collide. The Fed vessel fired and braked with its thrusters.

Piet didn't permit his gunners to respond. The *Wrath*'s best hope of survival was to stay buttoned up and pray that the hull withstood Fed battering. The damage Stampfer and his crews could do wouldn't repay the loss of one of Venus' first-line warships if a bolt entered a gunport at the wrong angle.

Before giving the *Savior Enthroned* his full attention, Stephen fired his flashgun into the cold thruster of the nearby featherboat. Tungsten puffed away in a green flash.

The crew who'd been positioning the safety net had vanished within the little vessel's cabin. If they knew what they were doing—and it was suicide to assume your enemy *didn't* know what he was doing—they could have taken the feather-boat into the through-hold to cleanse it with their exhaust. Now that a dollop had been ripped from the nozzle, asymmetrical heating would rupture it at the first moment of use.

Dole and ten or a dozen boarders had cleared bodies and trash from the elevator so that the doors would close. The cage began to rise, carrying the boarders to the next deck to continue the attack. The working party in the farther elevator had taken their cage down before Venerians could reach it. The shaft still provided passage, but boarders would have to cut their way through heavy doors and alerted defenders.

There was a better way.

The Molts who'd been moving the laser cutter were all dead with their human officer, literally hacked apart by a pair of boarders with cutting bars. The device, five hundred kilos of machinery under 1 g and no less massive for being weightless at the moment, had been tethered by a long cable to a ringbolt on the deck to prevent it from getting away from the crew as they shifted it.

The cutter had struck the deck when the Feds released it and was bouncing lazily upward. Stephen braced one boot against the magnetic grapnel and took the cutter's wheelbarrowlike handles. At first all he could do was to slow the device's rotation around its center of mass. Philips and Hadley joined him, one on either handle.

Neither man was as strong as Stephen, but they were sailors with far greater experience handling massive objects in zero gravity. The weapons and ammunition belts festooning them drifted in all directions as if the loaders were hoop dancers performing, but they anchored the tool firmly. Stephen lifted the cutting heads to the deck above and switched the cutter on.

The generator roared, making the whole apparatus vibrate through the flexible cable. The three-laser head sprayed luminescent vapor from the nickel-steel plating. Pressure of the gas thrust against Stephen's grip, but because of the cutter's size his feet were planted firmly against the deck beneath him. Superheated steel lit the through-deck in a huge flare.

The cutters had penetrated to the compartment above and let the atmosphere out to ignite the gaseous metal.

With his loaders steadying him, Stephen swept the cutter in a long circular cut that ended when a two meter disk of steel spun upward, driven by the pressure of its own dissolution. Stephen switched off the tool and gave it a push to send it through into the compartment it had opened. He followed it with a carbine in his hands.

The compartment had been a living and storage volume for fifty or sixty Federation soldiers. Most of them were still in the room, killed when the laser cutter detonated a large ammunition chest strapped to the deck. Shreds of flesh and fabric, equipment and blood, drifted in startling profusion. The laser cutter sailed in slow majesty through the carnage it had achieved.

Stephen ignored the bodies. Only a few of the Feds had been wearing breathing apparatus. Those without would have died when the compartment vented, even if the blast spared them. The hatch on the straight bulkhead, opposite the curve of the outer hull, was fitted with a rail around the jamb for use in weightless conditions. Stephen launched himself toward it, pushing aside floating debris.

Philips reached the hatch ahead of Stephen. He hooked the rail with a finger of the hand holding a flashgun and poised his free hand on the latch. Hadley gripped the other side and braced his boots on the deck so that Stephen could use him as a launching block.

Stephen poised the carbine and raised his left thumb. Philips jerked open the hatch. Stephen stepped through into the corridor beyond.

To the right, three Molts were clamping a net filled with storage drums to the bulkheads in order to barricade the passage. A dozen Fed troops with rifles and shotguns crouched farther on, looking toward the corridor that T-ed into theirs. Bullets from that direction splattered on the cross bulkhead.

To the left more Federation soldiers, all of them human, were bringing up a ten-barrel projectile weapon. Breathing apparatus dangled from their necks, but the corridor was still pressurized so they weren't wearing the masks.

They were landsmen and uncomfortable in weightlessness.

The heavy gun had touched the right-hand bulkhead and would shortly spin from the upper deck despite the troops' efforts.

A Fed officer in full armor had his faceshield raised so that he could use the communications panel in a corridor alcove. He goggled at Stephen, hesitating between slamming his visor down and raising the fat-barreled flechette gun slung to his left arm. Stephen shot him in the face—the light carbine bullet probably wouldn't have penetrated a hard suit—and shot the nearest of the white-jacketed soldiers to the right as the recoil twisted him.

Stephen had nothing to anchor him. He fired three times as quickly as he could lever rounds into the chamber. Each shot rotated him faster.

One of the Molts had a cutting bar. He lunged for Stephen as the gunman tried to twist the carbine to bear. Philips put the flashgun against the Molt's chest. The creature's thorax segment disintegrated in a bright flash, but the laser's cassegrain mirrors shattered also.

The hatch slammed shut behind Hadley when sensors told the mechanism that air was escaping through it. Stephen hooked his boot toe through the railing on the corridor side of the jamb and killed the crew of the multibarrel cannon with his last four rounds. Their blood-splotched bodies drifted in cartwheels compounded of their own dying spasms and the momentum of the bullet into each soldier's upper chest.

The heavy gun continued to trundle down the corridor. It brushed Stephen and would have crushed his thigh against the bulkhead despite the hard suit if the impact had been a little more direct.

Shooting and the momentary drop in air pressure warned the Feds on the other side of the barricade. One of them ran down the corridor in panic, forgetting the Venerian troops in the elevator at the other end of the intersecting passage. A bullet splashed her brains against the wall.

A projectile slammed Stephen just over the top of his breastbone. His gorget shattered and he couldn't see for an instant. The breastplate itself withstood the impact.

Hadley tried to hand him a rifle. Stephen grabbed the flash-gun instead, still slung to the loader's arm.

The multibarrel cannon drifted into the barricade. One of the bulkhead tie-downs broke. The whole mass, weapon and cargo drums caught in the net, swung majestically around the remaining tie-down and toward the intersection. Fed soldiers, crouching behind the barricade, backed away or tried to stop the cannon's slow progress.

Stephen fired the flashgun point-blank into the ammunition locker fixed to the cannon's trail. Over a hundred 2-cm cartridges went off with a red flash in the middle of the defenders, flinging bodies away. The blast would have sent Stephen down the corridor also, but Hadley was gripping a tie-down like an experienced sailor, and the flashgun's sling held. Dirty smoke bulged out on the shock wave.

Six men in ceramic hard suits sailed from the intersecting corridor to finish the slaughter. Dole was in the lead with a shotgun in one hand and in the other a cutting bar, still triggered and spitting blood from its edges.

A score of Fed soldiers came down the corridor in the direction the ten-barrel cannon had been traveling. Dole pointed his shotgun one-handed and fired. The charge of buckshot hit a bulkhead twenty meters away and ricocheted into the Feds in a cloud of paint chips. The soldiers hadn't expected to meet an enemy so suddenly. Only a few of them wore back-and-breast armor.

Six or eight more men in ceramic hard suits arrived from the elevator to add their fire to the volleys directed at the Feds. Stephen traded the carbine for the pump gun Hadley'd offered him earlier, but by the time he raised the weapon the Feds had vanished back the way they'd come. Eight casualties, some of them still moving, floated in a fog of blood.

"Lightbody, Jones!" Dole shouted through his helmet speaker. "Secure the back way. The rest of you whoresons follow me!"

"Stand where you are!" Stephen Gregg bellowed. "We're not going to kill them by love taps, we're going to tear their bloody throats out if they don't surrender. Guard the corridors while I talk to their captain! And Dole, there's a laser cutter in the hull-side compartment. Put a crew on it."

Stephen snapped up his faceshield and used the rifle butt to pole himself gently into the communications alcove. The Fed officer still gripped the handset in a gauntlet as he floated with a bullet hole between his startled eyes. The panel had a flat-plate vision screen. An officer in a blue jacket watched in horror at the carnage that drifted past the pickup lens at the base of the display.

Stephen ignored the handset and switched the panel to speakerphone. "Do you recognize me?" he shouted to the Fed officer. "I'm Stephen Gregg. Put your captain on and maybe you'll live through the rest of this day. Soonest!"

A sailor fired twice. One of the bullets struck the bulkhead at the end of the passage and ricocheted back, whanging several times on the upper and lower deckplates. Another sailor shouted a curse.

An older female officer took the place of the first at the commo unit. This officer's cap and left lapel were both gold. "Colonel Gregg," she said in a taut voice. "Your ship has been driven away and your small group will inevitably be wiped out unless you surrender. I have eight hundred heavily armed soldiers aboard. Do you yield?"

"You've got a hundred less than you had when I started, missy!" Stephen snarled. "Listen! I've got a laser cutter and all the other tools you were using for repair work. Unless you surrender *now* I'll punch a hole in every compartment of this ship and void it to vacuum. I've already started, missy! I'm Stephen Gregg and I'd as soon kill you all as take your surrender. By God I would!"

A body with no face drifted past the alcove, trailing five meters of intestine through what had been a white uniform. The captain of the *Savior Enthroned* saw the corpse and stiffened. Stephen laughed savagely at her expression.

"The lives of my crew and the troops in my care," the Fed captain said, her voice three tones higher than when she first spoke. "Honorable captivity for the officers and exchange if that . . . if that becomes possible. Yes?"

An explosion or a high-velocity projectile made the giant vessel's hull ring. Some other portion of the boarding party was in a vicious fight.

"Accepted," Stephen said. "But any of your people

who're still fighting in three minutes had better be able to breathe vacuum. On my word as a gentleman of Venus!''

The Fed captain grimaced and nodded. She turned a rotary switch and began to speak. Loudspeakers in every corridor and compartment of the *Savior Enthroned* crackled out her orders to surrender the vessel.

ABOARD THE *GALLANT SALLIE*.

"Three minutes to transit," Harrigan warned from the *Gallant Sallie*'s navigation console. "Lighting thrusters."

Sal drew Stephen's armored form firmly down onto the deckplate so that the 1-g acceleration wouldn't slam him there. His faceshield was raised, but his eyes focused a thousand meters out.

The boarding party had made a single transit jump to get the captured vessel clear before the Feds attempted to retake her. The Federation commander's draconian threats to any captain who failed to hold the preset order had stifled the individual initiative that might have overcome the attack on the *Savior Enthroned*.

The huge globular form of the *Savior Enthroned* drifted in a cloud of debris against an alien starscape. While they waited for a ship—the *Gallant Sallie*, as it chanced—to arrive with navigators and additional flight crew, Stephen's men had voided the trash of battle. If Sal looked closely, she could see that many of the objects floating around the captured ship were mangled bodies, Molt and human both.

The *Gallant Sallie*'s thrusters fired. Apparent weight returned; the deck was downward again. Objects ignored because there'd been forty extra sailors packed into the vessel now settled abruptly. The *Savior Enthroned*'s image became a diminishing ball in the center of the display.

Sal began undoing the clamps that held Stephen's hard suit together. Half the front of the gorget was gone. The sealant repairing the crazed remnant clung to the latch until Sal scraped a knifeblade through it.

Stephen suddenly looked at her. "Lord!" he said. "Sorry, I was a long way . . ."

He glanced wonderingly around the *Gallant Sallie*'s cabin. Sal lifted his helmet off, then the gorget.

"I don't remember coming aboard," Stephen said. He started to take off his own gauntlets, so Sal unlocked the three pieces that covered each arm. "I didn't realize your ship was the one that was going to pick us up."

"We'd ferried a load of ammunition from the Ishtar City Arsenal," Sal said. "Piet thought we'd be a good choice to take your wounded off. And bring you back particularly, Stephen. Piet was concerned that you might be carried to Venus inadvertently."

Stephen laughed harshly. "At least one of Pleyal's ships is going to reach Venus," he said.

"Venus orbit," Sal said. "I don't think there's a transfer dock on the planet that could take her. I . . . It's incredible that you captured her, Stephen."

The boarding party's ten wounded men were on stretchers in the hold with the *Wrath*'s own surgeon and one of his mates. Stephen and his two loaders had come across with their wounded by the same lines that guided the additional prize crew to the *Savior Enthroned*. Dole had come as well. The bosun was keeping himself as inconspicuous as possible because Captain Ricimer's orders had directed him to help take the prize to Venus.

"The Fed medics did a good job with their wounded," Stephen said. He'd forgotten that he'd been removing his hard suit. Sal unlatched the leg pieces. "With guns to their heads. It wasn't necessary, but I didn't try to stop it."

"Prepare for transit," Harrigan warned. Except for the mate, all the *Gallant Sallie*'s crewmen were watching Sal and Stephen out of the corner of their eyes. Nobody was going to say anything—probably nobody cared—but Sal didn't need others to tell her that a captain's place was at the controls during transit.

Human beings had duties also. When they conflicted with the governance of a starship, well, sometimes the starship had to wait.

Transit. Bleakness, grayness, nothingness. *Back*, and she

was holding Stephen Gregg's hands though she didn't remember taking them in hers. Transit.

The series was of eight in-and-out jumps, a thirty-second pause to calibrate for the observed position of the straggling Venerian fleet, and a final ninth transit pair to bring the *Gallant Sallie* within a kilometer of the *Wrath*. It was a clean piece of navigation. Sal had had plenty of time to program a back-course to the fleet while the *Gallant Sallie* waited, its hatch open, to receive the party from the captured vessel.

She hadn't known that Stephen was still alive until Dole raised the faceshield of the figure floating beside him like an empty suit of armor.

Attitude jets puffed, rotating the *Gallant Sallie* so that Harrigan could brake the freighter's slight velocity relative to the deputy command vessel. The *Wrath*'s image was the background to the mask of alphanumeric calculations filling the display. Patches of odd-colored ceramic covered battle damage. A crew was at work on the outer hull.

Stephen closed his eyes and took off the linked back-and-breast pieces of his hard suit. There was a huge bruise visible through the sweat-soaked tunic he wore beneath the armor. "Has anything happened with the fleets?" he asked without emotion.

"A lot of shooting," Sal said. "Less damage, and none of it serious. One of the Fed ships blew up all by itself, but you've won our only victory so far, Stephen."

He looked at her, really *at* her. Sal was lifting away the hinged groin and thigh pieces. Stephen put the tips of his fingers on the backs of her hands to hold her attention.

"Sal," he said, "the Feds surrendered because they thought I'd tear the whole ship open and leave even the crew to suffocate when their oxygen bottles ran out."

Sal nodded. "I'm glad they surrendered," she said carefully. "That saved many lives."

Perhaps yours among them, my friend. My love.

"They were right, Sal," Stephen said. "I told them that I'd as soon kill them as not, and that was as true as if I'd sworn by a God I believed in. I was ready to kill the whole thousand or more of them."

"You didn't, though," she said.

"No, they surrendered," Stephen said—not agreeing.

"Stephen, if it bothers you so much when you think of what might have happened . . ." she said. She paused, wondering if she was willing to go on. "Then the next time, don't do it. But it didn't *happen*."

"I'd have killed them all," he whispered.

Sal turned her hands to grip Stephen's as hard as she could. Part of her prayed that she wouldn't start to cry; but the tears would have been for both of them, herself and the man she held who couldn't weep for the soul he thought he'd lost.

ABOARD THE *WRATH*.

Piet saw Stephen's approaching figure reflected in the bright-work of his console. He spun the couch with a smile of greeting that hardened minutely as he rose to his feet. "I didn't know you'd been wounded, Stephen," he said.

"It's a bruise, Piet," Stephen said. Maybe he ought to wear something high-necked—though he really didn't want even cloth in contact with the swollen, purple-black flesh over his breastbone. "You should see the other guy."

Piet *had* seen the other guy, many times over a decade. The mangled bodies floating through the compartments of a captured starship were all the same, except perhaps to God.

"Glad you're safe, Colonel Gregg," Simms said quietly. The navigator turned back to his console immediately, as though he were afraid of the reaction.

It always puzzled Stephen that people really did seem to like him. Even people who knew what he was.

"Come view what's happened while you were gone," Piet said. He drew his friend down beside him on the couch turned crossways in respect to the three-dimensional display. "I'd like to get your opinion, and it'll be another hour yet before the Feds complete their calculations."

He touched a control. The blotchy appearance of the enemy after a transit series replaced a real-time image of the Federation globe reformed. The Venerian ships converged on their enemy in a speeded-up review of the battle. Vector lines careted six Venerian vessels moving in line ahead toward a gap in the Fed formation. A sidebar along the top of the display strung database close-ups of Captain Casson's *Free-*

dom and five similar vessels: spherical armed merchantmen, among the largest ships in the Venerian fleet.

The globe began to collapse on Casson's squadron like an amoeba ingesting prey. Four vessels from the Federation rear guard closed, maneuvering with surprising agility. Stephen frowned. Piet nodded, pleased that his friend had noticed. He touched another control. At the bottom of the display appeared an oddly angular vessel, a dodecahedron rather than a sphere.

"The Feds have brought four orbital monitors with them," Piet said. "The living conditions aboard on a voyage of this length must be indescribable, but—"

The monitors were designed for weightless conditions rather than to operate at most times with the apparent gravity of 1-g acceleration. Their decks were onionskins around a central core instead of perpendicular to the main thrust axis like those of spherical-plan long-voyage vessels.

For all their light frames and the discomfort of their crews, the monitors were dangerous opponents for Casson's self-surrounded squadron. The Fed vessels had many times the usual number of attitude jets to provide the agility Stephen watched on the display, and eleven of twelve facets mounted a powerful gun.

The remainder of the Venerian fleet swept down with unexpected coordination on the "east" quadrant of the Federation globe. Feds closing on Casson turned to meet the new threat. Cracks opened in what had almost become a crushing vise. Casson's squadron eased out of the trap.

Stephen looked at Piet with a faint smile. "Your idea?" he said. "Organizing the rescue instead of letting it turn into a mare's nest as usual?"

Piet shrugged, almost hiding his own smile. "I signaled—Guillermo signaled, of course—all vessels to conform to the *Wrath*'s movements. There wasn't time to do more . . . and somewhat to my surprise, most of the others did as I asked."

He looked at Stephen and shrugged. "We aren't as tightly disciplined as the Feds, Stephen."

Stephen shrugged back. "Tyranny has certain advantages in the strictly military sphere," he said.

Piet's smile became broad and as hard as a gun muzzle.

"Tell that to the captain of the *Savior Enthroned*," he said. "You might get an argument."

He returned the display to real-time images and pointed. Barges carried supplies and munitions from the Fed transports to the war vessels on the outer face of the globe.

"We can listen to their intership communications and know they're frightened," Piet said quietly. Guillermo and Simms were absorbed in their work; no one else was close enough to overhear. "Short transit series are a terrible strain. Metal doesn't craze the way our ceramic hulls do, but their seams are working badly and many of their ships have gunfire damage."

He looked at the friend beside him and went on, "Only sometimes I think—if we run out of ammunition before we break the Fed formation, what happens then?"

"Then you put us alongside them, one ship at a time," Stephen said. "And we board them. If that's what it takes."

"The commander acknowledges your communication, Deputy Commander," Guillermo said. The Molt raised his voice but didn't turn his triangular head lest he seem to be intruding his personality into a private conversation. "He is relaying it to the remainder of the fleet for action."

Stephen raised an eyebrow. Piet smiled with slight warmth. "We're three transits from a junction that will carry us to within half an AU of Venus, sixty-five million kilometers," he explained. "The Feds will certainly attempt that route. If we calculate our speed and position correctly, though, we can prevent them from taking the third jump unless they're willing to turn their thrusters directly toward our guns at a few hundred meters range. I suggested such a plan to Commander Bruckshaw."

"If they don't make that junction, then what?" Stephen asked.

Piet laughed. "More of the same, my friend," he said. "At least until we run out of ammunition. Then we'll see."

He preserved a light tone up to the final sentence. On the display beside him, the Fed formation looked as perfect as a poised axe.

ABOARD THE *GALLANT SALLIE*.

Sal finished her calculations, finished checking the AI's calculations, really. The display reverted from alphanumeric to its previous setting: a view of the Federation globe and, fifty kilometers to one side, the straggling Venerian formation.

Sal lay back on the couch with a sigh. A circle of white light marked the *Wrath*, otherwise an indistinguishable dot at this scale.

"So, Captain . . ." Brantling said from a seat at the attitude-control board. "We're headed back for home, then?"

Sal scowled and for a moment continued to face the display. She realized that she had to tell her crew sometime, and they deserved better than the back of her head when she did so. She got up and faced her men. The whole crew was in the cabin.

"I've decided that we'll hold position with the fleet for a time," she said as professionally as she could manage. "Although we—"

The cheers of her crew interrupted her. Brantling clapped Harrigan on the shoulder and cried, "Hey, I told you she had too much guts to run off when there was a fight coming!"

Kokalas clapped his hands with enthusiasm and said, "We're going to pay them bastards back for Josselyn, we are."

Nedderington, who'd learned everything he could from Godden when the gunner's mate was aboard, rose from the locker holding the *Gallant Sallie*'s meager store of 10-cm rounds and opened the lid.

"No!" said Sal. "No, we're not going in as a fighting ship. Christ's blood! we don't have but two hard suits aboard and one only fits me. All we're going to do is—"

Watch and pray.

"—render assistance to damaged vessels if necessary, and to carry out any other tasks the commander, the comman*ders* may set us."

"We'll be following the fleet's transits, Sal?" Tom Harrigan asked. "Or . . ."

"We've got the course plots, transmitted from the *Venus* and the *Wrath* both," Sal said. "We aren't . . ." She paused, wondering how to phrase the description. "We haven't been ordered to accompany the fleet, but we aren't acting against the commanders' wishes, either."

"Captain?" Brantling said, pointing over Sal's shoulder.

She spun. The Federation globe was dissolving in sequential transit. The *Wrath* vanished, then a dozen more of the largest and best-crewed Venerian ships.

"Stand by to transit," Sal said as she dropped back into the navigation console, engaging the AI. An orange border surrounded the display. Five seconds later, the *Gallant Sallie*—

Transit. Sal saw the cabin as a black-and-white negative, but that was only the construct her mind built of familiar surroundings to steady itself.

Starscape. The *Gallant Sallie*'s display was set for real visuals, not icons representing the confronting fleets, but at the previous range there was little visible difference. Ships had been glimmers in starlight, varying by albedo rather than absolute size.

Now the fleets and the *Gallant Sallie* with them had closed considerably. In the fraction of a second after Sal's eyes adjusted to the sidereal universe again, she could see the *Wrath* as an object, blotched from previous damage. Two of the starboard gunports were open because the lids had jammed or were shattered by fire.

Transit. Sarah Blythe had made her first transit when she was two years old. The feeling had never really disturbed her the way she knew it did others.

Starscape. The two fleets on the display were nearly a

single mass. The Federation globe very nearly rested on a lumpy plain of Venerian ships. At this moment Federation AIs would be screaming collision warnings.

The Fed captains knew the real threat was not impact with the tightly controlled first line of the Venerian fleet. They had the choice of overriding the next programmed transit or having their thrusters ripped out by point-blank plasma bolts. Some of the Federation officers were experienced enough to have expected this result as soon as they saw how much more maneuverable their opponents were. Their commander was sure to have a planned response.

The squished and gaping Fed formation vanished raggedly. The Venerian fleet didn't move. Sal disconnected the sequencer.

The *Gallant Sallie*'s AI was very nearly as powerful as those of the *Wrath* and her sister ships, let alone the armed merchantmen that made up the bulk of the Venerian force. Sal would have a solution within a few minutes, whether or not one was relayed from the dedicated warships.

"What's happening?" Rickalds said, panic growing with each syllable. "Ma'am, they're getting away!"

"They're not getting nowhere!" Tom Harrigan snarled contemptuously. "They're running with their tails between their legs 'cause we cut them off. As soon as the computer tells us where they ran to, why, we'll jump right after them. And I shouldn't wonder if we had 'em right by the balls, as strung out as they're going to be!"

The artificial intelligence bordered the screen with blue and threw up a blue sidebar. The complex calculations of the latter were too minute to read.

Sal didn't need to know where the course would take them. All that was important was that it would take them in pursuit of the Feds, in company with the men who would crush the tyrant's force or die.

"Prepare for transit!" she ordered, engaging the sequencer.

"Course received from the *Wrath*, ma'am!" Cooney called from the adjunct communications module at the back of the cabin.

"We've got our own course!" Sal said. The screen's border went orange.

Transit.

Starscape. She couldn't see the Federation fleet. The Feds had a lead of the minutes it took the *Gallant Sallie* to compute their course. A Venerian ship was present, though: the *Wrath*. A dozen more, a score more, Venerian vessels winked into sight.

Transit.

Starscape.

Transit. Brantling's reversed image stared tensely from Sal's mind, though she hadn't been looking at him or even toward the back of the cabin.

Starscape, but partly masked by a planet looming across the sky. The Federation ships were in orbit or already beginning landing approaches.

"Bloody hell!!" Tom Harrigan said as he made the identification a fraction of a second before Sal herself did. "That's Heldensburg! The port governor's letting the Feds land on Heldensburg!"

Venerian warships appeared and immediately accelerated through sidereal space toward the scattered Feds. The intended attacks were unplanned and thus far uncoordinated.

"The governor, La Fouche, he's a fan of Pleyal's," Sal remarked. "I remember what the cargo supervisor told us."

Her fingers set the AI to determine a course that would hold the *Gallant Sallie* stationary in respect to the planet below. "I wonder—"

One of Heldensburg's 30-cm cannon sent a bolt across the *Wrath*'s bow. The round probably wasn't aimed to hit. It was simply a warning that a Venerian attempt to interfere with the Feds here would have Heldensburg's ship-smashing port defenses to contend with. The *Wrath* drew away from its target, a big Fed vessel braking from orbit.

The Venerians no longer had to wonder how Port Governor La Fouche would interpret his nation's neutrality in a war between Venus and the North American Federation.

ABOVE HELDENSBURG.

"Oh, this is too bad!" Commander Bruckshaw said, glaring at the hundreds of ships indicated on the display in the conference room of the *Venus*. "Why, this should never have been permitted to happen!"

Stephen was more amused than not by the sight of so many private vessels, probably everything on Venus capable of the short journey to Heldensburg. The ships had come from every port on the planet as soon as a courier brought word home that the Feds had gone to ground on Heldensburg.

Some of the ships carried supplies and munitions, the way the *Gallant Sallie* had done a few days before, but many captains were motivated simply by a desire to get in a blow of their own against the Federation. The light guns the merchantmen mounted made them as useless in a real battle as their hulls were vulnerable.

The multitude of small vessels could get in the way, true; but so far as Stephen could tell, Bruckshaw's irritation was mostly because the newcomers weren't under his control and hadn't come at his request. The mass of ships was sure to have a psychological effect on the Feds, despite their knowing the influx had little military value.

"I believe most of the captains are here, Commander," Piet said, gently prodding Bruckshaw back to the real matter at hand. This was a live rather than video conference, because if Guillermo could eavesdrop on Federation intership communications, then the Feds—or their Molt slaves—could listen to the Venerian fleet.

Stephen grinned sardonically at Sarah Blythe beside him. She was too tautly professional to meet his eyes. Sal was present because Mister Gregg had brought her to the command group meeting. Stephen knew he was throwing his weight around to bring a friend into a conference called only for the captains of fighting ships; but he had the weight. A score of the gentlemen accompanying Bruckshaw on his flagship crowded the room with even less reason.

"Yes, I see that," the commander said sharply.

Bruckshaw had had a frustrating time. Though he'd closed with the enemy whenever possible, he knew the *Venus* hadn't done any marked damage. On a strategic level, the Federation fleet was unbroken and now in the process of refitting beyond his reach.

Besides those military considerations, the commander had to be galled to know that the only Federation ship captured had been taken by his famous deputy, Captain Ricimer. Bruckshaw had deferred to Piet's experience just as he'd promised he would, but—Bruckshaw was the governor's cousin, and Piet was a potter's son. Though the commander was a decent and intelligent man, he was human.

He grimaced and said in apology, "Factor Ricimer, would you please outline the situation for the assembly?"

Piet bowed to his superior and turned to the company. "We've tried everything we know to get the port commandant, La Fouche, to stop sheltering the Feds," he said in a pleasant voice. "Commander Bruckshaw has sent couriers both to Venus and to Avignon to get the decision reversed through La Fouche's superiors. At best that will take a week—as much time as the Feds need to refit."

A branch of opinion in United Europe held that alliance with President Pleyal was a better choice than the present climate of low-level hostility toward the North American Federation. La Fouche might well be carrying out the policy of his government under cover of personal whim.

"I'm convinced that to attempt to land in Heldensburg with the defenses alerted would be suicidal, not a matter of military consideration," Bruckshaw interjected. "I will not countenance such a waste of the state's limited resources."

Several of the veterans relaxed noticeably. There was mur-

muring among the gentlemen—stilled instantly when the
commander glared at them. Were it not for Bruckshaw's birth
status, someone was sure to have suggested a head-on assault
and damned as cowardly anybody who caviled. The commander had quashed that wrangle with a combination of
good judgment and the courage to voice an unpalatable truth.

"Yes," said Piet. "Venus has no lack of men ready to
charge thirty-centimeter guns. My friend Mister Gregg, for
example"—he nodded, smiling faintly—"and many others
in this room, I'm sure. But the Lord gave us courage to be
steadfast in His service, not to throw ourselves away."

"If we wait till the Feds refill their tanks and repair their
damage—and Heldensburg has a first-rate maintenance facility as I well know . . ." said Willem Casson. The old man
wore a mauve velvet suit and the jeweled awards three trading associations had given him for his explorations on their
behalf. "*And* refill their ammunition lockers too, I shouldn't
wonder, if there's any shells down there of the right sizes—
well, then, what do we do? Use up our air and reaction mass
stooging around out of range, then hope we can break their
fleet refitted when we couldn't do it before?"

Casson glared at Piet and added, "Because some folk
don't have the guts to carry the fight *to* the Feds!"

Sal stiffened. If Piet had taken more than a fraction of a
second to reply, there would have been a brawl between his
supporters and Casson's.

With his smile still broader, Piet said in a soothing voice,
"I didn't mean to impugn the courage or judgment of anyone
in this room, Captain. Your point is well taken: we can't
afford to permit the Feds to regroup at leisure. Though we
can't force them up from Heldensburg with ordinary warships, I believe launching unmanned vessels into the port will
send them flying in panic."

"The heavy guns can destroy a ship *as* a ship," Salomon
put in, "but it's still a couple hundred tonnes of hardware
following a ballistic course. A thirty-centimeter bolt doesn't
make a ship vanish."

"You talked about suicide," said Captain Montero. His
fists were unconsciously pressed together in front of his
chest. "If a ship isn't controlled down to twenty klicks al-

titude, it's not going to come close enough to scare anybody but farmers in the next province, we all know that."

He looked around challengingly. Montero wasn't a member of one clique or another, just an experienced captain stating a well-grounded opinion. "Coming that close, especially in the sort of junker you'd throw into the ground that way, well, the port guns are going to smash it to bits before the crew can get out."

"Not a ship with a modern navigational system," Sal said loudly, perhaps louder than she'd intended. Men craned their necks to see who'd spoken. The room was full, and Sal was shorter than most of the others present.

Stephen turned his head in unspoken challenge. Men who met his eyes nodded, smiled stiffly, or simply looked away.

"I can program the *Gallant Sallie* to land itself from orbit," Sal continued. She smiled tightly. There was sweat at her hairline, though her voice didn't sound nervous. "It won't be a soft landing, but that's not what we need here. I volunteer my ship for the mission."

"One ship won't do it," said Salomon. "It'll take half a dozen, and I'm not talking featherboats, either. At least a hundred tonnes."

Everyone spoke at once, to the assembly or to a neighbor. Bruckshaw and Piet leaned their heads together for a whispered conversation.

Bruckshaw straightened and said, "A moment!" interrupting the brief pandemonium. "A moment, gentlemen and captains. I've discussed this possibility with Factor Ricimer. We agree that we'll need six ships of at least a hundred tonnes burden to be sure of success."

Piet winced. Bruckshaw caught the expression and added, "With the blessing of God, that is. The Free State of Venus will purchase the vessels involved at a price set after survey by a board of senior captains, chosen and presided over by Factor Ricimer. Let me say that no shipowner will be the loser financially from his patriotism."

He smiled faintly and added, "We appear to have most of the merchant fleet of Venus to pick from, after all."

"Say, I've got a ship you can have!" Captain Groener

said from Casson's side. "Assuming the survey covers stores at listed value?"

"Captain Casson?" Piet called. "Captain Salomon? I'd be honored if the two of you would serve with me on the survey board. Will those present who own ships they'd like to volunteer please join us now? We won't go outside this group unless we have to."

There was a surge toward Piet. Most of the fleet's captains themselves owned one or more ships, part of the cloud of light vessels clogging the starscape about Heldensburg. With the survey done the way Bruckshaw implied it would be, this could be a very profitable way to sell a vessel that needed a total rebuild.

Sal shivered. She started to put her arm around Stephen for support but caught herself before the motion was complete. "I should have asked you," she said. "I'm sorry."

"You're the managing director," Stephen said. "And a very good business decision you've made. Go talk to Piet."

He nodded Sal forward. "I wouldn't argue with a choice you had a right to make," Stephen added softly, "any more than I'd expect one of my men to tell me who to kill next."

ABOARD THE *GALLANT SALLIE*.

"They're clear!" Brantling announced. He was in the cutter in the *Gallant Sallie*'s hold, speaking over the hardwired intercom rigged for the mission.

On the display, Sal could see the barge pulling away with most of the *Gallant Sallie*'s crew and personal effects. Tom Harrigan watched tensely from the attitude-control boards. He, Sal, and Brantling were all the personnel the old vessel had on her last voyage.

Ships didn't have souls; and even if they did, there were humans dying in this war also.

"All right, we're going in," Sal said. She pushed the EX-ECUTE key to start the program. Even that simple movement felt awkward in a hard suit.

Harrigan wore the *Gallant Sallie*'s general-purpose suit. He looked even more clumsy and uncomfortable than Sal felt. Stephen had offered to find armor for Brantling, but the sailor had refused. He waited at the cutter's controls in a helmet, a breathing mask, and a flexible bodysuit.

The attitude jets fired, then counterfired. The thrusters lit with a shudder, returning the vessel to an apparent 1 g of acceleration toward Heldensburg.

Words in white letters crawled across the bottom of the display. The message had been sent on the command channel, overriding the lock Sal had placed on the commo gear.

"*Wrath* sends, 'Our prayers go with you,' " Sal relayed to her fellows. The transmission was slugged "Piet," not "*Wrath*," but she would have felt awkward saying that.

Heldensburg was an ugly planet, yellow beneath the misty

blue scattering of its atmosphere. Sal hadn't realized quite how ugly the place was on previous landings here. A turgid pimple, swelling on the display.

Two specks swung toward the *Gallant Sallie*. Sal highlighted and expanded the images.

"I see them! I see the Feds!" Brantling cried.

"Brantling, keep off the intercom!" Sal snapped.

Because the hatch remained open, Brantling had been able to glimpse either the featherboat or the armed barge trying desperately to match courses. The Feds had a number of light vessels in orbit to prevent what the *Gallant Sallie* was about to do.

The thrusters cut out momentarily. The AI used the attitude jets to rotate the *Gallant Sallie*, then fired the thrusters again at an initial 3 g's. They were coming in very hard and fast. A technical expert from the *Wrath* had reprogrammed the artificial intelligence to permit it to execute maneuvers well beyond safety parameters.

Sal checked their heading. The point of impact was drifting west, though for the moment it was still predicted to be within the port reservation. She adjusted the program. Execution was in the AI's electronic hands, but Sal felt the ship quiver minusculely as altitude jets burped moments after she'd entered the correction.

Heldensburg filled the display, as vapid as an ingenue's smile. The port was on the opposite side of the planet. Sal angrily hit keys preset to a series, then another set. A corner of the display—an eighth of the total—became a close-up of the port, a real-time view as relayed from another Venerian ship. On the opposite corner, a Fed featherboat with a light plasma cannon protruding from the bow port accelerated to come up with the *Gallant Sallie*.

The number of Federation vessels crowded even the vast Heldensburg spaceport. From a score of locations, plasma exhaust bloomed like flowers opening. To react so quickly, the Feds must have been expecting, dreading, exactly what was about to happen. The *Gallant Sallie* and her consorts couldn't expect to destroy a significant proportion of Pleyal's fleet, but they could very easily induce a wild panic that threw the Feds into the arms of sharks like Piet Ricimer and his *Wrath*. . . .

Sal rechecked their heading. Below them, clouds swept swiftly eastward as the *Gallant Sallie* cut against the grain of Heldensburg's rotation. The predicted landing—impact—site still drifted west, but less swiftly. With Sal's correction, the ship would hit close to the center of the target.

The atmosphere was beginning to buffet the ship. Even though thrust had dropped to little more than 1 g, movement was difficult.

"Let's—" Sal said as she rose from the console.

The featherboat fired its plasma cannon. A bright ionized track showed on the display because the Feds as well had dipped into the atmosphere in pursuit. The bolt missed closely enough that hair on the back of Sal's arms rose.

"—go!"

Tom Harrigan grabbed Sal and flung her bodily down the passage ahead of him. The ship staggered like a drunken sailor, but Sal had a lifetime's experience on jumping decks.

She caught the lip of the cutter's dorsal hatch and hoisted herself into the cabin. She turned to help Harrigan, but the mate had paused to throw the hatch-closing switch.

Brantling lit the thruster. Plasma smothered the hold in a brilliant fog. The cutter lurched even though the nozzle was irised wide. Sal saw Harrigan's gauntlet flail through the iridescence. She grabbed him and pulled. Harrigan came aboard just as Brantling took the cutter out of the *Gallant Sallie*, ticking on the way against the slowly closing hatch.

Sal pressed her helmet against the mate's and shouted, "You idiot!"

"Sal," Harrigan said, his voice a buzz through the ceramic of his helmet and hers, "I was afraid the open hatch'd throw the AI off in the lower atmosphere."

The *Gallant Sallie* glowed across a broad segment of sky, plunging toward Heldensburg. Brantling was trying to climb out of the atmosphere, but the featherboat now kept company with them less than a kilometer out. Another gleaming reflection, probably the armed barge, was closing as well.

One moment the *Gallant Sallie* was a white-hot comet trailing a cone of superheated atmosphere. In the next the ship disintegrated as a rainbow flash, hit squarely by one of Heldensburg's 30-cm guns. The bolt was powerful enough to destroy the hull's structural integrity; friction and inertia did the rest.

Sal watched transfixed. They'd removed the cutter's hatch before the mission so that nothing would slow her and Tom when they boarded at the last instant. The cutter's attitude as Brantling braked the momentum transferred during the *Gallant Sallie*'s dive gave Sal and Harrigan a perfect view of the port.

The *Gallant Sallie* had broken into three large pieces, plus a score of smaller ones that were refractory enough to survive their bath in the atmosphere. Most of the smaller chunks were separated nozzles and plasma motors, each describing a slightly different trajectory toward the ground. The general effect was that of a shotgun charge, but the smallest of these missiles weighed a hundred kilos and travelled at orbital velocity.

A dozen Federation vessels were already climbing skyward, corkscrewing wildly because their officers hadn't taken the time to balance thrust. Two ships touched in a grazing collision. One continued to climb but the other, an orbital monitor with a lighter hull than the long-haul vessel, caromed out of the port reservation and dropped. The monitor came down in a swamp, only marginally under control.

The barge moved alongside Sal's cutter. The Feds mounted a twin-tube laser on a pintle in the open cabin. A man in metal armor and two Molts with asbestos padding over flexible vacuum suits swiveled the weapon to bear on the cutter.

Sal waved her hand. Harrigan clamped her thigh so that she could raise the other as well. The Fed pilot was probably using a laser communicator to order Brantling to hold station, but Sal didn't want the gunners to doubt her willingness to surrender.

Fifty tonnes or more of the *Gallant Sallie*'s stern hit near the center of the spaceport, narrowly missing a 1000-tonne giant just lifting from the ground. The shock wave sent ripples of dust across the surface.

A plasma motor ripped through the heart of a moderate-sized freighter half a klick away. The victim's thrusters were already lit. Kinetic and thermonuclear energy combined in a stunning fireball, dazzling even against the sunwashed expanse of the port.

Every ship in Heldensburg was attempting to lift. Two more unmanned Venerian vessels dived toward the port, though Sal was sure that at least one of them would miss by several klicks.

The barge edged within twenty meters, seesawing as the pilot tried to match velocity. One of the Molts flung a line belayed to a staple on the barge's hatch coaming. The throw missed ahead, but Sal managed to catch the line as the Fed overcorrected and the barge slipped behind the cutter.

She'd thought the Feds might kill them out of hand, but apparently the crews of the screening force wanted proof that they had done *something* to prevent the disaster taking place beneath them.

Sal gestured Harrigan, then Brantling, ahead of her. From reflex she held the line instead of tying it, since there'd be no one remaining aboard the cutter to cast it off.

Brantling paused at the hatch coaming with a reckless smile on his face. He pointed to the legend on the bow of the barge: A311, and below it in smaller letters ST. LAW-RENCE. He touched his helmet to Sal's and said, "Look, Captain! That's their flagship. Only the best for Mister Gregg's friends, hey?"

A 30-cm bolt lit the sky beneath the barge with the iridescent, vain destruction of another incoming Venerian missile.

ABOARD THE *WRATH*.

The purpose-built Fed warship closing to point-blank range was slightly larger than the *Wrath*. The name blazoned on her bows was *St. Lawrence*. She was the flagship of the tyrant's fleet, and her captain was putting her in the path of the Venerian vessel that had already ripped the thrusters out of three armed Federation merchantmen.

Stephen Gregg watched with professional approval as the *St. Lawrence* grew on the gunnery screen. Courage was easy enough to come by. The Feds aboard the vessels wallowing powerless—one of them dropping back toward Heldensburg with fatal inevitability—were probably brave enough. They'd just lacked the skill to deal with an expert like Piet Ricimer maneuvering beneath the stern of their ship and loosing a salvo into the most vulnerable point. This fellow knew his duty to the ships under his command, and he was able enough to at least make a stab at carrying out that duty.

He was a brave man also, for he surely knew he was about to engage Piet Ricimer, the terrible pirate conqueror.

Both ships were coasting on inertia, their thrusters shut down and shielded against hostile fire. Attitude jets puffed, changing the *Wrath*'s alignment slightly.

"Mister Stampfer," Piet announced over the intercom, "you may fire as you—"

The starboard gunport across the bridge cantilevered open. Stephen had known that the *Wrath* and *St. Lawrence* were on parallel courses; and known also that the two ships were close together.

Until the port lid lifted and he saw nothing but the Fed's

scarred, curving hull plates, Stephen hadn't appreciated how *very* close the ships were.

"—bear!"

The 20-cm gun fired, started to recoil, and shattered in brilliance. A plasma bolt had struck at the edge of the port and on the muzzle of the Venerian cannon, blowing glassy shards of both in all directions. The splinter cage vanished. The gun to the trunnions and three crewmen above the waist were missing. The remainder of each was vaporized or scoured away by ceramic shocked into high-velocity sand.

The blast wall partitioning the bridge held, though flying debris scored it foggy. The tube Stephen gripped broke, and he flew across the bridge.

There were dozens of nearly simultaneous shocks, cannon recoiling and plasma bolts hitting the *Wrath* in turn. Vaporized metal from the hull of the *St. Lawrence* spurted, still white-hot and glowing, through the blasted gunport.

The cabin lights were out, but holographic displays cast a pastel glow across the interior surfaces. Stephen scuttled around the blast wall, dabbing with all four limbs. He expected the *Wrath* to swap ends and pour her remaining broadside into the *St. Lawrence*. Instead, the ships continued their matched courses, hurtling through nothingness a hundred thousand kilometers above Heldensburg. Piet had lifted the access plate of his console and was aiming a handlight into the interior.

Stephen braced one boot on the remnants of the 20-cm gun and locked the other armored knee on the hull where the gunport had been. The present hole was easily large enough to pass his body. He leaned out, aiming his flashgun.

Great gaps glowed in the flank of the *St. Lawrence*. The blue-white light winking through a jammed gunport was clearly an electrical fire. Only the fact that the battle was being fought in vacuum kept the entire gun deck from turning into an inferno.

The Fed warship had lower-level boarding holds like those of the *Wrath*, though they were split fore-and-aft instead of being full-length on either side. The hatches were open. Half a dozen Molts wearing padding over pressure suits leaped toward the *Wrath*. Sixty to eighty human soldiers in full or half armor waited to cross on the lines the Molts were carrying.

Stephen shot instinctively. The nearest Molt veered upward, driven by the pressure of gas spurting from his ruptured air pack. Others aboard the *Wrath* fired also. A second Molt tumbled under the impact of a bullet; a third separated from his line, dead though undeflected, and bounced from the *Wrath*'s hull. The remaining Molts set their suction grapnels against Venerian ceramic before they could be stopped.

There was a three-meter hole in the *Wrath*'s midships hull, perhaps blasted by a 20-cm gun exploding. The Fed boarding party scrambled toward the opening, guiding themselves by the lines.

Stephen slung his reloaded flashgun and launched himself toward the *St. Lawrence*. If he'd had time to think, he would have been frightened. For all his years in space, Stephen Gregg was as much a landsman as the Fed soldiers creeping gingerly across the boarding lines aft.

The quickest way to stop the boarders was to sever the lines aboard the Federation vessel. That wasn't something to think about, only to execute.

Stephen hadn't judged well the angle at which he'd pushed off. He drifted high. A Federation soldier tugging himself toward the *Wrath* hand over hand looked up and goggled. Stephen shot the man through the faceshield and threw the flashgun away to change course. The cast made him tumble, but the weapon wasn't quite massive enough to bring Stephen in contact with the *St. Lawrence*'s hull.

Beneath Stephen sailed a man in a ceramic hard suit, moving faster and at a flatter angle. He grabbed the lip of the open boarding hatch with one hand and turned to snatch Stephen's boot. He was Hadley, festooned with weapons and ammunition. Philips crossed only a few meters behind. The loaders, both of them accomplished sailors, had followed their principal—and done so with a great deal more skill than that principal had showed.

Stephen gripped a rifle floating from Hadley. Hadley slipped the sling as he cast Stephen into the hold, among the dozen or so Fed soldiers still waiting to cross the lines. Some of the Feds didn't realize a Venerian had boarded, but an officer fired a charge of buckshot into Stephen's right hip. The impact flung him against the forward bulkhead. He shot as he rebounded, starring the Fed's visor behind a gush of escaping air.

Recoil kicked Stephen back into the bulkhead. He pinned himself there deliberately by emptying the magazine into the nearest Feds. An officer's breastplate withstood the bullet that spun the man out of the hatch. His arms and legs windmilled; his mouth was open in a useless scream.

A light plasma cannon, a boat gun rigged as an antiboarding weapon, fired from the *Wrath* into the *St. Lawrence*'s aft hold. Bodies flew out with the debris. More Venerian sailors were crossing to the *St. Lawrence*, using the Feds' own lines or throwing themselves unaided across the ten-meter gap. Muzzle flashes, huge for being unconfined by atmospheric pressure, fluttered within the *Wrath*. The fight on the gun deck wasn't over.

Stephen unclipped his cutting bar and pushed off. He couldn't find his loaders without more effort than he had time for, and the bar was the better tool for the moment anyway.

A Fed stood at the ringbolt to which a pair of boarding lines were snubbed, aiming a rifle at Stephen. The man wore full armor. His face through his visor was white because of the strain with which he pulled at the trigger. The rifle didn't fire. Empty, still on safe, simply broken—it didn't matter. Anything could happen in the panicked confusion of a battle.

Stephen slashed through the lines and continued his stroke upward. The bar's teeth spun sparks from the surface of the Fed breastplate, but they sheared in satisfactory fashion through the rifle's receiver and the thinner armor of the gauntlets holding the weapon. Air and blood sprayed from the cut.

Dole with his white-chevroned helmet sailed into the hold. Six more sailors followed him. The *Wrath* had been shorthanded since she took the *Savior Enthroned*. Casualties from the gunnery fight and now the lack of these men would leave Piet with a corporal's guard to conn and fight his ship; but he'd manage, as Stephen Gregg would manage, or die trying.

The hold was empty of living Fed soldiers. The deck shuddered. The *Wrath* had at last begun to rotate on her long axis, tugging the Fed vessel by the line still attached in the aft hold.

Stephen jumped from the ringbolt to the companionway up from the hold. The pressure door wouldn't open. The hold brightened by perceptible degrees. Stephen turned his body to look.

Dole was spinning the power-assisted wheel on the bulkhead between the fore and aft holds. The clamshell hatches were closing, so the hold's overhead illumination reflected from their inner surfaces.

The *St. Lawrence* rocked from six hammer blows, then a seventh. What remained of the *Wrath*'s port battery had been brought to bear. Ions glared through the crack still open between the mating hatches.

Hadley used the carbine to pole himself to Stephen's side. Instead of offering to trade weapons, the loader undogged the hatch with an easy spin. Air rushing from the companionway shook both men. Vents in the ceiling of the hold opened also to restore pressure.

A shock heavier than that of a 20-cm bolt whipped the vessel's hull visibly. Apparent gravity returned as the *St. Lawrence* got under way.

Stephen took the carbine. Dole jumped to his side.

"Feds have a lot of safety muck, sir," the bosun said. The partial atmosphere made his amplified voice sound like that of a child squeaking. "You can't open the companionway with the hold opened to space, that's all."

"Let's go," Stephen said. Hadley pulled the hatch fully back for the gunman to lead.

There was no one in the companionway. Like the *Wrath*, the Federation warship was built with holds and plasma motors on the lower level and all living and fighting volumes on the single deck above.

The companionway's upper hatch was closed. Stephen expected it to be locked or even welded, but the wheel turned easily in his hand. He gestured behind him.

A sailor stepped by on the narrow landing and pushed the hatch open so hard that he fell partway out into the corridor. Three half-kilogram shots slammed through his helmet and threw neon sparks across the armored hatch. The sailor's legs thrashed, tangling Stephen and dropping him into a squat on the landing.

Stephen fired twice, angling his shots to ricochet bullets down the corridor. The carbine's operating lever broke because of his hasty strength. Dole dragged the dead man back.

Something hit a huge ringing blow on the corridor side of the hatch, knocking it nearly closed. As Dole reached up to pull the valve the rest of the way home, a crew-served laser burned across the lip and coaming, missing the bosun's arm by the thickness of the dust on his armor.

"Rifle," Stephen said, dropping the useless carbine.

Open the hatch again and charge. The Feds might panic; the hatch itself was protection from whatever weapon they'd set up on the hinge side of the valve. Shoot a few, shoot at least *one*; and die, as the men with him would die if they followed, but that was their choice.

Stephen wondered where Philips was. Chances were that he and his loader would be together again in a few seconds, though Philips deserved a cooler part of Hell.

"Sir!" Dole said. "Please—let's go this way."

Dole had dropped his shotgun. He thrust the tip of his cutting bar against the ceiling panel with both hands. The decks were minimum clearance, two meters, so he had good leverage.

The ceiling was nickel-steel like the rest of the ship's fabric, but the plates were only a centimeter thick instead of the 10 centimeters of companionway armor. The cutting bar sliced through with a bloodthirsty howl. White sparks blazed as they fell.

Holds and power plant on the lower level. Living quarters on the main deck.   And in the upper curve of the cylindrical hull, the mechanical spaces. Tanks of air and reaction mass, and the pumps that circulated both throughout the *St. Lawrence*. Oh, yes. There was another way to deal with this one.

The Feds could hear the cutting bar's scream. Somebody must have understood what it meant, because a moment later the hatch opened from the corridor side. Stephen blew the head off the Molt that was half lunging, half being pushed toward the companionway.

Stephen continued to pump and fire the powerful rifle. Two other sailors were shooting. Hadley thrust Dole's shotgun between Stephen's legs and loosed both barrels under the valve, into the ankles of the man who'd pulled it open. The Feds still aboard the *St. Lawrence* were crewmen, sailors. They didn't have the armor of the soldiers who'd boarded the *Wrath*.

The Feds couldn't use their heavy weapons while the corridor was choked with their own people. The armored Venerians couldn't miss and couldn't be harmed in the packed chaos. Stephen closed the hatch again.

The hatch didn't lock from this side. The Feds would bring up their laser to face the opening and try again. They were already too late, because a square meter of the ceiling clanged from Dole's shoulders to the landing.

A sailor formed a stirrup of his hands and launched Dole into the mechanical spaces. Another sailor started to follow. Stephen pushed the man aside and put his own boot onto the linked gauntlets. "Hadley, you next," he ordered as he rose through the hole with a great thrust of his arms.

The space above was an unlighted warren of pipes and flocking-insulated panels. Stephen saw the treads of Dole's boots as the bosun crawled down a channel. Dole couldn't possibly see where he was going, but he'd worked the guts of starships enough years to have an instinct for their layout.

Hadley came through the hole gripping a handlight. Stephen took it, hesitated, and switched it on. Fed crewmen might have entered the mechanical spaces through an access port by now, but he'd rather take that chance than remain blind.

With the lamp's aid, Stephen wormed his way up to where Dole squatted in a meter-by-two-meter alcove sculpted in the side of a huge tank. Three arm-thick pipes fed into an armored regulator and out again through a multibranched manifold. Dole set his cutting bar against the regulator. The bar groaned and died. Dole had exhausted the battery in slicing through the ceiling plates.

"Gimmie your bar, sir!" the bosun demanded. "If we open this up, the ship's whole oxygen supply vents. We can take the barge in the aft hold and be long gone by the time the Feds realize they're all dead!''

Stephen set his rifle down to unclip the bar from his armor. He froze.

If you couldn't sleep with it afterwards, then don't do it.

''Dole, can you shut off the water to their thrusters from up here?'' Stephen demanded.

''Huh?'' the bosun said. His face went momentarily blank. ''Yeah, I suppose. Give me the light.''

More sailors had crawled into the mechanical spaces. ''There's a feed trunk here, Mister Dole!'' a man shouted. ''But there'll be another to starboard, like enough.''

''Cut that trunk and the rest of you guard it!'' Stephen ordered. ''Dole, Hadley, and me are going to take care of the other half of the system!''

It was three hours before Admiral Jean King, Commander of the Grand Fleet of Retribution, gave up. During that time the *St. Lawrence* drifted with only auxiliary power. Her tanks of reaction mass were draining into the belly of the ship via every crack and passage through the inner hull.

Crewmen making desperate attempts to retake the mechanical spaces failed bloodily. Federation personnel didn't dare use flashguns or even projectile weapons against enemies lurking amid the high-pressure oxygen pipes. The Venerians felt no such compunction.

When King saw a pair of Venerian warships easing closer to his own disabled vessel, he decided to surrender instead to the leader of the boarding party that had actually accomplished his destruction. To carry his offer, King sent one of the Venerian prisoners the *St. Lawrence*'s barge had brought aboard when the *St. Lawrence* reached orbit.

He sent Captain Sarah Blythe.

BETAPORT, VENUS.

OCTOBER 14, YEAR 27.
2217 HOURS, VENUS TIME.

The *Wrath* began to vibrate from the torque of the tractor motors transmitted through the drawbar. When at last the cradle wheels turned, the warship's massive whole rumbled from Transfer Dock 14 into the tunnel leading to the Halys Yard where she would be repaired.

Sal touched Stephen's upper arm. It took the big man's mind a moment to register the contact. When his eyes blinked back to the present and focused on her, the slabs of his facial muscles loosened slightly.

Even before the *Wrath* moved her own length forward, the tractor slowed. The driver had switched its motor to alternator mode to drink the warship's momentum. The cradle's ceramic disc brakes squealed as they heated and finally, white-hot, bit. Dock 14's huge inner doors thundered like the start of a volcanic eruption as they closed behind the halted *Wrath*.

"You know," said Dole in a conversational voice, "there was times I really didn't think I'd be back to see this again."

The bosun threw the switch controlling the doors of the starboard boarding hold. All six segments sprang open as they were designed to do. The wrenching the *Wrath* took from short-series transits and Federation guns had loosened her hull, sometimes in desirable fashions.

The crowd roared. The banks of additional lighting set up in the tunnel shivered to the echoing cheers.

It had been Piet's idea. There would be a formal service of welcome and thanksgiving at the Governor's Palace in three days time; but Piet Ricimer, his crew, and the *Wrath* itself were from Betaport. This was Betaport's celebration.

Stephen had been the one to suggest that the crew be locked through with the ship rather than enter the town in the usual way, by the personnel hatch on Dock Street. The ship tunnel was more spacious, and the patches on the vessel's hull were a more vivid witness to the battle than anything the surviving crew could say.

"God has blessed Venus!" Piet Ricimer cried from the front of the ship's company. "May we always be worthy of His care!"

Guillermo stood at an audio board in the rear of the hold. The Molt kept the directional microphone on the upper hatch aimed at Piet's lips, sending his voice through the *Wrath*'s powerful outside speakers. Even so, the words were a descant to the cheering.

Piet stepped forward, gesturing the crew with him. The crowd surged toward them through the marshals, meeting and mixing on the boarding ramp. Betaport dignitaries in finery more often gorgeous than tasteful mobbed Piet.

Stephen didn't move from the rear bulkhead, but Sal saw his mouth quirk in a smile. Piet wore his half armor for show, though the gold finish was pitted from when he and Stampfer alone crewed a 20-cm gun whose hydraulics had failed. At least the back-and-breast would keep him from being crushed by well-wishers.

Sal stayed beside Stephen. Betaport wasn't her town. Harrigan and Brantling had transferred to the *Freedom* and were probably in Ishtar City now. Sal would see her father and childhood friends in three days, at the formal service.

Floral wreaths and bottles of liquor greeted the crewmen. The marshals had given wives and girlfriends places near the front, though there was no lack of freelances to cherish men who'd returned unattached.

Twice Sal saw *both* a wife and a girlfriend greet the same sailor. Those weren't the only tears shed in the general joy. Piet had listed the butcher's bill and the *Wrath*'s remaining complement in the same couriered dispatch that announced the victory. There were women, one of them with a newborn infant at her breast, who'd refused to believe until the hatch opened and they saw the pitiful few within the *Wrath*'s hold.

Not all those missing were dead. Many were in prize crews, and there were a dozen wounded who ought to survive (though not always with the original number of limbs).

But there were also the men *listed* as missing. In a space-man's town like Betaport, everyone knew "missing" gen-erally meant drifting in vacuum somewhere more distant than light could reach in a million years.

As the crowd milled beside the *Wrath* in the greatest fes-tival the port would ever see, Stephen turned to Sal with an expression she didn't recognize and said, "I almost killed you on the *St. Lawrence*. I wasn't sure I was going to tell you that."

He had to speak loudly to be heard, even though they stood together.

Sal put her arm around his waist, shrugged, and smiled. His muscles were as taut as a starship's tow cable. "Well, there's risk in anything," she said, "but I agreed with King that I should take the surrender offer instead of him sending one of his officers. You'd have thought that was a trick."

"Not that," Stephen said. "We were about to dump the main oxygen supply, but I didn't. I—we, I didn't know which pipe was which. We cut off reaction mass to the thrusters instead. Because I decided I didn't want to kill a thousand people."

His voice was trembling. Sal tried to hug herself against his chest, but Stephen held her apart and tilted her face so that she met his eyes.

"Another thousand people," he said. Only then did he draw her close.

The expression Sal hadn't been able to recognize was hope.

"Stephen," she said. "Let me stay with you. All night."

"No," he murmured gently. "That—"

"*Please*, Stephen, for God's sake!" she said.

"Sal, it's not you, it's me," he said with his lips to her ear. "On the ground, I don't sleep well. I don't really sleep. I appreciate what you're trying to do, but I don't want anybody around me when . . . Not even servants. Especially not somebody I care about.''

Sal drew away and looked into his eyes again. ''You don't understand, Stephen. If it's not you, it'll be the man I killed on Arles. The liquor helped for a while, but I can't drink enough anymore. If you won't hold me, I . . .''

She flung her head forward and blotted her tears on Stephen's worn brown doublet. ''I don't know what I'll do. I don't know what I'll do.''

He stroked her back with fingers that could bend steel of their own thickness. ''You need *me*, Sal?'' he said. ''You need me?''

''On my life I do, Stephen,'' she said. She choked; she didn't know if he could hear her words or not. ''On my very life.''

''Christ's blood, what a pair of cripples we are!'' he said.

Stephen lifted Sal into the air so that her short blonde hair brushed the ceiling plates. ''But you ought to see the other guy,'' he added with a wry smile. ''And after all, I *didn't* kill you, did I?''

Stephen swung her in a circle around him as though she were a child rather than a solidly built adult. Piet Ricimer looked up from the crowd pressing him. Sal caught a glimpse of a beaming smile replacing the amazement that had flashed across Piet's face.

''I warn you,'' Stephen said, suddenly serious as he put her down. ''I've got two rooms with nothing but a bed, a wardrobe, and a lot of slash bottles. There won't be anything else available with this crowd in town.''

''We'll manage,'' Sal said. She hugged him close again. ''We've managed everything so far.''

BETAPORT, VENUS.

MARCH 15, YEAR 28.
1455 HOURS, VENUS TIME.

"I am pleased to see you again, Colonel," Guillermo said as he bowed Stephen into Piet's private office.

The Molt was the only one authorized to open the door nowadays. The door *keeper*, on the other hand, was Dole or another trusted sailor who'd been with Captain Ricimer too long to care who a would-be intruder might be. If somebody tried to push into the captain's office, he got knocked down—and lucky if he didn't get a boot in the ribs besides.

Of course, Mister Gregg wanting to see the captain—that was something else again. There weren't appointments between old shipmates.

Piet was hunched over a desk covered with shiny glassine printouts, trying to find a datum as he talked on the phone. He raised three fingers when he heard the door open, but he didn't look up from his search. Stephen moved a stack of flimsies and a sample case—microchips, of recent European manufacture from the look of them—off the chair and sat down.

Piet caught the motion from the corner of his eye. He glanced at Stephen, grinned with enthusiasm, and said, "I'm very sorry, Factor, but something's come up. I'll get back to you."

He hung up the phone and switched it mute. "Stephen!" he said, rising from his chair. "My goodness, I'm afraid I've been as busy as I hear you are yourself!"

"I came by with a business proposition, Piet," Stephen said as they shook hands above the cluttered desk. Piet looked like he'd gained five kilos in the months since the

Wrath came home, but the fire of his countenance burned just as bright as it ever had.

"I've got something I'd like you to look at too, Stephen," Piet said as they both sat down. "But you first, please. After all, you came to me when I haven't managed to get out to see anybody in far too long."

"Blythe Spirits Limited has six ships, now, Piet," Stephen said, leaning back deliberately in the chair. He'd learned that by feigning ease he could sometimes induce the actual feeling. "They're all of them ships taken in the sweep of Fed shipping we made after the Grand Fleet of Retribution came apart."

He made a face at Pleyal's grandiose title. "They can be had for a song, though the navigational upgrades are a significant factor."

Piet chuckled, then sobered. "Metal hulls aren't as strong as good ceramic, Stephen," he said. "Not that I'm trying to tell you or Captain Blythe your business, but . . ."

Stephen nodded. "Right, but metal degrades instead of failing abruptly the way overstressed ceramic's been known to do."

He smiled grimly. They'd seen it happen to a consort of their own vessel: what had been a ship after one transit disintegrated to a sleet of gravel during the next. There'd been no survivors, and no chance of survivors.

"At the point Sal no longer thinks the hulls are safe," Stephen continued, "we'll strip the electronics and scrap the rest. They're *very* cheap, Piet."

"I wouldn't venture to make business decisions for you, Stephen," Piet said with a reminiscent smile. They'd seen a lot of things together, Piet and he.

Outside the door a cultured, angry voice said, "I have an appointment with the factor, my good man, an appointment!"

Lightbody was on duty with Guillermo. Stephen heard the sailor's reply only as a truculent rumble, but he was willing to bet Lightbody slapped his truncheon of high-pressure tubing into his palm as he spoke.

"Cargoes are going begging," Stephen explained. "The Fed colonies don't make any complaint about trading with us no matter what Pleyal says back in Montreal. For a lot of them it's us or starve, and they know it. And I'm not talking short-term profits, either. The shippers who make contacts now will have a foundation to build on as the colonies grow.''

He leaned forward and stretched his hand across the desk. "Piet," he said, "you and I started out to be traders. Pleyal's beaten. Come on into Blythe Spirits with us."

Piet laughed brightly. Only someone who knew him very well would have heard the slight tension in the note. "All right," he said. He placed his hand over his friend's. "How much would you like from me?"

"Not your money, Piet," Stephen said. "I want you, doing the same thing Sal's doing in Ishtar City. Picking captains who'll get so rich on quarter shares that they'll buy their own ships and make everybody—themselves and Venus and the colonies they serve—that much the richer. Equal partners, Piet. The three of us."

Piet tilted back in his chair and laced his fingers behind his head. "Fernando Comaguena, the Hidalgo of the Southern Cross—the pretender, Pleyal would say—is in Ishtar City now. There's some suggestion the governor might permit him to recruit help on Venus to regain his rightful position in Buenos Aires."

He raised an eyebrow.

Stephen got up and stretched. "Not for me, thank you, Piet," he said. He smiled, wondering if the expression looked as sad as he felt. Though it wasn't a surprise . . . "The Federation's been beaten. Pleyal and his successors can never be a threat to Venus again. They'll never be able to dictate who goes to the stars."

Piet lowered his hands slowly to the desk and stared at them. "It's a little hard to be sure where to draw the line, Stephen," he said.

"Then draw it here!" Stephen said with a passion that surprised them both. "Piet, there'll never be perfect peace while there are men. But there can be peace for *some* men."

Piet pushed his chair back and stood. "Do you have peace, Stephen?" he asked softly.

"Sometimes," Stephen said. He felt the corners of his

mouth lift in a wan smile. "More than I did. You know, sometimes I think that eventually I may be able to sleep a whole night through without, without . . ."

Piet walked around the desk.

"Piet, I never knew how important it was to be needed," Stephen whispered.

Piet took Stephen's hands in his. "I need you, Stephen," he said.

"You needed somebody *like* me, Piet," Stephen said harshly. "You don't need me if you're going to put the hidalgo back on his throne—if that's even possible."

"I need a friend, Stephen," Piet said simply.

"Then listen to me, Piet!" Stephen said. "The best thing a friend can tell you is to get out now. Leave the wars to other people and invest in the stars instead. God knows they've cost us enough already, you and me."

He put his arms around the smaller man. They hugged like lovers.

"*God* knows what they've cost," one of the men repeated; but not even an observer in the room would have been sure who spoke.

AUTHOR'S NOTES

1) Readers may notice that the plot of FIRESHIPS is based largely on events in the life of Sir Francis Drake. I therefore think I ought to mention that Sir Francis wasn't an ancestor of mine, and I can prove it.

The Drakes from whom I'm descended (through, let me add, a long line of dirt farmers in the years since they emigrated to the American colonies) are the Drakes of Ashe, a very old and thoroughly undistinguished family of Devonshire gentry. The height of their achievement arrived when a member of the family became Sheriff of Devon; however their—our—coat of arms, a wyvern (a two-legged dragon) displayed, is attested back to 1307.

Francis Drake was the son of a shipwright and lay preacher. He grew up in a hulk in the mud of the Medway, where his father was employed in the dockyard.

When Francis rose to prominence, entirely through his own efforts, he began to use our coat of arms. One of my ancestors promptly complained to the College of Heralds and quashed this mere *mechanick's* claim to kinship—thus depriving the Drakes of Ashe of our one chance to embrace somebody important in our number.

The story doesn't end quite there, however. Francis Drake went from success to success. He was knighted and gained the right to his own coat of arms. The first, extremely ornate, design Sir Francis submitted to the College of Heralds had as its crest a full-rigged ship.

Caught in the rigging, dangling head down and helpless, was a wyvern . . .

2) I wasn't sure I was going to mention this further aspect of FIRESHIPS, but I think I should. When I decided to do a

series of novels using the Age of Discovery for plot para-
digms, I didn't intend the matter of what wars cost the people
who fight them to be a major theme. I'm not a writer who
claims his characters get away from him: mine don't. But
this aspect of the three novels grew unexpectedly from the
subject matter.

I've learned that the people who haven't been there themselves really aren't going to understand what I'm trying to
tell them, but to be very explicit: it isn't the things that were
done to you that are hardest to live with afterwards. It's what
you became and the things you did to survive, one way and
another.

For the folks who have been there—you've got friends,
you've got people who understand *even if you haven't met
them*. It's not just you. You're not alone.

We're not alone.

Dave Drake
Chatham Country, NC